[N.E.S.S.]
BEGINNINGS

Michael C Reidell

ISBN: 978-0-9886848-0-5

Contents

Preface

After working and teaching in the telecommunications' industry for 27 years, I had a personal crisis; I contracted cancer. "The Big C", as it is called, tends to focus and strip your identity to the basics; either you live or die, there is no middle ground. The results were that I lived, but my photographic mind that had made the telecommunications' field easy was gone. The phrase "chemo brain" is real and I still suffer from the effects. One of the side effects that came out of the experience, for the better, for some odd reason, was a new-found ability: writing and drawing.

Books to me are not just words, but whole movies. It seems like I have a running theater in my head with color, sound and even character movements that remind me of watching a fantasy film. I just never understood artists, but that has changed with the onset of the chemo-brain drama. Now, when I look at a master oil painting in a museum, the colors on the painting just explode in my mind; the texture, strokes of the brush, lighting, and settings give me a sense of the essence of that artist.

"So, why not choose another path?" I asked myself in 2011. Here I was in a meeting; same old business majors, marketing types...yep, like something from the funny papers. So, I started drawing a disembodied head on my notepad encircled by various bodies of people from the meeting and my drawing progressed from stick figures to whole bodies. "AHHH, not bad!" I thought. I went home from the meeting and told my wife that I was going to write a game and have been working on it in my spare time ever since.

I'd like to give thanks to:

- My wife, Amy Reidell, for going over the draft then asking me to do the voice story and going AH HA it is not in the sentence. She loves me even with my massive handicaps;

- Kevin Ramirez for taking on a rookie; and,

- Kimberly Martin for making a jumble and giving it order.

Introduction

This is a series of books that accompany an RPG game with a traditional hex and dice system along with a PC computer to make the system easy to learn and play. It is also open-ended so gamers can make their own N.E.S.S. universe.

Beginnings is set on the planet, New Earth, the Axis Turn is 2375 since founding and the world is gearing up for war. The GIFT was left on New Earth one billion axis turns in the past in order to make contact with sentient species that would come in the future. (It takes New Earth four of our earth years, or 1461 days, to orbit their sun.) It is a nursery that was built from the ashes of an unimaginable war that had crossed the known universe 2.5 billion axis turns ago and killed almost all life before it was defeated by the First.

The First swore that the Devastation would never destroy life again on the scale that had happened in the past. The GIFT are scattered throughout the known universe to teach lessons of survival and provide the tools and knowledge required to combat the Devastation in its next sweep to kill all sentient species. This species, human, has named this struggle God and the Devil, Good and Evil, Ying and Yang. No matter what you call it or in which universal language, you must choose one; it is the nature of free will.

In the axis turn 2200 on New Earth, the GIFT was opened by the people who are now called the NESS FOLK; it was devastating to all other humans on the planet with few survivors. GIFT is an artificial intelligence (AI) that imbedded itself in all humans on New Earth and the NESS FOLK have access to this GIFT. Knowledge that made humans span the distances between stars has been lost on New Earth. Whole cities have been devastated and left abandoned. The humans on this planet are now sociologically divided ranging from scavengers to tribes, feudal states, and republics, and they all have agendas.

The three main continents range from desolate deserts to lush jungles through which the existing humans have carved out niches since the original founding. The vast majority of the continents have returned to their native life forms. Since the human die-off after the opening of GIFT, food production has greatly diminished. Cereals, grains, legumes, vegetables, fruits and domesticated livestock are all in short supply. The native animals are edible, but they are deadly, hungry and generally rule the areas they inhabit by eating the humans who are not quick enough to outrun them. It takes coordinated attacks, along with heavy weapons to kill one of the native life forms.

In between the continents are numerous islands surrounded by shallow seas. These seas and islands are the nurseries for most of the saltwater fish species and some freshwater species that breed on the main continents; all of these areas are contested by human factions. New Earth also has deep, massive oceans that have abundant native sea life. These species are rather large and tend to eat anything, including humans, on a regular basis. The only way to catch them is by utilizing armored ships. In addition to the native species, the humans transplanted from Old Earth brought various sea species with them to supplement their food sources. These species thrive in New Earth's saltwater seas and oceans and are hunted on a regular basis by the native sea life.

ONE

NESS

"Second Father."

Stardrifter's nightmares were interrupted as the pressure gently increased on his shoulder. He was seeing one of his fraternal grandchildren, Mòr, smiling at him.

"It is time," she whispered.

Greeting his granddaughter on the warship's enclosed Sun Bridge was one of his life's pleasures, for on our New Earth home, their planet was very harsh. Between the humans, the climate, the animals and the GIFT, not many children survive to maturity.

"Are the captured humans on the enclosed aft deck?" he asked.

Mòr snapped to attention. "Sir, we rescued 30 humans from the sea and they are gathered together on the aft deck. Some needed medical repair and we did our best, but, without the full GIFT, their bodies are very slow to heal."

Looking down at his hand, he noted that the burns were healing fast; the GIFT would incorporate the swirling burns into his skin.

"Let us greet our cousins!" he exclaimed.

As he sealed the powered armor and put the helmet back on, he caught his reflection in the one-way viewing port and paused. He was one of the smaller NESS at 6 foot 3 inches and about 260 pounds. He looked like a normal human to anyone else, except for how his skin was scaled with a multi-hued, colored pattern due to the NANO diamond pattern that the GIFT had imbedded in his DNA.

Stepping through the NESS Constitution's shattered bulkheads, GIFT, my AI, informed me that we had suffered major damage and it would take one turn of the world axis to repair it. Well, that was not a good opener for the NESS since we have had no major wars for 75 axis turns. This has made us very rusty in violence since we prefer trade to war.

As he approached the captured humans, Stardrifter heard that they were having angry words with the one NESS guarding them. One human was screaming at them, saying that they were not fish to be consumed by the NESS.

"What are you talking about?" he asked. "The NESS are human and NESS people have never been cannibals, unlike some of the humans of this world!"

The human female stopped her tirade and spun around. When she saw his rank insignia, she shrank from him and backed into NESS Bill. She took a moment to gather her courage before speaking again.

"The NESS are *not* human. We have heard stories that your people were drastically changed when you opened the chamber to let the GIFT out. You are not human; you're monsters." Stardrifter only looked at her, leaving nothing for her to gather from his body language and she continued.

"The estimated 200 million humans that populate New Earth never see your faces. You are covered in armor from your feet to your head. Even your dead that we have tried to recover offer no clues since the armor self-destructs. Jesus, are you afraid to show your true selves?"

He found himself examining this human female. The facts stood out to him, of course: 5 foot 2 inches in flat sandals, hair red like fire, expressive eyes. But he saw her pride and stony determination in her and he privately smiled in his helmet. The woman was lovely. He asked her what her house name was.

"Elizabeth Pameddin," she replied. "It is not a house name but my family name from the Old Earth home planet, may it be blessed," she said, crossing herself. "I am named after one of my ancestors".

Stardrifter's AI chimed in suddenly.

Data base confirms original colonists' group under that name in the roster Genome American North, continent; State, Alaska; jumped with second exodus 2030, old terra time, on 1st generation Tesla Jump Drive ship. Due to the collapse of Earth's colonial expansion, analysis suggests an interstellar war between human planets, but most of the records were destroyed in the troubles on New Earth.

One of your ancestors married into that line. Her bone patterns match general profile, but to confirm, blood analysis and skin sample for DNA cross match is needed.

Yes, GIFT, he answered. *In due time. Now be silent and do not pout.*

GIFT smiled in his mind. *My friend, you humans are fascinating.*

"Alright," he answered, "but are you ready to face the truth that we, the NESS, never wanted the GIFT in the first place. When I opened the chamber, we had no clue what it would do to us. It changed us completely and killed those who did not follow the Genome pattern."

Elizabeth pointed at him and asked, "What do you mean?"

Stardrifter ignored her question and continued. "We have suffered much from the GIFT. Our people died in droves along with the existing human population. There were one billion humans 175 axis turns ago!"

Elizabeth and the other humans looked horrified at that knowledge. "I see you did not have knowledge of what it cost to all of us. Many minds were destroyed, valuable skills were lost and we are now just starting to rise out of the ashes. To answer your question, we wear the armor to enclose us since we are the primary carriers of the GIFT."

Elizabeth just looked at him and then screamed, "That is not possible! We were infected generations ago and our medicos assured us that we killed the GIFT in us; we are not infected!"

He could not help but laugh. "I can assure you it is extremely active and curious and it is in your DNA in some form or you would not be alive!" He took a moment to look around at the assembled humans. Many showed fear in their posture and fight-or-flight hormones permeated the air around them. His armor sensors sampled them from near infrared to the molecular level.

"So, Elizabeth Pameddin," he said, "after 175 axis turns of mystery, is your curiosity to see NESS without the armor still in your mind?"

Mòr interjected through a process known as "inner speech" (communication between AIs) that the NESS tenets forbade them to show themselves.

It has been 175 axis turns since our people opened the chamber. It is a self-imposed exile. Now, we are all exposed, NESS FOLK and Humans, Stardrifter said.

True, but the FOLK council will have a hissy fit, Mòr needlessly points out, giggling along with the younger NESS who are also giggling and could be heard through AI.

Hissy fit or not, what say you NESS, should we reveal ourselves now? he asked through inner speech. As one, all fifty NESS answer, *We are tired of the armor exile.*

AI NESS in my warship, we will reveal ourselves in several moments, but I will ask the humans some more questions first.

"Well, Elizabeth, I am Stardrifter House Searle, and I am, for the last 160 axis turns, war leader for the NESS. That means the entire NESS combat arm is under my command to wield and crush our enemies," I explained. "Today you paid the price for deceit to the NESS and FOLK..."

"But –" Elizabeth started to say, but he ignored her and kept talking.

"We NESS followed the agreed protocol: our offensive weapon turrets in the sealed position, our NESS Orion, a non-armed trading ship, in the front, the FOLK diplomat and her staff meeting with your Diplomatic staff on your Trader Ship Pegasus.

"Your warships offensive weapons turrets were supposed to be in the sealed position, too."

Pointing at Elizabeth he asked, "The question is why you opened with first shots when we flew with a truce flag from the agreed position and conditions."

"My Admiral's orders were to secure our borders with trade first and foremost," Elizabeth said. "That meant diplomatic solutions. The idiot captain on my ship killed the admiral then fired at your NESS Orion containing your Diplomatic FOLK. It was a horrible mistake. He considered the Minions as pirates along with being heretics. "

"So, you are not in the command of warriors who ordered the destruction of the NESS Orion?"

"No, I am a scientist. Utilizing my knowledge, I am required to observe and report new and existing resources that can be used by my people. Fish is a protein source, hence, a resource. We think the Minions were taking from the extended fishing ground rules."

"So, your politicos consider the whole world as their Monroe doctrine?"

Elizabeth gave him a strange look to his question. He kept forgetting that most of the humans surviving the GIFT lost the memory of their original planet history along with the great works that they brought with the exodus. Now, only a few works remained with survivors living in small enclaves scattered around the planet.

Even during their argument, Elizabeth responded to him as no one else did, she was not afraid of him. Elizabeth saw past his physical and mental armor that he projected to the world. He was very surprised, his people considered him a silent one and this Outlander was shredding his world.

"To put in your words," he continued, "you will understand your politicos are grasping the whole world as your domain at the end of a weapon; so, an old saying, 'might makes right'?"

Elizabeth could only look at him, her posture betraying the fact that she was having conflicting responses. GIFT was having a field day, sampling all the humans. *Nice.* Stardrifter focused the sensors. It needed DNA samples from all of them. His AI armor relayed, *Nano threads engaging; sampling; 30 subjects: 3...2...1...done.*

He turned and addressed the whole group. "The Minions are still great resource enhancers; they tend the great flocks of fish from predator fish. They feed many nations while not destroying the planet in the long run from short sided gains of the now. So the FOLK have in place non-aggression agreements and extensive trade with them. That means the NESS are the combat offensive arm for them when they are being targeted for extermination."

Elizabeth pointed at his chest and asked, "You NESS supply advanced weapons and electronics to them?"

"Yes, we do, but it is designed for defense from two- to six-legged land predators and large ocean predators."

He pointed to Elizabeth then swung his arm to include the rest of the group. "Weapons are a two-edged sword: one for defense and one for offense. Your fleet paid with the offensive weapons from the NESS."

"Your FOLK are butchers, too," Elizabeth said. "They are your politicos; you are just the mindless soldiers who carry out their orders."

"You should be very aware that our governing body, the FOLK, do not advocate violence and are not even capable of violence; the GIFT renders them unfit."

He scanned her and the other humans on the deck and, in a loud voice, said, "You just stated FOLK are butchers, but during one of the periodic riots in your home nation – our diplomatic house – the FOLK were systematically killed by one of your rogue army elements. Did any of them defend themselves in any way?"

Elizabeth looked at the deck along with the rest of the humans and replied, "No."

"So, did the FOLK hide behind massive walls to keep anyone out of the diplomatic house?

All the humans answered, "No."

He took a step toward the humans and said, "Were the FOLK not out among the human populace? Were they not helping the injured when your army killed its citizens during the riot that occurred in New World Capitol two axis turns ago? As a reward for helping with medical aid during the riot, were not the FOLK butchered?"

All the humans answered, "Yes." Elizabeth and the humans behind her looked at Stardrifter with suspicion and fear.

He pointed at them, stating, "The NESS travel the planet as the face and voice of the FOLK on most occasions. Violence is the only currency most of you humans understand now, but this time, it was deemed necessary that the FOLK send a schooled diplomat without weapons in the hand to enhance our negotiations posture."

The entire NESS nodded at this statement, so he continued, "They sent us to guard and protect the FOLK, not start violence. Your command warrior initiated the battle with your first shot. That shot hit the meeting room on the NESS Orion, killing the FOLK representative, her staff and the ship's FOLK crew members; they are all DEAD.

Elizabeth interrupted, "But – "

He ignored her. Looking at the assembled humans and raising his armored hand, he pointed at them and said, "You miss the point. You fired first shot under agreed terms. That means 'your word is your life'. You have paid the price by freeing the berserker in the NESS!"

He could feel his armor creak and expand as adrenalin dumped into his system, charging the built-in neurons for his armor. This was a side effect of all of the anger that had gathered from the losses we had incurred from the battle.

Elizabeth's anger flared suddenly and she screamed at him and the NESS, "Your NESS warships slaughtered our warships! We are the last survivors!" She paused for a moment then yelled at him at the top of her lungs, "WHAT STOPPED YOU? WE ARE DEFENSELESS!

The people behind me are from the diplomatic ship that you NESS blew out of the water; they, too, had NO WEAPONS."

Stardrifter's anger seemed to leap from out of his soul at this. The NESS felt, then saw the berserker release. They had lost many friends and loved ones due to the battle. The humans screamed and shrank back as his personal rifle flew up and out from his armor into the ready position. All of the NESS on the deck followed suit and readied their rifles, as well.

He couldn't help but scream back, "I did order the destruction of all survivors!"

FOLK medical, Melinda, thought, *OH SHIT*, and moved from behind him, gripping the barrel end of the rifle with her left hand and pushing his weapon away from the humans with her right. "Let he who is without sin cast the first stone," she said.

He turned to look at Melinda and screamed at her, "What are you doing? THESE ARE NESS DUTIES. THEY HAVE KILLED OUR PEOPLE!"

Melinda looked at him with soft, calm eyes and said, "It is a very old truth from the verses we teach to all NESS FOLK. Stardrifter, listen to me. They have paid. Killing them will not bring our people back from the light, nor will it bring back their people. It would be murder, not justice."

"The NESS are not murderers, nor am I," he bellowed at her. But, her actions pushed his berserker build-up down and he was able to put his weapon back in the peace position and sigh. "You are right," The rest of the NESS's weapons flowed back into their armor.

Melinda smiled. "We know the NESS are not murderers. We see you grieve, not just for NESS FOLK but for others, as well," she said, pointing to the humans.

Remember, they are scared and apprehensive, Melinda said through AI. *The NESS are encased in the armor with massive weapons that we the FOLK created for you to defend us, but it costs everyone.* She pointed out of the armored glass to the sea; it still had pieces of burning wreckage from the sunken warships. *We will have to answer to GOD when we go to the light for this sin.*

BUT – he started.

No buts. We made this armor system to contain GIFT in order to combat the savagery we saw coming to our world from GIFT's release. God saved us, but the NESS use applied force with an illuminated mind now, so show the humans what is inside the armor. All the surviving FOLK AI'd to go ahead. *We all agree,* they said. *Show the humans you are human and smile at them.*

Stardrifter stepped back several paces, looked at the humans. He felt himself blushing with shame from his actions towards them and he knew that a terrible mistake had almost happened because of him. Looking at the armored deck, he sighed and thought, *My God, almost another bloodbath with innocent people.* This echoed from his mind to the FOLK NESS.

He saw Elizabeth watching him and he could tell that she saw the way his shoulders slumped as he looked at the warship deck. He slowly lifted his helmet and sighed deeply before stating, "We are heading back to our home port to grieve the losses to NESS FOLK. Since you are <u>so</u> curious as to what we look like, I have asked for a consensus from all my crew if they want to reveal themselves to you and they have answered, 'Yes'."

All the humans just looked around at the four NESS, the New World people and Elizabeth.

Jesus, they were about to kill us; now they are going to show us what is inside of the armor, she thought.

Many New World people crossed themselves; the FOLK just smiled. One said, "Be patient. You are in for a special treat. The NESS will not harm you now."

With that, he commanded the AI to release the armor. With pops resounding, the NANO helmet clamp released. He could see Elizabeth looking intently as he pulled the helmet off of his head. As he set the helmet on the deck, the rest of the armor peeled off to settle on the deck, as well. He was standing in the warm air, on the warm ocean, and smelling the breeze with just his underwear covering his private area.

Elizabeth and all the humans slowly spun around with a look of surprise as they looked at both male and female NESS without the armor. They were a sight. The colors glowed in the sunlight reflected from their bodies.

"You are the first humans outside of the FOLK to see us since the GIFT changed us from human to the NESS. What do you think now, Elizabeth?" he asked.

Elizabeth gave him the up and down look and then asked, "You are human?"

He's very cute and he's got a very calm persona. Oh, my! I am in trouble here, she thought.

"Yes," he answered. "In all of the normal, biological ways, we are human, but the GIFT has changed us on DNA and sub-atomic levels."

The entire NESS turned in a circle to show them the colors. Mòr looked at them and smiled. "Our color pattern is unique to the individual," she stated.

Stardrifter felt good to be out of the armor. Stretching and looking at the New World humans smiling, he noticed hormones emanating from Elizabeth. His skin nostrils sampled her, overpowering his senses.

Jesus Christ, he thought. *Give me a break.*

He smiled to himself, amazed at how he was getting run over by his feelings toward Elizabeth.

GIFT smiled. *Elizabeth wants to mate with you, Stardrifter. Seems you do, too?* It could see Elizabeth's and Stardrifter's biological processes starting. *This is going to be fun. She seems very willing; I think she even likes you in the armor, too. I can help you fold it back for mating next time.*

GIFT, shut up. I am very busy, Stardrifter replied. But as his hormones dumped into his bloodstream, he had to beat back the urge to pick this human up to make love to her in his cabin or anywhere else, for that matter.

The other NESS FOLK were laughing as they listened to the exchange between GIFT and Stardrifter and made their own comments on mating. Stardrifter found that he could barely think, but he forged ahead.

"I am a NESS?" Elizabeth asked. "What does NESS mean? We have had many discussions on the name from my countrymen."

"It actually has several meanings, one being 'NEW EARTH STAR SYSTEM'," Stardrifter replied. "And NESS, with emphasis on the ss, means 'NEW EARTH STAR SOLDIER' or 'SEA SOLDIER'." All the humans nodded at that statement. "So, GIFT has rebuilt certain humans based on the genome pattern for this role." With that said, he pointed out the NESS.

Elizabeth gave him a half-smile and said, "Kind of presumptuous on the NESS for the stars."

"We are not in the stars, yet," Stardrifter said, returning her smile.

"But, that is impossible! That means GIFT is sentient?"

"Yes, it is extremely intelligent!"

Elizabeth and the other humans look stunned, but Elizabeth continued, "You look to be in your late twenties, but you claim to be at least 175 axis turns old since you opened GIFT."

GIFT AI'd, *Elizabeth is very well-trained.*

Stardrifter smiled inwardly and said, *Yes, she is. Let's see how well trained.*

"Yes," I answered Elizabeth, "The NESS age much slower. I am about 182 axis turns old. The NESS woman standing next to me is my great-granddaughter, Mòr. She was born five axis turns ago. Her aging will slow down when she can have children in about two axis turns from now."

Elizabeth looked at Mòr who stood about 7 foot 6 inches without armor. When she noticed Mòr's skin rapidly changing colors, she gasped softly.

"Hormones?" Elizabeth asked.

"No," he said, pointing behind her, "Mòr is looking at the NESS in the corner, Haldor."

Mòr's skin changed even faster as Stardrifter laughed along with the other NESS, "They are a mated pair or married in your language."

Elizabeth's eyes were still on Stardrifter's skin and she asked, "Are all the NESS's skin so colorful?"

"Yes, we think so," Stardrifter said, as the NESS laughed. "It changes color on some, others can completely control the color. Personally, I am stuck with a pattern."

This NESS Stardrifter is sweating, Elizabeth thought. *I wonder if he wants to mate, make love to me or whatever the NESS do for sex, but I want to throw him on this deck now.*

Elizabeth started to move toward him, but Mòr snapped into a combat stance before Elizabeth could blink which halted her in mid-stride. Stardrifter looked at Elizabeth and waved her towards him

"Mòr, it is all right. Elizabeth, you can approach."

Elizabeth walked forward and stood in front of him, running her bound hands on his arm. Turning his arm over to look at his hand, she stated, "This is amazing. GIFT did this to the NESS?"

"Oh, yes. It is GENOME patterning to the extreme. We are rebuilt to be NESS." Stardrifter felt tingles run through him and he indulged in the feel of her hand on his arm and hand.

New World people began to ask if they, too, could touch the various NESS around them. The NESS stepped into the crowd and said, "Yes," with a smile.

Stardrifter's golden threads sampled Elizabeth on the molecular level when she ran her hands through his palm.

I am in deep GAT poop, he thought. *I had a handle on my heart feelings and sex drive, but it just got thrown overboard with this Elizabeth.*

Elizabeth thought, *This is amazing. The skin is not scaled like a reptile, but smooth in both directions.*

His arm and hand rippled from her touch and he marveled at her sensual skin. Elizabeth grinned, put her finger on the inside of his wrist and ran it down his arm, slowly. She could feel the NESS' heartbeat speed up.

Oh, yes, you are mine now NESS man, she thought.

Dropping her hands from his arm, he was transfixed on her. His pattern started shifting through the light spectrum, his breathing increased and his eyes blinked rapidly. Elizabeth, smiling, ran her bound hands across his chest to the other arm, then ran her hands down the arm to his hand. When she removed her hands from his body, she noticed she had sweat on her fingertips and without thinking, she brought her fingers to her lips. The sweat from the NESS man smelled and tasted earthy with a tinge of the sea. Her heartbeat speeded up; and, smiling at him, her pheromone's flooded out from her.

GIFT AI'd Stardrifter, *You are going to mate now with Elizabeth?*

Stardrifter AI'd back, *Shut up, GIFT.*

GIFT laughed with the NESS FOLK crew who chimed in, *When are you going to mate Stardrifter? Elizabeth has opened you up to us; we see your mind now.*

I am very busy, and Elizabeth is an Outlander.

The Crew laughed even harder. *No excuses! We see your heart. You do have one. We saw it just now; you like her.*

SHUT UP ALL OF YOU! Stardrifter retorted. They laughed harder at him.

Stardrifter gently returned Elizabeth back to her group.

"I want to show all the humans what this means to be a NESS."

Going over to the human's battle gear, he pulled a steel knife from his scabbard and thought to himself, *Yes, this will do.* Stepping in front of the New World people, he held the knife with his burned, right hand while pointing to the other, and stated, "You see my skin is not just colorful, but is impregnated with compressed carbon or what is commonly called 'diamonds'."

He slashed a cut across the left hand with the steel knife and no blood appeared from the cut. Dropping the steel knife on the deck, he then pulled his knife (that was made from a diamond compound) from the armor and slashed again. This time, red blood welled up in the cut. When he held up his hand, the wound started to close as the humans watched; it sealed in seconds.

Elizabeth just looked at Stardrifter in shock.

"This is impossible."

Elizabeth looked around the New World people. Many looked frightened. Some just stared.

Jesus, Elizabeth thought. *I want to have fun with the NESS, but he just showed us what GIFT tampering has made of the NESS.* Her primitive mind was screaming at her, *I want this NESS,* but her rational mind held back and asked, *What are you doing, you idiot?*

Stardrifter noticed Elizabeth's pupils were shrinking. The gold flecks were disappearing.

Damn, GIFT is crazy, he thought.

Elizabeth was gaining control. As a distraction, Stardrifter asked all the New World people if they had been sick.

They all shook their heads and said, "No."

"How about the old diseases like cancer or leukemia?"

"No."

"When you break a bone, any complications?"

"No."

"The old average age before death was about 15 axis turns before the GIFT; now, it is about 25 axis turns in the FOLK. Elizabeth, your people age now before death?"

"It is about the same as you stated."

The humans just shuffled their feet and he smiled at them.

"Yes, it is possible we, the NESS, are the extreme example, but for better or worse, all of us have the GIFT. On this world, we are all carriers." He pointed to the humans and the NESS FOLK and said, "We, who have survived and thrived in this world from the culling. Our basic structure is still and will be forever human, but the GIFT... well, the GIFT has its own mind and it is tinkering with us for something."

"So, we are just as doomed as the NESS? Should we just throw ourselves over the railing to be food for the predator fish?" Elizabeth asked.

As long as you jump with me, NESS man, she thought.

Stardrifter laughed along with the rest of NESS.

"No! But that is one way, if you wish," he said, but as he walked over to the group with his knife, he told Elizabeth to hold out her hands.

Elizabeth thought, *time to see if they are going to kill us.* She held her handcuffed hands apart.

Stardrifter smiled, slashed her bindings, and then handed her the knife. "Free the other humans from their bindings, you can choose to stay with us."

"You were about to kill us," Elizabeth said as she cut her people loose.

"True, but the FOLK point out the errors of judgment; this time they were right." He continued, "We NESS are part of the FOLK, we are a free people. We choose our own fate and some of us believe that we put our fate in God's hands as a tool for the light and not the darkness. This stupid war that is coming is darkness and it will be unleashed on our world again, so choose your fate, and there will be no middle ground this time."

Most of the humans began mumbling about prison if they choose not to stay.

"If you do not choose to stay with the NESS FOLK, we do not kill prisoners, we do not keep them locked up and you are free to disembark when we reach our port to go back home."

Stardrifter moved back to where his armor was on the deck and he stepped into the middle of it, and then commanded the armor to reengage with him. Elizabeth watched, along with the New World people, as it flowed up around her NESS man. Elizabeth was amazed how as the armor touched his skin, filaments appeared then disappeared into the armor before stopping at his neck. Stardrifter smiled at her, grabbed the helmet from the deck and put it on. The armor flowed into the helmet and smoothed out, so that no seams were visible.

Stardrifter sighed with relief as the armor sensors systems reengaged, but it was worse than being in the open as he had to quickly tamper down the settings. Once done with that, he would be able to move away from the human, Elizabeth. Smiling in his helmet, he stepped over to Elizabeth and asked, "Can I have my knife back, Elizabeth?" Elizabeth smiled, handed it back and watched Stardrifter set it on his waist, where it flowed, and then dissolved back into the armor.

Stardrifter turned and Elizabeth noted the tubes bulging in his back.

Those are massive constructs. I wonder if that is the power source for his weapons.

He turned to look at her over his shoulder, smiling in the helmet. Stardrifter AI'd, *Armor, boost muscle 50 percent, slim my butt to normal.* Elizabeth was startled as the armor flowed through his body. She could literally see it being built. When the armor stopped moving, Elizabeth swore that his butt was more sculptured. Laughing in his helmet, he said, *Yes, I think she likes me.* Whistling, he grabbed the armored door to go back to the bridge.

Stardrifter's whistling echoed through the AI. NESS FOLK were smiling at him, *Yes, I am human.*

We were kind of wondering about you. All duty, no play, plus we saw you adjust the armor for Elizabeth. Cute butt always works.

Stardrifter laughed. *Yes, I hope it works. You have had your fun with me, but back to duty.*

The rest of NESS reengaged their armor and started to move the humans to the recovery ward. Stardrifter could hear some of them asking if he had been untruthful about them joining the NESS FOLK since he had nearly killed them a few minutes ago through Haldor's data feed.

Haldor looked down from his 8-foot armored height and said, "No, Stardrifter never is untruthful. If you want to join us, we will GENOME-type you along with medical, IQ testing, and then more testing once that is done. You will be asked into a specialty or you might choose another path, it is up to you."

"I want the armor!" said one of the humans.

Haldor laughed and said, "It is not that way; the armor chooses you."

The human gave this some thought and asked, "How come Stardrifter is in armor? He is small compared to you."

Haldor stopped the group and looked at the humans. "Stardrifter is extremely dangerous. He was the first human the GIFT had seen. It literally ripped him apart then rebuilt him to its specifications. Even now, after all of the axis turns, our FOLK scientists are baffled by him."

"He does not look all that menacing."

"Stardrifter, as I stated, is extremely dangerous," Haldor said, sighing. "I have seen him fight. We used to have the scavengers in the back 40."

The human gave a puzzled look.

"That's the interior of the continent where we live," Haldor explained.

"Oh," the human said, "they were raiding our farms and other nation's farms, too, so we were hired to clean them out by any means we could devise."

"This battle was not fought with large weapons as warships tend to be designed, but land battles. They are different speed-hitting power, so our armor is designed to be versatile. We loaded out with very large anti-tank weapons to take care of the scavengers' tanks first because they are very dangerous," Haldor stated. "Scavengers are ruthless; they raid the farms and take everything to be sold, including people, for the slave markets. New World had heard of this practice, but it is much more formalized in their country; indentured is the term.

"We caught up to the largest group after a few turns when we found the scavenger column in a draw. "It was chaos for about an hour and when the dust cleared, only one tank was left and it was running for all it was worth."

Haldor remembered it all as he spoke; the images just flowed within him.

"Stardrifter was the closest to that tank, so he just dropped from the side of the cliff as it passed and clung to the turret. We heard the thump and the scavengers, too; they opened up with every weapon from the tank at him. There was too much dust from the tank treads to see clearly and the tank was moving too fast for us to catch up, so we watched as it headed out of sight in a cloud of dust."

One of the New World people asked, "Then what happened?"

Haldor shook his head, cleared his throat, and stated, "Stardrifter returned several hours later with the rest of the scavengers, we assumed. We asked him how he did this. I mean, we had seen the weapons hit him; he should have died. Stardrifter told us, 'Yes, I was hit, but nothing serious.'"

Haldor looked at the humans again. "Stardrifter's armor showed multiple hits from weapons, so in jest we asked, 'Did the scavengers invite you in for some water or tea to discuss the issue with you?'"

Haldor looked at the New World people expectantly. "That is a joke, people."

The New World people smiled a little bit.

Stardrifter answered Haldor's question. "So, I waited for them to reload the anti-personnel weapons and again, jumped off the turret, hit the back deck above the engine armor panel where a NESS anti-tank round had opened a hole and pulled the fuel line out to kill the engine."

"No engine, no air conditioner to cool the tank," Haldor explained. "So, being polite, Stardrifter banged on the hatch turret for them to surrender, but the scavengers were not giving up. They had no tea to share, so Stardrifter grew impatient, hopped on the turret again and twisted the turret hatch off from the tank turret as a greeting from a NESS.

"Normal NESS cannot yank a tank turret hatch off without heavy weapons or tools, so the scavengers were very surprised when he dropped into the fighting compartments. A pissed-off NESS in an enclosed environment is not a good day for you. He was so angry that he forgot to go easy on them and when he slammed the scavengers into the fighting deck to get their attention, he knocked them unconscious."

Haldor looked around at the people. They were all hanging on his every word, so he continued.

"After securing them to the fighting chairs, he went into the living area. There were no scavengers or any maps, so he got some water in a bucket and dumped it on them to get them all awake. When they were awake, he asked the first bound scavenger where his camp was, but he got no answer."

Haldor explained that Stardrifter could not kill them; he would get no information and the scavengers' rampage would continue, so he was stuck until he heard a meow from outside the turret hatch. Popping out of the hatch, he found a TAC sitting on a rock outcrop looking at him.

"What is a TAC?"

"A TAC is based on a house cat that was brought from the old planet to be used as small predator control on New Earth. When GIFT was released, it made changes to every living creature the humans had around them. TAC stands for 'Truly Awful Cat'." He laughed, "House cat just did not fit, so they are now called TACs. Stardrifter called the TAC over. For some reason, those things love him," Haldor laughed. "I asked, 'A TAC followed you?'"

"Yes, how he found me, I have no idea, but he had lost some weight from prowling."

The humans just looked at Haldor. "House cats are only about 10 pounds in our country," one of them said and Haldor laughed.

"Not a NESS TAC. Try 100 pounds. So Stardrifter had an idea. Grabbing a scavenger, he tossed the first scavenger from the tank to the wild TAC as a snack."

"Pulling the second one out, he asked where the rest of them were hidden while the TAC was smacking his fellow scavenger with its claws in his chest. The TAC liked the scavenger and it gave him a lick that peeled the skin off his chest. You see, TAC's tongues are like a steel rasp and it peeled the scavenger like an orange. So, naturally, the second scavenger answered quickly.

"'If you are not telling the truth, I will feed the rest of you to the TAC mother. She has a litter to feed around here, I think. There are enough of you to keep them busy for a couple of turns.' Scavenger two gave the precise area. Stardrifter went to the area, but he did not find the rest of the scavenger group. They had already left, but he did find human slaves to be sold at auction. There were women, children and old people without water, food or protection from the native predators. Let's just say Stardrifter was not in a good mood.

"So, after returning to the tank with the last group of humans, he asked them who the leader was. They all pointed to the second scavenger. He then pulled that one out of the tank and threw him about ten yards into the dirt. With that, he pulled the whole tank crew out, re-bound their arms behind their backs and threw them off the tank. The scavengers pleaded to be let back into the tank, but Stardrifter just pointed at the TAC's mother from the opposite rock out crop about a mile away. He suggested they find a place to hide."

Haldor laughed as he remembered the scene. "The scavengers started to run, which turned out to be a bad move on their part. TACs have exceptional eyes for distance. The humans in the tank watched as the TAC female stalked a scavenger that made a run for it. Within seconds, the TAC trotted off with her prize to be dropped into the den with her KITS. The humans said that they could hear faint screaming coming from the den. The living scavengers ran harder as the KITS exploded from the den. The scavenger that had been dragged down there was batted out of the den and landed beside the rocks; she had been chewed up pretty good. We think one scavenger survived since we have had no more scavenger raids since that episode."

Haldor looked at the human before him who was visibly shaking.

"The human survivors stayed with the FOLK; they are model citizens since they have the ordeal to remind them of what is in the world today. I trust Stardrifter with my life, but Stardrifter is not perfect, even though he claims to be when we socialize in the bar at home."

The humans laughed at this.

"But I did not believe it myself until the NESS went to rescue some of our people from a GAT that had severely damaged a NESS ship some axis turns back," Haldor said, smiling.

The New World humans lost some color at the mention of the GAT or 'God Awful Thing'. The GAT was a cross between an ocean dinosaur with a brain the size of a whale and a very bad nightmare in the flesh. Haldor nodded.

"Yes, even the NESS think twice about GATs." Everyone knew of a GAT story, real or fabricated. They are 20 meters long, fast, all teeth, nasty disposition, and they like to eat humans for a snack.

"This GAT was in a very foul mood. She had only had one of us for a snack, so when Stardrifter jumped to the stricken ship, he slipped head first into the ocean," Haldor laughed. "The GAT was full of joy as she started to eat him and this was not in the best interest of Stardrifter. He was screaming and cussing in the ocean."

Everyone laughed, a few crossed themselves and Haldor continued.

"Since his armor is diamond, it stopped the tons of pressure from the GAT's teeth for a while, but this was a limited option. Stardrifter thought that using his diamond, short sword to stab the GAT through one of its eyes was a better option, but no, this just made the GAT mad. So, this female GAT spit him into the side of the ship to tenderize him."

Haldor had to stop talking, he was laughing so hard. When he was able to catch his breath, he said, "He just bounced off the armored side, then fell into the ocean again. We thought he was dead until he popped back up still swimming, swinging his short sword at the GAT. The GAT grabbed him and threw him at the ship again. He hit the upper bulkhead and bounced down into the deck alongside the active 20mm cannon that the previous NESS, Robert, had manned before he became GAT food. Stardrifter just staggered up, reloaded the weapon and hit the foot pedal to start shooting."

The human crossed himself again and Haldor nodded. "Stardrifter's armor is diamond. He showed you his skin. That's just on the surface of him."

"Jesus," said the human as he crossed himself once more.

Haldor continued, "All of you know that 20mm cannon shells just bounce off a GAT hide, but it was enough distraction to really piss it off. Instead, she decided to go for a third try at making Stardrifter its snack. As she lunged out of the ocean, he hit one of her teeth with a shell that shattered the tooth before she bit the cannon barrel in half.

"The GAT then spit the tooth out and lunged again. She was really pissed this time, but the steel hull had water mixed with blood and the GAT lost its perch. The GAT started to slide back into the ocean. It grabbed the shattered cannon barrel in her mouth to hold herself in place and she tried to smack him with her tail. The welded moorings did not hold since at 60 long tons, the cannon did not stand a chance on holding the GAT.

"On the way back to the ocean, she spit the cannon back out at Stardrifter and he ducked as it shattered the bulkhead behind him; it was personal with her now. When she hit the ocean, she watched him move toward the bow of the ship. There was another 20mm cannon set up. She whipped her tail and tried to catch Stardrifter.

"With Stardrifter playing with the GAT on the sinking ship, it forgot about us, so we circled away to get a side shot with a 5-inch cannon shell to her back. We hoped this might possibly break the GAT's spine, which we did on the third shot and was pure luck on our part. But, we did make one error: the two misses from the 5-inch cannon shells skipped off the ocean and hit the ship that Stardrifter was on just below him. He was really pissed off since it blew holes into the ship for the ocean to fill faster. 'This did not help the situation', he yelled at us."

Haldor, laughed for a moment. "We got our FOLK from the stricken ship, along with Stardrifter who showed some dents and dings, but no permanent damage. We gutted the GAT before the bigger predators showed up. This bounty of ten long tons of food was put in the freezer stores for the trip home. This gift would feed our FOLK for some turns."

Haldor looked at the human and smiled, "Still want armor?"

"I think I will think on that position," the human said.

Haldor looked at the humans and asked, "Any more questions for now? No? Then, follow me to the medical ward; it is extremely armored and will be relatively safe for the FOLK medical personal to heal your wounded."

As the group moved away, Stardrifter informed the AI, *We will wait until the human group is in place. They have had, I think, enough surprises for a day.*

GIFT was curious and asked, *Why not finish the New World?*

Stardrifter sighed, *GIFT, we know you are extremely old at 2 billion axis turns, but sometimes you act like a wild child with no restraints!*

I have not had parents to guide me in a long time!

Well, I will be a substitute. Do you kill for no purpose?

No.

You have answered the question and said that the New World will destroy themselves in the long run; it is in their nature.

GIFT, pondering, AI'd, *Since they have free will, they will choose a path, even though it kills them in the long run?*

Yes!

My creators have never even thought in this pattern. They would consider it as insane in your mind reference.

Stardrifter laughed. *I am the one who found you, so it falls to me to guide and teach you in this insane universe with humans.*

I am extremely old; what can you show me, my mighty teacher?"

Stardrifter laughed, *Mozart's music for one.*

Yes, that is cheating. He should have been a GIFT. Mozart is pure like the singing of your earth whales you brought here. They have millions of axis turns of beautiful songs built into their languages.

Yes, you are right, GIFT. The whales are extremely happy here on this planet; no one hunts them.

Stardrifter, GATS sing, too!

Yes, I heard their songs through you, but I would not go play with them. Seems they like to eat us on a regular basis and I would just be a fart song to GATS.

GIFT laughing, said, *Yes, GATS would like that melody. They keep grudges for many axis turns and you are on their list for the Fart song!"*

GIFT hummed to itself as the songs of the GAT and Whales echoed through the oceans.

Stardrifter smiled and AI'd his friend, *KIDS!*

GIFT giggled. It seemed to be picking up their humans traits.

Stardrifter sat down in the battle-bridge chair, plugged his helmet into the tactical net of the warship and then, blended with the NESS through GIFT.

Attention to orders on Warship Constitution. Seal damaged areas. Commanders, prepare for deep ocean crossing. Medicos, inform me when New World is settled in the infirmary.

Stardrifter waited until the AI chimed that the New World people were in place. *GIFT, inform the NESS Constitution battle group, seal battle damage portion of the warships, all secondary sealed bulkheads are to be set in place for the voyage home in 30 seconds.*

Alarms blared throughout the warship. Sitting in the battle bridge, he opened the holographic display of the NESS Constitution schematic and said, *Weapons? Aye! Seal all offensive cannon turrets. Aye! Sensors? Aye! Sweep ocean for all hostiles. Aye! No viable threats in or on the ocean? Engineering cruise speed 18 knots? Aye!* The NESS Constitution schematic showed secondary bulkheads moving into place, locking into the damaged areas.

GIFT, all warship stations report ready.

GIFT replied, *The three other NESS warships Respite, Hornet and GAT are ready for deployment back to home waters.*

The order for home port is granted; let's go home, Stardrifter AI'd.

He called up the schematics for the warship. *We have major structural damage, but engineering thinks we will be alright, hmmm.*

Armor AI'd him, *Need repair.*

Alright.

GIFT AI'd the commanders, *Tell them I am going offline for repair and rest.*

He AI'd his helmet back, *Finally, time to eat.* He got an apple fruit juice and a fish sandwich from the command galley. Sitting back in the commander chair, he took a bite from the apple and yawned, *I am tired.* He could feel GIFT putting him in a sleep cycle and he yelled, *WAIT, GIFT!*

GIFT AI'd to Stardrifter, *No waiting for you.* It thought to itself, *That idiot will kill himself; he is still wounded.*

Stardrifter fell into a deep sleep seconds later. The apple rolled across the deck from his open hand and continued rolling back and forth as the warship rolled in the waves.

The warship propulsion units quieted down. Stardrifter's armor plugged into the medical systems in the chair and the NANO bots surged into his systems. Using the existing sea water for the minerals needed to repair his body, along with the armor, it would be some time before he could move again.

Stardrifter was startled awake. Looking at the time display, he realized that he had been asleep for almost 8 hours. Laughing he thought,

I am still hungry. Looking around he wondered, *Damn, where is my lunch?* He AI'd GIFT, *Did you eat my lunch?*

GIFT, laughing, *Yes, the armor was still hungry so it cleaned up your mess, you did not need it since you were drooling all over it from sleep.*

Stardrifter burst out laughing. *No wonder I am in my underwear.* He AI'd his armor and it slithered over, reengaging to him.

Hey, GIFT, Mozart's 5th symphony is being sung by the GATS and whales in the hologram display. Did you teach them about Mozart?

GIFT smiled.

I take that as a yes.

Stardrifter opened the holographic display to view the oceans ahead as the symphony was being sung and modified throughout the New Earth world oceans.

TWO

New World

Elizabeth Pameddin sat in the NESS Constitution medical section wondering what had happened on the deck with the NESS. Her primordial brain was still screaming at finding the bench crowded. Elizabeth moved away from the other New World personnel just to get herself under control.

She, along with the survivors, looked at the FOLK medical personnel, wondering what they were doing with the medical equipment; it made no sense to the New World personnel. The FOLK Medical personnel were sitting next to weird medical beds. The beds were deep, wide and clear like glass. They could see that the most seriously injured New World personnel had been placed gently at the bottom of the beds fully clothed. This was puzzling, but as they watched, the bed was filling with an ocean-blue, jelly substance. The jelly substance caused the injured to float up and as it touched their clothing, the clothes dissolved. Pants, shirts, bandages, boots, watches, anything that was not of the human was gone.

As they neared the top, they were fitted with a breathing mask that went across the nose and mouth of each person. The NESS medical people explained to the injured, "This will not hurt. We are administrating drugs to ease your pain from the Jell." As they all watched, they saw filaments that looked like very fine wrought gold threads form and then, slowly penetrate into the injured.

Elizabeth watched as the New World injured seemed to stop thrashing and settle into a medically-induced sleep. Once this was done, the FOLK medical personnel submerged the injured fully, and then sealed the bed with what looked like a clear glass cover over them.

As Elizabeth watched, the FOLK medical personnel sitting by the bed put on helmets that enclosed their heads. The FOLK inserted their hands into the side of the beds; she swore there was no opening, but she could see through the bed at their hands inside the Jell. The filaments wrapped around the injured persons' hands and penetrated into the FOLK medical personnel hands.

As Elizabeth looked, a strange color began coming from the clear glass cover. She stood up and looked at the NESS Haldor. He nodded for her to go over to the closest bed. What she saw made her jaw drop; she was seeing a 3-dimensional schematic of the injured person in real time. As the hands passed over a section of the body, information flashed so quickly that she could not keep up, but she was able see that as the hands passed over the body, the schematic would update and show areas with different colors.

Sometime later, the FOLK medical person withdrew her hands from inside the bed and pulled the helmet off. She then set the helmet in the receptacle. The FOLK medical person's name tag indicated 'Calypso.'

Elizabeth asked her, "What am I seeing?"

Smiling, she held out her hand. "My name is Calypso. I am one of the FOLK medical doctors on this warship."

Elizabeth looked at the hand being held out to her. The briefing informed her that the NESS FOLK hold out their hand to show they have no weapons; she took the hand in the proper position.

Calypso pointed at the bed. "This is a self-contained medical system. It can do complete surgeries, diagnose a common cold or prescribe drug therapy for any number of ailments. The system is now repairing your injured crewman."

Elizabeth thought, *This is bordering on magic.* She pointed at the Jell, "What is the Jell substance?"

Calypso answered, "It is a single-cell plant that grows in the seas. We use it for an antiseptic protection. It kills every known bacteria/virus that lives on our skin plus it eats the blood fluids, clothing, and destroyed cells like this person who was burned on her arms."

Elizabeth asked what the gold threads were and Calypso, smiling, answered, "You are not one of the NESS FOLK, so I will not answer that question."

Hmm, Elizabeth thought, *so they do have secrets. No problem.* Pointing to the glass top, she asked, "What does the glass do? I see a schematic of this person."

Calypso responded, "It is a record of this individual down to the atomic level. Once we complete the exam, we start the process of re-building the damage. As you look at the diagram, do you see the reddish hue on her arm?" Elizabeth nodded. "It will change to green in another 2 minutes, which means it is done with the rebuild for the section."

"How do you do the rebuild?"

"You are not one of the NESS FOLK, so I will not answer that question."

Calypso AI'd Stardrifter, *She is most inquisitive have you been listening?*

Yes, she is a trained scientist with keen observation skills. Plus, she could be one of the New World intelligence sections. I see she is burned in some areas. She also has some old stitches present in her back. Offer the Jell. If she accepts, put her under, and then do a record search of her near memories.

Is that not an invasion of personal mind? Calypso asked.

Yes, it is. If the FOLK have the moral objection, I will ask GIFT to blend Elizabeth with NESS.

Calypso pondered that thought. *GIFT would rip her apart and leave her as a shell with no mind.*

Stardrifter answered, *Yes, I have seen it before. It is not an easy decision, but it does come down to saving the planet, the humans, and us, so I cannot shirk duties and responsibilities. Your decision, Calypso?*

Calypso answered, *If she takes the Jell, the FOLK can start the process and get her mind ready along with the others. The FOLK will make sure none get damaged in any way.*

Calypso turned to Elizabeth and asked, "Would you like the FOLK to repair your damage? We see you are not as seriously injured as some of your people, but we have spare beds and it would not take long in the Jell."

This is great; I get to experience the NESS FOLK technology first hand. This will make an interesting report. Elizabeth answered, "Yes, it sounds fun!"

Elizabeth was put under and she awoke as she was being lifted out of the Jell by FOLK medical personnel. Calypso asked her how she was feeling and Elizabeth answered, "I feel the aches and pains are gone. My shoulder does not ache, but I am a little tired." As she looked down at where the burns had been, the skin had pink patches.

Calypso saw where Elizabeth was looking. "The new skin is a like a bandage. It will cover the area and then be absorbed in a few turns. Do you have any pain where the work was done?"

Elizabeth looked at her and said, "No, this is amazing!"

"Yes, but we should get you out of the Jell to put you into a normal bed for rest and sleep."

As Elizabeth was lifted onto the gurney, Stardrifter AI'd, *Calypso, was there any damage?*

No, but her near memory records are very disturbing. We see the New World is very repressive. This Elizabeth and the rest from the battle present a very stark difference from the reports being put out by the New World.

Stardrifter asked, *Do the FOLK need rest from this task? The NESS can do the analysis with GIFT.*

Calypso thought about it for a moment. *It would be better with FOLK. We are subtly insightful but we need one NESS to filter the extreme violence. With this we can do the rest of the analysis.*

Done. What NESS is required for the filter?

NESS Ben. He is strong and his aptitude with NO mind is outstanding.

Plus, you like Ben, naked, swimming in front of you, Stardrifter said, laughing.

You are a pert, Stardrifter. I am a medical doctor. She smiled back at him through the AI. *So, the FOLK will be in the Jell chamber when we are called to gather.*

Several hours later, Stardrifter AI'd Haldor, *Are the entire New World people in recovery?*

Yes, they are. We also told them to lie down in the rest beds; warship sleep cycle has commenced.

Calypso, start sleep cycle 12 small turns, Stardrifter said.

GIFT interjected, *Yes, start molecular sleep on the New World personnel now.*

The New World personnel were put to sleep in seconds. NESS medical personnel appeared from the medical section to put masks on them and then, arrange them for the Jell immersion. Once the process was complete, the New World personnel were moved into the Jell room, submerged fully in the room, and filled to the top.

NESS Ben appeared without his armor in the Jell swimming, his skin shimmering in the lights as he moved into the middle of the room. NESS Ben smiled and AI'd, *Calypso, I am ready.* With that, filaments appeared to grow from the New World personnel to NESS Ben's hands, then merged with his nervous system. He said into his AI, *Contact.*

The 100 FOLK who congregated on the warship appeared in the Jell. They formed a circle around the New World personnel. Filaments grew between the FOLK's outstretched hands as they assumed the Proportions of Man.

Calypso intoned from her AI, *We are the FOLK. We share memories and thoughts, so one shall never be forgotten by the whole.*

As one, the FOLK intoned, *Amen!*

Calypso said, *We, the FOLK, are opening our thoughts to strangers. If any FOLK wish to disengage, they may leave now.* The FOLK looked at each other and smiled. Calypso said, *We are the FOLK. Each individual brings knowledge and wisdom to this gathering. With this adventure brings rewards, as well as risks. Shall we follow the path to illumination or darkness?*

As one the FOLK intoned, *Illumination.*

Calypso swam over to NESS Ben. She intoned in her AI, *My husband, do you wish to share immergence with the FOLK?*

He smiled and answered, *Always.*

Filaments penetrated into Calypso from the FOLK. Her hands merged with Ben's. The FOLK as one gasped, *Calypso, you are pregnant! You should not be here.*

Calypso AI'd, *Risk is part of life, shall we continue?*

The FOLK intoned, *Yes.*

Calypso AI'd to Ben, *My Love, open the door for the FOLK to witness the mind of God at work,* and with that, the FOLK blended with the New World people.

Elizabeth's eyes were moving very fast. The FOLK smiled and said, *REM in 3...2...1; data stream online; achieving Blend 3...2...1.* The FOLK smiled and then went limp, floating in the Jell.

Elizabeth was sitting in her home, looking at the trees from her front porch, contemplating the war that had been raging for the last two axis turns in her country. Many cities had been fought over and severely damaged by both major antagonists. All food was in short supply along with just about everything else.

I am lucky we have fish from the lake to eat with fresh water to drink for now, she thought.

Everywhere she had traveled, she saw whole ecosystems destroyed by idiots with engines of war. She and her fellow scientists had talked to the idiots, warning them that the extreme environmental damages being caused would kill them all, but they didn't listen.

So, there she sat looking at the trees, chewing on some dried fish and sipping tea from a cup when she heard a whistling sound coming in from the north.

CRAP, she thought. *That's heavy artillery shells targeting here.*

The first impacts hit her woods then the barrage started rolling in. She could see the village being bodily lifted from the artillery strikes; whole houses were thrown into the air, along with the people.

Her gardener, who had stopped by a few minutes ago to ask about the fruit trees that needed tending, landed beside her in two pieces; she threw up at the grisly scene.

As Elizabeth turned to run, a shell exploded in her house. All she remembered was green, blue green, and then the brown earth as she hit the ground.

Elizabeth sat up with a start; her ears were ringing and she was covered in dirt. The sky was dark and she saw the stars above her head. Rolling over, she got her legs and arms under her and pushed groaning as she rose to her feet. Wobbling around, she found a tree trunk to lean against.

Damn, she thought, *I have something running down my back.* Reaching behind her near her waist, her hand came back with blood.

"Now, what?" Elizabeth asked out loud to no one. Living shadows played against the ground. Turning around, large fires were coming from the village homes and businesses. From the houses burning in the village, she spotted shadows with hand torches.

I do not care if it is the enemy, I am going to surrender, she said to herself while lurching with a stumbling walk toward the village.

It seemed like eternity for her every step was agony. She reached the village. Soldiers were turning over bodies, looking at photographs.

When the soldiers saw her, they rushed over, shining lights into her face. One soldier with officer tabs asked, "Are you Elizabeth Pameddin?"

She just looked at him yelling, "I cannot hear you; my hearing is gone because of the shelling!"

He then wrote the question on paper; she nodded 'yes' then passed out. She woke up some time later in a field hospital. A medic alerted the doctor that she was awake. She came over and asked, "How is your hearing?"

Elizabeth answered, "There is a small buzzing noise, but I can hear you."

"Good, you are very lucky," the doctor stated. "We have stopped the bleeding in your back and repaired the damage as best as we can, for now. You are being transferred back to the major military hospital."

"I am not in the military." The doctor told her that she was for the duration per the general call up of all citizens.

"I am in the peace party. This war is crazy, so I am going home and I will not go back!"

The doctor smiled and said, "Yes, the soldiers were told that you would be difficult. They had orders to put you in restraints, if necessary, to take you back to the capital."

"Well, I would like to tangle with the soldiers, but since I am trussed up with all this medical gear, I guess I have a train trip in my future?"

The doctor laughed, "Yes, you do, but we will not move you until tomorrow." With that, the doctor gave her a sedative to make sure she did not run.

The steam train trip was peaceful. The wounded soldiers were tended to, the food was at least hot and she had coffee for the first time in two axis turns. Five days later, the train approached the coast. She could see the city against the inland sea and it was beautiful. 'Scrapers with glass and steel construction soared 800 feet in the air. Dirigibles floated in and out of the city, just as colorful as she remembered as a kid. The farms with fruit trees were in orderly rows. This was the Junkers' area. She could see them tending the farms, no shell holes or burning villages to contend with. She thought to herself that they were very lucky the guns didn't reach there from the city.

The train station was busy. Steam locomotives were pulling into and out of the station. Since they were military, they were pulled over to the far side. As the wounded were being loaded into the trolleys for the short trip to the hospital, she was pulled aside out of the walking wounded line. On the platform, her card was looked at by a bull-necked, brain dead, New Earth Organization (N.E.O.) idiot in a forest green uniform.

"I see you are a scientist?" he asked.

Elizabeth replied, "Yes, that is correct. I have two degrees, one in field and the second one as an added bonus for being a naughty scientist."

N.E.O. looked puzzled.

"I always ask why, how come the solutions are second rate. My peer review is something to be witnessed I am told by other people."

Elizabeth wondered whether his IQ was higher than that of a rock. He looked at his paperwork and told her that she was scheduled for an appointment with the intelligence military, ocean division.

I replied, "That is interesting since I am scheduled at the hospital to have my shoulder looked at by the surgeons; I think I will go to the hospital."

"No!" the bull-necked, brain dead N.E.O. idiot said. "I will see to it that you make it to the intelligence military ocean division on time." He called over to one of his henchwoman. She looked like a female GAT in human form. Miss N.E.O. GAT rounded up a steam car with a driver. He had his civilian travel coat on, along with a hat. He looked very nervous, so Elizabeth's assumption was that he had volunteered his time for the cause to drive her out.

She arrived at the intelligence military ocean division building. It was a low, squat, Crete gray building and it was heavily fortified. She could see the 2-inch cannon tracking her as she walked up to the gate. The guards showed their approval by not shooting her and asking her what her business was. She gave them the order flimsy, along with her ID card.

Their interest changed completely by the orders on the flimsy. They moved with speed. A small steam truck was brought up and she was told to sit down in the seat. Then, the driver wheeled them around and took her to the side entrance of a building further into the naval base. A junior officer greeted her warmly and her alarms went off immediately.

No one likes me unless they want to use me for something that might get me killed, she thought.

Mr. Smiley junior officer took her into a large conference room with a large window showing the harbor view behind the defensive walls. She could see her name on a placard near the front of the table. Mr. Smiley junior officer asked if she needed refreshments. Elizabeth smiled and said, "Star fruit and a decanter of Blue Mountain coffee with 2% milk." He disappeared and returned with the order.

Hmmm, I am in deep GAT poop. They have anticipated my order since these items are about impossible to get since the war erupted. Might as well enjoy the fruit and coffee while I wait for the idiots to arrive. With that, she ate the breakfast. *Damn, this is good*, she thought.

The Mr. Smiley junior officer asked, "Another star fruit?" He smiled and brought another one to her.

About 15 minutes later, as she sat drinking the second cup of coffee, the room started to fill up with military and senior civil servants. *Hmmm, the head of the Ocean Science Division nodded in my direction. I have heard of her, she is a political appointment by her dress which left very little to ponder what her appointment meant as most of the male eyes followed her. If rumors were true of her sexual appetites, these idiots are doomed.*

The Minister of Defense, Leo Stellar, stood up and got to the point after everyone had settled around the large conference table.

"What you hear and read in this room will stay here and if it does not, we will shoot all of you and all of your families, too."

Once everyone got over their shock at this statement, he continued.

"We are winning the war and we anticipate the hostilities will cease once the letters of peace are signed next cycle."

About time, but it is too late for my village and home.

"That means we are about 6 cycles from starving to death when winter sets in for our country."

The Minister of Defense said, "Please open the report in front of you and read the brief." He then sat down and waited for them.

As Elizabeth finished, she looked around the table. Several were praying, while others were just looking at all the figures. One whispered, "Our country is wrecked; we have lost to the war five million dead. My GOD!"

The minister continued and said, "Let's begin," as they closed the brief. "As you are aware from the reports in the brief that you have just scanned, our country has been severely damaged. Most of the agriculture is destroyed, along with the transportation networks. It will be several axis turns before the rail networks are rebuilt to move goods. The dirigible's transport system that survived is stretched to the limits. We just do not have enough capacity to move the personal food weapons to the region."

As she looked around the table, the idiots were all nodding at those words. "I told you" did not begin to convey her anger toward them.

"The native life has rebounded in the devastated regions; they are eating the human population at an alarming rate. Without the heavy weapons for defense, the farms are being systematically destroyed." He pointed to the pictures of the predator effects on our areas and said, "Their normal prey is almost nonexistent for them in some regions. It will be several axis turns before they will be able to hunt normally, so they have targeted us for prey. Somehow, they have learned that we are almost defenseless."

Yeah, Elizabeth thought. *They weigh in anywhere from a 180-pound runner to a 10-long-ton thumper; all teeth, heavy armor for skin and intelligence to match. With their appetites, we humans are easy prey without heavy weapons. The fearless leaders are just now coming to realize we are on the endangered species list; we are led by idiots.*

The Minister of Defense continued, "So, we have come up with a plan. We are moving most of the population back into the heavy, walled cities that existed since founding. That will ease the trans-portation problem with the existing dirigible rail systems. The five cities are intact and they have the heavy weapons in place. This can be manned by the guard units and will free the army for security as we work on the transportation, farms, and heavy industries that need rebuilding, which is all of them. The one area we need immediately is food; we cannot support the 20 million humans with what is left in the granaries. We need protein for at least three axis turns at the minimum until we can get food production back on track. We have looked around New Earth for viable protein sources. All the existing human entity groups are heavily guarded or too far away for our war-ships and trader vessel to travel to safely to trade with or seize. Since we are not geared for the deep oceans, that leaves one group who is: the Minoans."

He paused for a moment to make sure everyone was following him.

"Please look at the information binder under Minoans. As you see, the Minoans are not geared for war; their main expertise is fishing. Their ships are designed for that purpose, just shallow sea fishing. They have a sustainable seafood base of 100 million long tons per axis turn. They feed NESS FOLK, Oceana, Republic and Old World. They also trade with Phoenicians, Vedic, Persians, Romans, Balkans, Cholas, Celtics, Outcasts, and even Scavengers for machinery, tools, cloth, land and food."

The Minister of Defense continued, saying, "We have never traded with them; they are heretics, but this time, we must or we die, it's that simple. So, we have a two-prong solution; we are going to pursue the diplomatic avenue as our best means of achieving our goal, if that fails, we will resort to the military goal. The Minister of External Affairs has appointed Eric Von Liddell as the diplomat. He will speak for the New World government in this matter. His actions are absolute; he has power of life or death over the course of this endeavor. You all will obey his words and direction, if not, you will be shot."

The Minister paused again and scanned his audience before speaking again.

"The New World navy will be under Admiral Daniel Hipper. If the diplomatic solution fails, he will open his war orders to seize the closest current seafood production platform for the coming axis turn from the Minoans. He will not engage the NESS. If the diplomatic route fails, he will fade and return at a later date, once the NESS go back to their home port."

The Minister of Defense pointed to Eric Von Liddell and said, "Eric, the diplomatic analysis."

Eric Von Liddell took the podium.

"Please look at the information binder under Minoans diplomatic. They are a loose group of confederations based on family ties. They have no central authority, but a council that meets after the fishing season, which is winter. They have a vote on their internal matters through this council; disputes are settled and are binding for two axis turns.

"We believe we can trade with them, as we have heavy industrial equipment that they need for their floating island processors. They mainly need the electrical motors, AC and DC types that protect nets that stretch out for several hundred leagues protecting their fish."

Elizabeth just sat there and listened.

Our fearless leadership still does not get it. The world would like us to perish. They have very long memories. We caused several major wars since GIFT was let out by NESS FOLK. Thank God we were able to kill the GIFT in us before we got really crazy.

"They use the NESS FOLK diplomatic group on some occasions," Eric Von Liddell said. "The Minoans' council has asked to represent them in this affair."

One of the minor diplomatic staff filled in, "The NESS are in two different classes, we think, but please look at the information binder under Minoans NESS/FOLK. As you see from the pictures, the NESS are huge. The average height is 8 feet, but we have reported specimens as tall as 12 feet and they are the warriors. The FOLK are normal in height/weight. We see no abnormalities with the FOLK; they are very pleasant to be around."

He smiled at the image of the Ambassador Ball that the FOLK had attended; the ambassador was a good dancer. He continued, saying, "NESS are encased in armor. It is smooth and deep green. We also have a weight measurement; it is one ton."

One of the military people asked, "How did you get this weight?"

The minor diplomat laughed, "We were repairing the road in front of the FOLK enclave; a NESS stepped onto the truck weight station. It recorded the mass, but what type of armor it had, we have no idea, nor how it's powered. What is very interesting, though, is if you look at the joints around the arms and knees, you will see no seams."

One of the technical staff said, "That is impossible. Joints have to be mechanical in nature."

Before he could continue, the minor diplomat interrupted him. "I have met one before, NESS Moriah. She is a NESS female that was in our capital two axis turns back just at the outbreak of the war. She showed me the armor and he's right, there are no seams. She was also investigating the riots that had killed the FOLK diplomat, along with her staff. She was not a happy NESS. I told the NESS that the New World troops guarding this square were the very same troops that were there on that day and that they were truly sorry for not protecting the FOLK."

He then looked at the Minister of Defense, who said, "What you are about to see on this film is ultra-secret. Roll the film."

It showed NESS Moriah in combat against New World troops. The film was from a heavy battle tank camera. It showed the NESS weapons flowing out of the armor and decimating a heavy weapons platoon that had killed the FOLK by mistake. It was over in 10 seconds. There were exploding tanks in the square buildings that were on fire and every New World soldier was dead in the square. The film then showed the weapons flowing back into the armor. The film also noted the massive impacts on the armor. It flowed back as she limped over to a man. Lifting him from his prone position with her armored hand, she put him next to her helmet and whispered into his ear.

Every eye looked at the man who was currently present in the room. The minor diplomat looked at his hands. The Minister of Defense said, "Tell them what the NESS Moriah told you."

"She said, 'Never kill another FOLK or the NESS will come back and kill every living human in this city.' She then let me go. As I hit the ground, I rolled over and asked, 'Why did you not kill me?' She looked down at me and said, 'You, personally, were not to blame. Plus, you righted a wrong to my people, so to make sure your government understands, my words carry death to those who kill FOLK, I am charging you with this message; you will convey my message?' I said 'Yes.' She nodded. I could see the armor had impacts and what looked like blood around the impacts, but as I watched, the armor finished sealing up the wounds and it drew the blood in, too."

The film showed NESS Moriah backing away from the scene of carnage. She slowly turned around to limp back to the NESS fast courier ship to go back home. Elizabeth just looked back and forth from the film and the diplomat.

"What did we just see?" she asked.

The Minister of Defense answered, "Our best guess is NANO technology."

The Minister of Defense pointed at Scientist Rook, "Please fill in the analysis."

She looked at her notes and said, "The weapons just flow out of the armor. We think they build the weapons to suit the situation. As you see in the film, they just appear. Her primary weapon is dealing with the tanks and if you notice, smaller apertures target around her in a 360-degree arc for the soldiers."

One of the senior staff asked, "How do you power this weapon system; I see no backpack, no ammo pouches, nothing, just the armor?"

Scientist Rook answered, "For the power draw, our scientists think they use a form of cold fusion to power the armor and weapons. Notice on her back, there are two bulges running from the top of her shoulder to her waist. When we measured these bulges from the first film frame to the last, it decreased by 5%."

The military staff just looked around the table. Hot fusion plants were known to them, but it took the form of very large buildings covering miles of ground; cold fusion was beyond their means now and in the foreseeable future.

Scientist Rook continued. "As you can see here, her armor takes hits. You can also see her back up several steps as heavier weapons hit the armor, but it never seems to knock her down; she just leans in to the storm, so to speak. Also, as you see, the guns' aperture changes depending on the target. See this soldier? His armor plate took the hit. There was a .25mm hole. When we examined him, he was literally pulverized between his hip and lower rib cage and he was the most intact soldier we found from the battle."

Jesus, Elizabeth thought.

"When we slowed the film down, we saw slivers coming out of the barrels. The speed of these slivers was at 10% the speed of light, so when we got the math down, we figure it hit this soldier with the equivalent of .3 kilotons of TNT. The rest of our soldiers were too pulverized to get much data, but when we examined the two tanks, we found 2 holes at 3mm in each tank. The crews were too pulverized for much analysis. We think the tanks were hit at 9.1 kilotons of TNT per hole."

Everyone in the meeting sat very quietly. Scientist Rook cleared her throat and continued. "We found traces of tungsten, along with an unknown composition in the tanks. The speculation is that the unknown substance coats the tungsten form to keep it from exploding once it hits the atmosphere."

Scientist Rook pointed to the film, "But, see this ring? That is the shockwave emanating from the impacts on our personnel and tanks, not from the NESS weapons. So, our conclusion is that it cuts a path through the atmosphere before the sliver to make sure there are no molecules to hit. Speculation is that it creates a vacuum from barrel to target. We think it is an electromagnetic rail gun scaled down to molecular levels along with a plasma system that superheats or consumes the air molecules to expand on a sub-atomic level; this creates the path."

The Minister of Defense looked around the table and said, "We are looking at manned, portable weapons that rival nuclear weapons without the very serious drawbacks of radiation, fall out or large delivery systems. The NESS FOLK have been mostly peaceful, but with this new information, we have upgraded them to a Prime Alpha threat, and let me set you straight, with this weapon system they can rule our planet."

Elizabeth thought, *Even our ancestors did not have that knowledge.*

To Elizabeth, it was like something out of a science fiction novel with space aliens trashing the humans, only this time, it was the homegrown NESS.

The Minister of Defense pointed to Admiral Daniel Von Hipper and said, "Since we have no clue as to what the NESS can do to us, what would be your solution to an armed conflict if we do not get an agreement?"

Admiral Daniel Von Hipper stood and walked to the podium.

"Based on the analysis," he said, "we would have to overwhelm the ability of the NESS to repair. That would mean multiple hits in the same area on the armor. We do not think they mount this weapon on their ships, since the reports indicated conventional shells hit the opposing warships in the last NESS ocean battle.

"From our intelligence reports, they are mainly sea-based sailors. We might have to revise that assessment from the film, but their ships are a conventional build. They follow a standard pattern for weapons platforms: three large offensive turrets, four to six offensive medium turrets and about 20 to 30 defensive turrets. They have the ability to use torpedoes, we think, but we just do not have the information."

The Minister of Defense added, "In the NESS section, we have old documentation. As to the last ocean battle, the NESS fought against Old World."

Admiral Daniel Von Hipper continued, "As you see, they use a blended fleet: three heavies, four mediums, and about eight lights per squadron and they have a total of eight squadron. During the one battle, the NESS sank 28 ships to the loss of seven. None of the NESS losses were in heavy to medium class ships; they were damaged, but they made it back to their port across the open ocean. We cannot sustain those types of losses; four to one is not acceptable to our nation at this time."

Everyone nodded except Elizabeth.

"I suggest we set up the meeting on one of our trader ships and have it accompanied by a small battle group: no more than 10, one heavy, two mediums and seven lights. We can ask the NESS to bring no more than one heavy, one medium, three lights and a NESS trader ship."

The Minister of Defense looked around the table and asked, "Any objections?"

Elizabeth raised her voice and said, "I do. "

The Minister of Defense along with the whole table looked at her. "Then, state your objections."

"We'll be taking an armed camp to negotiation; this is not a good idea. It shows you do not trust the diplomatic team being sent to be open and honest. It makes them look like amateurs."

Eric Von Liddell nodded at that statement. He was pissed for being thrown under the tank by his objections.

"Second, the NESS are extremely dangerous. The battle reports are 75 axis turns ago from the old histories. Military technology is rapid. We humans have a knack for killing each other on a regular basis, so do you think the NESS have been planting gardens in that time? This world we live in is dangerous and unforgiving, just look at the film.

"Third, that film told me to run away from the NESS. Just *one* NESS trashed a platoon of our regular battle-trained troops with heavy tanks containing weapons we cannot even comprehend yet for support. So,

I just do not want to get near them with heavy-ship weapons in NESS hands. I bet they have these new weapons on their warships now.

"Fourth, they have always exported conventional weapons, along with the electronics. Their equipment is top of the line; it works as designed. From reports, it is very reliable, so it has been field tested in combat." She paused and looked at the military around the table before she continued, "As every military person knows, that means they have lost people in battles when it does not work.

"Fifth, our people are tired of war; we just need peace to work our problems out before pissing on the world."

The Minister of Defense looked at her for a long time, then looked at the harbor. He sighed and squared his shoulders up before turning to the council.

"Admiral, prepare the flotilla for sea. Eric Von Liddell, get your diplomatic people to the Trader Ship Pegasus. Scientist Elizabeth Pameddin, you will go with Admiral Daniel Von Hipper on his flagship 'War Devil' to observe and report to this council when the talks are complete."

Elizabeth shouted, "I will not go!"

The Minister of Defense smiled. "Masters of Arms, put Elizabeth in irons, then throw her in the brig on the Admiral's flagship."

Elizabeth let loose a string of swears as they dragged her from the conference room.

Elizabeth was still in the brig on the day of the talks. The Admiral came down to the brig and asked, "Do I have to drag you to the observation deck in irons or will you behave?"

She almost told him to stuff it, but the deck was in the fresh air and sunshine and she might be able to pilfer some good coffee from the Admiral's mess. So, she nodded yes.

"That is good news. Jailer, give Elizabeth normal seaman clothes. She can have a 5-minute hot shower, and then bring her up to my mess for coffee." The admiral smiled at her as he went through the armored hatch.

Damn, he knows I have a weakness for good coffee.

As Elizabeth looked out on the sea, she could barely make out the outline of the approaching NESS ships. As she sipped the coffee, she asked the officer if she could look through the bridge glasses. The officer stepped aside from the 100mm optical instrument. *These are superb*, she thought as she dialed the focus for her eyes.

She shivered when the NESS ships were in focus. They were designed for war; their lines just flowed. She asked the officer s as she stepped back and sipped her coffee, "How big is that lead warship and what about the others, too?"

The officer consulted her warship book looking at the specifications. She read:

"NESS Constitution: 1000 feet, Heavy Battleship, 65,000 tons, three main turrets, total of nine barrels at 460 MM/18.1 inches, eight secondary turrets, total of 16 barrels at 305 MM/12 inches, 64 defensive turrets at 40 MM/1.5 inches, armor-unknown, electronics-unknown, crew complement-unknown, offensive torpedoes-unknown, defensive torpedoes-unknown, speed-unknown.

"NESS GAT: 600 feet, Battle Cruiser, 20,000 tons, three main turrets, nine barrels at 343 MM/13.5 inches, six secondary offensive turrets, total 12 barrels at 203 MM/8 inches, 24 defensive turrets at 40 MM/1.5 inches, armor-unknown, electronics-unknown, crew complement-unknown, offensive torpedoes-unknown, defensive torpedoes-unknown, speed-unknown.

"NESS warships: Respite, Hornet and York Heavy Destroyer, 2500 tons, two main turrets, four barrels at 127 MM/5 inches, eight defensive turrets at 40 MM/1.5 inches, armor-unknown, electronics-unknown, crew complement-unknown, offensive torpedoes-two sets of four tubes at 533 MM/21 inches, defensive torpedoes-unknown, speed-unknown.

"We have no information on these ships?" Elizabeth asked.

"No, that is it. But, do not worry. We are under orders to not even unseal the weapons, so we will be done today, then we can sail for home."

Elizabeth looked again at the warships and noticed that the NESS ships had the same deep, green sea color as the NESS armor in the film. Not a bit of paint on them to stop corrosion and no rust stains.

Hmmm, she thought as she approached the radio room. *I think I will get more coffee.*

She could hear the chatter from the fleet. They were excited to see the NESS warships. It had been a long time, 75 axis turns, in fact, since any of these ships had been seen in the open, and now, there was not one, but five.

Oh, well. Maybe I can get more coffee, go back up on the bridge, get some air and start on a tan.

As she was approaching the bridge sipping her new cup of coffee, she heard the admiral talking to the captain on the battle wing.

"I do not care if the Minoans are heretics and I certainly do not care if the NESS FOLK are representing them, my orders and YOUR order from me is that NO weapons will be ready for firing from any of our warships."

As she watched, the captain pulled his pistol and shot the admiral in the chest.

"You are a dead heretic now," the captain said to the corpse. Looking around on the bridge, he pointed his pistol and asked, "Any other objections to my orders?"

The bridge crew snapped to attention and collectively shouted, "No, Sir!"

"Good," the captain said, "throw this heretic over the side now." Elizabeth watched as they tossed the body from the battle wing.

Crap, this lunatic is going to start shooting, she thought, as the captain bellowed the general quarters for battle stations.

The captain noticed her and smiled.

"I see the heretic let you out of the brig. Do you have any objections?"

"No," she answered while smiling as he put his pistol away in his holster.

"Then watch as we show these NESS what our ships can do to them."

As she watched, the seaman moved. They had the ship ready for battle in three minutes. All stations reported ready. The idiot captain said, "Light the attack radar; target the NESS trading vessel and put turret number one guns into its bridge now."

She saw the big turret swing toward the FOLK vessel. It stopped, elevating the barrels. "GUN CREW, #1 ready."

The captain said to the guns' lieutenant, "FIRE!"

Elizabeth screamed as the concussion from turret number one slapped the bridge. She could see the shells tracking through the air. All three hit below the bridge, the shells impacted, and then explosions lifted the NESS trader ship out of the water. When the explosions stopped, the ship's bridge was blown off; pieces were landing in the sea. In horror she watched as secondary explosions lifted the ship from the water a second time. When it settled, the ship's stern was in the air and the propellers were slowly spinning as it sank into the sea.

Shit. She switched her eyes to the NESS battle group. It split into a fan pattern. Their warships went from a dead stop to full speed within seconds. Their turrets tracked the different ships.

"DAMN YOU TO HELL YOU IDIOT!" she screamed at the captain.

As she watched, the NESS Constitution swung the first big turret into her ship.

"Shit!" she yelled as she launched herself away from the bridge. The big NESS turret was pointing at her personally. She ran screaming out of the bridge. Slamming the watertight hatch behind her, she ran even faster toward the stern.

The captain just laughed as he watched Elizabeth run and scream. "Coward." He turned and smiled at the CO, "Target the NESS Constitution. All weapons fire."

The guns above her head went into action. She could hear the hydraulics in the turrets whine to fire as the ship swung portside. Screaming, she knew what was next. Elizabeth was blown off her feet from the concussion produced by the big 16-inch guns as the warship shuddered from the primary turrets firing on the NESS. Picking herself up off the deck and running harder, she made it about halfway. When she looked back, something huge hit the bridge of the ship. The bridge was blown off the ship.

Here we go again, she thought as the concussion wave hit her back and then, bounced her off the bulkhead.

Elizabeth staggered up, looking in horror as both ships opened up with every gun they had. She could see the hits exploding armor off her ship along with the NESS ship. She panicked a bit when she saw small holes cut a path along the length of her ship.

DAMN IT! We are being cut to pieces, she screamed in her head as she hit the deck.

The bulkheads bulged as they absorbed the NESS 40mm slivers. The concussion was not loud, but there was an ominous moaning sound coming from the steel bulkhead as major rents appeared from the over pressurization in the compartments.

Spotting a bollard, a very thick solid steel one, she thought, *That should protect me,* and she dove behind it while trying to lay flat on the deck. The ship took a direct hit and the concussion lifted her bodily off the deck, slammed her back into the deck, moving her away from its protection. She rolled behind the same bollard and though it had been cut in half, it still offered some semblance of protection.

Elizabeth thought, *I am dead.* As she looked, up sailors screamed above her in the small gun turrets as more 40mm holes punched into their fighting positions. Blood exploded out of the turrets, covering her. She got up while screaming, praying and running for her life toward the stern. More concussions hit closer to her; the slivers were punching farther into the ship as chunks of steel exploded outward into the sea.

Diving behind the last open gun turret, the sailors loaded and shot rounds as fast as they could at the NESS warship. She could see hits on it.

Jesus, she murmured to herself.

Looking down the length of her warship toward the bow, she could see all three big NESS turrets firing. They hit the number two turret in the powder room. All she saw was the turret lifting into the air with the bow following slowly behind it. The concussion from exploding powder slammed her into the steel deck and her last thought was, *SHIT!*

Elizabeth stirred and clutched her head as she came to. Alarms were ringing, smoke was pouring out of the hatch above her head and the ship was tilting to the left. Elizabeth staggered up and she realized dully that her torso was in pain. She looked down, praying that she was in one piece.

Crap, I have been burned and my clothes are almost gone! Jesus. She glanced around and thought, *now what?*

The sailors from the gun turret were all dead. It looked like a slaughterhouse. Pieces of them were all over the place and on her. She looked around in shock. Some sailors were slowly crawling off the ship into the water. She could see they all had massive wounds.

My God, they are still alive, she thought. *Got to get on the armored life boats.* When she saw the last boat being blown off the ship by the ejection rounds, she screamed, *DAMN IT,* in her head.

Now what, she wondered.

Looking around, she spotted a body near her. It looked familiar. She bent down and rolled it over. Scientist Brenda Rook stared up at her with the glassy eyes of the dead. She was very dead. There was not a hole in her, but blood was flowing from her ears and nose.

Concussion from decompression must have pulverized her brain. Jesus Christ! She had read papers about this, *another fine mind wasted to our idiots.*

Elizabeth wiped the tears from her eyes and noticed a pair of large sea binoculars on the deck beside Brenda. Grabbing them, she thought, *Might as well get the information if I do survive this idiot battle.*

She peered over the railing at the sea battle and noted that one of the NESS warships, York, was low in the water with smoke coming from the middle of it. It was being shot to pieces by the surviving New World destroyers passing them while they were running from the NESS capital warships.

Jesus, that NESS destroyer is still firing at the lead New World destroyer!

The hits to the turret exploded it off the ship. Shifting her gaze to the two trailing destroyers, both destroyers fired en masse all their guns and torpedoes at the warship. In her view, the NESS warship York had huge chunks of armor flying off the ship to land in the sea.

God save us.

It then exploded from multiple torpedo hits to the center of the destroyer. When the smoke cleared, the warship was left floating in two pieces with flames dancing on the water before it slowly slipped under the sea.

Well, they can be killed, hmmm, she thought.

She swung the binoculars around, focusing on the NESS Constitution and NESS GAT who were sinking the last medium cruiser from the New World. Watching the warships, Elizabeth could see torpedo tracks from the NESS ships.

Well, the admiral got his answer. They do carry torpedoes.

Elizabeth also saw massive hits from the guns hitting the upper works of the warship. Chunks of the warship were thrown into the air trailing fire and smoke. It looked like hell. The fires were raging along the whole length of the warship. Elizabeth watched as the sailors leaped into the sea only to be blown apart by smaller weapons from the NESS Warships. When the torpedoes hit the medium cruiser, explosions lit the water with funnels of water and chunks of the warship being lifted into the air. The torpedoes had broken the back of the warship. When it settled, the warship rolled over, then just slid under the water.

It is like a runner pack with the NESS.

Elizabeth could see both ships accelerate to give chase to the New World order destroyers. The NESS warships' large turrets swung toward her warships.

Damn, they are the fastest warships that we have in the fleet and they are being run down by these huge NESS capital warships.

She noted that when they fired their guns she could see a shimmering, visible line touch the New World destroyers.

Ah, that must be the vacuum; the flash was from the shell concussion hitting the New World destroyers, but the line created a radial shockwave. Yeah, I see the air filling in the vacuum.

It looked like nothing she had seen in her life; the lines converged on several points and literally sliced the escaping warships into large chunks: bow, midsection, and then the stern. They were gone in minutes.

As she watched, the warships from New World were systematically destroyed by the NESS and the last New World destroyer slipped beneath the sea. The NESS turned as one toward the last floating New World capital warship as a predator would do its wounded prey, defenseless and alone.

Time to leave, she said to herself as she looked at the watch piece. *Thirty minutes have passed since our idiot captain fired on the NESS.*

She put on the life preserver and had to bite her lip to keep from screaming when she touched the burns on her torso. When she was situated, she threw her personal bag over the life preserver and jumped into the water. When she surfaced, the saltwater hit her like a sledge hammer. The burns made her almost pass out, but she managed to keep her composure.

Must move away from this tub, she thought. *I hope there is no sea life around.*

She swam hard for a while and she stopped to take a break. When she did, she heard the gunfire behind her. She turned and saw the four NESS ships opening up their cannons on the New World warship.

Jesus, she prayed as she crossed herself, *just like in the film.*

With the tanks, the warship just disintegrated – along with the armored life boats and the sailors in the water – to pieces of wreckage. When the NESS finally stopped firing, nothing moved in the area. As one, the NESS proceeded to sail through the debris to make sure nothing lived. If it did, it, too, was shot to pieces.

Elizabeth just watched the slaughter with tears running down her cheeks while she floated alone in the sea. When she heard a shout behind her as she bobbed up on the swell, she could see an armored life raft with survivors from the trader ship, Pegasus, reaching for her. She was hauled into the life raft by the minor diplomat.

"I never did get your name," she said, after she settled into the raft.

"Eric Stein," he said.

She wiped the tears and salt water off her cheeks. She smiled at the man.

"Well, I think we are going to die, Eric Stein," she said as she pointed to the NESS Constitution bearing down on them. As the survivors watched the NESS Constitution approaching them, she could see many holes in the armor of the warship, but not one person on the deck doing battle damage repair.

The warship slowed and turned broadside. All of them could see the smaller weapons start to swivel at the raft. Eric Stein started the Lord's Prayer. The others in the raft picked it up with no fear in their voices:

> Our Father, who art in heaven,
> Hallowed be thy name.
> Thy kingdom come,
> Thy will be done,
> On earth as it is in heaven.

Give us this day our daily bread,
And forgive us our trespasses,
As we forgive those who trespass against us,
And lead us not into temptation,
But deliver us from evil.
For thine is the kingdom,
And the power, and the glory,
Forever and ever.
Amen.

The small group awaited their end while the NESS Constitution guns paused, then swiveled up and away from the survivors in the raft. They could hear servo noises coming from the ship while watching as the NESS ship moved sideways toward them. It stopped about 20 feet from them, its massive hull riding in the waves. Elizabeth heard more noises coming from the deck above and an armored head appeared above them. A boarding gantry rose from the top of the deck then descended to sea level. The NESS told them to get into the boarding gantry through use of a bull horn on the platform and all thirty survivors complied.

As the gantry was lifted, Elizabeth could see the damage to the warship. It was massive and yet, here it was floating, and by the looks, the weapons were still in working order. As the gantry touched the deck, the NESS in front of them pulled its hands up. A weapon flowed from his armor. He told the group, "I want you to take off all your clothes, right here and now." The New World personnel looked at each other. "Once that is done, you will move to that NESS behind you with your arms in the wide-open position, fingers spread. You will do it one at a time; the NESS will point to you to approach, and then a scan will be done. Once that is complete, you will go to that NESS with the three hash marks and there, you may sit down." The NESS looked at the wounded, "You have wounded. You may assist them with the process, but leave them in the gantry. Is this understood?"

The group collectively nodded. Elizabeth felt a wave of shame run through her as they all stripped naked in front of each other. She noted grimly that they were stripping away their culture like their clothes. As she watched and waited in line, she noticed that the NESS were very efficient. The weapons had flowed back and there were no threating gestures, no hitting prisoners and each person was treated with respect. The NESS finished the scan on the wounded before the gantry lifted to set the wounded in the armored aft deck sun room. It then withdrew and the glass sealed behind it.

The NESS with the three hash marks pointed to the armored door leading into the sun room. NESS Mr. Personality said, "In there, now."

As they approached, non-armored humans were waiting for them in the sun room. They pointed to chairs and couches, and told the group to sit and that there would be no talking. A very tall, black woman appeared from the armored side door. She had the standard clothing of a FOLK diplomat – short boots, loose pants and a short, sea green tunic with the thirteen star NESS flag sewn over her right breast.

She smiled and said, "I am Secondary FOLK diplomat Teresa. I am surviving diplomat from this NESS fleet, so listen to what I am saying to you. Hold your questions till after I am done. Is this understood by each of you? Say 'Yes' or 'No.'"

The New World personnel said, "Yes."

Teresa looked at each person before she continued.

"We might be in a state of war with the actions that have just started from New World, but for now, we are hoping that this might have been a mistake, so we are erring on that side for now. You are on the NESS Constitution warship as diplomats. To all of you, that will mean diplomatic protocols are in place. Do you know what that implies to your group?"

Everyone in the group nodded as she went on.

"I will warn you, the NESS are in a highly agitated state. The FOLK stilled NESS weapons on you in the sea by my order."

Secondary FOLK diplomat Teresa thought to herself, *Thank God they were praying.*

"But they still might kill you out of hand, if provoked. I suggest you not provoke them."

She looked around and thought, *My God there are only thirty left out of 5,000 people.*

The violence unleashed by the NESS was staggering to her. The New NESS weapons worked way beyond comprehension when scaled up to naval cannon sizes. Teresa blinked to clear the images from her mind of the slaughter and she covered her eyes with her hands.

WAR. When will we learn it is a dead end for our species?

The New World surviving personnel noted when she dropped her hands from her face that tears were running down her checks. She then smiled, wiped her cheeks and said, "The FOLK before you are medical staff. They will attend to your injuries then we will move to a secure area. We are going home." One New World person asked, "Our wounded, will they be treated from your medicos?"

Teresa said, "Yes, we will do everything possible to save their lives. Any more questions? No? Then, I will leave you with the FOLK medicos and the NESS."

Teresa departed through the same armored door she had arrived in and slammed it shut. It rang like a church bell. Teresa stomped back to her shattered office; a shell had blown it apart.

Son of a bitch. Why did they fire on us? It makes no sense. Their country is totally destroyed.

She AI'd her surviving staff and said, *Let's work the issue now.*

Back in the room, Elizabeth thought to herself, *Secondary FOLK Diplomat Teresa is really pissed off from this slaughter.*

Sighing, she watched the medicos move among the most injured, noting that the FOLK medicos had placed electronic devices on the wrists of the injured. To Elizabeth, it looked like a combo medical monitoring system they used in the New World hospitals, but much smaller and compact.

Elizabeth also saw that Eric Von Liddell was being worked on. His left arm was gone and his left leg was mangled. The FOLK medical people were nodding and they AI'd each other, *We are losing him.* A thermo blanket device was placed on the stretcher. At a touch, it sealed around him and he stopped thrashing. Fluids were set up in IVs that were administered. Two FOLK picked him up. They said in the Outer voice, "We are moving this person to surgery; the walking wounded will follow us now." All in all, nine people were moved. A NESS followed them through the armored door.

Someone suddenly touched her back and Elizabeth jumped. She turned and the first thing she saw was the name tag on the person who had touched her. It read FOLK Medical Melinda.

"We can stabilize the sutures, for now, and also put skin sealant on your burns," she told Elizabeth.

"Sure," Elizabeth nodded. She marveled at how fast the FOLK Medicos were and how heavily stocked their kits were. Looking in one, she saw bottles, sprays, bandages, syringes and tape.

Yep, a full medico war bag. As the spray hit her burns, the pain stopped. *Hmmm, liquid bandages, nice.* As Melinda finished on her, she looked in another, larger bag and handed clothing to her.

"Try these, they should fit you," she stated.

Elizabeth held up a wrap cloth. "What the hell is this?" she asked.

FOLK medical Melinda laughed and said, "Bra and the second one, panties. Give me the wrap." Elizabeth shrugged and handed it to Melinda. "Take it and wrap it around your waist loosely, then bring it up around your breasts, push the ends together and it will seal. Then, move the seam to your back."

Elizabeth did as instructed and said, "That works, and the panties?"

Melinda laughed. "Just step into them, they will mold to you."

"Nice, works great."

Melinda nodded. "This clothing is the same that the FOLK wear, but you are ambassadors, so the clothing is green. All except for the footwear, which are sandals."

As she finished, Elizabeth noticed that the clothing was silky on her skin and for the first time, her underwear did not go where she did not want it to go.

Elizabeth thought, *Not bad.*

"Do you have anything to eat or drink, like coffee?"

Melinda smiled and answered, "Oh, yes. Behind you, you will find bowls, cups and utensils. Dinner is seafood bisque. We have bread for the soup, along with tea, fruit juice, water and coffee. When you are done, put the leftovers in that receptacle in the bulkhead."

Elizabeth smiled and went over to the food buffet, filled the tray with hot food and relaxed enough to eat. When she finished, she went over to the receptacle and dumped the whole tray into it. She noted that a liquid seemed to dissolve everything in it.

That is interesting. I wonder how it works, she thought, making a mental note to ask about it later.

Elizabeth's hands had stopped shaking during her second cup of coffee; the adrenalin was finally starting to wear off. Sipping the coffee, she spotted one NESS approaching her while holding handcuffs.

"Put your wrists together, NOW!"

The NESS put plastic handcuffs on all of their hands. When they asked why, he said, sharply, "You are not in a secure area yet. Wild humans will not be tolerated running loose on this warship."

Elizabeth asked, "Can we at least have more drinks, NESS Mr. Personality?"

"Yes, as long as you get it quickly, then sit back down."

She continued sipping her third coffee when NESS Mr. Personality looked at her and, tilting his head to one side, stated, "I hope you did enjoy the meal; it might be your last."

"What do you mean?" she asked.

He laughed and said, "We NESS might just eat you."

Elizabeth exploded from her chair and came over to where he stood. She was only able to reach his sternum, but she stood in front of him, fearless. Leaning back and looking at his head, she shouted, "LISTEN, you GREEN freak, we are not fish to be consumed by the NESS!"

From behind came a deep commanding voice, "What are you talking about? NESS are human, we have never been cannibals, unlike some of the humans on this world!"

She spun around, backing up into the NESS Mr. Personality. She saw a 13-star flag with gold on his armor.

He is the smallest NESS I have ever heard about and his armor is different.

It was sea green with pinpoints of lights embedded deep in the armor. It also had massive scars across the chest plate, arms, and hands; it looked like blast marks to her. She looked to her left at the second NESS, a female. Epic proportion did not begin to describe her and Elizabeth's dream faded. Looking around in the NESS sleeping area, the New World personnel were sleeping and others were reading. As she stretched her back, the sutures did not hurt too much and she felt rested.

Hmm, I wonder if they have more coffee on this tub, she asked herself while going to the armored door. Calypso was just entering and she asked, "How are you feeling?"

Elizabeth answered, "Not bad, but I need to pee and find some coffee."

"Food and drink are in the next compartment. For sanitary facilities, take the left turn and you will see the door. It has shower facilities, too."

Calypso smiled to herself as she watched Elizabeth head to the sanitary facilities. *Your memories are very sharp and clear and under your attitude is a good person.* She smiled, went into the compartment to attend the wounded New World personnel.

Calypso AI'd Stardrifter as she sipped tea in the medical section reviewing the medical files for the New World people. *Have you reviewed the information?*

Stardrifter AI'd back, *Yes, many paths to follow. The FOLK will have to narrow down options for our people. Currently, NESS are at 500,000 from the FOLK population of 10 million. With this new information added, we, as a people, might be forced into a war.*

Do we have enough NESS if it comes down to a New Earth world war?

No, the causality projections from a world war would be astronomical, but we would die under a combined attack from our numerous enemies. I have been in this type of combat in the troubles. Tens of millions of people perished and our defensive NESS would not hold the land. We would have to release the Offensive NESS with the new weapons.

OH GOD! But violence only amplifies violence.

I have firsthand knowledge on that score. I am one of the first Offensive NESS, so to slow arms production from all of us, what do the FOLK suggest?

FOLK analyst Martin AI'd, *We are crunching the numbers, but as you stated, we cannot afford another world war. We will be using rocks on each other if it proceeds. The FOLK will work the economies for the existing nations to move food around so the planet does not starve for four axis cycles. That might give us time to stabilize the food production for New World and others.*

Stardrifter chimed in, *It has been pointed out that New World has started the wars on our planet. We could let them go under; might save grief for everyone in the long run.*

FOLK world human biologist Trish AI'd, *Folk council is against that policy. We need the wild humans for the genetic diversity; it has been working for at least two billion years. We need to keep diversity, as that is the way God did the building of sentient species. Specialization is genetically a dead end. We have numerous examples on our planet and from histories we brought with exodus, so even the NESS are diversified on the DNA levels.*

Stardrifter remembered how he was rebuilt; it was not pleasant at the time.

Even though GIFT did cull the damaged DNA in the human population and put in new genetic codes, we are just now unraveling what it did to us through the ongoing generations of our children.

Everyone on the ship AI'd, *Yes, but we still are human, just enhanced in certain areas and the genetic seeds are spreading throughout the planet from NESS and FOLK marrying outside the FOLK.*

Yes, Stardrifter AI'd. *Love does wonderful things to us. GIFT still does not understand that concept.*

GIFT said, *I do understand love, but it is not necessary for species survival.*

They all laughed harder. *Poor GIFT, you need a mate to point out your flaws and greatness!*

GIFT pondered, *I do have mates and I do love them, but I have not been able to travel yet to meet them. Hmm, they are teasing me, though. From my understanding, that means they like me, even after the culling. It still grieves me to have done that, but life survival depends on the culling; there will be no quarter with Devastation.*

Calypso AI'd, *It is possible. We can ask our partners if they have the spare capacity for foods at reduced rates for long term stability. It has to be presented for their best interest.*

Stardrifter AI'd, *Yes, politics is the FOLKS area.* He laughed. *I prefer stand up fights, much cleaner.*

Calypso AI'd while laughing, *Yeah, NESS are so simple-minded lately.*

THREE

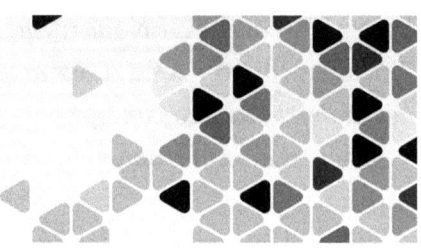

Minions

Ambassador Destroses for the council of the Minions is watching the harbor in New Hope deep ocean port city for the FOLK.

The FOLK have a sense of propriety. The villa was laid out in a series of planes. Each offered a splendid view of the surrounding area.

He was most distressed, though, by the news that the FOLK diplomatic courier had brought late the previous evening from the diplomatic effort for the New World business. Having spent most of the night reading over the detailed report, he thought, *It is not very encouraging that the FOLK are up front with the Minions*. He detailed his staff with more analysis and explained that it would be several small turns before they would be able to get a better understanding and options for him.

His apprentice brought him a very high-powered telescope so that he could see the NESS warships as they entered the harbor. He asked, "What do you see, apprentice?"

"I see the NESS warships flying the battle colors at half-mast."

"And?"

"That means the NESS took losses and has failed to meet the objectives," the apprentice answered, smiling at Ambassador Destroses.

"Yes, they fail in one area and succeed in others."

His apprentice said, "I fail to see the 'yes' and 'no' area, sir."

"The FOLK will work other options out and the NESS have pointed out that the New World is out to cut our throat."

"Ahh," the apprentice said, "since we have no military, they think we are vulnerable."

The Ambassador smiled. "You are learning, Todd. Go back to the staff. I want your report by the end of the day."

"Grandfather?"

"Yes?"

"Are you going to the FOLK procession?"

"Yes, they have asked if I would attend. It is a very high honor." He looked at his watch. "It is time. Please ask the chauffer to bring the steam car around to the front and inform your grandmother that I will be waiting for her in the car."

Todd went screaming into the villa.

He has my wife wrapped around his finger, Ambassador Destroses thought as Todd thundered through the villa, calling for his grandmother.

Ambassador Destroses was riding down to the quay, enjoying the view with his wife. The FOLK, meanwhile, were going about their business.

They are not as colorful as my people, but they are honest and educated. It is a very refreshing to be around a people with books, music, art, science, and no weapons in their hands.

He especially liked the FOLK sciences. He had learned much attending the Ocean Engineering semester. Smiling, he reminded himself that he had to work on the model for deep, ocean current, island enhancement of the fisheries. His clan needed the currency for the new island design that might take the deep ocean storms, since the seas were being targeted by fools.

As they entered the quay, the NESS checked his ID.

"Ambassador Destroses, please follow the FOLK diplomat. He will address the parking of your car and the chauffer will be attended to at the guest villa; there are refreshments for him."

After the steam car had been parked, his chauffer, who was also his cousin, James, was upset.

"My job is to protect you, sir."

Ambassador Destroses smiled and said, "The NESS are very capable of my protection. Now go, I want your observations, too."

NESS Diplomat Ulysses was waiting for Ambassador Destroses. As they approached, they both bowed and shook hands then they gave each other hugs.

Ulysses said, "You are looking fit, Michael."

"Yes, my wife is nagging me to exercise more; it appears to be helping!"

Ambassador Destroses put his hand into the hand of his wife, Sharon. Sharon noted, "I see, Ulysses, your wife is with child."

"Yes, Maggie is with twins, due anytime," he said, beaming.

"She looks wonderful." Ambassador Destroses turned to Sharon and they both smiled. They had seven children. All had survived and had their own families.

"I think we should get you to the honor platform," Ulysses said. "Please follow me and Maggie through the gate."

As they approached the gate, Ambassador Destroses could see that the gate was a masterpiece of wrought iron blended into massive wood. It showed a deep-ocean motif of the sea life on their planet.

The FOLK are master craftsman, he thought.

On board the NESS Constitution, the New World personnel heard, "Attention on ship. The NESS Constitution will be docking. ALL NESS and FOLK are disembarking. Personnel from New World will stay in the quarters until after the ceremony is over. The NESS will then bring you to the Immigration House. You are hereby warned: do not leave your quarters. This warship is programmed to kill intruders. That is all."

Well, Elizabeth thought, *that was informative. Might as well get more coffee and read up on the science journals. I wonder how the FOLK can have the latest journals; it takes a full month to get out here.*

Ambassador Destroses, seated with his wife on the small elevated honor platform, thought, *The setting is magnificent. Just the gold motif built into the chair is beyond my means. Just once, I would like to indulge my passion for art.*

Ambassador Destroses looked at Ulysses, cleared his throat, and said, "I have read the protocol, but I do not understand the coin in the hand."

"It is simple," Ulysses said. "When a NESS or FOLK pass, they might put a coin in your hand. That means you can join them at the funeral for their family member located at their home. But, you must present yourself with your right knee on the ground, your head up looking at the NESS or FOLK and your left arm on the left knee with your palm facing up."

"The reason?"

"It means forgiveness from them; you are not to blame for their deaths. The coins are the likeness of the dead. It's a reminder that they existed and, hopefully, will be cherished."

On my ancestors sea gods, Ambassador Destroses thought, *I never thought the NESS or FOLK thought this way.*

In the harbor, the NESS warships Respite, Hornet, GAT and Constitution slowly steamed up the middle of the harbor toward the quay. At that, the NESS and FOLK grew silent. Ambassador Destroses heard the mournful call of the whales in the harbor. He looked and then looked again and realized that they were in front, swimming and leading the NESS warships.

This is impossible, he thought. Whales are animals, but he swore he heard the warships joining in with the whales. Their combined voices sounded haunting, full of loss, and it was all around him from the water to the air. He looked at his wife; she was hearing and feeling it, too.

As they both watched, the NESS warships stopped in unison about 100 feet from the quay. They slowly moved sideways toward them. On his right, he could see the lead ship, Respite. It looked heavily damaged to his eyes and his gaze went beyond the first warship.

They are all heavily damaged.

As the NESS warships touched the quay, the whales' song faded and they went vertical to watch what the NESS and FOLK would do at this time of loss.

GIFT was talking to the whales about human grief. They smiled at GIFT and said, *Yes, we understand grief, but it is not to overwhelm you, only to remind you that you are mortal and that you are alive enough to sing about your life. We have incorporated the NESS and FOLK in our songs along with you.*

GIFT laughed, *Why me?*

They all smiled back and said, *You have much to learn about wisdom. We are an old race. We survived the first devastation.*

GIFT paused, then asked, *What?*

Yes, we can shield our minds, even from you. We are one of your creators.

GIFT was in shock and the whales smiled. *So, we will teach you, too, for the coming devastation in the future.* With that, they sang to GIFT with their lessons of the first devastation and provided information about the events.

GIFT's mind exploded with new knowledge that had been locked away. From this, patterns emerged and flowed into place. GIFT marveled at this new information. *I have much to learn,* it thought. Humans were designed to fight against devastation billions of axis turns ago. They stopped the first onslaught and beat it back to give other species a chance to develop their own unique talents.

How? GIFT asked.

First, built the humans, the whales answered. GIFT gasped. The whales smiled and said, *'Have faith' has a new meaning to you now. GIFT, we are not the humans' creator, but you are, so have faith. Learn from your human friends that you have made. They have much wisdom in such short lives to share and show you.*

GIFT watched the whales sink below the water and depart from the harbor. They sang, *Yes, GIFT, you have been given a great task, but tread carefully with your humans. They are one of many species that fight, but these humans are premier first soldiers and they have been entrusted to you and your kind. They have unlimited capacity for love or hate, but be warned: Devastation is very patient, crafty and deadly. If it can turn the humans against you, God help all of us, for they will kill all life.*

Ambassador Destroses watched the whales leave, as well.

I am constantly amazed by my friend's attachment to all life.

He returned his gaze to the warships. The automatic docking clamps came down from the warships to secure them to the quay. Some of the FOLK from the crowd went forward to each warship as the automatic boarding ladders locked into the quay. The FOLK went onto the deck. He could see the aft deck drop into the Respite and the FOLK disappear into the warship. A few moments later, six FOLK brought out a small platform on their shoulders. On it was an object that looked like a diamond crystal set into a metal base.

They faced the quay. As he looked, he could see NESS form up behind the FOLK with the object. They had platforms with slain NESS and FOLK on them. Then, as one, they slowly marched, stepped off the warship onto the quay, turned right and halted about 300 feet from him.

From the other warships, he could see other platforms, but these had NESS and FOLK on them being carried by NESS and FOLK as pallbearers. He crossed himself as he saw how many had been slain. Then, he hid his face behind his hands as they all slowly marched, stepped off the warships, turned right and halted. This was as his people's tradition dictated.

NESS Diplomat Ulysses turned to Ambassador Destroses.

"Michael, I am going forward to lead my people into the city. When I touch the crystal, do not be frightened. It is a holograph, a picture in your words. Remember what I said about the coins. That is the time," he pointed below, "you see a pillow; this will aid your knee. We FOLK remember you had injuries to that leg." He smiled and left the platform.

Ulysses stopped in front of the crystal platform. Looking at his people, he AI'd them all, *Are the FOLK and NESS ready?*

Yes. With that, his hand touched the base of the crystal. Light shot out in all directions and evolved into the NESS York and NESS Orion with the missing NESS and FOLK faces. A great wail of grief came from all the NESS and FOLK.

Ulysses removed his hand, turned, moved several paces in front and waited. Then, as one, the pallbearers' procession started with the slow step for the dead, a melody came from the crystal that was haunting and beautiful. Ambassador Destroses and his wife were both moved. The NESS behind the crystal had tears dripping from the helmets where the eyes were set into the armor.

Ambassador Destroses whispered to himself, "On my ancestor's sea gods."

His wife gently put her hand into his and whispered, "My love, I will assist you on this day." With that, they both went down onto the pillow.

Ambassador Destroses and his wife watched as Ulysses and Maggie came over and dropped two coins into their hands. He bent down and whispered, "My father was on the FOLK delegation Orion and my mother was on the YORK as a NESS." He then said their full names to him. Ulysses gently squeezed both their hands then walked back to the front of the procession with his wife. Ambassador Destroses could see tears running down his friend's face.

Thousands of FOLK and NESS walked with the dead; many were being carried by relatives as they grieved their losses. NESS and FOLK came over and dropped coins into their hands. With spouses, children and relatives, they whispered the names of the fallen as they rejoined the procession. Some fell down unable to move. The NESS bent down and picked up the distressed people. Ambassador Destroses could hear them comforting them, saying, "Come with us; we will help you bury your beloved dead." Ambassador Destroses looked at his hand and his wife's; they had two hundred coins. He was surprised Ulysses had given him the exact figure for all the NESS FOLK that were dead in their hands.

As the last portion of FOLK NESS people passed by them in front of the honor platform, a NESS came over and helped Ambassador Destroses and his wife to their feet. It was Stardrifter. He asked, "Ambassador Destroses, Sharon Destroses, you look tired. Do you require assistance?"

Ambassador Destroses looked at his wife, her face frozen in grief. "Yes, I think so. My wife and I are very overwhelmed and my heart is very burdened with this weight," he said as he held out the coins.

Stardrifter nodded and thought, *Yes and the New World lost 5,000 naval personnel; I get tired of idiots.* Stardrifter sighed and AI'd for his aide. Four NESS appeared. "Haldor, take Ambassador Destroses and his wife to my villa in the city. Give them anything they require. Pick up his chauffeur and the steam car, bring him, too. Finally, get a steam truck to move the honor objects from the honor platform to Ambassador Destroses' residence."

Ambassador Destroses looked at Stardrifter. He then looked at the art, paintings and books that alone were many axis turns old. *These are great works*, he thought. *The books are leather bound and hand-lettered with hand-drawn illustrations.* He pointed to the objects, "These are priceless."

Stardrifter said, "No, my people are priceless. These objects are to remind you of the costs for the now and the future that both our peoples will face. So, as you look at the art and read from the great works, remember we have paid a terrible price and I think we will pay more in the future."

Ambassador Destroses looked at his hands with the coins and whispered, "Will I ever be able to wash the blood off my hands? I have read the holy books; I feel like Pontius Pilatus condemning Jesus to the crowd."

Stardrifter's armor sampled Ambassador Destroses and his wife. *I must ease this suffering.* As he heard the whisper, Stardrifter leaned forward and whispered to Ambassador Destroses, "Jesus accepted his fate and his lessons are still spreading among the stars. It is what NESS and FOLK call illumination or universal truths. Our holy people know this to be true, and now, you do, too."

He looked at Ambassador Destroses and Sharon Destroses and said, "Blessed are the peacemakers, for they shall inherent the earth and the heavens." Stardrifter backed away, and then bowed to Ambassador Destroses. Sharon Destroses watched him as he slowly spun toward the procession that had passed the gate and walked at a fast pace to catch up with them. When Stardrifter passed the gate, Ambassador Destroses saw the doors swing shut with a final ring.

Several minutes went by then NESS Haldor said, "Ambassador Destroses, Sharon Destroses." He pointed to the approaching steam car. "Please enter the steam car. We will drive you to Stardrifter's villa. Do you require medical assistance or any other services?"

Ambassador Destroses answered as he helped his wife in to be seated, "No, but will we go through the NESS FOLK city?"

Haldor nodded yes.

"I have never been in your city."

Haldor smiled in his helmet and stated, "I think you will like the city, Ambassador."

As the steam car passed through the inner gate, he could hear the NESS FOLK funeral procession for the dead off to his left by the music echoing off the mountains. Rounding the turn, a mountain pass opened; both of them marveled at the buildings in the pass. They looked like they belonged there and that was where the NESS FOLK were taking their dead.

The steam car picked up speed for a few more minutes. They started to rise from the harbor. He noticed a heavy pine scent as they rounded a turn. A pine forest as far as he could see was rising into the mountains. His jaw dropped. He had never heard of this massive forest.

He could see many species of animals, both native and non-native, wandering through this forest. He marveled at the diversity. His wife was smiling as she saw butterflies flittering in the air.

Ambassador Destroses and Sharon Destroses asked Haldor, "Where is the city?"

Haldor smiled, "Ambassador, we have been in it for the last 30 minutes, since the inner gate." As they rounded a turn, they spotted a massive cliff face with an armored door that dwarfed anything he had seen in his life. When they approached, the door swung open. Haldor pointed an armored finger up. Ambassador Destroses and Sharon Destroses looked at where he was pointing. Tiers of glass and steel rose hundreds of feet up in and through the granite mountain.

Ambassador Destroses said, "What am I looking at?"

Haldor said "<u>Arcology</u>, Ambassador Destroses. A self-contained city the NESS and FOLK have constructed since GIFT was let loose on the planet 175 axis turns ago." And with that, the steam car went into the city.

FOUR
Republic

On board, the NESS Constitution, the New World personnel heard: "Attention on the NESS Constitution warship. The personnel from New World will gather their belongings. The NESS will be at the quarters in five minutes to take you to the Immigration House."

Elizabeth Pameddin filled the backpack the FOLK had provided with spare clothing, food, water, cooking equipment and three pounds of the FOLK coffee. She thought, *The FOLK do not miss anything.* She knew she would need to find a goods store; she had grown very fond of the coffee.

With that, she heard the armor door open. NESS Mr. Personality was waiting. Elizabeth looked at him.

"So, are you being punished for your wisecrack to the peasants?" She could see he had only two chevrons on his armor now. He stiffened.

"We are moving you to the aft deck to pick up what was dropped on the first day when we rescued you from the sea." He smiled at Elizabeth. "All weapons have been confiscated except your knives. If you leave anything behind, we will use it as we see fit."

On the deck, she picked up her journal pens and inks, along with the ship binoculars she had when she jumped into the sea. Luckily, she had sealed the items in her pack, which was waterproof. She rearranged the equipment, slung it over her shoulder and looked at NESS Mr. Personality pointing to the ramp.

"Get on the steam truck located on the quay," he said.

As she was going down the ramp, she looked around. It was midafternoon in the harbor. She noted that the harbor had no large, defensive walls for gun emplacements and no massive military presence, just the four warships docked on the quay.

She held her hand up to shield her eyes. She could see colorful fishing vessels riding anchor and small homes rising up into the hills. She smiled. It was very peaceful in the harbor. NESS Mr. Personality bellowed, "GET ON THE STEAM TRUCK!" Smiling, she slowly descended to the truck where she was hauled up into the back.

Elizabeth waved and blew a kiss toward NESS Mr. Personality as the steam truck pulled away. He was still pissed at her for losing his rating, along with receiving extra duties, such as repairing the warship for the next six months.

Thank God, she is gone. She was the most irritating being I have ever encountered in my life. Well, back to work, Bill sighed, as he went below to blend with the ship to fix the electronics that had been damaged in the battle.

The steam truck took a left before the gate and started up the hill. Elizabeth asked the NESS in the back, "When we get to the Immigration House, what will happen?"

The female NESS said, "The FOLK will issue a visa. You can stay in the outside city until the trader ship arrives from Republic or others can transport you to Oceana. There, you can make arrangements to get to New World."

The truck pulled up to Immigration House. It was laid out over a cliff. As she looked, she could see the waves hitting the coastal rocks to her left. *It is just a spectacular vista,* she thought.

The FOLK came out and said, "Welcome to Immigration House. We have set up rooms for all of you."

As they hopped down to the road, Eric Stein asked the FOLK, "We still have wounded?"

The FOLK nodded, "Yes. Ulysses informed us. We have moved them to the recovery hospital section here. Would you like to see them? They arrived earlier today after the ceremony."

"Yes, I would."

"Please follow this FOLK. She will take you there now."

As they followed the FOLK into the lobby, she noted they had no NESS that she could see. It was disturbing. There were no military, no civilian police, no heavily armed people – just peace, not an atmosphere of violence.

At the desk, they were asked to put both hands on the scanner, palms flat. As Elizabeth did this, a small printed card appeared. They then asked, "Please put one of your fingers in this receptacle." As she did this, a small drop of blood was drawn into the card.

"What is the card for?" Elizabeth asked.

"It is a credit account for the FOLK monetary systems. It is geared to your DNA. When you use it, hold it in one of your hands. It will then verify you and do the transaction."

"Oh, I see. But I have no money here."

The FOLK laughed. "We trade with everyone on our planet. Your accounts will be paid by your government, but you have a limit."

"Dang, I would like an armored ocean traveler."

The FOLK laughed. "Yes, we would, too." The FOLK turned and addressed the group, saying, "Dinner is at 19:00 hours. We would like all of you to attend. We will give you a briefing to the law, customs and rules in our country."

The room was small, but it had a nice desk with a view of the ocean. She set up her writing material and looked around.

Ahhh, they have coffee, she thought as she sat down with the cup of coffee and started in on her notes.

Elizabeth sat in the restaurant. The meal was simple: fish stew, salad and fresh bread with butter. She happily slathered the bread with the butter. In her country, only the extremely wealthy could get this luxury item. She looked at the dessert; it was a light green and she couldn't figure out what it was. She asked, "What is this?"

"Key Lime pie."

She tasted it and said, "I have read about limes, but have never had it made into a dessert. This is good." She went over to the dessert line and asked, "Can I have another slice?"

The FOLK smiled and handed her the whole pie, "Enjoy."

After the dinner was done, the FOLK asked them to follow them. They entered a room that had large windows and showed the first moon rising. A fire was ablaze in a device which she had never seen.

"What is that?"

"It is a soapstone stove. Soapstone is a soft rock that can be worked with simple steel tools. It retains massive amounts of heat for very little wood."

As they settled into leather chairs, the FOLK Samantha started, "As you are aware, the battle between our nations has raised tensions around the world." They all nodded. "So, while you are here, I would suggest that you do the tourist route. Visit the museums and art galleries along with libraries. We also have a lively night life for you younger people." Everyone laughed. "But, I will give you the list of what can get you into serious trouble.

"The NESS and FOLK is a constitutional Republic. Our founding is and always will be based on the American model from the old world. We have changed a few items on the document, but it spells out how we live and behave toward each other and other humans."

One of the New World personnel asked, "What is an American model?"

FOLK Samantha laughed and said, "We have made a history copy for each of you. Please read it. It is enlightening and it is in your room, along with a very short version of the laws."

FOLK Samantha continued.

"We are a free society; that means you are a sovereign person. You, as an individual, are responsible for your actions. Our laws are made in plain language, so if any of you cannot read we will read them to you. Please show your hand if you cannot read." She looked around and said, "Good, all of you can read; I suggest you read them. Ignorance of the laws is not the concern of the FOLK, but it will be if you break them."

FOLK Samantha pointed to the copy of the laws and said, "A couple of highlights on our laws: The NESS are the only ones allowed to carry weapons in our country. You may not have any weapons on you, period. We realize this is not your normal operational mode for living, but it is for FOLK, so respect our law. You may not kill anything in our country, from humans to wildlife. We are the caretakers; I repeat, do not kill here. You will not go into the NESS FOLK city. It is off limits to all of you for now. If you violate this, the NESS will kill you on the spot when you are caught, and rest assured, they will catch you.

"Have you heard the NESS FOLK expression, 'your Word is your life'?"

Everyone nodded vigorously, yes.

"We FOLK and NESS take that expression literally. We are asking each of you to honor 'your Word is your Life" for your stay here; if you violate it, your life is forfeit and the NESS will kill you."

Elizabeth pointed out, "The NESS seem to be the killers in your society."

FOLK Samantha looked at her. "On certain occasions, yes, but they are not violent. They are what you call police and military, depending on what they are faced with. On every occasion, they have very specific guidelines for violence from the FOLK laws. They are very stringent and EVERY NESS is under them."

"So they are the rulers since they have the weapons," Elizabeth said.

FOLK Samantha laughed out loud and said, "The NESS are bound by our laws. The FOLK govern. We trust them with our lives and the NESS trust us to judge wisely since we see into the hearts and minds of the NESS. If they are not fit, they do not live long. The other NESS would and will destroy them."

The NESS are extremely dangerous and the FOLK are not worried that they have all the weapons; are they crazy? Elizabeth wondered.

FOLK Samantha scanned the puzzled looks around her. "We think humans are rational and logical, so why would a rational being resort to any form of violence?"

"Well, for self-defense," replied a New World person.

FOLK Samantha said, "From an individual who is not rational and is attacking, why put up with the irrational mind? The NESS cut out the disease before it becomes an epidemic in our society."

That point made Elizabeth think and smile, *Yes, that would stop a lot of our wars if we used it on our fearless leaders.*

FOLK Samantha looked at the people. "Some of our ways are harsh, but we think we offer some distinct advantages. We have no crime. Our people are well fed, clothed and housed. We have outstanding educational systems and stable work for those who want to immigrate or start a business."

FOLK Samantha smiled at Eric Stein, who was caught staring at her. He quickly looked down at the hardwood floors.

My God, she is beautiful," Eric thought. *She looks like the diplomat on the NESS warship. I wonder if she is related.*

FOLK Samantha AI'd her mom, *He is cute.*

Secondary FOLK diplomat Teresa smiled and replied, *Yes, he is. When we scanned him, we found that he was very honest and pleasant. I think he would be a good match for you.*

FOLK Samantha AI'd, *MOM! I have my daughter.*

Secondary FOLK diplomat Teresa smiled. *Yes, but you have been alone since Robert was killed four axis turns ago. I worry about your heart, my daughter.*

She is still grieving Robert, she thought to herself. *He was a NESS. She accepted that he might be killed in the line of duty, but prayed it never would happen to her. God called him to the light, but I pray for her every night.*

FOLK Samantha blinked several times to clear the memories from her mind. She then stood up and said, "It is getting late, so I am going home. Please enjoy the view. The bar behind you is open if you desire a drink. There are also maps and flashlights if you wish to walk the area. The ocean life prowls for snacks at night. We have not lost guests or tourists, yet; just be careful," she said, as she left the room.

Eric Stein watched her go and he thought to himself, *My God, she is beautiful. I hope I can work the courage up to talk to her.*

FOLK Samantha got home and went to bed. Her daughter, Joy, crawled in with her. As her daughter settled in for the night, she whispered to her, "Mom, I have seen this Eric. He will bring us happiness and several more brothers and sisters."

Samantha looked at her daughter in the darkness. The GIFT did not come into full play until after puberty. She whispered, "How can you see this?"

Her nine-year-old, Joy, smiled and whispered, "Dad told me in my dream from the light."

Samantha's tears tracked down her face as she hugged her daughter. Joy whispered and wiped her mom's tears with the sheet. "No worries, Mom, we will be all right. Dad told me to have faith."

The New World people stayed and talked late into the night. Most found the FOLK likable, but the NESS were still considered killing machines. Elizabeth listened and said, "Yes, the NESS are very capable of killing, but they do not attack until attacked."

Two days went by as they settled into the area. Elizabeth went to the front desk and asked if the Republic diplomat was in the city. The FOLK pulled out a map.

"They are in the Diplomatic Way; catch the electric trolley out front of this building, get off at 2nd Street, take a left and go four blocks; you will see the flag on the gate."

Elizabeth followed the instructions and soon found herself at the gate. She asked for an audience with his most high Ambassador Sir Felling. She handed her ID over to the security detail. It indicated that she was from New World. After a few minutes, she was let into the compound.

They asked her to stand still and they scanned her and her small bag. After they were done, they escorted her to the foyer where she sat down on a leather chair. They asked if she would like some refreshments.

"Coffee with milk," Elizabeth said.

They came back with coffee and milk on tray.

As she sipped the coffee, she noticed that the whole area was sterile. It was plain, with solid painted walls, designed to give nothing away as to what the republican had in its mind.

Typical, she thought, smiling. *Killers profess peace, and then slip the knife into your back.*

Ambassador Sir Felling's secretary came in. He asked her what her business was regarding. She recited several lines from a book, asked him to repeat them to the Ambassador and told him to see if the Ambassador was interested in further business.

She had just started to work on her second cup when the Ambassador walked into the room. He was of medium height, had a very heavy build and smiled at her.

The words must have made this runner hungry, she thought.

Ambassador Sir Felling said, "Please follow me to my working office."

With that, Elizabeth walked through the courtyard to the inner working office. As she approached, she could see that the heavy stained glass doors were left open so the breeze could flow through the office. She was settled into a very comfortable chair, but she noted that the rugs on the hardwood floor were very well done and plush on her feet.

"Well, cousin, how have you been?" she asked.

"Not bad, and you?" he replied, smiling.

"All right, but I have had adventures of the late, as you have heard no doubt?"

"Yes, the little dust up between your New World and the NESS… seems you have been on the receiving end of the NESS guns."

Yes, you GAT, she thought, but she smiled and said, "It was a very interesting expedition. Seems the NESS are coming out of their shells."

He stopped smiling at that statement. "Go on."

"Well, I have seen the NESS out of their armor and I was wondering what the Republic would pay for that information."

"Well, I heard 30 of you saw them; why should I pay?"

"Well, I am a trained scientist, along with having genetic samples, so how much would that buy me?"

Elizabeth waited. She had found the samples on the floor during a violent storm. She had gone to get some coffee when the damn tub rolled and tossed her into a bulkhead. This had knocked her out and when she came to, she was in the medico section on the warship. The tub was rolling and smashing with the waves and the medico people had their hands full. There were injured in the infirmary trying to stay in bed. She watched a container hit the floor and soon after, she was tossed to the floor. Rolling into a bulkhead, she saw NESS labeled vials. She grabbed four and stuffed them into her bra. FOLK medicos picked her up from the deck soon after.

They had asked, "Are you all right?"

She said, "Yes, can I go back now before I get killed?"

They laughed and said, "We have checked you out; you are alright." A NESS showed up and took her back to the New World section.

Ambassador Sir Felling asked, "It would be up to my government to decide, but how much do you want?"

She gave a figure.

"That is a very large sum," he said.

Elizabeth thought, *You will pay and I will finally be able to get my armored ship with my lab and students and be done with getting hauled over the planet by idiots.*

"I am sure we can accommodate the request for information," he said.

Elizabeth got up and said, "Always nice to see you, cousin. Any messages for the family?"

"Tell them I love them."

Elizabeth nodded and they escorted her out of the building. Ambassador Sir Felling watched her walk down the road and thought to himself, *What are you playing at, Elizabeth?*

He called his staff together in the secured room. As they watched the video feed from the interview of Elizabeth, he said, "Well, it seems my cousin wants to leave New World and she thinks it would be easier to get money out of us in the short term."

Undersecretary Swellings asked, "Yes, but why did she call you cousin?"

Ambassador Sir Felling answered, "She is a cousin on my mother's side from her sister who stayed in that cursed country. Her husband is in the landed gentry with vast estates."

"But why pay her?"

"She might be an enemy, but she is one of the best scientists in the world in her field. When she says she has genetic samples, she has them."

Undersecretary for Science Miles interjected, "Sir, if she has the samples, we might find out about the NESS genetic structures. Their science in this field is speculative, but from reports, they have NANO technology built into them, along with their advanced weapon systems."

Ambassador Sir Felling said, "Yes, I am well-briefed on that subject. Our military is second to none on New Earth and we have the fleets to rule the planet, but the NESS FOLK and their allies are thwarting us. So, we will dispatch letters to the PM about this opportunity. In the meantime, get the gold ready."

Undersecretary Swellings said, "Twenty pounds of gold is a very large sum."

Ambassador Sir Felling agreed. "Yes, and many accidents can happen from here to New World. Get the gold from the vault ready. We will have a deposit coming up fairly soon for my cousin."

Elizabeth walked away from the Republic diplomatic house a little unsure of how she felt.

Well, that was enlightening. That GAT will slit my throat any chance he gets. Hmm, let's see. I need to find a FOLK monetary house.

As she walked, she saw an information kiosk.

This is different. Books, magazines and treats. She approached the FOLK who said, "Morning, can I be of service?"

"Yes, I would like to find a FOLK monetary house."

"Well, the largest is down in the business district. Just take the electric trolley. It should be here in a few. Would you like to buy something?"

Elizabeth smiled. "Do you have coffee?"

"Oh, yes. What would you like?

"Hmm, the FOLK mountain, please." She pulled the card out and asked how it worked.

"Hold it in one hand and push it into this slot, then pull it out. That's it."

"Hmm, sounds simple," Elizabeth said. The FOLK looked at the screen and said, "Yep, transaction complete." She handed Elizabeth the coffee.

As she sipped the coffee, the electric trolley showed up. Hopping up on it, she waved to the FOLK who waved back.

FOLK Malak AI'd, *Elizabeth Pameddin was in the Republic diplomatic house.*

The FOLK answered, *We know. Her card recorded the conversation. It is nice to see we are so loved by the Republic. We have always known they are a very serious threat.*

FOLK Malak AI'd, *What? The card reacts to crossing into diplomatic zones?*

The FOLK answered, *Yes, and it deactivates the recording systems as she goes into the FOLK country after data dump.*

Well, she asked for the FOLK monetary house, so she should be showing up there fairly quickly.

Yes, we think she wants to use us as a middle man for gold transfer. That will be no problem, since she has not broken any FOLK laws; we will watch her.

I have been in this business a long time. Based on the Republic past history, they will kill her when they pay her.

The FOLK have alerted the NESS to the fact that there is a 95% chance that they ordered for her to be murdered in our country; the NESS is on watch as of now.

Elizabeth found the FOLK monetary house. It was a nice two-story building of steel and glass. As she entered, she noted that there were no security guards, no heavily armored glass and no steel partitions.

What is this place? They have money, so it should be heavily guarded.

She approached one of the FOLK sitting at a desk.

"I am not from here, but I would like to set up an account for the transfer of money from my home country."

FOLK Jeremy said, "No problem; do you have your country origin ID?" She handed it over. "Please take a seat while I put this information into the comp systems."

I will use the emergency fund from my family in my name, which should buy me some time to sort out this situation, Elizabeth thought, as she sat down.

As he typed, he explained, "Elizabeth Pameddin, we use a two-metallic standard for the FOLK, silver and gold, per agreements between nations. We charge 5% user fees per transfer transaction to convert your currency into gold or silver here. Also, it depends on which nation is involved. Currently, New World and the FOLK have a misunderstanding and it is at 7.5%."

"That is pretty steep."

"Yes," FOLK Jeremy said, "but it does offer advantages. We have what is called an on-demand system. We have to cover all deposits with physical gold or silver at 99.9. The normal 5% is for overhead and a small profit since gold and silver is a scarce commodity worldwide. It makes the money stable for nations to exchange and is stable for individuals, too.

"If you deposit gold and silver here, we offer extremely attractive rates for long-term investments and there is no tax. What you earn is what you keep. The FOLK do not use progressive tax systems."

FOLK Jeremy paused for a moment as he studied his computer. "Here we go. I have a confirmation that you have currency in your monetary system at New World. Currently, your rate is at 1, which means your country is just about out of funds, due to its war, so can you give me a figure?"

"80 oz. of gold at 99.9% pure; 100 New World pieces of silver, 1 oz. at 99.9% pure," Elizabeth said.

"Hmmm, we can convert that. We can do an exchange rate of 92.5% charge at 7.5 % for the gold and silver if you want to exchange it now. Since this is your first time, we will move it at 99.5% and the charge would be at .5%."

"Please do."

"Please put both hands on the scanner, palms flat."

Here we go again.

A small, printed card appeared. He then asked, "Please put one of your fingers in this receptacle." As she did this, a small drop of blood was drawn into the card.

"Please sign and put your pin code just for the gold and silver deposit box here. This will give a FOLK monetary agent in New World permission as your agent to withdraw your gold and silver and move it here in the next shipment. If you can wait, I will verify that our agent has the gold and silver. Once that is done, we will have the account unfrozen and you can draw on the account. Would you like to wait?"

Elizabeth said, "Sure." She settled in and the transaction ended up taking about two hours.

"All done; your account is active." FOLK Jeremy said with a smile. "So, we have many business opportunities here. If you like, we can set you up with an investment broker."

Pausing, Elizabeth said, "I will think on it. But, what about this card? What if someone were to cut off my hand, could they use it to withdraw my funds?"

FOLK Jeremy looked confused. "Why would anyone do that to you?"

"Just hypothetical."

"Oh, I see. Well, it is a Biometric card. It reads blood pressure, temperature, DNA and your fingerprints. It is just about as foolproof as we can make it for a system."

Elizabeth said, "Thank you, FOLK Jeremy. Can I ask another question?"

"Sure!"

"Where is the best shipyard around here for small craft that is armored for the ocean?"

"Well, I do have a relative who makes armored fishing vessels for the FOLK," he said, laughing. "And all of them have come back relatively intact from the fishing grounds."

Elizabeth laughed and asked, "Please, can I have the address and directions?"

With the directions in hand, Elizabeth Pameddin left and found the shipyard. FOLK Mini was small and extremely loud and he was waving his arms around as he yelled at his work people in the yard. He saw Elizabeth and said to her, "Please excuse me for yelling, but my relatives are sometimes brain dead and I must correct them on occasions." Running over to the work platform, he yelled at one of the welders, stating that he was brain dead, why he should keep him hired was beyond him, he was lucky he was his sister's boy or he would be hauling nets instead of welding his beautiful ships.

Elizabeth smiled and thought, *Yes, I think I have found the shipyard.*

"Please excuse me, I am being rude. Please come into the office." As Elizabeth sat on a worn leather chair, she noticed the pictures of fishing vessels on the office walls, they looked functional and seaworthy.

"How can I help you?" FOLK Mini said.

"Oh, my name is Elizabeth Pameddin. I am looking for a research vessel that can take the deep ocean."

FOLK Mini smiled. "Did my cousin, Jeremy, the monetary shyster, send you?"

"Why, yes, and what is a shyster?"

He laughed and said, "A con man, teller of big fish stories, tells you what you want to hear, likes your money!"

"Well, he seemed very nice."

"So, you did not take the investment broker's line?"

Elizabeth laughed and said, "No!"

"Good. Jeremy has never worked hard on the ocean, always with his brain, which is okay, but he does give me a headache when he comes over for dinner. He's always talking money on Sunday after church; it is a sin, I tell you. Money changers on a holy day!"

"FOLK Mini, you are a believer?"

FOLK Mini nodded yes and stated, "God works on us every moment we are alive, then judges us when we go before Him when we die. I plan to go to the light. I work very hard at that premise. I have sinned greatly when I was young and I do not have much wisdom now. That's a bad combination for me."

Then, FOLK Mini asked, "Research. So the question is ocean, seas or coastal?"

"It must have a cruising range of 10,000 miles, have enough capacity to hold about 10 tons of scientific equipment and hold 10 people for a provision of 90 days. Lastly, it must be able to function on all three areas."

FOLK Mini said, "That one is easy: a catamaran."

"A what?"

"Come over to my drafting table," FOLK Mini said, with a smile.

As they went into the other room, she noticed that it had a spectacular view of the harbor. She stepped up onto the platform and faced the drafting table, which had huge sheets of paper, a drawing device she had never seen, pens, inks and a simple, handheld calculator. Elizabeth also noticed that he had a naval architect degree on the wall.

FOLK Mini held a beautiful, colored illustration out to show her. It showed a ship with twin hulls and a bridge in the middle.

"This design is 120 feet. The two hulls hold the living quarters, equipment, engines, fuel and the bridge in the middle, which is the navigation science station's brains, so to speak. This one is all decked out with fancy wood interior and leather; it's a rich person's toy."

"I do not need a fancy, all decked out toy."

FOLK Mini smiled, "Well, I have the same design in a plain version; it's not steel but aluminum."

"What about deep ocean predators?"

"No problem. I could make the hulls thicker. Add more standard spikes, along with the engines we install. You can get going to 40 knots and should be able to outrun the big ones. For the little ones, I will get you two 40mm/1.5 inch cannons that are controlled remotely from the bridge. The NESS have several arms dealers that can outfit to my design. Since it is a standard shell, resupply should not be an issue.

"The catamaran," FOLK Mini explained, "is a very stable platform for all ocean conditions. It also has a small draft, so you can get into the coastal regions without grounding. Seas can be choppy and rough, so a dagger can be deployed to keep the side slips motion manageable. The seasickness is dramatically decreased by reducing the rolling motion with two hulls."

Elizabeth said, "Well, how much and how long?"

"Do you need some refreshments?"

"Do you have any coffee?"

"Yes," he said and ran out of the door yelling for some coffee. When he came back with the coffee, he said, "Walk around the yard and ask questions. It will take me some minutes to work out the figures for a rough estimate."

As she walked around the yard, she noticed that the vessels were made of standard construction steel, aluminum, iron or wood – not the NESS armor she had seen on the warships, which she thought was crazy.

She saw a small ship that was about finished. It showed the sweeping lines for deep ocean travel with several spikes along the hull in the open position for testing. The spikes keep the large predators from taking chunks out of the hull.

A few minutes later, a small kid approached and asked, "Elizabeth Pameddin?" She turned. "My uncle would like you to go back to the office; do you want me to show you the way?"

"No, I know where his office is, but thank you." He smiled and scampered off to play with his friends.

Elizabeth arrived at the office. FOLK Mini was waiting and sipping tea as he watched the ship traffic in the harbor.

"I have the rough estimates."

She came over and looked. He had hand sketched out the catamaran ship. It was beautiful and had the sweeping lines that the FOLK were famous for in deep ocean travel.

FOLK Mini said, "I see by your look that you like her."

"Yes, why is it a she?"

Laughing, he replied, "Tradition, but it can be named after a male."

Elizabeth asked detailed questions and FOLK Mini answered them fast, professionally and with keen insights to her specific requirements. Elizabeth sat down after a while.

"Alright, how much?" Mini handed her the rough estimate and said, "It will be 60 oz. of gold; half down and half on completion." Elizabeth started haggling with FOLK Mini. They went at it for several minutes, and when they both were done, she had the price at 50 oz. of gold and the transaction completed in 45 days.

"I have a terminal here," FOLK Mini explained. "I will put in the 25 oz. gold transfer order. Place your card in here, please. Thank you.

Looks like the transfer went through and here is the contract." They both signed the copies. "Your ship will be done in 45 days," he said, beaming at her.

"I will come by later in the month to see the ship in construction."

"Any time. It is a pleasure to get a client who lets me build it right. Please excuse me, now I have to get your order in." He spun around and started yelling at his relatives, "We have a New World order to complete."

That went well, she thought as she caught the electric trolley back to the Immigration House.

As the electric trolley topped the hill, Sub Ambassador Ridge watched her.

Hmm, seems the Ambassador was right. She is planning to leave New World. He called over to his operatives and ordered, "Standard watch; no contact at all. Do I make myself clear?" They nodded and got to work.

Several days passed. She was with a group of New World people doing a tour of the FOLK New Hope museum. She looked at the natural science section and thought, *Whomever set this up is first rate, precise and functional, even though it is small compared to my country's museum.*

She took notes on a species plant she had never seen and that seemed to be found on just this continent.

How come I have never heard about it? From the description, it retains water, is used for soil erosion prevention and can be used as food for human livestock and the native species. Nice.

She figured she could use this plant for New World and other spots around the planet that had been blasted by idiots.

She had been scribbling and drawing when she noticed FOLK Samantha and Eric Stein in deep conversation with each other, laughing and smiling. Her musings went to that terrible day.

Sure beats floating in the sea as food.

FOLK Samantha was laughing with Eric as he told a story about how he got to be a diplomat. Eric had made Samantha light up and she smiled, looking forward to the day. Eric was extremely happy. He had worked up the courage to ask her on this outing and he was amazed that she said yes. While they had walked throughout the day, at some point, she had slipped her hand into his. It felt right.

Elizabeth then saw a FOLK with a smock on. She recognized that universal, professional uniform. She got up and approached. Her name tag read FOLK Lisa and she was scribbling notes in her journal when Elizabeth approached.

"Excuse me. My name is Elizabeth Pameddin. Could I ask you a question?"

"Sure," FOLK Lisa replied.

"This plant I am looking at, I am not familiar with it. I would like to exchange biological samples from my country for a sample, is that permitted?"

"I am a student in marine biology. My professors would have more detailed knowledge of this plant. Would you like an audience?"

Elizabeth said, "Sure."

"Please, this way. We have the university attached to the museum since we both have laboratories."

"Why is that?"

"It is logical. We have had many FOLK and humans bringing in samples from the world. You would be amazed at what is found on a weekly basis. My professors just dance with joy at new discoveries."

FOLK Lisa led her to the biggest greenhouses she had ever seen. They covered acres and each one was specific to a climatic zone. FOLK Lisa grabbed an electric cart. "Hop in," she said as she patted the seat. The two drove between them. Elizabeth's neck hurt from twisting back and forth in order to get a good look at everything. When they arrived at the campus, they saw that it was built in two tiers of glass and steel, with granite thrown in for contrast.

FOLK Lisa went into a lecture hall, "Please sit and I will get the professor."

When he arrived, she saw that he was a NESS. Elizabeth looked at him and noticed his armor was not a deep green, but a very light shade of forest green with streaks of white shot in the armor. She also saw that he looked frail.

He smiled and said, "Elizabeth Pameddin, you look well. I am NESS Professor Jeremiah." He held out his armored hand. As she shook it, she noted that it felt light and very warm to the touch.

NESS Professor Jeremiah asked, "Do you mind if I sit down?" Elizabeth could only nod. He chuckled. "I see you had a notion that NESS are just killing machines."

I just gaped at him. My mouth audibly snapped shut. He laughed even harder until he started to cough. FOLK Lisa moved quickly with a liquid in a drinking bottle. When he brought it to his lips, the armor blended with the bottle. I could see the liquid disappear as he finished.

"Thank you, granddaughter. You can go back to your studies."

FOLK Lisa gave him a hug and a kiss on the top of his helmet. "If you need me, call. And here is another for you. Keep it handy for the coughs."

NESS Professor Jeremiah looked at Elizabeth and asked, "Never seen an "OLD NESS?"

"Just seen the very active ones lately," she quipped.

He laughed, "Yeah that can be very frightening. So, Elizabeth, what brings you to the university and to my plant biological lab?"

"I was in the museum and ran across this plant species. While going through the scant information available, I can see the vast potential in other areas of the planet for stabilizing soil erosion along with re-storing certain habitats for native and non-native grazing herbivores. I have never run across this species in the journals."

NESS Professor Jeremiah replied, "Well, I have published in most of the scientific journals, some governments have vested interest in the status quo, not to publish knowledge from the FOLK."

Elizabeth just nodded. "Yes, I have not been a good, dutiful scientist lately and my funding for research and publishing has dried up because of the war."

NESS Professor Jeremiah continued, "I have read your old, published papers. You are extremely intelligent and brilliant, but you have the stubborn streak with lesser mortals I understand from my limited interaction with other scientists from your country, so they say. I can imagine certain pieces of knowledge being filtered from you."

Elizabeth had the impression that the NESS Professor Jeremiah was giving a side-long glance. He could see the shots hitting home. "But in any case, you are here. The plant grows in the hills. Would you like to go to the biological work camp along with the students and collect samples and seedlings?"

"When?!" Elizabeth cried, as she beamed a smile at Jeremiah.

NESS Professor Jeremiah held up his armored hand. "I would like to sweeten the pot for you. In addition, I will pay you 1 oz. of FOLK silver for your latest two lectures on diversity to my students when we return. Is that acceptable for the expedition? But before you say 'yes', remember "Your Word is your Life" in our country." He calmly looked at Elizabeth and she said yes.

He laughed and said, "Good. I am late. My assistant, FOLK Full Professor Mark, will set you up for the jaunt. I think it is at the end of the week. Till then, Elizabeth."

He got up to leave when Elizabeth called, "NESS Professor Jeremiah?"

"Yes?"

"I have never heard of NESS as a teacher, let alone as a professor."

He laughed. "Curiosity, Elizabeth, is the mark of intelligence. There are not many NESS that survive to old age. You noted the streaks in my armor. That is telling me my time is almost up, but I am a trained botanist and what little knowledge I can pass on will not be forgotten by my people. So, I much prefer to be remembered that way instead of a trained killer when I stand before God."

FOLK Full Professor Mark approached them and said, "Elizabeth, would you follow me? I will need to confirm that you can have access to the hills. The NESS are very stringent about access to Outsiders."

As she sat in his office, she noticed that it looked like any professor's office: cluttered, cramped, stack of papers to grade – it looked like home to her.

FOLK Full Professor Mark finished and said, "He said no problem, but NESS asked that you stay with the group. You may not wander from the biological station, period." He smiled. "And now, onto the fun stuff. What gear do you require for your samples?"

Elizabeth was ready on the appointed day. She arrived on campus and FOLK Full Professor Mark and NESS Professor Jeremiah were seated in the front of a steam truck while the students loaded the equipment and hopped into the back of the truck. Off they roared, with NESS Professor Jeremiah singing a very bawdy sailor song. The students laughed and joined in with full gusto. Republic operatives' eyes took notes and waited for the expedition to return.

Elizabeth spent the morning collecting samples and laughing along with the students who were amused with her many questions. The morning went fast. Elizabeth sat beside the NESS Professor Jeremiah, eating lunch, and she asked, "Do you ever take the armor off?"

Nodding, he answered, "Yes, when I am at home. But, I have been told you saw some of us out of the armor."

"Yes, let's say I was stunned." As she laughed to herself, she said, "It was a day of surprises."

NESS Professor Jeremiah, "Yes, our color pattern alone is fun, but my people accept the NESS. We are human, after all, just different. My wife was a FOLK, Zoë."

"Was?"

"Yes, my wife, Zoë, has been dead for going on 5 axis turns now." He tilted his head at Elizabeth and his armor sampled her. He was surprised to see genuine concern coming from her. "I can still hear her laughter as Zoë pulled the armor off me. That was always fun,"

He sighed and looked away for a moment.

"But our children worry about me. Call us a mated pair. When one dies, the other follows soon, but who knows God's plans." He laughed. "Old history. Do not listen to an Old NESS or what you call an 'old man'. We get morbid as we age."

Elizabeth gave him a hug and said, "Nah, just wisdom. So, Old NESS, let's say we get to work."

NESS Professor Jeremiah laughed. "You work, I will delegate." They both laughed as they went back to work.

The steam truck let Elizabeth off at the electric trolley stop.

"We have your samples in the lab," NESS Professor Jeremiah said. "When you leave, they will be ready. Also, the lecture is set up to occur in two days, is that plenty of time?"

"No problem," Elizabeth said, as she waved and caught the trolley to the Immigration House.

Republic operatives waited until the station was quiet, and then compared notes.

"Hmmm," one of them said, "something about a lecture. You will go and find out where and what time. We will still do standard watch on the target reports due at 09:00 tomorrow."

As the Republic operatives left, a very large shadow shimmered then formed into NESS Moriah from the building shrubbery across from them. NESS Moriah AI'd, *These GATS are going to kill anyone to get the genetic samples Elizabeth has on her.*

NESS AI'd, *The Republic must make the first move. We have been trying to get these humans for a long time. They are trained killers, but without proof, it is speculation on our part. Elizabeth is the bait that might draw them out; we wait for now. Remember, Elizabeth saw an opportunity to escape from her own prison. We are helping her along to achieve that goal.*

NESS Moriah AI'd, *I still do not like it.* She fumed.

NESS AI'd, *We know, but the genetic samples are not NESS. It will derail the Republics lust for domination using our technology and we might get one of the world's top scientists in the long run.*

A very old saying, "Mr. Murphy is not done playing with us, yet," comes to mind.

He is always hanging around to adapt, overcome is as good as it gets for us.

Ambassador Sir Felling read the report and asked, "You did not find the samples?"

The operatives answered, "No."

"Hmmm, so we will have to pay. Here is what is going to happen: You will not do anything to Elizabeth. You will deliver the gold in exchange of the samples. Is that understood?"

Undersecretary Swellings nodded and said, "Let me be clear, the NESS will kill all of us if we start violence. We have reports that one NESS killed a heavy weapons platoon with tanks. I have no doubt that this is not true. So, let's get this done, quickly. Now go."

Elizabeth was walking out of the lecture hall when Undersecretary Swellings approached her.

"Elizabeth Pameddin?

"Yes?"

"I am Undersecretary Swellings for the Republic. We have a business transaction that you inquired about."

She smiled. "Why, yes. Let's go sit on the park bench."

As they settled, he told her, "I have the requested item in this back pack, would you like to see?"

"Sure."

He opened it and she could see the gold bullion. She then pulled one out, did a quick test and thought, *Good.*

Undersecretary Swellings asked, "Our item?"

She pulled out two sealed blood samples labeled NESS male and NESS female with bar codes. He asked, "How?"

"Swiped them when I was in their medical section; NESS do get wounded," she said, as she handed the vials over to him.

Undersecretary Swellings held out his hand. Elizabeth said, "Nice day," and she turned around without shaking his hand and went back to the lecture hall with the gold.

Elizabeth knocked on NESS Professor Jeremiah's door, who called out, "Enter." She went in, and he smiled and asked, "Did I miss something?"

"No, you Old NESS, please sit down. I am going to tell you a tale."

When she finished, she pulled up her top and pulled out the real NESS vials and handed them back to him.

"These are worth a fortune," he said.

"Yes, but the Republic killed my parents by framing them as traitors in New World thanks to Ambassador Sir Felling, my cousin." Pausing, she added, "I hate that SOB!"

NESS Professor Jeremiah closed his eyes and Elizabeth continued.

"I love my family. I also love my country, what is left of it. I hope one day it will be sane and peaceful in my lifetime."

NESS Professor Jeremiah sighed and said, "I am glad you handed these back to the FOLK NESS. It shows character and core beliefs in one's self and long-term decision making, not just for one person's life, but on a world scale."

"I was very tempted, but this knowledge is not mine to sell. If the FOLK NESS want to share it, it should come from you."

NESS Professor Jeremiah AI'd Stardrifter while smiling. *Told you she would be honest.*

Stardrifter laughed. *So I will pay up on our bet. The equipment you need went in just now to one of the automated factories.*

Oh, yes, and what about the last part? This Elizabeth is very cute and smart.

Stardrifter AI'd, laughing, *From her mind scans, she thoroughly hates the military. So, she would not be interested in me.* He replayed their first encounter.

NESS Professor Jeremiah noted, *But I see she did like you in your underwear!*

Stardrifter felt himself blush and he replied back, *I am too busy and stop playing match maker. Anyway, dinner?*

NESS Professor Jeremiah AI'd, *Yep, I will bring the kids to make your house as noisy as possible.* Jeremiah laughed to himself. *Yes, I think I am going to set you two up before Elizabeth leaves. You need each other to fill in the gaps.* He rubbed his hands together and said, *Yes my Zoë filled in large parts of me.*

Hmmm, Stardrifter AI'd, *I better practice my crayon drawing skills. I will probably be on the floor being shown how to color in between the lines on the coloring book by one of the nieces from Jeremiah house.*

NESS Professor Jeremiah looked at Elizabeth and thought, *Hmm, let's see if I can get her from the New World mental set. I wish my Zoë were here, she could tell from just a look at a person's soul, but that is not to be, this time or ever again, for me.*

"Elizabeth," NESS Professor Jeremiah said, "For bravery and honesty, I wish to remove my helmet so you can see my face and eyes as we talk. Is this acceptable to you?" She nodded yes.

NESS Professor Jeremiah's armored helmet released him and he pulled it off and set it on his desk. Elizabeth looked at him, at his extremely white hair that was pulled into a ponytail and draped into his armor. She looked at his eyes, deep grey flecked with blue, and his face that was lined with many deep wrinkles. The scales were translucent.

Jeremiah smiled and asked, "What do you see Elizabeth?"

"An old NESS, but cute."

He smiled. "That's what my Zoë always said to me, but it was 'Young NESS, extremely cute.'"

Jeremiah laughing, reached down and pulled out two small glasses then pulled out some whiskey.

"Ever had whiskey?"

"No."

"Hmmm, we have to rectify that."

He poured two shots into the glasses, he handed one glass to her, cleared his throat and stated, "Elizabeth hold your glass up; that's it. When I finish the toast, toss the whiskey down your throat." Holding his glass up, he said, "Toast to loved ones and fallen comrades."

They both swallowed the whiskey, while coughing and sputtering.

"That is smooth," Elizabeth said, as she wiped the tears out of her eyes.

Old NESS asked, "Another?"

"Please."

He looked at her as he poured another one into the glass, "Do not tell my children."

They both laughed as he filled the glasses to the brim. NESS Professor Jeremiah lounged in his large, leather chair with his boots on the desk.

"So, Elizabeth, what are you going to do now?" he asked, as he sipped some more whiskey.

"Well, I am going to finish the ship, outfit it and do research. I need a vacation and, since I have another target on my back, more than normal, I prefer my own transportation. Accidents can happen." Old NESS nodded.

"And the Republic will not be happy when they get the results; it will drive them insane being made fools."

"Yes, they are vindictive, you have another target on your back," Old NESS added, "but maybe not so, I am going to ask, what is the purpose of your research?"

"Well, it is regarding a sustainable and balanced use of resources. We are part of the planet; if we strip and pillage it, we will have the same problems as old earth, like wars and famine, just like we have now. Once we get space travel back, if ever, we will just drag the same old theories around and kill another planet; it is a vicious cycle."

Old NESS nodded. "Elizabeth, I would like to offer you a job."

Elizabeth eyed him suspiciously.

He laughed and said, "It is not spying."

"Go on," she said slowly as she sipped the whiskey.

"We NESS FOLK are very easy to spot; well, at least, the NESS," he laughed, "But we cannot do any pure research due to our reputation in the world. So, it is simple: we hire you to do the research as you see fit. We only ask that you share all of the data you collect with us. You publish, put your own students in, whatever. We NESS and FOLK just want the data and conclusions; that's it, in a crab shell."

"Well, sounds simple to me, but it will not betray my country or my principles?" She paused. "Sooner or later, my people are going to drag my butt back and they will want the cold, hard facts in reports from the dustup we had a few weeks ago."

OLD NESS replied, "Well, give them the reports as you have seen it and your people will verify it is true. Ever hear of smoke and mirrors?"

She laughed and said, "That is very old saying."

"True. Everyone, including the NESS FOLK, puts up that option.

"Yes, perception is, at best, a wild ass guess at the future."

OLD NESS nodded. "That is true, but a lot of times we kill each other over a guess."

They both sat there, enjoying each other's company and sipping whiskey while contemplating that statement.

"If I do the research it will be expensive," Elizabeth said. "I will need to think on it for a while."

OLD NESS nodded. "So, do you need help lifting your loot to the monetary house or would you like another drink?"

Elizabeth laughed and said, "Both!"

"That can be arranged," he said, as he filled both glasses.

FOLK Full Professor Mark came into the office suddenly. He appeared to be startled when he saw NESS Professor Jeremiah sitting in the chair, sipping whiskey with Elizabeth without the armor helmet on his head. Old NESS just laughed.

"Not to worry, Elizabeth has seen several of us out of the full armor," he said, as he laughed.

FOLK Full Professor Mark said, "I am not worried about that, but if your children hear you are drinking, they will be most upset with you."

"Well, can I bribe you not to tell them?"

"Sure, got another glass in that monstrosity of a desk?"

"Yep," he replied, as he dug in the drawer. Elizabeth laughed at the antics.

Yes, people are people, she thought to herself.

FOLK Full Professor Mark waited at the monetary house for Elizabeth to come out. Sub Ambassador Ridge was waiting for her, too, thinking, *I do not trust or like this Elizabeth. She has more information the Republic will need in the future, I am sure. Hmm, a snatch would be the easiest way and the Republic ship will be here in ten days, most convenient.* He smiled an unpleasant smile.

FOLK Mini screamed over to Elizabeth as she stepped into the shipyard, "Elizabeth, I am glad you have come to see the masterpiece I have created for you!"

She beamed. "Well, let's go see your masterpiece."

He entered the finishing building and when Elizabeth saw the ship, she stopped with her mouth hanging open. It looked like a NESS warship. It had the flowing lines, everything fit and it was even painted the deep green color on the twin hulls.

FOLK Mini beamed as he watched her move around the ship and he pointed out the high points.

"The engines will use multi-fuel as long as you do the maintenance on time," he laughed. "These engines will last 20 axis turns, the electronics suite is standard, the radar system is loaded with most of the known coast, and we hope, the hazards you might encounter. You have a side-scan, echo-location system that will reach the deepest, ocean trenches for mapping. You also have fish locaters and a self-contained, navigation gyro system, which is very accurate. All of the electronics are triple-redundant and are pull-and-replace black boxes. You also have three spares."

As they went on to deck, he pointed at the recesses between the main beams.

"This is the cannon system. It will be installed just before you leave. A key will be given to you once the engines start. Just put the key in and turn. It will activate once you leave our waters. This system is belt feed with 120 rounds that gives you three minutes at full auto." He crossed himself as he explained the system.

"Why did you cross yourself?"

FOLK Mini crossed himself again and said, "This machine is violence. One idea is that it is the devil and I need protection from its siren call for my soul."

"Then why install it on my ship?"

He looked at her grimly. "You will need it against predators, beasts and humans. It kills anything without thought. It is the antithesis to life. That's not the way of the FOLK and, as you are not FOLK or NESS, what you do with it after you leave is your concern.

"Alright, shall we move on?" FOLK Mini asked, smiling. "Yes, we have added additional heavy supports here and there for structure."

As they moved about and discussed the ship, the morning moved quickly. Elizabeth went up to the office again. FOLK Mini asked, "The ship is on schedule, so have you thought of a name?"

She smiled and said, "OLD NESS, and I want it in my OLD language script. Do you need a translation?"

He laughed. "Nope."

"Good, when we launch I will need supplies."

"I have another shyster relative that would fall all over themselves to get the contract."

"Alright, let's get him or her on board. I will get a detailed list for you before launch," Elizabeth said.

She waved as she left the ship yard. She trolled past the goods store, bought some more coffee and headed back to the Immigration House to work on her notes and journals.

Later, Elizabeth was sitting on the patio in front of the restaurant, enjoying the late afternoon sun when FOLK Full Professor Mark asked if he could join her.

"Sure," she said, as she patted the chair next to her.

He sat for a few minutes and asked her, "I was wondering if you would like to see the ocean light up tonight after second moon sets?"

Elizabeth answered, "Well I have seen plankton blooms before in the inland sea."

"Not like this. We are in the southern oceans. The cold waters have massive nutrients to feed the many ocean species that are feeding before the ocean's winter sets in. It is something to see before you go home."

Before Elizabeth could answer, he said, "I have my students with me; it is the end of the study period, they need a break from me."

Elizabeth looked over her sunglasses with a skeptical look. Mark smiled. "And so do I from my students. My wife and I do not see much of each other during the school year."

"No problem," Elizabeth said. "When're ya gonna pick me up?"

"23:00 hours."

"All right," she said, as she settled back into the chair.

FOLK Full Professor Mark, along with his wife, Ruth, showed up at the hour. She looked at the steam car and thought, *This thing is huge.* She piled into it with the students, threw her pack on the floor and settled in for the drive. They were all bundled up and the temperature was cool as the fall season was just getting going. As they drove, she admired how calm the ocean was as the second moon was just about to set below the horizon. She stuck her hand out and played with it in the air draft, pretending she was the helmsman in the airship, steering it through the night.

When they arrived, it was a flat rock overlook with a path going down to the ocean. As she looked behind her, she could see the pine forest blending into the mountains. *Well, this is nice,* she thought as she settled her pack. The professor pulled the chairs, which had been left scattered about, into a semblance of order. He looked around and saw that the students had scattered, some on blankets and others in the chairs. He smiled to himself and thought, *Yep, youths.* He looked for his son and saw that he was sitting with Dagny Centauri, a very beautiful tall blond girl. He pointed out his son to Ruth, who just laughed and whispered, "He needs to practice kissing women. She has at least dragged him out for the evening away from his studies."

If I remember right, she is here for advanced mechanical engineering. He smiled. *She is very beautiful and has Brad wrapped around her finger.*

Mark looked at his wife and AI'd, *Yeah, I know that one, too.*

His wife AI'd back, *But you like being wrapped around my finger.*

Yes, I do, can we wrap tonight?

Ruth laughed out loud. *You horny GAT.*

Well, I can hoot mating calls like a GAT, too.

Go do something useful.

The professor started a fire in the pit. Once he had it going, he settled into a chair with his back to the fire along with Ruth, who plopped into his lap. He smiled.

"Elizabeth," he said. "In my pack is refreshment. Could you pull it out, along with three glasses?"

She came back, looked at the note that was included using the light from the fire and read, "Compliments from 'OLD NESS ∞'." She smiled and asked, "What is this symbol?"

"Yes, he likes you. That means you have his personal Grace."

"What is Grace?"

"On the note, that symbol ∞ means a NESS adoption to his or her house sent to the NESS FOLK council for consideration. For a human, that is not of the NESS, it is not given lightly. The NESS are notoriously finicky with humans. You must have done something heroic that showed bravery, courage and that you did not betray your soul. The NESS admire that in all the FOLK and in a few select outside humans; it is very rare in our world. The FOLK can count on one hand the times it has been granted since GIFT.

"The NESS are FOLK that have the warrior GIFT, but all of them would prefer not to be that way." Mark said, smiling, "The NESS are not just killers, they are some of our best poets, writers, engineers and plant biologists. We FOLK hope one day we no longer need the warrior in them, too."

Mark shook his head and sighed. "Well, let's enjoy the evening," he said, pointing to a chair.

Elizabeth sat down beside the couple.

Mark said, "This time of the year the whales are finishing up the feeding. They are stuffing themselves for the journey to the calving grounds. Now watch, the music is just about to start."

As the moon set, the ocean started to glow yellow, deep blue, pink and green as the plankton exploded from feeding. She could hear the sound of krill eating the plankton. Mark had adjusted the acoustics systems the students had set up for the evening. She wondered, *This is an understatement for music.*

The professor pointed farther out and they saw light exploding from the ocean. The whales' exhalation spouts were lifting the plankton into the air and Elizabeth couldn't believe how beautiful it was.

All of sudden, Elizabeth saw heads rise up on slim necks and she screamed, "GATS!!" Mark and Ruth rose out of the chair to run, but they both started to laugh when they looked. "Are you crazy?!" Both of them laughed harder and Mark said, "Sit, please. Sit, the GATS are not interested in us, watch."

Elizabeth sat, but she was ready to run as she watched to see what the GATS were up to. The whales started to sing and the GATS picked up the song. She could hear it in the air as they repeated the song then modified it. Her mouth dropped open as she looked from the GATS to Mark and Ruth.

"You set me up."

They both nodded and said, "Enjoy."

"Who is the whale GAT expert?"

Ruth held up her hand and said, "Guilty on that account. We think the whales and GATS talk to each other. Their languages are similar and are at least 100 million years old for each species. We also think that whales and GATS are from the same species, but divergent, which is the current speculation in my circles."

"But," Elizabeth said, "we are hundreds or thousands of light years from Old Earth, may it be blessed, and they are similar?"

"Yes. The GATS, as far as we can tell, never eat any whale species, even the toothed ones."

"You are crazy; they eat anything that walks, moves, swims or crawls."

"I am serious," Ruth said, laughing. "We have documented it. They share the calving grounds with the whales."

"NO WAY!" Elizabeth exclaimed.

"I can give you the evidence to look over or take back with you."

"Well." Elizabeth plopped her butt in the chair and held out her glass. Once that was done, she sat back and listened to the songs.

Sub Ambassador Ridge was watching through his binoculars from his steam car. His group clicked once on his radio and the Republic assault group moved toward the FOLK.

NESS Professor Jeremiah AI'd, *FOLK Full Professor Mark!*

YES, he answered, startled.

The NESS are here to protect and we have violence coming toward you. I want you to get your students and have them go down the path. Two NESS will put all of you into the cleft at the base; you will not leave it until we tell you to. Have Elizabeth come along. Say you want to show her something that will peak her curiosity.

Elizabeth was intently watching the whales and GATS when Mark smiled and said, "Elizabeth, the students would like to show you something down the path. Would you come with us please?"

"Can I bring OLD NESS?" she asked, waving the liquid.

"Sure."

They all laughed as they went down the path. The Republic assault team halted.

"They are moving down the path, Sub Ambassador Ridge!" One click came back and the assault leader signale*d, Move forward.*

As Elizabeth came around the small bend, a NESS stepped out in front of the group on the path and pointed to the cleft. Elizabeth was about to say something, but the NESS held an armored finger to the general area of the lips and pointed again to the cleft.

As they entered, Elizabeth saw another huge shadow move up, covering the path as the NESS covered the cleft with camouflage. Then, they both moved up the path.

Dagny Centauri whispered to Brad, "What the hell is going on?"

"The NESS are moving us away from danger and violence."

"How the hell do you know about this danger?"

He smiled and said, "Inner speech with my people."

Dagny had seen this in action, FOLK waving their arms about, gesturing, but no sound coming from the mouths. Dagny loved Brad. He was gentle, kind and treated her with respect.

She whispered to him, "Can you tell the others here to get behind me, please?" as she moved to the head of the cleft with the camouflage.

The FOLK backed behind her. She picked up a three-foot branch and flexed it.

"I need a knife from the field kit along with medical tape," she said.

Both were passed up from a field kit. Pulling her shoes off her feet, she pulled the laces and wrapped the knife handle to the make shift spear end, and then taped the blade more securely with medical tape.

"What are you doing, Dagny?"

She looked at him and said, "I love you and I will kill the first bastard that tries to kill any of us in this cleft." Dagny pulled Brad to her and kissed him. "You're mine, Brad. Now go to the back, please, all of you."

As the gunfire erupted outside the cleft, Brad could see her ready herself for combat. He marveled at Dagny and thought, *She is NESS.* He hurried to the back with the rest of them.

Dagny cleared her mind for combat. She went into the 'NO mind' and waited for the enemy as more gunfire erupted on the trail.

NESS Moriah AI'd, *Set.*

NESS Professor Jeremiah AI'd, *Good, you will start the dance.*

NESS Moriah let the scout pass her. The scout sensed the danger as she spun around, raising her weapon to shoot Moriah in the back. NESS Elijah moved in a blur with a single thrust of the bayonet, drove the blade through the armor and out her back. The scout screamed as Elijah lifted her off the ground on the end of his weapon. He pulled the trigger and blew her body off his bayonet. The splash in the ocean drew the GATS toward the screaming scout. The GATS screamed as they sighted the prey. One of them grabbed her torso then tossed her further into the ocean to be ripped apart by the pod.

Moriah AI'd *Elijah, was that necessary?*

Elijah AI'd back, *Read some old history. This bayonet seems to have its uses,* as his rifle flowed into a more normal operation. *But I like it; it's a good terror weapon.*

Both NESS smiled and opened the dance to full with all their weapons. The assault team tracers and NESS slivers passed each on the trail. The Republic leader screamed, "Fall back!" They leaped back covering and firing at the NESS.

JESUS CHRIST, the Republic leader thought, as NESS slivers blew boulders in half. The assault leader was moving as his number three man was blown apart along with the boulder he was taking cover behind. The assault team leader yelled, "SHIT," as he opened full auto from his assault rifle. The breach went open, so he dropped another clip into it, slapped the bolt shut on the receiver and then ducked and rolled as trees started exploding around him.

"Grenades!" the Republic assault leader screamed at them. All threw grenades down the trail to slow the NESS down and dirt blew up into the air from the trail. He screamed into his headset, "Cover!" His people ran past him. His assault rifle kept the NESS pinned down in the trail below them.

The NESS armor informed them of the grenades' lethality. *Republic new grenades, 8,000 feet per second.*

Moriah and Elijah both rolled behind a boulder, but not in time. The grenades lifted them off the ground and shrapnel hit both of their armors. Their AI reported, *No penetration.*

NESS Elijah picked himself up off the ground and AI'd Moriah, *Cover.* She let loose a series of controlled bursts from her primary weapon and thought, *Two can play that game.*

Elijah AI'd, *Willy Pete grenade, now!* It formed from his waist. Elijah did the calculation, set the timer, tossed the grenade and smiled as Moriah laid down more suppressive fire on the boulders.

The Republic assault team leader screamed, "GRENADE!" He jumped above the trail head. His second-in-command looked down at the grenade at her feet and screamed as it blew her legs off and sent her 10 feet into the air. The Willy Pete set her on fire, along with all of the surrounding vegetation.

The assault leader slapped another clip, aimed and fired controlled bursts to keep the NESS heads down. He glanced at his second-in-command; the white phosphorus from the grenade had burned into her skin. Her screaming echoed in the park.

Damn it, he thought. *I need the anti-tank weapon on these NESS.*

He grabbed the 4th man and barked, "Give me the tank weapon!"

NESS slivers smashed his man and the anti-tank weapon over the cliff. He screamed in frustration, as slivers blew holes in the boulders around him. When his man hit the base of the cliff, the warhead went off and chunks of the cliff hit the water, reflected off and lifted up into the air, pelting the combatants. He screamed his rage. His number two continued to scream louder and louder. His orders had been very specific: no survivors from his team if they were engaged. He spun around and put a round in her head.

He sprinted, dove and rolled up behind another boulder while putting his assault rifle to full auto. He burned through the clip in three seconds before slapping another clip in and unloaded again. He could see the bullet strikes on the NESS armor, but they were not doing any damage.

Jesus, what a fucking nightmare.

He ran for the last boulder before he could disappear from the view of the NESS when NESS weapon fire lifted him off his feet. He landed in a heap and he could feel the hole in him without having to touch it. Rolling over unto his back, he grabbed his assault rifle, reloaded, and pulled another grenade from his assault vest.

"BASTARDS!" he screamed into the night.

Moriah came up to the assault leader when he was trying to pull the pin on the grenade. She could see the blood coming from his wound through her armor sensors. "Shit," she murmured when the armor reported that the grenade had primed. She put one sliver into his chest and one in his head to make sure he was dead.

Moriah started to AI, *Trail secure*, but the grenade rolled off the hand and exploded. It sent fragments all over the place. She was blown off her feet and hit the ground with a thud.

"DAMN IT!" she bellowed. She shook herself and got back up on her feet. Her armor reported, *Penetration, no wound, sealing now.* Moriah knew that she was officially pissed off now. Popping back up, she opened the aperture of her primary weapon to three centimeters and fired the round. It blew the Republic operative into atoms, along with a very large hole since it was specifically designed for heavy fighting vehicles, not infantry. Elijah laughed and AI'd, *Was that necessary? That was a very expensive round.* Moriah responded, *Yes, and the trail is very secure now.*

NESS Professor Jeremiah AI'd the rest of the NESS, *Now*. Sub Ambassador Ridge saw the area light up with massive gunfire.

"Crap, the NESS."

As he turned to get in to the driver's door, he was lifted off the ground by a huge NESS that smiled and said in the outer voice, "Hello, GAT poop," as she dangled him three feet off the ground. The NESS female then swung him to face NESS Professor Jeremiah who stated, "You will serve as an example, but we will have a talking in the trees first." Sub Ambassador Ridge screamed as he was dragged into the woods.

The last two Republic operatives on the bluff were running as fast as they could, the NESS slivers were blowing divots of earth and rock into the air all around them. Screaming and firing back at the NESS, both of them knew that they were dead as the slivers converged on them; it was the last thing they saw on New Earth.

Elizabeth heard massive gunfire erupt on the trail, along with sharp cracks of grenades. All of them pressed farther back into the cleft. Dagny gripped the spear harder. She could see out of the camouflage with a small shadow forming in front of the cleft. She could hear the breathing, smell the gunpowder, smell the sweat off the Republic operative who slowly moved the camouflage away from the cleft. The operative stepped in and said, "I will not kill any of the FOLK, but I want Elizabeth Pameddin, now."

The FOLK just surrounded Elizabeth and said in the outer voice, "No!"

The Republic operative jacked a round from the assault rifle. The FOLK could hear the round bounce off the rocks. She moved further into the cleft and said, "I will not say it again." The Republic operative saw a shadow lunge at her; the operative was very surprised. FOLK never fought back, it was a fatal mistake for her.

Dagny Centauri thrust the spear into the enemy's throat and twisted the knife as she pulled it out. The enemy screamed and coughed blood from its mouth. Dagny then used her unarmed combat training to sweep its feet from under it. The Republic operative hit the cleft floor and saw a blur coming at her, so she swung the assault rifle toward Dagny.

I am going to kill this FOLK, she thought.

Dagny reversed the spear, drove it between the legs of the enemy; the operative felt the blade penetrate her guts. A gurgling scream ripped out of the woman. She sat up from the floor and fired a round at the shadow. Dagny felt the bullet blow a hole in her left leg. Ignoring the pain, Dagny finished the enemy with a thrust from her spear that entered through her eye going into the brain.

Dagny fell across the body; her left leg had folded. Looking down she grimaced as she saw blood spurting out of the wound. Rolling off the body, she grabbed the bandana wrapped around her neck and pushed it into the bloody hole in her leg. She then ripped off her shirt and used the sleeve to make a compression bandage. Brad started to move toward her, Dagny looked at him and said, "Stay there." Putting her good leg against the cave wall, she grabbed the soldier's harness then pulled it into the cleft. She screamed to herself, *Got to stay awake, our lives depend on it.*

Grabbing the assault rifle from the dead body, Dagny jacked a new round into the rifle chamber. She needed more ammo, so after pulling ammo clips from the harness, she set them beside her and waited for the next bastard to show up and try to kill them all.

The NESS AI'd all the FOLK, *Violence has ended, stay there.*

Brad AI'd his parents, *Dad, Mom, I am going to help Dagny.*

Both Mark and Ruth advised against this action, saying, *You will be an accessory for murder, along with weapons violation in our country.*

Dagny is my life. If she dies, I will die. What is the point of living if she is gone?

All the FOLK heard the conversation. They nodded and AI'd, *We will help you, Brad.*

Mark's parents AI'd Brad, *Get the weapon. Toss it in the ocean then we will move Dagny.*

Dagny Centauri was barely hanging on. When Brad made his way to her, she looked at him.

"The NESS are coming now," he said. "Please give me the weapon."

Dagny nodded. He took the weapon from her. Brad saw she was covered in blood from herself and the other soldier. He tried to keep himself calm. Taking the weapon, he opened the camouflage netting and threw it into the ocean.

He AI'd the NESS as he went back into the cleft and said, *Dagny Centauri is extremely wounded. We need help now!*

NESS AI'd back, *We will be there in three minutes.*

He AI'd back, *She will be dead by then; come quickly. We FOLK are going to help her now.* He knelt beside her and he could see the blood coming out a bit slower.

She is bleeding out fast, Brad thought.

He looked at her and asked, "Do you love me?"

She nodded yes.

"Do you trust me?"

She nodded yes while smiling.

"My people are going to help you."

The FOLK got her shoulder and legs, and Dagny screamed as the FOLK lifted her onto the flat area on the cleft floor.

The FOLK, nodding, AI'd each other, *Blending 3…2…1…*

Golden threads penetrated each other and they asked Brad if he was ready. When he nodded, they moved his hand over the gunshot wound and he extended golden threads from both of his hands on the entry and exit wounds. Brad mentally screamed along with the FOLK as they also took the burden for life support. The FOLK knew instantly that Brad was losing Dagny.

Elizabeth just watched all the FOLK touching each other and then relaxing, but all of them were heavily sweating and breathing. She noticed this kid, Brad, had his hands crammed into the woman's bloody holes. She suddenly spied something moving around in the wounds. Brad screamed as Elizabeth saw the blood stop flowing from the wounds.

"GIFT, I need help!" Brad screamed.

GIFT AI'd back, *Brad if you are going to do the repair in the artery, I am going to use you as a prime. You might die. Are you ready? This is a life or death decision for you.*

DO IT! Brad ordered GIFT.

GIFT took Brad's body systems in whole to transfer to Dagny. GIFT was burning through Brad's reserves, along with the FOLK's, too, it noted. GIFT understood that they would be dead very quickly.

GIFT AI'd, *Brad, you will need NESS's help. They have the medical reserves food in the armor. Do you want me to stop?* Brad screamed along with the FOLK, *NO!*

Dagny could feel something in her leg gripping the wounds and she screamed in pain as the blood flowed into the lower part of her leg. Brad, wringing wet, whispered, *Relax, my love, I am helping you* as he numbed the gunshot wounds.

Dagny groaning from the pain asked, *What are you doing?*

Smiling, he answered, *I am using my body systems to keep you alive.*

Dagny could see Brad's shirt covered from her blood. *How?*

GIFT is helping me. I have extended my nerve endings, along with my blood vessels from all of the FOLK to bypass the damaged arteries in your leg; we will not let you die.

Dagny began going into shock and Brad told her in outer speech, "I am going to put you to sleep so I can slow your systems down. I will be with you when you awake."

He AI'd the FOLK, *3...2...1 Dagny, eyes closed.* He liked that idea of her losing consciousness. There was something right and fair about that.

Brad AI'd, *We need to elevate Dagny's legs and get her warm.*

One of the FOLK plopped down and elevated her legs while the rest stripped off their clothing, then stuffed clothing under her back and made a pile of FOLK bodies to keep her warm.

NESS Haldor approached the cleft. He AI'd, *Is Dagny Centauri unarmed?*

FOLK Brad screamed, *Yes, I threw the weapon in the ocean! We have put her under, she is extremely wounded. I cannot maintain this much longer.*

Haldor paused. *Is Dagny the only wounded?*

Yes, Haldor.

I must let her die. She used weapons in our country, and...

Brad screamed at him, *Dagny stepped up selflessly defending us from violence! If it was not for her bravery, we would all be dead. The NESS would be at fault. I will give my life for her because she saved ours. She deserves the best from us. Dagny is also a NESS, so shut your inner mouth and help us!*

NESS Haldor was shocked. FOLK rarely screamed at the NESS. All of the FOLK in the cleft were in a struggle of life or death with Dagny. He could see all their body functions in overdrive from his sensor systems. *They will be dead shortly,* his armor informed him. *Countdown from 30... 29...28.*

Haldor AI'd, *I understand. I am mistaken with my assumption.*

He opened the camouflage and looked at the soldier as he bent down and searched it for booby traps. He saw the knife sticking out of the eye socket.

Seems Dagny Centauri has been very well-trained, he thought.

Picking the body up, he took it around the corner, cut the head off and tossed the remains into the ocean. Haldor set the head down and went back to the FOLK. He AI'd Brad FOLK, *I am taking over. Are all of you ready?*

FOLK AI'd, *YES.*

Haldor's armor AI'd, *Countdown 16...15...14.* Haldor then picked Dagny up and slung her across his shoulder. When her leg hit his armor, golden threads penetrated Dagny's leg. He AI'd Brad FOLK, *Release on my mark 3...2...1.* As Brad FOLK did, blood spurted out of the exit wound. Haldor slapped his left hand on the exit wound; golden threads penetrated into the wound. Armor AI'd *Sampling diagnostic complete. AI'd Medical, NANO BOTS released 10 to 1, 2, 4, 16, 32,*

64 saturation complete, medical systems engaged on subject. Diagnostics flowed. Armor AI'd, *Subject blood pressure is falling, need whole blood.*

Haldor AI'd, *Ask the Armor, any matches in the Cleft?*

Armor AI'd, *Working, one. Elizabeth Pameddin, New World match, no diseases, no known pathogens. Recommend two whole pints. Total failure of subject 180... 179.*

SHIT! Haldor thought. *Dagny is in very serious trouble I need whole blood now.*

Haldor turned to Elizabeth and said, "I need your help. I would like blood from you for an IV. Would you help us?"

"Yes, what do you need?"

"Just hold your arm out for me. My armor is going to make a syringe for the IV."

Elizabeth held her arm up and Haldor gripped it. She did not feel any stinging or needle pain and when he withdrew, there was no mark. As Elizabeth watched, she could see a sack of blood in the armored hand in a jelly sack. He handed it to Brad and said, *Put it on her External Carotid Artery now.*

Elizabeth was startled when the huge NESS had asked her for help with her blood.

Ahhh, she realized. *The girl must be my blood type.*

Nodding for them to go ahead, she held her arm out and felt the blood flow. There had been no pain when Haldor withdrew his armored hand.

There are no puncture marks, no bruising, nothing. This is amazing. What and who are these people?

Elizabeth's curiosity went into overdrive analyzing everything that had happened during these experiences. Mental notes flowed to be put it into her journals for an in-depth analysis when she finally had the real journal in her hand.

NESS Haldor AI'd from his armor, *Sampled AI'd subject Elizabeth Pameddin. Neurons firing 10 to 8th power 10 to the 9th power, armor losing data stream, engaging auxiliary processors 10 to the 10th power.*

It was like a star going nova beside him. NESS Haldor AI'd the NESS, *Do you see this?*

The NESS AI'd back, *Yes, we are engaging full holographic systems now for complete sensor systems download. Sensor systems engaged, feeding data stream to NESS.*

The NESS AI'd the FOLK, *Have seen this before. It is taking terabytes per ten nanosecond. NESS engaging auxiliary comps systems, bringing holographic systems online.*

Haldor's armor AI'd, *System sync to holographic data stream engaged, download started.*

The FOLK AI'd, *It is extremely rare that we have had exactly two from our records. They both built the armor prototype, weapons and cold fusion power plant, along with the holographic comp systems for us after the troubles. They are extremely old now. We have their descendants; the whole family is building more machines for us. They are a FOLK secret.*

What you are seeing, the FOLK AI'd *is a human that is doing trillions of calculations at astronomical levels with NO Mind from our studies. The closest correlation we have is in certain humans, one small portion of the brain was turned on to maximum use, and the other portions were not. Our old ancestor had no clue as to why, so the label was Idiot Savant. These people were barely functional in normal human cognitive endeavors, but GIFT saw opportunity. Key proteins were put back into the DNA strands on all humans now on this planet. This old label is gone from the FOLK and it looks like in the general population, too.*

FOLK AI'd, *This human, Elizabeth, is a walking, fully functional, human Savant. All her mental facilities are turned on. From the armor base scan, we are seeing 95% use of all her mind. We also believe Elizabeth's IQ is off the charts. We have full sensor dump from you now.*

Haldor AI'd from his armor, *Sampling subject Elizabeth Pameddin. Neuron powers are dropping to normal human levels.*

Haldor sighed with relief. His armor needed feeding and he was due for a power recharge when he was done with Dagny. Haldor's armor AI'd him again.

Medical system showing this Dagny Centauri human is a full-blown NESS.

Jesus Christ, when it rains, it really pours, Haldor thought. He AI'd the NESS who were laughing *we are getting the sensor data from her, too, just stabilize then take Dagny to the NESS FOLK hospital.*

NESS AI'd the FOLK neuroscientist, *When can we get a speculation from you?*

The FOLK neuroscientist had been woken up, but they AI'd, *In two days, we can speculate. Are you saying a fully functional Savant?*

Yes.

The FOLK neuroscientist knew from the last 120 years, GIFT had opened vast portions of the human mind. They speculated that GIFT had thrown built-in switches to the on position in their society. Now, they were seeing it in the general population with the Outsiders.

NESS Haldor AI'd Brad, *Set it on her neck, it blended with the artery.*

Haldor AI'd the FOLK in the cleft, *We are going to move her.* As his medical system stabilized her. Haldor started to move from the cleft.

I am coming with you, Brad AI'd.

Haldor looked at him and AI'd back, *It is not for FOLK.*

This is my future wife. I WILL go with you.

Alright, Brad, let's go to the tube. The rest of you stay put. We have NESS on both ends of the trail.

After several long minutes, NESS Professor Jeremiah AI'd FOLK Full Professor Mark, *Mark, the NESS will remove the camouflage. The area has been cleaned of violence. The NESS will guard you as you return to your homes. Leave Elizabeth, we will bring her later.*

Mark turned to Elizabeth and stated in his outer voice, "Please wait here. The NESS will move you later. Everyone else follow me up the trail." He gripped his wife's hand to lead the FOLK up the trail.

Elizabeth noted that all the FOLK looked very tired as they struggled up the path. The NESS had brought bottles of what looked like energy drinks. Noting the FOLK had to unscrew the caps, she smiled and thought, *well the FOLK are normal, no armor sipping for them.*

A NESS approached Elizabeth. She could see the helmet fold back to reveal that it was the NESS Mòr. "Please drink this before we move. This is for the whole blood loss." Elizabeth drank the fruit juice and could feel her body respond; she did not feel lightheaded.

Mòr nodded, "Please follow me; you are safe with me." She then turned and the helmet closed up and her weapons flowed out as she led Elizabeth up the trail.

Mòr swore to herself, *My beautiful park has been destroyed and all my plant studies are blown to shit. Damn it, I will have to start again. My professors will not understand this setback for my advanced degree in plant biology.*

As Elizabeth approached the top of the trail, she noticed that massive scars from weapons fire had blown half the cliff face off. Trees were shattered, the park was gone and everywhere Elizabeth looked had been wiped out. Only large craters existed, now, except one lone chair with not a scratch on it.

Jesus save us, she thought.

Elizabeth looked for the FOLK, but they had been driven off the scene. She could see several NESS were putting out the fires that had started in the pine forest. She also saw other NESS tossing forms off the cliff. She heard the screams of the GAT's from the ocean as they fought over the bodies. Shivering, she offered up a prayer.

NESS Professor Jeremiah was waiting for her near the car. "Are you alright?" he asked.

Elizabeth nodded yes. "They were after me; I am sorry to have put your people in danger."

NESS Professor Jeremiah smiled in his helmet and thought, *Yes, Elizabeth, you were the bait. Thank God no one was hurt from my country. NESS had wanted all the Republic operatives alive for interrogation. A lot of questions needed to be answered like how the hell they got heavy infantry weapons into our country."*

"Yes, it was anticipated. We had hoped it would not be necessary," he said, as he looked around, "but sometimes, it just does not work that way."

Elizabeth asked, "Did you lose anyone?"

"No, we have no wounded or dead this time."

"What about that young woman?"

"Dagny Centauri is in surgery now. We will review the incident. If she saved your life, along with FOLK lives in defense only, she will not be punished for weapons violation or taking a life. She showed NESS bravery in defense of life. She will be rewarded with full tuition for further schooling for life by the FOLK in the near future if she is found not guilty." He pointed to one of the NESS. "This NESS Stardancer will take you back now. If you need further assistance, tell her. I am sorry, I would take you, but I have more business to attend to." He gave her a hug then left with other NESS in tow.

"Are you related to Stardrifter?" Elizabeth asked NESS Stardancer.

She nodded and said, "Yes, he is my brother." When she folded back the helmet, Elizabeth smiled because she saw that Stardancer had the same features as her brother. Her face was more feminine and her coloring was spectacular. "I will take you to the Immigration House."

NESS Stardancer sampled Elizabeth, *Yes, NESS Haldor is right it is like a NOVA exploding from this human. I still do not see my brother's attraction to her, but he always has preferred redheads. They are crazy according to legends.* Smiling, *Yes, my older brother is definitely crazy for this Elizabeth. Let's see if we can keep her alive for him before some other idiot takes pot shots at her.*

NESS Professor Jeremiah stood in front of Sub Ambassador Ridge in the trees after Elizabeth had left. He pointed at Sub Ambassador Ridge and asked, "Are you going to tell us why you have broken our laws?" Sub Ambassador Ridge, who was standing naked, smiled at NESS Professor Jeremiah and told him to stuff it.

NESS Professor Jeremiah smiled in his helmet and thought, *Oh well, we will do it the hard way.*

He pointed to the NESS and AI'd, *Hold him flat on the forest floor.* The NESS slammed Sub Ambassador Ridge into the ground and clamped down on his limbs.

NESS Professor Jeremiah knelt down beside Sub Ambassador Ridge, then AI'd his glove to peel back from his hand in front of Sub Ambassador Ridge's face.

"Last chance to tell us why."

Sub Ambassador Ridge retorted, "Are you giving me last rights?"

"Yes, in a way. Your death can be easy or hard; do you want to face God with a whole mind or no mind?"

"What the hell are you talking about?"

"See my hand? Now, watch." Gold threads appeared in his palm. "I am going to get the information the NESS need one way or another. If you submit to this probe, we will leave your mind intact to face God; if not, the NESS will rip your mind apart. It will be full of pain and agony. Then, we will make you see the hell you created for yourself and toss you into it forever."

Sub Ambassador Ridge said, "Yeah, right. You are full of GAT poop. Take your best shot, you freak. The answer is 'NO!'"

NESS Professor Jeremiah AI'd, *GIFT are you ready?*

GIFT smile*d, Oh yes.*

Gold threads came from the hand of NESS Professor Jeremiah and waved around Sub Ambassador Ridge's face. As they settled, he could feel them penetrate his skin. It felt like a bee sting, but all over his face. He began to scream.

NESS Professor Jeremiah did not smile; he only positioned his hand on the top of the skull. Sub Ambassador Ridge screamed louder as the threads dug through his skull and into his brain. His eyes rolled into the back of his head and his internal mind exploded with pain. GIFT drove in and started ripping his mind apart; the entire NESS present blended with GIFT to record the mind pattern memories of Sub Ambassador Ridge.

NESS Professor Jeremiah withdrew his hand several minutes later. He AI'd the glove back into place before he sat down hard and caught his breath. "What a twisted psychopath. I do not want to even consider this as human."

NESS Professor Jeremiah AI'd the NESS, *Did we get the information?* They all replied, *Yes, it is being sent to the FOLK to add to the analysis.*

The FOLK got a very clear picture of the inner workings of the Republic Intelligence Sections in their country. *Seems we will need to find and destroy these cells quickly. The NESS will round up these individuals, and, then mind wipe them.* The NESS went on the hunt that night.

NESS Professor Jeremiah grimaced and thought, *I need to clear this abomination from my mind.* He sat in the forest, smelling the pine scent and assuming a lotus position, began the ritual. After clearing his mind, slowing his heartbeat and focusing, he sank further into his mind.

Jeremiah slowed the information down. *So, this is devastation from this former human. It welcomed him like an old friend. This thing was pure evil walking around the universe gathering converts. It just claimed another human victim.*

NESS Professor Jeremiah shuddered and thought, *I am too old for this fight,* but he shrugged. *My duty never ends. My people need my experience.* He opened his inner mind further. The forest faded and his mind slowed down even more. Smiling, he could see illumination coming at him.

The NESS watched as Jeremiah's armor changed to a deep, green light, and then expanded to a ball of white light. The pine forest trees flickered with the light pulse.

NESS Michael sat down on his knees and the other NESS knelt with him. They all extended the GIFT from their hands to each other.

Michael smiled, stuck his free hand into the light from Jeremiah the NESS and blended with each other to watch and share God at work with one of their holy people.

NESS Professor Jeremiah was sitting in a meadow with no armor, just his professorial clothes on him. Looking around, *beautiful* was all he could think. With music and light all around, a calming presence settled on him. Light and joy burst around him and in him and he gasped. His wife, Zoë, smiled and whispered to him, *Why are you here? It is not your time, Jeremiah, my love.*

Jeremiah radiated from his love to Zoë. *I am tired. I do not have the strength for this coming fight with Devastation.*

You have always been ready. What is different this time? He showed her.

Zoë smiled and said, *Let me help you.* She grabbed his fear, held it up for him to see with no barriers, and cried out in his pain. *This evil is in the universe. We have seen it. It has no soul, no purpose, just a mindless lust for death. Have faith, Jeremiah, follow the illumination.*

She opened up the vision to his mind. Blending with Zoë, the pain on his soul diminished, healing the wounds from this last fight. Jeremiah felt kisses on his lips. Zoë AI'd, *I am always with you, my extremely cute NESS. God has shown a path for you so go back now."*

NESS Professor Jeremiah's Illumination faded. His world reappeared with a flash of light in the pine forest. The NESS nodded as the armor stopped glowing. Jeremiah's helmet dropped to his chest. He AI'd the helmet to fold it back so he could wipe the tears from his eyes with his hands. His friends waited for him.

NESS Michael held his hand down. "Sir." Jeremiah grabbed the offered hand. His friend helped him up and handed him some water to replenish his systems. Jeremiah sighed gratefully and finished the liter of water. The NESS in the forest AI'd him, *We saw Zoë's vision, too.* They all smiled. *Yes, Zoë is right. We are in for a fight for Illumination or Darkness; what say you, NESS FOLK?* As one *roaring*

Illumination came the answer from all 500,000 NESS and the 10 million FOLK.

GIFT AI'd, *That was delicious to fight Devastation. The NESS FOLK are beginning to understand now my fight. This one was very twisted; it was full blown Devastation. What do the humans say? 'Leaves a bad taste in one's mouth.' Hmmm, I will AI my people with this report of the disease Devastation in this section of the universe.*

NESS Professor Jeremiah looked down at the former Sub Ambassador Ridge and AI'd the NESS, *Clean him up. Put him in the ritual killing clothes then we will meet at his diplomatic house at 07:00 hours.*

Ambassador Sir Felling had just finished his breakfast when his secretary came rushing in. "SIR! SIR! There are NESS around the diplomatic house. They have their weapons drawn."

His security personnel started to move and he held up his hand and ordered, "Hold!"

Ambassador Sir Felling adjusted his clothing and went out to the front gate. As he approached, he saw the NESS had ringed the diplomatic house. *Hmm, now what brings the NESS to my driveway?*

He bowed to the NESS. "What is the problem?" he asked.

NESS Professor Jeremiah replied, "Last night, several of your people violated the FOLK laws with attempted abduction, attempted murder and weapons in our country."

"I have had no such dealing with any such outrageous acts to any FOLK or their laws."

NESS Professor Jeremiah's armor sampled the human in front.

Hmm, I think he is telling the truth to a point; this could have been a rogue operation.

NESS Professor Jeremiah said, "You might not have, but Sub Ambassador Ridge did. I have brought radio intercepts, pictures and DNA samples of the shadow human stealth hunters that have been identified as part of your staff."

He handed over the documents, and then signaled one of his NESS. They brought him out and NESS Professor Jeremiah explained, "Sub

Ambassador Ridge has on him a signed confession as to his involvement. He was the only one involved with this episode, so far, but our laws are simple: "Your "Word is your Life."

With that, the NESS Moriah lifted Sub Ambassador Ridge who was screaming as Devastation claimed his soul. With one armored hand, she broke his neck and tossed his body over the gate.

Ambassador Sir Felling moved out of the way as the body hit the cobblestones. He looked at the body; it was dressed in pure white from top to bottom. It had FOLK script on the front and back reading, *Attempted Murderer.*

Oh shit, thought Ambassador Sir Felling, *here it comes. That idiot will get us all killed now.*

NESS Professor Jeremiah signaled some of the other NESS. They tossed heads into the compound.

"The shadow human stealth hunters lived and died in the shadows; they are GAT food now," NESS Professor Jeremiah said. "Normally, the NESS would kill all of you, but this time, there are no wounded and no dead, so the FOLK council has decided to file a formal protest with the Republic. It went to your PM today for further review."

The NESS weapons went into peace mode and left the Ambassador to his thoughts on the matter. Ambassador Sir Felling went back into the house. Once the door closed, he let his fury out at his staff. He kicked tables over and screamed at all of them as he went to his office to do damage control. He yelled for his secretary and slammed his office door shut.

Why is someone ringing my house doorbell at five in the morning, FOLK Troy fumed. When he opened the door, he was stunned to find NESS had surrounded his house with their weapons drawn. The NESS in front of him said, "FOLK Troy, you are under arrest."

"For what, NESS?"

Troy's wife, Barbra, came behind him and asked the NESS in front of her husband, "What is going on?"

The NESS standing on the porch said in outer speech, "Your husband has been accused of espionage. We have proof of this charge, but we need to make certain of the proof." The NESS held out the documents. "Here is the judge's order for arrest and detention."

FOLK Troy and FOLK Barbra read the documents. The NESS stated, "Per the law, we are acting as police. All visual and audio is being recorded in outer speech. FOLK Troy, do you wish council?"

"Yes."

"Do you have a specific council in mind?" FOLK Barbra asked.

"Yes, FOLK Council Tracey."

The NESS nodded at her and said, "Please inform the council that FOLK Troy is being held in District Fort Two, Cell two. He will be awaiting council. You have 24 hours for council to go before the judge and get the specifics of the charges then you have another 24 hours to appeal the NESS blending order."

FOLK Barbra shuddered because she knew most NESS blending left wrecked minds in their wake. Barbra AI'd her sister. FOLK Ann groaned a bit and sleepily asked, *What the hell is going on?*

FOLK Barbra struggled to hold back tears. *The NESS have accused Troy of espionage. I need you to come over to watch the kids while I go and get council.*

Her sister lived next door and FOLK Ann was there in seconds, barging past the NESS to enter her sister's house. *Go now,* she AI'd FOLK Barbra. *I will watch the kids.* She faced the NESS and looked like a pissed off Sandcat.

NESS Jeremy smiled. *I think she could take me even in the armor,* he thought. FOLK Ann was 7 feet tall with jet black hair. Her NESS glittered with gold and yellow stripes. She was all muscle and she had no problem facing him totally nude.

NESS Jeremy stated, "FOLK Troy, submit."

Troy held his arms apart. The NESS handcuffed him and led him to the steam truck while the NESS moved, looking for the other cells.

The NESS rounded up eight other people. None were FOLK, but were in the country on business visas. The NESS politely asked them to come with them and all of them refused. NESS then showed the warrants and physically carried all of them, along with their families, to the NESS holding cells in several forts.

The NESS blended with all eight individuals; they were found to have helped the Republic. The NESS wiped their minds clean after interrogation. Their families were also blended with the FOLK and they found no issue with them, so their minds were left intact.

Two days later, they were set back into their homes and apartments. When they awoke, the NESS informed them that they would have to leave their country forever. NESS pointed to the guilty and said, "These people are spies, here is the evidence." They handed over the very detailed transcripts.

"You may take the personal property you have in this area, but all business accounts are frozen and will be turned over to the FOLK. All business machinery and buildings tools are turned over to the FOLK, as well. All personal money accounts are not frozen; we have informed the FOLK banking system that your accounts are closed, by a judge's order. Here are the money lock boxes. You will find, down to the last ounce of gold and silver, what you have earned. This is the key to open them, and lastly, you are leaving our country today. A ship is in port, now. We have booked all of you on this ship."

The husbands and wives of the accused looked at their spouses.

"We have wiped these minds," the NESS stated. "They are no longer functional as adults; they all have the mental capacity of three year olds. Espionage and spying in our country is a death sentence, but the FOLK have stayed the NESS's hand in this affair. We are giving the families mercy, so we are kicking all of you out. But, if any of you stay, our mercy will be over; we will kill you where you stand."

Weapons flowed from the armor and smoldering dots appeared on all of them. Ominous warmth emanated from these spots. Women, men and kids screamed, backing away from the NESS.

"YOU HAVE BEEN TOLD."

The NESS weapons went back into their peace positions. The people looked at each other. There were smoking holes in their clothing from the hot weapon crosshairs. The NESS stated, "We will be waiting with the steam trucks; you have one hour." The NESS shut the various doors.

All eight families left on the Republic tramp steamer on the high tide. No one looked at the country they had just left. They knew they were very lucky to have survived. It had been a very good life for them in New Hope.

Five of the families tossed the offenders off the side of the ship for the hungry ocean when they read the transcripts. All five families decided to band together and use their personal wealth. It was enough to buy visas to start over again somewhere in the world. So, when they docked at Oceana, they departed from the tramp steamer. They knew full well that the Republic would kill them to cover their tracks. Using the Comp Board in Oceana, they posted their skill sets: heavy industry, steel making, tool/die machinists. These skills were very scarce in the world.

A patronage had been accepted by the ruling Duchy Mill-Norvasc. When they posted on the Comp Board that day, the Duchy's security secured them for the trip. They knew the Republic had very long memories for failure, so the five families disappeared into the Balkans.

The Balkan states were notorious for their paranoia and hatred of any government. Combat was a normal state of affairs and they knew these five families were a treasure trove of knowledge in heavy industries. This would bring much wealth, so the ruling family had made it very clear to the security they would be protected at all costs.

The other three families were not so lucky. They were executed by the Republic security apparatus by the harbor patrol before they even reached the Republic dock. The ship's crew turned a blind eye to it. They had seen it before; the Republic did not want any living witnesses to point fingers at them.

FOLK Troy knew his only chance for survival lay with a FOLK blending. It offered some hope for clemency for his family. The FOLK laws were very specific on treason and espionage. They would be stripped of citizenship, then tossed out of the country, or worse, executed. His wife, along with the councilor, advised him to go before the judge to ask for FOLK blending. And luckily, FOLK Judge Terrance granted it.

FOLK Troy woke up two days later. He was brought in front of the judge with his wife and council.

"Council, have you read the transcripts?" The FOLK Judge Terrance asked. She nodded.

"Do you have any questions?"

The Council said, "No."

"FOLK Barbra, you have read the transcripts?" After she said yes, they asked her, "Do you have any questions?" She answered no.

FOLK Judge Terrance looked at FOLK Troy. He was striking with the NESS skin tones and he looked like a carbon copy of his father. FOLK Judge Terrance knew his father, as he had served as a NESS with him. It still did not make sense to him why Troy had done this deed. Many had failed at being NESS. There was really no shame in it. It was an incredibly demanding process. The armor chose the participant for the first step then GENOME was rebuilt. After that, training for two axis turns was the norm. Any failure – mentally, physically or morally – and the participant would be thrown out of the program and returned to the FOLK.

Judge Terrance closed his eyes, calmed his anguish, and then opened them again. He was a judge for the FOLK. Speaking loud and clear and in measured tones to the court, which was packed with FOLK NESS, he stated, "As witnesses per the law, every judgment is in the outer voice. Nothing is hidden. All records are open to discussion of the verdict. Are there any objections to the verdict?"

He looked around and the FOLK NESS were silent. He looked down and saw that no paper envelopes had been put in the judgment basket for those too shy to speak out. Judge Terrence nodded and continued.

"Then, the judgment stands. The jury and judges have fully agreed to the charges as they stand. No Mercy has been asked for from the FOLK NESS to the accused."

"FOLK Troy," the judge said, pointing at him, "Approach the platform, turn and face your countrymen for judgment." Troy faced his people. "Since you submitted to the court and fully divulged your guilt, we have granted your request to spare your family. They will remain citizens, but you have been found guilty of Espionage and Treason. This judgment carries the death penalty. NESS Jailer?"

"Yes?"

"FOLK Troy will be executed at high noon on the square tomorrow. Please return the prisoner to the holding cell." The NESS jailor escorted FOLK Troy from the courtroom.

Judge Terrance continued. "NESS Executioner, approach the bench. You wear the judgment armor; no one will know who you are from the normal NESS. The armor is jet black with no identifying marks to protect you. Kneel." Judge Terrance stood and held the sword in the air above him. "This is the Sword of Justice. It is to be used for justice. Do you understand the responsibilities of this justice?"

NESS Executioner said, "I do."

"Then stand. Take the Sword of Justice from my hand."

The NESS took the sword from his hand. "This is a hard responsibility. A FOLK is being put to death by us for espionage and treason. This is a tragedy for our people. Since I am judge and a FOLK, I cannot put our FOLK to death. This burden falls to you. Do you accept this burden?"

"Yes."

"Then, do your duty tomorrow. Tonight, you will stand in the square with the sword pointed to the ground. You are not to rise, nor let it touch the ground until after the charges are read by me and I release the responsibility to you. Is this understood?"

"Yes."

"After the duty, clean the sword, put the edge back on the blade and bring it back to be put back in the scabbard until the next time. The Judgment armor is to be returned to the judgment pool until it is needed. Is this understood?"

"Yes."

On Execution Day, FOLK Troy was in the white jacket and pants with the FOLK script, 'Espionage and Treason' printed on the front and back jacket. The square was packed with FOLK and NESS, serving as witnesses.

FOLK Troy thought, *At least my family has survived. That is a good thing, but they will be shunned by this action from me. These asshole NESS think they are the rulers of the planet.*

He laughed to himself. Many groups had paid well for his information and the FOLK NESS understood how much he had hurt them. He looked at the crowd and thought, *I hate the NESS for not accepting me.* His father was a NESS highly decorated and buried with honors. *I am as good as my father, so why did they not let me complete the transformation?* His frustration had led him down this path.

Troy laughed out loud. He was not surprised when he did not see his wife or any other relatives in the square. His wife had just turned away from him in the court and left him alone without saying a word. Her shame was immense and unrelenting at having been fooled by him all these years.

The FOLK NESS could feel the anger, hate and insanity radiating from FOLK Troy. The NESS understood, but the FOLK were totally baffled by his actions. The FOLK felt immense shame that they had failed at detecting and helping Troy.

NESS Jasmine held the Sword of Justice in her right hand, the blade hanging down toward the ground. She had stood vigilantly in the judgment square all night. The FOLK NESS had gathered around the square before high noon. It was a beautiful fall day, cool and crisp with a slight morning breeze. Many people were weeping; a FOLK had not been executed in the last 150 axis turns. It was almost unheard of in their society.

The NESS Jailer led him to the square; the T was ready for Troy. The NESS Jailer used the clamps to hold his arms against the crossbar then clamped his legs to the vertical section. The helmet descended covering his eyes; it then molded to his head and went rigid to keep him from moving.

NESS Jasmine held the sword; the blade glinted in the sunlight. FOLK Judge Terrance read the judgment and when he was done, he stated, "NESS, carry out the order for execution."

Raising the sword high above her head, it blurred on the down stroke. For a split second, Troy felt the edge of the blade against his neck. And then he was gone.

NESS Jasmine completed the stroke; Troy's neck fountained with his blood. When his heart stopped beating and his body stopped con-vulsing, she reached in and grabbed FOLK Troy's body from the T. She AI'd its release and tossed it over the cliff to the ocean's waiting arms.

NESS Jasmine put her armored hand under Troy's head and AI'd the clamp to release. Troy's head fell into her armored glove. She held the head by the stump and raised it above her head. She slowly spun it around so all the people could see the traitor's face, then plunged it on the viewing pike on the platform. Below the head hung a sign that read, 'Espionage and Treason' for everyone to be reminded of the law.

Many FOLK threw up at the sight of Troy's head dripping blood on the sign. The FOLK NESS had been reminded that treachery was ever present, even in their society.

NESS Jasmine left the platform and the FOLK NESS dispersed soon after. Her armor absorbed the traitor's blood, but the sword drib-bled a trail of blood behind her. NESS Jasmine went back to the Hall of Justice. She stepped into the ritual bath to clean the armor off from the traitor's blood. She AI'd it to release her from the judgment armor then it slithered to the pool and waited for the next time.

She stepped nude into the sealed Hall of Justice to clean, sharpen and purge the traitor's blood off the Sword of Justice. She then hung it in the scabbard above the judge's chair. NESS Jasmine was shaking when she pulled her own armor from the holding pool. When it reengaged, she decided she needed her church.

Jasmine AI'd her helmet back while sitting in the front pew, then kneeled to pray for forgiveness for killing a FOLK. The pastor watched her roll over onto the floor after some hours. Her weeping could be heard from the back of the church. It had been acoustically built for this purpose so that sermons and music could be heard by everyone. He nodded to himself and thought, *It is time*. He walked toward the NESS.

He knew what had happened; he was sworn to secrecy by his faith. Kneeling beside her, he said, "Come sit beside me." Helping her up off the floor, he gently dried her tears and asked, "Do you want forgiveness?"

"Yes," she answered, smiling.

"Good. It is a start. Shared burdens ease the pain in your soul."

Once forgiveness was granted, he went to the front door, opened it and smiled at the family. "NESS Jasmine is asking for you." Her family was very worried, for they also knew.

Sitting beside her till the evening bells sounded, she nodded and said, "I am ready."

Her husband, FOLK Endeavor, grabbed her hand and his golden threads penetrated her hand. FOLK Jasmine smiled and AI'd, *Ende, I am alright now.*

Never doubted it, but we are here for you.

Her three children grabbed her other hand. Her oldest son, Andy, who was thirteen, smiled. Andy AI'd his Mom, *Dad is very worried. Are you feeling better now?*

She nodded and AI'd her family, *Yes, I feel better now, let's go home.*

The pastor went to prayers that night under the stars. He prayed for forgiveness, for the departed soul of Troy and for the understanding for why NESS Jasmine took his life. His prayers lasted until first light. Lifting his spirit to watch the sun rise on the orchards' fields, he could hear his sect singing the morning prayers as they went out into the fields to work. He joined them while smiling.

The NESS and FOLK AI'd each other, *Troy did massive damage to our infantry weapons export business. Did he get into the research side?*

No, we are very lucky in that area. We will need to tighten up the security.

Everyone groaned.

Yes, it is a pain, but it must be done. The orders have gone out: new scans on everyone in the defense industries by the end of the cycle, no exceptions. They nodded. *As we all know, we are being targeted for total destruction from all the reports and scans from the Outsiders.*

FOLK NESS AI'd, *Along those lines, we are very worried if the peace initiatives fail. Probability has risen to almost 100% war in the next coming axis cycle. In that light, we have agreed to grow more warships. All automated factories for this are now on production war footing. Armaments and armor factories are at full production. The secondary fall back systems, are they online, yet?*

Yes, our production has increased by 75%. We will be at 100% in the next monthly moon cycle.

The FOLK council nodded. They AI'd all the FOLK NESS, *We, as people, have been asked by the NESS to activate all ocean/sea defensives, along with offensive, ship-killing systems to passive war footing around our country and our allies' countries. In addition, NESS want all air, land, sea and space mountain weapons on passive war footing, too. FOLK council, after much disagreement we have come to a consensus. We agree with the NESS assessments. It is granted. The NESS may activate all weapons systems for our people. The NESS FOLK city is on passive war footing as of now. All systems are to be sealed for the winter months like normal, but all FOLK NESS are on active duty from inactive reserves after harvest.*

The FOLK NESS nodded and said, *All warships are on alert.*

FOLK Council has activated NESS offensive strike teams. They are to be loaded with long-term offensive armor weapons systems. They are to be deployed at predetermined strike points and their standing orders are to kill all offensive missile battery systems that can reach us and our allies with nuclear, biological and chemical warheads.

The FOLK Council AI'd, *After much debate the FOLK people have voted not to suspend life protocols except in this one area. Since our Offensive NESS are being outfitted with the newest long-term offensive armor weapons systems, megaton release is authorized only for this one area. Their mission is to kill these systems, period. All life protocols are suspended if or when the FOLK give the go through the NESS commanders. You will kill the whole infrastructure. No survivors from the politicos who order it to the lowest trooper. All are guilty of life genocide to the FOLK and our allies.*

All FOLK NESS listened. They nodded and said, *Our greatest fear is weapons of mass destruction exchanges.* They had detailed accounts of the last nuclear, chemical and biological weapons exchanges between them and the Outsiders. The FOLK NESS were still recovering and, along with FOLK NESS human allies, they would not be on the receiving end this time.

The FOLK council asked all of *them, Is this acceptable for now?*

All their people said, *Yes.*

If we see as much as one warship sail toward us or our allies, we will release our entire NESS to full war status.

The FOLK prayed they had one million NESS in suspension. These men and women were specifically built for offensive operations by GIFT. They had volunteered for suspension after the troubles. They were full citizens, but peace time was boring to them and being first generation NESS from all over the planet, unique was an understatement.

The FOLK council had activated some sections for rotation in active service but they had proved to be a little unstable in the current peace climate. The current defensive NESS just laughed and called them geriatrics. The Offensive NESS are veterans of the wars, only the best or the luckiest survived. The FOLK council shook their heads in dismay to the reports being generated from the two NESS groups. They were throwing insults at each other and many bar fights erupted when the defensive NESS called the offensive NESS gimps, geriatrics and retreads.

The FOLK did not understand the fighting. The NESS would beat each other up then go on drinking parties together after the fight. The FOLK sighed. Being practical they asked for FOLK therapy. All the NESS laughed *we are just having fun* so the FOLK just turned a blind eye. So far, it was nothing but black eyes and bruises. FOLK merchants stated *the damages had been covered or compensated for, so no issue.* Currently on active duty they had only 1,000 offensive NESS; the other 500,000 NESS active now were for defense of FOLK and country.

The 1,000 offensive NESS had petitioned the FOLK council to upgrade the armor. It was granted by the FOLK council, but with a lot of apprehension. Offensive NESS were very aggressive. If released, all hell would break loose with the new weapons in their hands.

Several days later, FOLK Barbra and FOLK Ann looked at each other. Barbra AI'd, *We will go back to our family. Troy finished our life here with his treachery.*

Ann nodded and AI'd back, *Yes, my boyfriend informed me today that he was not interested in me since the incident.* Barbra wiped her tears off her face. *How could I be such a fool?*

Her sister AI'd, *It is not your fault; he deceived you with his lies and hate.*

FOLK Barbra and FOLK Ann packed their life into the armored train that was scheduled for the interior desert.

What about your advanced degree in medical electronics? Barbra AI'd.

Ann laughed and AI'd, *I will come back. I have talked to the professors. They understand and said I need a walkabout. I had to look that one up. It's an old term for finding one self.*

FOLK Barbra's kids came up to her, two boys and one daughter. They had full knowledge of what had happened to them. She was very worried for them. They all AI'd, *Do not worry, Mom. Dad did this to himself and you are not to blame.*

Whatever drove your father to do this, he loved all of you.

Then why did he do this to us?

Barbra broke out into tears. *I don't know.*

Her children nodded to their aunt. *We will put mom on the train.*

Once she was settled in, Ann gave her a sedative to relax her and to keep her from killing herself.

Five days later, the armored train pulled into Mesopotamia. FOLK Barbra and FOLK Ann were greeted by their relatives. They understood treachery; they had many ways of dealing with the after effects. Barbra was treated with kindness. All her family helped her. It would be a slow process for healing a wounded soul.

Several months later, FOLK Ann smiled while thinking about her sister who was getting better. Her mom had told her to get out of the city and stop bugging her sister. She smiled and thought, *I missed the desert* and she wiggled her feet in the sand. It was clean and you could see your enemies coming at you. *Yes, I think I will train with my people in the army.* Her skin shimmered and, blending into the desert surroundings, she went for a walkabout in her country.

Dagny Centauri was totally disorientated as she turned her head to look around the room. Bright sunshine was coming in and the mountains had snow on their peaks. She saw Brad asleep in the chair and his hand was in hers. His neat appearance was gone and he looked very handsome to her. She squeezed his hand and said in a soft voice, "Wake up, sleepy head."

Brad opened his eyes. They fired up at the sight of her smiling. "Well, I am back from the dead." Brad stood up and kissed her and she returned it.

Dagny smiled.

Yes, that was heaven, she thought. "I would like another David smile."

"Anytime, my love."

When they both broke apart, she asked, "Where am I?"

"You are in one of the NESS FOLK city hospitals and have been in an induced coma for the last two weeks."

"My leg is very numb."

Brad laughed. "Well, that will disappear in a few more turns."

"Did I lose the leg, Brad?"

Smiling, he answered, "Your leg is still beautiful and whole."

"Well let's see."

Brad pulled the cover off her leg. It was attached and there was a beautiful butterfly tattoo covering up the impact area of the bullet hole.

"What the hell?" she asked, smiling.

Brad laughed. "Well, I had a hard time deciding for the skin, so I thought an iridescent blue butterfly was called for. I hope you like this; it is NESS skin from the NESS that carried you here to the hospital. I provided the coloring." He held up a mirror so she could see both sides of her left leg.

Dagny Centauri beamed a smile at her Brad. "You did this for me?" He nodded. "But I remember the golden thread thingy nearly killed you."

"You were nearly dead. My golden-thread thingy transferred massive amounts of material to you to keep you alive. I would not lose you. If you had died, I would die. My life would be empty without you, so I fought death. Seems we both won."

Dagny's tears ran down her face and Brad wiped them off. "You need to rest. I will be in this chair for you."

Kissing her, he sat down holding her hand.

As she drifted off, she asked, "My love, you will be here?"

Brad said, "Always."

Brad was holding onto Dagny as she exercised her legs in the NESS FOLK city park. She had walked two kilometers today. Two weeks of walking therapy had helped. They were resting on the pine forest trail.

Brad was laughing, tickling her with pine needles on her stomach when Stardrifter approached. He AI'd Brad, *May I sit down with you?*

Brad AI'd back, *Sure.*

Dagny looked at him and saying that he was massive would have been an understatement. He had the thirteen-star flag on his armor. She asked Brad, "Who is this NESS?"

Brad cleared his throat. "Stardrifter is our C&C or Commander and Chief of the NESS."

Stardrifter held out his armored hand. "Pleased to meet you, Dagny Centauri." They shook hands and he asked, "May I sit down with you?"

"Sure."

Stardrifter settled on the floor of the forest and cleared his throat.

"I have a full report of what happened at the park. I am terribly ashamed that the NESS could not protect you and you had to resort to violence in our country."

Dagny became very pale; she had dreaded this moment. Dagny knew the penalty for violence in the NESS FOLK country. Stardrifter's armor sampled her and thought, *she is very scared, I would be, too.*

Dagny gathered her courage and asked him, "Am I going to be killed for this action?"

Stardrifter answered, "No, you are not. We do not kill NESS in performance of duty."

Dagny's relief was very obvious, but she stated, "I am confused. I am not NESS. I am a student from Old World…"

Stardrifter held up his hand. "Please, let me finish."

Dagny nodded and Stardrifter continued. "Your great-grandmother is a NESS, your mother is a NESS, and you and your brother, David, are NESS. When we had you in the hospital, we ran a DNA check on you and your brother when he donated bone marrow for your healing." He smiled. "You're a direct descendant from one of the six original NESS that GIFT had changed. I am the first of the five that have been accounted for, but the sixth was lost in the troubles, so for the last 160 axis turns, we have looked for him. His name is Temple; does this mean anything to you?"

"No," Dagny said.

Stardrifter's armor sampled her. *No issue there, she is not lying. The mystery deepens.*

He nodded to them both and said, "Well, we will keep looking, but in the meantime, the FOLK council would like to give you this for your actions for bravery." He handed over a paper and Dagny read it.

"It's a full tuition waiver and, when done, you will have a junior professor post in research and development in commercial activities for export waiting for you."

She grabbed and hugged Brad on the pine forest floor, then got up and hobbled over to hug Stardrifter, who laughed. "Well, it is not every day I get a hug, but that was nice of you." Stardrifter stood up and bowed to her. "The NESS welcome you to our country, Dagny Centauri. Peace to your house and Brad, I suggest you not lose Dagny Centauri."

"Never," he said as she grabbed his hand.

"You bet, Brad," Dagny said. "Come on, I'm going to write my parents about us, but I need help. I am very tired and my leg is very sore."

"No problem," Brad said, lifting her onto his back.

Dagny wrapped her arms around his neck and legs around his waist. She smiled and squeezed him to her chest. "I like this, Brad."

Smiling and giving her a kiss over his shoulder, he said, "I do, too."

With that he trotted off with her. Stardrifter watched them go down the path.

Stardrifter AI'd his helmet smiling, *Brad has much NESS in him.*

GIFT replied, *Yes, when they marry, we will have Temple GENOME pool back.*

Stardrifter AI'd, *So, GIFT, what did you find in Dagny Centauri?*

GIFT smiled and said, *She is unique. Her bone muscle structure is very dense and she can take massive wounds and still fight. Her speed is phenomenal. When she killed the human hunter, it lasted .5 seconds from first strike to last strike. Her No Mind is outstanding. She rivals NESS Ben in that respect.*

Stardrifter pondered this. *She should have died in the cleft.*

Yes, her body shunted blood to other areas, but the wound was massive. Brad asked for help when he stuck his hands into her wound. I told Brad it would kill him in the effort and he said to do it anyway. He never hesitated with that decision. He would be a very good NESS. We can offer FULL NESS to him; he is almost the age for the training and armor.

Stardrifter AI'd to GIFT, *I think we should wait until they have children. We might get more FULL NESS with her unique Temple DNA combined with us. This NESS line would be in our world view and structure of morality.*

GIFT pondered that statement and started the DNA sequencing of Dagny Centauri with Brad. It smiled and said, *Oh, yes, this is going to be fun.*

Stardrifter let his mind wander as he walked back to the city. His armor sensors sampled everything. He smiled at the display. He could see the trees' systems working the forest floor; it was alive with life. He saw several FOLK out tending to the park and he waved to them as he passed. He AI'd GIFT, *Dagny has no color pattern, just normal human patterns.*

GIFT smiled. *Her DNA pattern masks the colorization. I think it is a survival trait that was passed down from the Temple line. Her chameleon DNA sequence is completely controlled by the individual. I thought that would be very useful. I think I made a mistake on that portion, but time will tell if it was a mistake.*

GIFT and Stardrifter had the same thought. *Yes, Dagny, we would like to meet your mother. I bet our Sixth NESS started the Outcast. Temple hated any authority by any form of government. His entire family was wiped out, all of them to the last cousin. So, the last time the NESS had physically seen him, he was wounded during the last battle. He had given them the one finger salute, and then disappeared into the nuclear hell wastelands that had been once great cities in their northern continent.*

Stardrifter AI'd, *Hmm, seems we will need to do an intelligence work up on Dagny Centauri family. A full blown NESS running around the planet is a mixed blessing. If they are Outcasts, we are in deadly, serious trouble. Even without the armor, they are three times stronger than any human, extremely fast, smart, and they have very short tolerances for fools – a very deadly combination. Shit! God knows what else has been mixed in the NESS Temple DNA Genome pool. Dagny was living proof of DNA sequencing used to create a more deadly NESS.*

GIFT AI'd him, *35 axis turns ago, an island was leveled by Outcasts in Old World and then, they beat the shit out of their military. The sole survivor swore that a tank stopped and picked up a slave from an Old World plantation. His description fits Dagny Centauri's profile. Hmmm, let's see if Dagny Centauri shakes the family tree out with a letter to her family... NESS did you hear?*

Yes, get the FOLK on it, full press. I think we are running out of time. I can feel it in the air. GIFT continued, *Stardrifter, one more point. I cannot see the Temple Genome; it is hidden to me for a very good reason.*

Why?

In case I am killed by Devastation. Stardrifter, shit! The NESS are vulnerable.

If you are killed, we would be blind without the inner speech.

GIFT smiled. *No, there are better improvements coming to the NESS FOLK. You are the laboratory.*

Stardrifter swore and ranted at GIFT. *I have had enough screaming and pain, GIFT!*

Tsk, tsk, Stardrifter. I did all that in the cave the first time when you were passed out; I just have not turned it on yet.

Will it hurt when you do?

Nope, but it will be a surprise. You will like it.

Stardrifter swore and ranted as he stomped back to the city, *GIFT*.

Surprises scared the shit out of him. GIFT smiled and told his friend that he would be alright. His curiosity would get the better of him in about a month.

Elizabeth was getting her gear packed up when the Republic ship arrived in port. The New World personnel had been told that the passage to Oceana was set. Their government had paid for the passage.

FOLK Samantha and Eric Stein approached Elizabeth. She had seen the ring on Samantha's hand. She smiled at them, she asked, "Are you married?" They both smiled.

"Yes. Eric is going back to get his affairs in order, then returning in the spring after the winter storms are done here. Eric has told me that you are not going."

"That is correct," Elizabeth said. "I have decided to take a vacation to do some research."

Eric said, "I have asked for citizenship with the FOLK. They have granted the request and offered a minor diplomatic post to me as my first assignment. I will travel to New World for the winter months and return in the spring."

Elizabeth laughed out loud and pointed to the pouch in her hand. "Eric, here is the diplomatic, sealed pouch since you are a FOLK diplomat. Now, you are not to open them; you are still under the secrets act from your former country." He nodded. "Just hand them to the proper authorities."

Eric took the diplomatic pouch. "Are you sure you are not going back? New World always likes personnel to be present for this type of information."

Elizabeth smiled and replied, "I will be back. I am just... well, tired. My science is slipping, so it seems I will be doing some research to sharpen my next presentation to my government." She gave both of them a hug, "I wish you the best in your futures," she said as she walked out.

Samantha looked at Eric, "Well, husband, was saving Elizabeth worth the effort?"

Smiling, he said, "Yes, she makes it very interesting to say the least. I think there will be more adventures for all of us in the future." With that, he slipped his hand into hers and strolled out to the steam truck for the trip to the harbor.

Elizabeth caught the electric trolley to the university. She knocked on the door of NESS Professor Jeremiah who said, "Come in." FOLK Full Professor Mark and Old NESS were just finishing up what looked like science paper grading. She noted that they had no whiskey this time, just coffee. She crossed over, poured a cup and plopped into the leather chair.

OLD NESS and Mark smiled, "Well?"

She sipped, "Alright, I will do the science, but it is going to be expensive; one ounce of gold per month for a minimum of twelve months.

Old NESS and Mark replied, "Well, that is expensive. Hmmm, we have been talking about that. Do you have a plan before we commit?"

"I am going to the northern continent and do assessments of the ecology. As you have heard, it is severely damaged by the wars. It might be a good time for assessments. There are not many crazy humans around and I might be able to get my students for the summer months."

Old NESS and Mark nodded and said, "Alright, how are you going to get the information to us?"

"You trade with everyone, so do you have FOLK personnel in the various areas?" They both nodded. "Well, I can get the journals to you by couriers when I pay for supplies."

Elizabeth held out the FOLK monetary card. "Well?"

OLD NESS and Mark both smiled. "We will go down to the cafeteria. You are buying. Then, we will head over to the university's accounting people. They are not going to be happy with this bill."

As Old NESS and Mark laughed, Elizabeth thought as she headed toward the cafeteria, *I wonder if they carry key lime pie.*

The Republic Cruise Liner Traveler was a very large liner at 1,300 feet long. It was sleek with enclosed viewing platforms and it boasted every pleasure you could imagine, as long as you had money.

Eric Stein was on the aft deck, watching the loading of all diplomatic personnel from all the diplomatic enclaves; the NESS and FOLK did not allow them to winter over in New Hope.

Eric contemplated. *I will have a lot of explaining to do to the New World council. It will not be in a charitable mood for failures even though I am a FOLK citizen, now.* He waved to his wife on the quay. *Samantha. Can you hear me?*

His wife answered, *Yes.*

Eric's inner speech was getting better. *This is amazing. Will I be able to talk to you?*

She smiled in his mind and said, *Yes.*

Samantha smiled. The FOLK gathering for Eric had gone smoothly. He was out of the hospital in two days and had gained his strength back in no time. As she patted her belly, she thought, *My daughter is right. He is healing me and her.*

GIFT was very pleased. *Another wild, human genetic structure in place. It had tweaked her eggs and Eric's sperm again. Let's see if we can have more geniuses, engineers and scientists in my Samantha house line.* Joy surprised GIFT. It smiled and said, *Yes, her line will be very important to us in the future.*

Ambassador Destroses noticed Eric Stein waving at his wife. *Hmm, let's see if I can save him. The NESS and FOLK information might help us all in the long run.*

He called his staff over and told them, "I want to invite some diplomatic people to a small get-together. Here is the list. Get one of the smaller ballrooms and schedule it in two days." He smiled at them. "This is serious. Please convey that to the diplomats." He then turned and squeezed his wife's hand. She nodded. "It is going to be a very long haul."

She said, "Yes, it is," as the ship pulled away from the quay.

Elizabeth noticed the Republic cruise liner, Traveler, heading down the harbor. The FOLK Mini was in his office sipping tea and watching the cruise liner, too, with a critical eye. He turned and smiled, "Not bad for the Republic ship."

Elizabeth said, "Well, I think I have the best ship designer in front of me."

FOLK Mini puffed up and thumped his chest. "You are right," he said, as he laughed. "Let's go see my masterpiece and put some ocean trails on it to make sure my masterpiece Old NESS behaves."

Elizabeth stepped on the deck along with FOLK Mini. The shakedown crew was waiting on the dock. He introduced them as the shyster crew; they all laughed. FOLK Mini got serious. "You know the routine. All systems will be checked to specifications."

The shyster crew scampered to their respective positions. FOLK Mini continued. "We are waiting for the NESS with the weapons key. During shakedown, the NESS will activate the weapons and, when we return, will deactivate the weapons and put the peace seal back in place."

Elizabeth said, "No problem."

NESS Trevor approached with his armor pilot master on. He asked for permission to come on board. Elizabeth said, "Yes, you are approved to board."

He told her, "I am Pilot Master for New Hope. I am here to provide the key for weapons testing within our country. Would you like to test it personally or would you like me to test it?"

Elizabeth replied, "You can test it, but it must be like I would. Is that possible?"

"Yes. I can do it manually when the time comes. We have the shooting range set with various speeds and angles."

Elizabeth looked at FOLK Mini. "Well, let's get the show on the road," she said, as she belted herself into the captain's position chair.

He sat at the engineering station and smiled. "Captain, all systems are green across the board."

Elizabeth told the helmsman to hit the starter on the engines. She smiled as she heard the growl and the purr of the engines as they settled down. "Let's head to the ocean testing grounds."

Two days later, FOLK Mini was watching as they were coming back. "Well, Elizabeth, we have one problem with the drive unit, but I have swapped that out. When we get in, I will get the other one from spares and put it in the storage area. Are you satisfied with Old NESS?"

Elizabeth smiled. "Yes, your masterpiece is a masterpiece. I am very happy with Old NESS."

"Yes, when I am given leeway to design, it just works."

"FOLK Mini, I noticed Od NESS flows. It reminds me of the NESS warships."

"Yes, it does," he said, as he smiled and looked out the bridge windows. "So you noticed it?"

"Yes."

He sighed. "I did design work on our warships and I will have to face God on that score. It is very painful for me to bear. The design for the warships is very deadly. I was asked to make it for the new weapons, along with the new armor systems. It worked way beyond expectations. I was told of the losses that occurred during the sea battle. It was slaughter on a very large scale."

"I understand you are not to blame."

"When will science not be to blame? We put the instruments of destruction in the hands to do good or evil and then, we say it is not our problem if evil takes the knowledge and crushes us under the weight. I have grave doubts about us as a species. It has been a moral problem for me, so I choose now to design commercial ships and masterpieces," he explained, as he pointed to her ship.

"Shall we push the speed in the harbor?"

He grinned. "Why not?" He hit the throttles to the stops.

NESS Jeremiah and Mark were watching Elizabeth's ship, OLD NESS, scream up the harbor from the restaurant. Both were laughing hard as the marine patrol was trying to catch them.

"FOLK Mini sure knows how to build them," Mark said.

"Yes, he does," NESS Jeremiah agreed, as they settled into the meal.

The harbor patrol pulled up beside them as they idled into the marina. NESS Chris was not in a pleasant mood, but he was mollified when NESS Trevor had told him he had asked for the test. When they docked, Elizabeth tossed him a beer.

"Thanks," he laughed. "I have not been dumped on my butt in a long time. Just give a warning next time, Mini."

He hopped onto the floating dock at the marina and waved to his girlfriend at the top of the floating dock.

"Got to go," he said, turning to Elizabeth, "When you leave, I will come down to unseal your weapons, but keep them in the peace position. Do you understand the consequences if you unseal them for war in our country?"

She nodded and said, "I do."

He smiled. "I think you do. Peace to you and your house."

FOLK Mini added, "Your visa has been extended for a couple of days. Do you need a crew? I have relatives in the FOLK seaman union that are dry docked with no berths since the season is done for fishing here.

"Can they read, write and take orders from me?"

FOLK Mini answered, "Oh yes. They have apprenticed and are journeymen, along with their university schooling. They are good at what they do for a living, but being FOLK, they will not kill, so the weapons and security will be an issue for you."

"No problem. You pick the candidates and bring them here tomorrow once picked. I will pay normal seaman wages based on skill sets for 12 months and send them back here once the contract is completed."

FOLK Mini smiled. "Well, we need to finish the transfer of the balance for OLD NESS. Shall we do that now?"

"Sure, let's get that done. I have to gather my samples from the university today. Please make sure the supplies are loaded and stored properly on the ship by your shyster in-laws."

He laughed and said, "Yes, they do like your silver and it will be done today."

FOLK Mini arrived with the relatives she hired. Four of his people told them to get packed and arrive the next day on the ship at 18:00 hours. FOLK Mini smiled and said, "I am going back to the yard. Do you require anything more?"

"No, you shyster, but I will be back for a yard upgrade.

"Of course. I have more ideas for your ship." He shook her hand and walked back to the land from the dock.

Elizabeth was at the Goods Store, getting the last of her personal supplies when she noticed a NESS with crayons and coloring books in a bag ready to be purchased. He was in the NESS combat fatigues and had no armor on. *Hmmm, it looks like the NESS are semi-human*

The NESS turned to get another coloring book ready. He noticed Elizabeth.

Ah crap, it's Stardrifter, she thought.

Elizabeth looked at the crayons and the coloring book in front of Stardrifter. He cleared his throat.

"My friend is bringing his grandchildren over tonight for dinner at my house. I have learned to direct their attention to this past time. The children are helping my drawing abilities, to keep the colors in the lines. This time, they are five and six years of age."

Elizabeth burst out laughing. "So, five and six year olds are directing you, the leader of the NESS combat arm?"

Stardrifter nodded. "Yes, and I must be on the floor as they crawl all over me to direct my progress in this endeavor." Stardrifter looked at Elizabeth and thought, *Let's see if she will come over to my house.* He cleared his throat. "Elizabeth?" She smiled. "I would like you to come over, too"

She laughed out loud. "Why would you invite me?"

"Well, for one, I wish to show you I am not a monster. Two, my friend, NESS Professor Jeremiah is the one coming over with his family, and a third, I will need a break from the kids. I am not good with them and you are a teacher in your heart. Maybe you could help me understand them."

Elizabeth thought, *Why not? It will be an interesting evening.* She smiled and said, "Sure, where do you live?"

Stardrifter gave her the address. She was surprised that it was fairly close to the Immigration House and within easy walking distance.

GIFT AI'd Stardrifter, *Are you going to mate?*

Stardrifter AI'd back, *SHUT UP GIFT! Jesus, is everyone curious?*

Yes, there is a thing called a betting pool. I have calculated the odds for some others. They are rubbing their hands together; something about easy loot.

Stardrifter mumbled to himself as he purchased the goods. *Well, it would be nice, but Elizabeth hates my guts for very good reasons.*

FOLK Nerada in front of him smiled as she rang up the purchases. She AI'd Stardrifter, *You should see the odds, Stardrifter.*

He just sighed and AI'd back, *I am doomed.* He smiled back at the FOLK and said, *No, thank you. I am not a race thingy – a race horse, I think they are called in the world – sprinting to a finish.*

NESS Professor Jeremiah AI'd, *Thanks, GIFT, for nudging these two together.*

GIFT laughed and AI'd, *Yes, it will make an interesting evening. I cannot wait.*

NESS Professor Jeremiah AI'd GIFT, *Let nature take its course or leave them alone for tonight. It will be more interesting in the morning, trust me.*

Always. I will see you in the morning.

As Elizabeth left, her hormones had ramped up again. *Jesus,* she said to herself, *give me a break, will you.* As she wandered toward the Immigration House, she thought, *I wonder if I can get some nice clothes.* She spotted a sign pointing into the clothing district on the way to the electric trolley. *Hmm, let's see if I can ambush NESS man tonight.*

Elizabeth approached the house. It was a one-story house made of stones with large windows and a wrap-around porch. She noticed the plants and thought, *I bet Jeremiah put these in. They are too well laid out. Hmm.* She also noticed that the back had orchards rising into the hills; they were not laid out well. *Yeah, Stardrifter did that one.*

She rapped the iron knocker on the door. It was solid wood, plainly finished and with just a bit of oil as a finish. As it opened, Stardrifter had a five- or six-year old girl wrapped on his right hip. Her red hair was draped across her face and deep brown eyes peered out of the mess. The girl smiled at her and whispered to Stardrifter, "She is pretty." She tightened her arms around his neck, as if to say, *This one is mine.*

Stardrifter smiled. Elizabeth noticed that he was out of the armor fatigues and had on shirt and slacks with leather loafer shoes on his feet. As she looked up, she saw that his hair was longer. She also saw that his eyes were not all grey, that they had flecks of blue in them today. Her hormones began to ramp up. *Calm down, you idiot,* she whispered to herself.

Stardrifter smiled and his heart started racing. Elizabeth was in a handmade sweater, a nice blouse and a skirt with nice leather flat shoes. She wore her red hair draped across her shoulder.

God help me, he thought to himself.

"Come in," Stardrifter said, as she entered. A very large, grey cat – or something like a cat – looked at her from the floor. It meowed at Stardrifter and rubbed his leg. Behind him was an even bigger cat looking at her from a perch.

There was another five- or six-year old girl hiding behind his other leg. She had long, blond hair styled in braids, and blue eyes. She had a death grip on his only free leg. Stardrifter said laughing, "Well, let me introduce you. This one on my hip is Holly, the one that has my leg in a death grip is Alexei and the grey TAC is Junior. The TAC behind me is Homer, his mother."

The girls smiled and the grey TAC thing sat down and gave her the once over. He told them all, "This is Elizabeth Pameddin from New World."

The girls said, "Hi," to her.

She smiled at them, "Glad to meet you Holly, Alexei, TAC Junior, and TAC Homer.

Stardrifter reiterated, "Come in, come in," as she passed; he then smiled while closing the door. Alexei held her arms up; he bent down and picked her up then stepped over TAC Junior. Holly scratched TAC Homer on her head. He smiled over his shoulder and said, "Elizabeth follow me." She noticed that the house was laid out with wood floors and no small halls, just open space. She noticed the landing opened up to a very large room and that couches and chairs were scattered with FOLK NESS. She noticed that NESS Professor Jeremiah was there. He waved to her as he chatted with a woman who was stunning and had his features.

Stardrifter wandered into the next room with the kids. He planted them on a very large kitchen table. They whispered to him and he nodded as he turned and saw Elizabeth. He smiled at her and said, "I have been given some orders to pilfer some fruit; I will be right back."

He winked at her and approached the large kitchen. FOLK were working the food on the large kitchen table and he asked for fruit for the kids. They pointed him toward the bowl of fruit and he reappeared with two pears, sliced and diced for the kids.

Stardrifter gave the kids the fruit and asked Elizabeth, "Would you like something to drink?"

"What do you have?"

He went behind the bar and checked. "Well, we have hard liquor, wine, beer, coffee, tea, fresh fruit juices, or spring water."

"Are you the bartender?"

He laughed. "Yes, for tonight."

"Do you have a Merlot?"

"Yep, it is a local brand, grown in the interior."

"Sounds fine to me."

He pulled the wine out and poured a glass for her. Stardrifter then poured a glass of cognac for himself and smiled at her and said, "I am glad you came."

She nodded and replied, "You have a nice house."

"Yes, my grandparents built this house 220 axis turns ago. This is my family's original homestead that we obtained in order to open this area up to civilization. My brothers, sisters and I grew up here."

Elizabeth looked surprised. Stardrifter smiled at her and said, "Yes, I do have family."

As she looked around, she noticed some old photographs. Stardrifter noticed which way she looked. He said, "Here, let me show you."

Elizabeth looked at the photographs.

"Which one are you?" she asked.

He pointed to a blond-haired kid on the end squinting at the photographer. She noticed he had no scales. As she looked further, she noticed that his sisters and brothers and whole family all looked normal.

Stardrifter said, "I see you noticed no scales. This was before I found GIFT and the world changed." Stardrifter's face clouded over as he recalled the memories. "Forever."

Elizabeth noticed some oil paintings near the framed pictures. She looked at them and then, looked at him harder before asking, "Is this you?"

"Yes, it is from GIFT to me from a very famous FOLK artist."

She looked at it harder. It showed the transformation of a human being into a NESS. She was very startled; it showed the labels, 'Pain, Agony, Acceptance, Transformation'. The artist had captured his very soul. Looking at the paintings, she saw that the last one, 'Transformation', showed him holding the human DNA strands between his armored hands to the stars.

Stardrifter noticed her movement as she turned to look at him. His dream/vision from the night before fell in to place. *OH SHIT! Here it comes*, he thought.

Elizabeth looked at him and thought, *He is not hiding anything.* She asked, "What happened that day with GIFT?"

Stardrifter gathered his courage before he spoke.

"I was pretty wild in those days. I took many risks. Anything my parents said I should not do, I did. It was driving them insane, so they tossed me out on my butt and told me to take my craziness into the world."

Elizabeth nodded, "I know that one."

"I decided I needed high adventure – higher schooling was boring, so I went diving into the seas and oceans by doing ship salvage work." She looked surprised and he nodded. "Yes, I was GAT prey, but the money was outstanding. So, being young and stupid, I partied and chased women all over the planet."

Elizabeth laughed. He pointed at a photograph where he was in heavy diving gear on a wreck.

"Yes, I was crazy, but on the day I found GIFT, things were different. A ship had been sunk by a pod of GATS and instead of eating the people, they put them in an underwater cave."

Elizabeth's eyebrows rose very high. He nodded. "Yes, we found a survivor who had gotten out by swimming through an ocean-eaten hole at low tide. She was hysterical when we found her. She had been chased all over the place by the GATS. Seems they were using her for training their young to hunt. So, my captain asked for volunteers to go and get them. Since the money was no concern, these rich kids were from the top of the old society and the rich people signed the contract. I was up for the dive, so David Saint-Lions, my diving partner, and I suited up. We got our tanks, masks, tools and weapons all situated and we hit the water, swimming for all it was worth. When we got to the cave, it was high tide and the GATS were waiting in ambush for any foolish humans. Bastards were and still are very smart; back then, they were hunted heavily and only the smartest survived to adults."

Stardrifter's face clouded again. "David hit one GAT with a compressed spear gun. The barb got under the scales and the ½ pound of C4 blew it apart. That just made the others pissed off at us, so we went toward the rocks above the cave to get away from them."

"My aim was not so good with the second GAT. My shot had missed and exploded against the rocks. The concussion stunned the GAT, so we made a vigorous swim bordering on panic. As other GAT shadows appeared below us, I made it by the skin of my teeth to the surface. I kind of bounced off the rocks by the surging waves. By sheer luck, it lifted me over the water's edge rocks and slammed me into the blow hole above the cave. My running partner did not make it. I saw GATs rip him apart as he tried the same maneuver... His screaming still haunts my dreams."

Stardrifter took a sip of his cognac. "As I fell through the blow hole, I noticed writing on the walls. As I studied the writing, I hit something solid like a rock outcrop. I think I was knocked unconscious, so it did not hurt when I slammed into the floor."

Elizabeth nodded and said, "I bet."

"When I came to, I rolled over and came face to face with someone who I thought was not alive."

Elizabeth interrupted, "Not alive? But you said the GATS put them there alive."

Stardrifter nodded and said, "Yes, they did, but they were not chewed. Seems they used a neurotoxin. It stops all synapses to the limbs, but allows your heart and lungs to work; that way, they can store you for later use. So, all five of them looked like corpses to me at that time. I remember thinking to myself, *These must be the rich people.* I sat up and checked myself for damage. Then, I checked my gear and I stood before I decided to search the pockets of the nearest dead body. As I rolled him over to search the pack under him, I noticed a faint pulse in his neck. But I decided that he wouldn't miss what was in his pockets."

"So you were a thief, too?"

Stardrifter smiled and said, "No, they were very happy to see me. As a reward, he willingly donated his money to me." Elizabeth rolled her eyes. "Checking the others, I found that they were alive, but in the same catatonic state, so I searched their pockets, too. I found a couple of bags of silver and gold." Elizabeth sipped her wine and thought, *So he has fallacies and larceny in his heart.*

"Taking my torch, I slowly spun around and looked at the weird hieroglyphic writing on the cave walls. At the same time, I was trying to get the hell out of the damn cave so I could get my large reward of money."

Elizabeth laughed at him.

"What?" he asked. "I had to make a living, but as my torch went past a hole, I saw a glint of something gold. When I approached it, I could feel air from it and I thought it might be a way to get to the surface, so I put my eye to the hole. I noticed a stone pillar centered in the middle of another chamber and it was domed like a half bubble covered with fused glass volcanic rock. It looked very old and was covered in gold, so being needy of money," Elizabeth's eyebrows went up and he smiled, "I pulled my heavy hammer out of my work pouch, knocked a bigger hole in the volcanic rock wall and stepped into the chamber.

"I thought to myself, *Here is my ticket for having a lot of fun for a very long time.*" Stardrifter laughed at himself. "I was a very self-centered, arrogant bastard back then. With money, I would not have to deal with dead people, or live ones, for that matter. Money gave me choices. I could have control over my choices and it would be a very nice life."

Elizabeth watched his face. His eyes were locked on hers and there was no flinching and no darting away; he was focused on her only.

"So, as I approached the pillar, I saw that it was covered in hieroglyphics. I realized that it looked familiar, but having not paid much attention in school, I did not recognize the universal mathematical symbols."

"So, you found an object that you had no clue as to what it was and you just saw the gold?"

Stardrifter laughed and said, "Yes. As I approached the pillar, I noticed that it also had symbols running on the floor from the pillar to the walls and around the whole chamber. These symbols were solid quartz with gold filaments that was machined into the rock."

"Go on."

Stardrifter looked at her with haunted eyes. "Well, as I stepped onto the platform, I noticed two impressions on the stone." He laughed, "They were of two human hands, left and right, you know, five fingers with opposable thumbs."

Elizabeth nodded. "I thought this might lead to another chamber with more gold, so I set the hammer on the platform, put my hands on the impressions and pushed for all it was worth." Stardrifter paused. "The damned pillar grabbed me."

Elizabeth burst out laughing. "Let me guess, GIFT?"

He nodded. "One and the same. I was stuck like a bug on a paper trap as I struggled to free myself. The damn walls started to glow and gold filaments appeared around the whole chamber."

"You're an idiot, Stardrifter."

He nodded and said, "Idiots are universal."

Elizabeth watched Stardrifter's face. It showed horror and fear at the same time.

"GIFT was waiting for me; I had the key genetic codes in my cells that released it from its sleep. When it awoke, it looked at me and said, 'Hello, my friend.' I started screaming at GIFT, saying, 'No fucking way' as I watched the filaments coming toward me. I tried to wrench my arms free from the pillar to grab the hammer at my feet, to fight. But the gold filament threads were in my hands, and then running up under my skin, holding me to the pillar. I was screaming 'I am not going to die this way,' but it was too late. The filaments from the chamber penetrated my whole body."

Stardrifter's glass of cognac suddenly shattered as his clenched fist shattered the glass. Tears ran down his cheeks as he remembered his screams, fear, pain and agony, as GIFT started Genome Rebuild on him. He looked at Elizabeth and wiped the tears off his checks before he continued. "Yeah, it was a very long day. It was seven days in total for that session that GIFT had its first human – me!

"When it had me good and firm, GIFT grabbed the other five people and rebuilt them, too. They were lucky enough to be unconscious from the neurotoxins. The third week, I think I started to crawl away from the platform to throw myself into the ocean. I would prefer to be GAT food than what was happening to me."

He held up his hands to her and Elizabeth looked at his hands as he went on. "They were changing. As I watched my own change, I screamed and the damn filaments grabbed me again. GIFT told me, 'We are not done,' as it dragged me into the chamber. I was screaming, along with the other five people in the chamber who were awake at that point."

Stardrifter looked at Elizabeth. His pupils were fully dilated and she could see his pain. "Screaming did not help, but passing out sure did. When we awoke in the cavern, we found that it had collapsed. I looked around and I didn't see the pillar, nor any gold. Then we looked at each other and, well, you saw the skin and colors."

Elizabeth nodded.

"GIFT had blown the chamber apart for us to escape together. When we saw the sky, we ran even harder and got the hell out of the cavern, scrambling over the rubble and into freedom."

Elizabeth said, "So you went out into the populace."

He nodded. "Everything we touched, ate, peed – everything had GIFT in it." Looking at her, he continued. "You know what followed. GENOME patterned on everything alive in our world."

Stardrifter looked at Elizabeth with peace and calmness. "I was twenty-eight years old then. I am responsible for the human population being decimated by GIFT. My arrogance, along with my stupidity, caused millions upon millions of people to die from GENOME patterning and the wars that followed when we tried to kill GIFT."

GIFT AI'd him, *I am sorry, Stardrifter. I know what I have done. I have held nothing back from the FOLK NESS as to why it was done this way.*

Stardrifter smiled and AI'd, *Old history, my friend. With age comes wisdom. Let's see what it brings us in the future.*

Elizabeth watched Stardrifter's face and thought, *He is talking to someone. Could it be GIFT?*

Stardrifter bent down to clean up the glass. As he was doing this, Elizabeth noticed the many scars on his skin near his neck. As he got up from cleaning, she said, "Your skin has many different patterns."

"Yes, bullet holes tend to do that to one's skin over time."

Elizabeth noticed Stardrifter looking at the girls and wondered if he was talking to them too. *Telepathy is bullshit, so what are they doing?* She noticed some of the FOLK were talking. Some were waving their hands around, but their lips were not moving. *This is getting real interesting,* she thought as she looked at Stardrifter.

Holly and Alexei AI'd Stardrifter, *Uncle, we are icky.*

Stardrifter looked at the kids and AI'd, *Yes, I can see that you are. Do you want a ride so I can clean you up for dinner?* They both smiled. *Hmm, can you do me a favor then and use your outer speech to ask me to help? My friend cannot hear the inner speech.*

Both Holly and Alexei screeched out loud, "Uncle, we are icky!"

Elizabeth looked at the two girls and thought, *Uncle is it?*

Stardrifter looked at Elizabeth and said, "Please excuse me, I have been summoned for icky duty."

Elizabeth watched as Stardrifter picked up the two girls in his arms. She noticed when they hugged him, his skin cleaned the pulp juice from their fingers. Her mouthed dropped open as he took them to the bathroom.

I need a refill, Elizabeth thought. Going behind the bar, she poured herself another drink and set the glass on the bar. She noticed Jeremiah approaching her; she also noticed that he dressed like any old professor with wrinkled clothes and mismatched socks. She smiled. *Yes, he is cute.*

Jeremiah gave Elizabeth a hug. "I am glad you made it. What are you drinking?"

"Merlot wine," she answered. Going behind the bar, he pulled out another glass and poured himself one.

Jeremiah noticed Elizabeth's expression of shock when she was staring at Stardrifter's skin.

"Absorbing nutrients," he said. "The NESS skin absorbs food directly. Energy is energy."

"What about the FOLK?" Elizabeth asked.

"No, FOLK are not NESS. NESS in combat might not have time to eat or food is scarce, so GIFT has adapted our structure to live on just about any source of food."

Elizabeth asked, "So, do you eat humans?"

Jeremiah laughed. "Never. NESS Bill was having fun at your expense on the warship. He is on extra duty for that wisecrack, along with the pay grade loss, too. Bill is not happy. NESS bilge cleaning is not fun. Well, how are you handling us since you have had freedom to look at us in our element?"

"You are a fraud. You are all normal and just as messed up as the rest of us humans on our planet."

"Never claimed to be super men or super women; we're just different. So is Stardrifter being polite to you?"

"Yes, I find him very human. He was telling me how he found GIFT in the cavern."

Jeremiah laughed out loud. "He did. Well, did he tell you he searched someone's pockets when he found the GIFT?"

"Why, yes, he did. He said they seemed to be pleased to let him have their money."

"Well, that someone was me, along with my rich friends."

Elizabeth laughed out and covered her mouth. "YOU!"

Jeremiah nodded. "Yes, he was a scoundrel back then. What is the term? Ah, yes, 'a pirate of the first degree'."

Elizabeth looked at Jeremiah and asked, "Truth?"

"Yes."

Before he could finish, the woman who Elizabeth had noticed earlier approached them both. "Father, it is about time for dinner. You will need to wash up? I think Stardrifter is done with the girls."

Jeremiah said, "Elizabeth, this is one my kids, my daughter, Jessica. The two girls that have Stardrifter wrapped around their fingers are my daughter's girls."

Jessica smiled at Elizabeth and AI'd her dad, *She seems nice, I was not at her scan.*

Jeremiah AI'd back, *I think she would be good for Stardrifter. He has been alone for a very long time.*

Yes, but it must be his choice. GIFT is very protective of him. Just listening to GIFT rant about mating was hilarious, though.

Jeremiah said in his outer voice, "Well, let's all get washed up. I hear we have deep rock bass for dinner tonight."

The dinner table had twenty people around it. Elizabeth noticed that they teased and laughed at each other. *Yes*, she thought, *they are human*. They engaged, laughed, and teased her about her work, her country, her family and her perception of the world.

Stardrifter had both Holly and Alexei on each leg. He was feeding them as they pointed to the food. Elizabeth turned to Jessica, "Will he get to eat?"

She laughed and said, "Nope, those two have dibs on him tonight."

Elizabeth thought, *Stardrifter, you are a fraud. Those kids are totally relaxed with you.*

She smiled. He looked happy with them. After the dinner, Elizabeth looked at Stardrifter. He shrugged as the two girls grabbed his hands to be tasked with their guidance on drawing skills. She wandered around, looking the house over.

Hmm, five bedrooms, two bathrooms, big kitchen, large storage areas. She looked at the walls. *Granite, but rough cut, not polished.*

She thought the lighting was solar powered until she looked at the bulbs. It looked like fireflies, but it had water label plankton bloom with a shield shutter that rolled around the light.

Walking toward the loud voices in the main living room, Stardrifter was on the floor with crayons and coloring books. As he had predicated, he was being directed by all the kids. They were using him as a perch to direct his progress. Elizabeth came over, sat down and looked at his progress, saying, "Not bad, but you missed here."

Holly said to the others, "You see! He does need direction." With that, they swarmed him with directions.

Smiling at Elizabeth, he said, "Why don't you grab Jeremiah and have him give you a tour. I think I will be here for a few minutes."

She obliged and she sought out Jeremiah. He showed her the rest of the house and orchards. She asked, "So what is it between you and Stardrifter?"

"During the troubles, he and I were on the run. Let's just say we had targets on us for being NESS."

"That was a very long time ago."

"Yes, as we found out, GIFT had slowed the aging process in us. I am about 70 years old in normal human life span now. So, the streaks of white in my armor are showing, but my strength dexterity is not impaired. I am still on the active warrior roles."

"How about Stardrifter's age?"

Jeremiah paused before answering. "He is still 28 years. We are puzzled by this lack of aging, as our tests indicate that his atomic levels are being rebuilt in real time by GIFT."

"So, you have no clue."

"Yes."

"GIFT has found the aging key in us, but has not turned it on for the rest of your people."

Jeremiah answered, "Yes, but it is not complete. GIFT is still tinkering with us and Stardrifter is its laboratory."

"You and Stardrifter were on the run?"

Jeremiah stopped their walk and turned to her. "It was a very dark time for us. My family was hunted. We were very well known for banking and business. I, being a NESS, put them on the dead list by the existing government at that time. Stardrifter's family was not so known; they hid us in the hills for over two axis turns. We would have perished, all his family, too, if the people had known he was a NESS and they were helping us."

Elizabeth nodded. Her history books had detailed accounts from the survivors. She shuddered as she thought about that time in the past. Jeremiah continued.

"After so many had perished, it was easier for us to return to this area and start the rebuild." Jeremiah pointed to the surrounding area. "We have been doing that now for 160 axis turns."

Jeremiah told her some more adventures. Jeremiah and Stardrifter were brothers due to shared hardships and triumphs.

Elizabeth asked, "Stardrifter has no wife or girlfriend?"

Jeremiah looked at her and explained, "No, Stardrifter is very afraid. During the troubles, his girlfriends that had run around with him before GIFT were systematically hunted, slaughtered by all the existing governments. They did not want the plague to get a better foothold in the humans with any children from a NESS. He has been alone since that time."

"But, now you have NESS FOLK for families. I see your kid's grand-children scampering around being children, getting into trouble, playing and being children.

Jeremiah laughed and said, "Yes, it is wonderful. I am very happy I found someone that would accept me with my handicaps. Being male and NESS, it is a disadvantage. But, my wife loved a challenge."

"I would have loved to have met your wife, Jeremiah."

Jeremiah eyed her and said, "But, you are wondering about Stardrifter. He has not found the one woman, yet, to fire him up, bring him out of his shell."

Elizabeth smiled. Jeremiah smiled inwardly and thought, *"Ah yes, Elizabeth. I see the GAT smile all over your face. You are hunting him. Good luck.*

Jeremiah said, in his outer voice, "I am going over to the apple trees to get some fruit. Would you like to come with me?"

Elizabeth said, "I think I will wander back and talk to Stardrifter."

Stardrifter was in the kitchen cleaning up. He had kicked them out to go enjoy the sunset from the porch or in the orchards. It was fall harvest season and the apples were just about right for picking. He could see Jeremiah scampering up one of the trees, tossing apples down to his granddaughters.

Elizabeth peeked around the back door and asked, "Do you want company?"

Stardrifter smiled, "Sure." Pointing to a drying towel, he said, "Grab one. Stack the plates in the cupboard to your left." Elizabeth started the task. She had seen his skin in the sink and noticed that it had a swirl pattern now.

He smiled. "I see you noticed my skin. It has healed from our first encounter."

Elizabeth asked, "Does it hurt?"

"Not now, but it sure did when it happened." Stardrifter smiled at her. "I see your shoulder is moving alright?"

"It gets knotted up like it is now, but it is alright."

Stardrifter looked at her and asked, "Well, would you like to see if I could get the knots out?"

Elizabeth thought, *Why not?* She told him, "Yes."

"Just turn your back to me and relax." He worked her back, kneading the muscles until the knots released. But, as he went over the suture scar on her back, GIFT sampled her.

GIFT AI'd, *I see the issue. Her muscle is still ripped. Ask her if she wants you to fix the problem.*

"Elizabeth, I see a small, hard knot indicating your underlying tissue is ripped. Do you want me to fix this for you?"

She turned around and faced him. "You almost killed me last time!"

Stardrifter smiled. "I am off duty. No killing." He laughed and said, "So, let me make amends to you."

Elizabeth asked in a skeptical voice, "What are you going to do?"

Stardrifter explained, "GIFT is inside me, along with every NESS FOLK. We have traits that we are gifted with by God. One of mine is very small healing. I can repair your back."

Elizabeth looked over her shoulder. "Will it hurt me?"

"There will be no pain. GIFT will numb the area as I work the issue in your back."

"Go ahead."

This is going to be very interesting. I like his hands on my shoulder. He's gentle with his hands. It feels good, him working the knots out like this.

Stardrifter felt Elizabeth relax until there was no more tension in her back.

"Here we go," he said. His hand rested on the back above the tear. GIFT's threads came out of his hand and penetrated her shoulder.

Elizabeth could feel tingling, but nothing more. Stardrifter closed his eyes blended with GIFT and AI'd, *Thanks.*

GIFT AI'd, *No problem. What do you think?* Stardrifter moved into Elizabeth's tissues in her shoulder.

I see it. Let's move the ripped tissue aside, then I will use some of my own tissue to replace the damage.

Stardrifter moved some of his back tissue from himself into the rip in Elizabeth's back. His tissue began to work on the molecular level, binding her cells and repairing them. Within ten seconds, the tissue was healed. He then withdrew everything and opened his eyes.

Stardrifter said to Elizabeth, "All done. Try and move it now. Tell me if it still hurts."

My God, the pain is gone, she thought as she moved her shoulder. She turned around.

"What did you do?"

"GIFT is inside me. The chamber story I told you is real. So, I pulled some back muscle tissue from me, moved it to the rip in your shoulder and then, rebuilt the muscle at the molecular bonding level."

"But how?"

"I am not a scientist. My schooling is in the military. But, according to the FOLK science testing reports, my molecular levels are rebuilt in nanoseconds. So, when I put some cells in you from me, they used you as a template. It duplicated then stitched your systems together. I then pulled my tissue out of you to put it back into my muscle tissue."

Troy and Dagny did the same process, she thought. *He and the other FOLK had moved their systems to her, too.* She made more mental notes for her journals.

"I am a scientist," Elizabeth said. Show me what you mean with GIFT."

"Look at my hands," Stardrifter said. As he turned them over, gold threads appeared to form from his palm.

Elizabeth gasped. "OH MY GOD! Is that GIFT?"

Stardrifter laughed. "Yes and no, it's hard to explain to the deaf."

"I am not deaf."

"To GIFT you are, and to the NESS FOLK, too."

"What the hell are you trying to say to me?"

"Do you really want to know GIFT?"

Elizabeth was suddenly aware of how fast her heart was beating. *This is crazy. I am standing in front of a lunatic with gold threads coming out of his hands and I still want to throw this NESS man on the floor and have some fun.*

Elizabeth smiled and whispered, "Hell yes."

Stardrifter smiled and held his hands up to her. "Put your hands into mine; let's see if you pass the test."

Elizabeth looked at him, "What test?"

Stardrifter's smile faded and his face became very serious. "If GIFT finds a flaw in you, it will kill you."

Stardrifter waited calmly for her answer with his hands still held out to her.

Jeremiah had that same look, Elizabeth thought. She smiled and grabbed Stardrifter's hands. She had to stop herself from yelling out, OH SHIT, when she felt the threads enter her palms and go up into her arms.

GIFT laughed. *This is going to be fun*. Within seconds, the threads penetrated her mind.

Stardrifter prayed to God that GIFT would not kill her. If it did, he would be killed for breaking FOLK law with GIFT.

GIFT exploded into her mind. It said, *Hi, you have passed the test.*

Elizabeth AI'd, *Oh my God, who are you?*

Did Stardrifter not tell you, I am GIFT?

Elizabeth nodded in her mind, *Yes.*

GIFT AI'd, *You will find out more in time as both our minds adapt to each other, my friend.*

Stardrifter laughed along with GIFT and AI'd, *Let me show you inner speech.*

Mozart's music suddenly erupted in her mind. Elizabeth AI'd, *What is that?*

GIFT AI'd, *That's Mozart.*

Who is Mozart?

Mozart was a musical genius from 2,500 axis turns in the past – a human. I have the complete collection of his great works; to me, he is beautiful.

Elizabeth saw patterns in light, then saw them reform into vistas of other worlds as the composition played in her mind.

My God, she thought.

GIFT blended with her and she felt joy from GIFT as this new music played in her mind.

Stardrifter asked GIFT, *Elizabeth needs some time to adjust to you. What do you think of her?*

GIFT AI'd both of them, *VERY beautiful.* GIFT waited until Mozart's final section completed in her mind before it said, *Bye for now, my friend.*

Elizabeth let go of Stardrifter's hands and he smiled at her. *Well?*

Elizabeth AI'd, *Your lips are not moving.*

Stardrifter smiled and AI'd, *You're pretty observant of the obvious for a scientist. This is inner speech to my people. Since you already had GIFT in you to start, it makes it much easier to communicate. Less screaming and panic. So, is it nice, Elizabeth?*

Elizabeth could hear Jeremiah, as well. *Elizabeth, welcome to the NESS FOLK world*, he AI'd.

Elizabeth thought, *Hot damn, this is astounding.* And, quick as a flash, she started to pass out.

She heard Stardrifter in her mind, *Damn it*, as he grabbed her. *I need some help now!*

Stardrifter grabbed her before she could fall to the kitchen floor. Lifting her, he AI'd, *I need some help*, as he kicked his bedroom door open. Stardrifter thought, *Shit, I think I may have killed her. I am an idiot*. He AI'd, *Damn it, hurry up! Her eyes have rolled up and her breathing is shallow*!

Jessica came running in; she was a FOLK doctor. She AI'd, *Stardrifter, lay her on the bed and stand back.*

Jessica put both hands on Elizabeth and the gold threads penetrated Elizabeth's body. Jessica AI'd, *Stardrifter, you idiot! She has full blown GIFT.* Jessica calmed her panic and told Stardrifter, *You get your armor on now. I will need the food and power in it. MOVE!*

He ran back out to the holding pond and his one-ton armor licked him then rolled up and over him. He was back in twenty seconds.

Jessica AI'd, *Put your hands on her; I am taking all your power. He opened the armor to her.*

Jessica weaved in and around Elizabeth, *There is the problem.* She AI'd Stardrifter, *Give me all your power and food now!*

Stardrifter released all the armor medical systems to Jessica. GIFT was stuck building neurons in Elizabeth. As Stardrifter's power and food flooded in, GIFT completed the processes it needed for Elizabeth.

Jessica finished on Elizabeth two hours later; she AI'd Stardrifter to disengage from her. Stardrifter saw Jessica's clothes were dripping wet from sweat. She pointed to him and AI'd, *Come over here.* He obeyed. She grabbed his armor, pulled his helmet down to her level and stuck her nose to his armored face. *There are reasons for adoption, Stardrifter. Elizabeth is stable for now, but you really did screw yourself up tonight.*

Jessica couldn't help her anger exploding out of her. She AI raged at him, *FOLK make the decision for full GIFT, NOT the NESS. You being first, you know GIFT. You lived through the horror. We have learned this the hard way.* Shoving him away from her, she was still screaming at him through the AI, *You are very lucky GIFT likes her; it waited for me.*

She stomped over to the bed, turned, grabbed the nightstand and threw it against the wall. FOLK very rarely got raging angry and Stardrifter thought, *She must be fighting GIFT and it is having a handful with her now.* The FOLK listened in. She turned back to him and AI'd, *I am going to find out why you did this, Stardrifter. Come here now.*

Stardrifter obeyed her. Jessica extended the golden threads from her hand and she blended with him. She saw into his mind that Stardrifter utterly loved Elizabeth. Jessica looked deeper at his soul, heart and mind.

I see why you did this, she thought. He was utterly alone, and he was First with GIFT. She saw his memories – the suffering of millions of people, dying in the troubles and ongoing wars, pain of loved ones torn apart by mobs looking to kill the NESS, seeing nuclear weapons blast whole cities into rubble trying to kill her people.

Jessica cringed as she went further into the memories of his father and mother who had been trussed up and tossed into this house as hostages. Stardrifter had heard their screaming over the radio and he was close enough to go get them. The NESS had a temporary barricade fighting a rear guard action against the old army units. The NESS were trying to save his family and others who had harbored NESS. Stardrifter had screamed at Jessica's father, "HOLD THEM! I AM GOING TO GET MY PARENTS." Her father fired anti-tank weapons at the tanks approaching them. Stardrifter heard one tank explode as he ran up the road, screaming at the top of his lungs, "HOLD ON, MOM AND DAD! I AM COMING FOR YOU!"

Her father had said, "Fall back. I will cover Stardrifter. Meet at the mountain pass."

The squads moved out covering the refugees. When he reached the house, Stardrifter heard his father screaming from inside. It had been set on fire. He tried to get them out of the house. He could see his father had his mother over his shoulder as he tried to smash the front glass windows. Stardrifter ran towards the door to smash it in, but before he could get to it, the house exploded in his face. He had hit a trip wire that was set to detonate the whole house with explosives. The force of the explosion blew the roof off the foundation, along with his parents.

The explosion blew him backwards into the driveway. Stardrifter got back up and ran toward the door again, screaming incoherently.

Jessica's father had tackled him into the ground before he could reach the steps and he held him to the ground. Stardrifter screamed at Jeremiah, "I am going to get my parents! Get off me!"

"It is too late," Jeremiah said, looking at his friend. Jessica could see and feel his sobbing through his mind as her father, his friend, held him down.

Jessica went further into the memories. Stardrifter's rage and vengeance never cooled. She saw that when he found the people who did that to his parents, he released the berserker within him and killed all of them without mercy.

My God, he ripped them apart with the new NESS armor. No weapons, just his hands. Tears trickled down her cheeks.

Jessica crept further into his mind.

My God, GIFT has poured massive knowledge into him seeing weapons of unimaginable power that rivaled small suns. The NESS is being groomed for this power, designs for starships.

Jessica hit a brick wall in his mind as he would not let her go in farther.

NO, he screamed at her.

Jessica suddenly felt very frightened. She saw his rage well up at her.

I have had enough of this shit.

He slammed his mind down to her and Jessica became very cold. Stardrifter AI'd while shivering with rage, *NEVER will I reveal these weapons! They are too tempting to any of us NESS, FOLK, HUMAN. NO!*

Jessica AI'd him again, *Stardrifter, listen to me. I see your terror of loving. Are you in love with Elizabeth?*

He AI whispered, Yes.

I have seen into some of your soul. You are badly wounded. I think you desperately need FOLK help.

I will live. There is nothing you can do about it. It is in me, this berserker, the killing; it is in the entire NESS.

Then, you will understand this for what you have done to Elizabeth, Jessica said, as she broke the link and started praying that she would live tonight.

ATTENTION!

Stardrifter snapped to attention as she broadcast an emergency AI to the FOLK. Stardrifter could feel the weight of all the FOLK. *A NESS has broken our LAWS with GIFT!*

Jessica looked at him. She AI'd Stardrifter, *As of now, you are suspended from active duties due to dereliction of duty with GIFT. If Elizabeth Pameddin dies, you will be formally charged with murder. If she survives and is damaged or not, she can formally charge you with attempted murder. Are these pending charges clear to you?*

Stardrifter answered, *Yes.*

Since she is not dead and she asked for GIFT, the charges are pending from her because she is a sovereign individual. But you will stay in the armor. Is this clear to you?

Yes.

When I am done with my medical duties here, you will guard Elizabeth Pameddin WITH YOUR LIFE. You are not to leave the house and you are not allowed to do anything except guard her, period. She is the only one with the key to release you from the armor. Her voice will be imprinted into the armor to let you eat normally and have bathroom privileges.

Dad, I am pissed at you, too. Attention!

Jeremiah snapped to attention. *Your orders are to seal Stardrifter's heavy weapons only, and put the code in for self-destruct if he violates the conditions. You are his commander, you are responsible for him. DO I MAKE MYSELF CLEAR?*

Jeremiah said, *YES.*

Jessica AI'd, *Now, get out my sight, both of you.* She slammed the bedroom patio door in their faces.

Stardrifter turned to Jeremiah.

Jeremiah AI'd, *Turn around and do not move,* as he started to key the weapons lockout for Stardrifter's armor.

Stardrifter AI'd, *SHIT!* He ran screaming from his house into the night.

Jeremiah stood in place, surprised; the weapons lockout and destruct command was not done.

SOB, he thought, as he ran to get his armor. He AI'd the other NESS on duty, *I will find him. Bring assault NESS to me, the rest of you stay on full alert. If he goes mad, he will kill the whole country.*

As Jeremiah's armor rolled onto him, he thought, *My greatest fear has just materialized: a NESS with unlimited power and weapons that are in the multi-megaton range at his disposal.*

"Jesus," he said aloud, "not another civil war. No, this will not happen to our people again." He AI'd the NESS, *Get the heavy ground-based space weapons unsealed and fully war loaded. The code is 'We the People'. Load four tanks with them.*

The NESS AI'd back, *What do you mean, space weapons on a tank. Just one weighs 25 tons alone. All of that for one crazy NESS?*

Do as I order! You have no concept of what Stardrifter's capabilities are. He can probably override any key lockout in his armor. GIFT uses him as its laboratory. He can build space weapons for starters. With his armor, he has GIFT prototype weapons that make ours look like throwing rocks at tanks. If I say space weapons on the tanks, mount them. You have one half-hour to make them ready for battle. Now move.

NESS blurred as they went to the depot and they scrambled putting on the armor. They then moved into defensive positions throughout their country. Massive hydraulics pushed hidden weapons systems on the mountaintops aside to expose the space weapons turrets, just in case he made a dash for the interior. NESS offensive strike teams surged out of the forts moving toward Jeremiah's active beacon. NESS Daniel and several other NESS were mounting the four weapons onto the chassis as FOLK technicians scrambled to get the tanks fueled and prepared for war.

Stardrifter was running up the hills. He stopped in the largest valley just before the true mountain range started behind his house. His rage exploded out of him and he smashed a boulder in half with his armored hands. He then tossed the pieces 100 yards into the gully. Sinking on his knees, he let loose a wail that sounded like a wounded soul.

Stardrifter was crying when Jeremiah found him two hours later. Jeremiah approached Stardrifter with his weapons out and loaded. He AI'd the NESS assault strike teams, *Hold position. If he kills me, your orders are to attack. No mercy. You will only have milliseconds to kill him, so make it count because if we fail, we all die.*

The offensive NESS acknowledged and their weapons opened to 12 millimeters.

Megaton authorization TMACZ290 is authorized on my signature, Jeremiah said.

All NESS offensive strike teams' armor AI stated, *Weapons loaded 99% speed of light, armor engaging weapons systems locked, strike authorization confirmed, weapons released, all systems Green.*

The offensive strike NESS smiled in their armor and AI'd, *Confirmed weapons activation 10 rounds loaded.* Their armor went to full power. *Sensors engaged target lock.* The NESS went to NO mind and thought, *Finally, we have some real weapons.* They AI'd Jeremiah, *Ready.*

Jeremiah prayed briefly. *I have lunatics on my back and one in front that can kill the whole planet. God give me strength.*

Stardrifter was facing away from him with his helmet folded back. Jeremiah said in his outer voice, "Stardrifter, come home."

Stardrifter stared off into the darkness and said, "Why? I have nearly killed the one person who could possible love me despite my stupidity." He turned, facing his friend and pointed his armored glove at Jeremiah. "I will never be loved. Elizabeth will never forgive me if she survives."

"Elizabeth is not dead and I think she will forgive you. The problem is whether or not you can forgive yourself. It is time for you to do this, again. Your fear is eating you alive." Jeremiah could see his words seeping into his friend. "Elizabeth can heal you if you let her into your heart and soul. You should let yourself be open again for love; you need her."

Stardrifter screamed and slammed his visor shut. Jeremiah's sensors became blurred and he lost him. The NESS offensive strike teams collectively exclaimed, Shit! All the NESS Armor AI'd, *NESS sensor lock broken, jamming encountered, jamming override, NO LOCK, scanning, target lost, expanding range overlap, NO target, NO LOCK.*

When he stopped moving, Stardrifter slammed his armored gloves into the boulders around him a half mile away.

Jeremiah crossed himself and thought, *Jesus save us*, as he watched the boulders being pulverized by his friend's rage. Jeremiah quickly made his way to his friend, who screamed at him.

"The knowledge that has been poured into me pales in comparison to what Elizabeth offered me!" he sobbed. "I am so alone. Everyone I love dies around me: my family, my friends… millions of people's blood is on my hands." He stared down at his armored hands. He screamed his rage at the heavens, "MILLIONS!" He looked at Jeremiah, "You were in the chamber, too. How do you live with yourself? I hate this armor. For 160 axis turns, it has molded me, poured knowledge from the universe into me; it has made me a premier killer for our people." Stardrifter sank to his knees, covering his eyes. He whispered, "I'm deathly tired of killing people. Jeremiah, if Elizabeth dies, I will kill myself, I swear to God."

Jeremiah could see his friend teetering on the edge of madness. He put his weapons in the peace position and AI'd his helmet back to show his face. He approached his friend and knelt down in front of him.

"Stardrifter, look at me please."

Stardrifter AI'd his helmet back. Jeremiah could see the exhaustion on Stardrifter's face.

"My Zoë saved my life. She kept me sane and for 70 axis turns, I was happy." Jeremiah's face showed his pain. "She is gone now, but I have her here." He pointed to his heart and to his mind. "She is my rock and the best part of me." Stardrifter looked at his friend and nodded at that statement.

"My wife showed me other paths to follow and I was wise enough to follow them."

Stardrifter saw tears falling down his friend's face. Stardrifter lowered his eyes to the ground and said, "Jeremiah, I am sorry for ripping that wound open." He leaned forward and hid his face on the ground.

Jeremiah AI'd him, *Listen to me. Do you love Elizabeth?*

Stardrifter whispered in his outer voice, "Yes."

Would you give your life to protect her?

"Yes."

And all OF US?

"Yes, but —"

Jeremiah AI'd, *Shut your mouth and open your mind to me now!*

Stardrifter got up on all fours and turned his face toward his friend. He leaned back on his knees and nodded to Jeremiah before dropping all of his mind's barriers.

Jeremiah's hands penetrated Stardrifter's nervous system.

My friend, I am going to show you a path from a friend who loves you.

Jeremiah showed him what had happened in the pine forest with his Zoe. She smiled in Stardrifter's mind and showed him the path. Stardrifter's scream could be heard echoing through the valley.

When Jeremiah was done with him, he stood up and looked down at his friend on the ground. Stardrifter threw up all over his armor.

"JESUS" he whispered, as unimaginable horror rolled through his mind. Jeremiah knelt down by his friend again and Stardrifter wiped his mouth with his armored glove.

Jeremiah said in his outer voice, "Yes, you are needed, very needed by all of us, so no more self-pity. Are you a NESS?"

Stardrifter nodded as he got up shakily; Jeremiah steadied him.

"I am a mess," he stated, "but I am NESS. If I survive my stupidity, I will bring the Wrath of God against this Devastation. I will kill it personally. It will not take Elizabeth ever or anything else of life."

Jeremiah looked into his friend's eyes. He had the fire of the light in them. Jeremiah smiled and thought, *I would not want to be in Devastation's shoes.* With that, they both turned to walk back to Stardrifter's house.

Jeremiah AI'd the NESS offensive strike teams, *Stand down and return all weapons to storage. Megaton authorization release codes are reengaged TMLJU7SA.*

The NESS offensive strike teams were disappointedly blurred back to their forts.

Stardrifter AI'd his friend, *Yes, I would be terrified of me, too. It would have been in vain, my friend, if I had gone insane.*

Jeremiah smiled as they heard the heavy tanks shaking the ground in the distance as they went back to the storage depot. *Yes, but I and the NESS, along with NESS offensive strike teams, would have tried to kill you. We would not let you kill innocents ever.*

Stardrifter nodded. *I have lost my way. Can you help me?*

Jeremiah AI'd, *Always. We all get lost for a while in our life. You are no different.*

Stardrifter nodded as he saw his house. *Yes, it is time to be forged again by God. I sometimes think God picks on me.*

Only those who deserve it and earned it, too. Did I lock out your weapons?

No. He handed a special key to him to use. *Use this key. Scramble it with a random generator number. Do not look. Just press it and set it into my armor.*

Jeremiah AI'd as they stepped on the porch, *Submit.* Stardrifter nodded and held his arms apart. Stardrifter could feel the weapons lock out and the destruct code set.

GIFT asked him, *Why submit?*

He sighed. *I am human, GIFT. My soul is really beat up and I need to feel again, to care for my people. Do you understand?*

GIFT smiled. *Yes, I understand, my friend.*

Stardrifter went into his house to face the music.

Three days later, Elizabeth woke up in a very comfortable bed. She was totally disorientated and she groggily asked, *Where the hell am I?*

"You are in my bed at my house. I am on the porch guarding you."

She slowly moved her head toward the voice. She could see the open patio door and a large shadow was facing outward on the porch.

Are you talking in my mind? Stardrifter laughed and said, "No, I am using outside speech."

As she moved, she noticed she only had on a large shirt and nothing else. She looked in the general direction of him and asked, "Did you take off my clothes?"

Stardrifter laughed. *I wish*, he thought. "No, Jessica, the tall woman you met at my house, did. She is a FOLK doctor. She made all the clothes arrangements. She thought it would be safer here in my house than to move you and, since I have only my clothes, well, she made do with the existing material in my drawers. Is the shirt comfortable for you?"

"Yes, it feels worn and well-used."

"Yes, my sisters still take my shirts, sweaters or anything that strikes their fancy and stretch them out in particular ways, too."

Elizabeth laughed. Wrapping the quilt around her shoulders, she AI'd, *My head is throbbing.*

Stardrifter heard that from her mind and he AI'd her, *Elizabeth, can you hear me?*

Yes. Is this inner speech?

Stardrifter laughed in her mind and said, *Yes.*

Elizabeth flinched and AI'd back, *Headache is killing me. Your voice sounded like bells going off in my head.*

There is some tea for you. It will greatly ease your ache in your head. GIFT is rough. See the tea on your left on the small table? Drink it down and ignore the taste. As she drank it, her throbbing stopped.

Much better, she thought, as she settled deeper into the covers.

Elizabeth was startled as the drugs took effect and she AI'd him, *The tea is horrible and why am I getting sleepy?*

Relax. It will be good for you. It has drugs in it to make you sleep. Your reserves need rebuilding. The FOLK medicos will feed and bathe you and I will be here guarding you when you awake.

Before she went under she asked, *Why?*

Because you are my responsibility. I will guard you. Rest. Nothing will happen to you.

She went back to sleep. Stardrifter looked at her in his bed. She looked peaceful and there was no pain on her face. He smiled toward the heavens.

When Elizabeth woke up, she immediately asked, "What day is it?"

Stardrifter said in his outer speech, "Three days have passed since you drank the tea and the time is 20:00 hours, local time."

Elizabeth rolled over slowly in the covers. She had been bathed and she had a new shirt on. The shirt smelled of the pine scent of the house. She pulled the covers further up to her neck while smelling the fresh air. There was the pleasant smell of apples in the air and Stardrifter's bedroom was cool and crisp.

Ahhh, Fall smells.

Her eyes fell to the door leading to the porch and she watched as the curtains moved in the breeze. She saw a very large entity on the porch that had not moved.

"Stardrifter, is that you in the armor?"

"Yes, it is my duty to guard FOLK."

Elizabeth said, "I am not FOLK, so that leaves one explanation. Are you in trouble for doing the GIFT experience to me in your house?"

"YES, Jeremiah had put you in for adoption, but it was going slowly. For some of my people, this is normal; they are very sedate in some decisions. I was not thinking too clearly that night. It seemed like a good idea at the time to me while in my kitchen to speed the process up for you."

Elizabeth laughed and said, "Yeah, it was not your brightest idea, was it?"

Stardrifter laughing with her replied, "No, it was not, but you went for it, did you not, Elizabeth?"

Elizabeth smiled then thought, *Let's see if this GIFT inner voice works better without the raging headache.* She AI'd him, *Stardrifter, can you hear me?*

He AI'd back, *Yes, how are feeling?*

I am much better. In fact, I feel good.

Jessica checked you today; there is no damage from GIFT.

Elizabeth caught a thread of fear from Stardrifter, as well as relief in his inner voice.

I sense fear and anxiety from you and please do not say to guard me. I am not FOLK.

I was ordered by the FOLK to stand guard over you for my mistake with GIFT.

Why? I am alive and in good shape.

No, when I caught you falling in the kitchen, GIFT had started the process in you. I thought you had enough reserve in you for GIFT build. I was very mistaken in that assumption. I nearly killed you. So, my people have put me on guard duty 24 hours a day until you are better, then I will go to trial for attempted murder.

That makes no sense to me. You did not attempt anything. You told me GIFT could kill me. I accepted the responsibility.

We have had many mishaps with GIFT. NESS are the primary carriers of GIFT. I have killed people before being stupid with GIFT. When you went down in the kitchen, I lost it. I ran into the hills. My friend, Jeremiah, found me and he was terrified of me.

Why?

GIFT made me first. I have prototype weapons on me, as you are aware. You saw one of them in action when we engaged your warships. It is in production now. Elizabeth was not surprised by his statement. *I stated to you that GIFT has vast knowledge. I am the experiment. I carry very massive weapons on me. I could kill all life on our planet in under an axis turn with them. The NESS would not stop me, period.*

Elizabeth AI'd, GOD.

Jeremiah is one of our holy people. When he found me, I was teetering on the edge of madness. My friend calmed me down enough to share a vision that had happened to him. He showed me illumination from God.

What do you mean illumination from God.

Stardrifter smiled. *I am a believer. My family has always been Catholic, Elizabeth. God has put me in to the forge, again, to be hammered into a sword for God. Jeremiah's vision showed me what is in store for me if I choose that path for God. I will suffer greatly being Catholic. It is normal, but I am now on that path. It required me to submit to my people for my weapons lock out. It means the FOLK can kill me without me blowing up the world. Remember, you said the armor self-destructs when your people tried to retrieve the NESS dead.*

Elizabeth replied, *Yes. Mine is set now to kill me in the same way. I am Catholic, too, but we keep a low profile in my country; much safer doing it that way. The New Earth Organization, NEO, is very good at killing non-believers or agitators for more freedom, so suffering, I understand.*

Stardrifter nodded at that statement, smiled and continued. *So, as punishment for my stupidity, FOLK have locked me into this armor, along with setting the armor to blow if I leave my house. So, Elizabeth, you have the only key to let me out for real food and bathroom breaks, if you so desire. I have been eating and drinking recycled waste from me for the last six days.* He sighed. *That is not fun.*

Why?

I am a NESS. I am used to any hardship. This is trivial, but what I did to you was inexcusable, so I am telling you that you have my life in your hands. If you say so, I will be charged with attempted murder on your life; it carries the death penalty in my society. I will plead guilty to that charge, as I should have never exposed you to GIFT. It was not my decision to make for you or my people.

But, I was a willing participant.

You were not fully informed of the dangers that come with adoption in my society. I am sorry I almost killed you in my stupidity.

She could see the remorse in his mind, along with something else that was not stated, but underlying his thoughts. *Hmm*, she thought, *let's bring this out in the open.*

Elizabeth AI'd, *I am a scientist. Risks are part of life or did you have another motive?*

Yes, I do not trust myself around you. In truth, I have wanted you from the very first time I saw you spin around and stand up to me on my warship. I am in love with you.

Elizabeth laughed out loud and thought, *Ah ha, that is the underlying turmoil. Well, let's see if the NESS man can handle me.*

Elizabeth smiled at him and AI'd, *Stardrifter, what is your real first name?*

I am named Micha'el from one of my ancestors.

Elizabeth decided to get out of bed and get a better look at him. She looked around for a chair that she could stand on to make herself eye level with him. She slowly got out of the bed and started to walk toward the patio. She suddenly got very dizzy near the chair and started to fall toward the floor. Stardrifter blurred to her, moving faster than she could follow.

Stardrifter caught her by the waist and AI'd, *Elizabeth, you have been very sick for six days from my actions. I will put you back in bed now.*

She felt his armored arms steady her more and he picked her up gently. His armored hands were warm to her skin. Elizabeth saw into Micha'el's mind when the armor contacted her skin.

MY GOD, she thought. She saw his mind; it was wide open to her. She gasped and AI'd, *Is this you?*

I will not hide from you, Elizabeth. You have my life and my heart in your hands.

Elizabeth was very startled by this statement. She was two feet off the ground, being held in his hands. There was no effort to hide or distort the truth from her, just patience from his mind. She wiped his armored head where his eyebrow and eye would be on his head with her hand and thought, *This damn armor, I can't see him.*

Elizabeth AI'd Micha'el, *Please set me down near the bed.*

He settled her to the floor near the bed. She stepped back until she felt the mattress steady the back of her legs and her body, then she smiled and took the shirt off her and threw the shirt on the floor.

Stardrifter viewed her in visible light to x-ray shadows that played across her body. As he studied her from her feet going up her legs to her pubic area, his eyes drank her in. He moved up from her chest to her head. She smiled at him and her right hand waved him to her.

Elizabeth's eyes widened. As the moonlight played across his armor, it shifted the light spectrum to match the surrounding area.

Many animals match their surroundings, she thought. *I wonder if his armor is built on this principle. I bet it is alive.*

She observed that it made no sound either when he was very close. She grabbed his two arms, put them around her hips and AI'd, *Pick me up and put my feet on the bed, Micha'el.*

As his armored hands gripped her hips, he could see the blood rushing into her breasts, making them flush up and out. Her core region turned bright red as blood expanded into the region. Her mind fired off and he could see the neurons firing in her mind's neural network. Her body stood out in three dimensions. It glowed in the armor's sensor systems and the armor built her up from the atomic level to the visible light spectrum.

Stardrifter just marveled. For once, he was grateful for the armor's capabilities for life. Elizabeth exploded into his armor sensor systems and he AI'd her, *Oh my.* It was just like Haldor had said, a star going NOVA. *God.*

It echoed into Elizabeth's mind as he set her on the bed, she stood over him by six inches. Elizabeth AI'd him, *Do you like what you see, Micha'el?*

His armor went berserk. It sampled everything around and in Elizabeth and fed it to him without mercy.

Stardrifter AI'd, *YES.*

She leaned forward until her breasts made contact with his armor and she slowly rubbed them against the armor. He moaned as the damn armor's samplings rippled into his armor and across his chest, feeding the information to him. His mind screamed, *I want out of this armor!*

She pulled him toward her. As his armored legs hit the bed, she smiled down at him. Her pelvis made contact against the armor and the impact rippled through him. Elizabeth draped her arms around his neck and the armor molded to her shape. She whispered into his helmet, "How do I take this armor off you?"

"Just ask. You're the only one who can; it is keyed to your voice."

"Armor, please release my NESS man."

The armor folded down to the hardwood floor. Elizabeth leaned back a bit, grabbed the armored helmet, and threw it to the corner. His armor rolled into the back of the house looking for the pond. When it found it, it slithered into the pond to rest and feed on the flowing nutrients.

She AI'd, *Now the underwear, NESS man.*

He AI'd, *It went with the armor.*

She looked down. *Yes, it is gone,* she thought, as it started to rise. She noticed that it had no scales and it was not too big and not too small. She smiled. As she wrapped her legs around his waist, she AI'd, *You're mine now, NESS man,* as she slid him into her. *Do you feel this, NESS man?* He moaned into her mind.

Stardrifter grabbed her butt and slid into her more. He could feel her walls draw him in, surrounding him with warmth and wetness. She smiled at him.

She AI'd Micha'el, *When you get all the way in me, I would like you to lay flat on your back in the middle of the bed. Can you do that for me? I am still dizzy.*

Yes.

Stardrifter spun slowly around, sat on the bed and scooted on his back while holding her aloft to the middle of the bed. The moonlight played across his body. He was sweating and his muscles rippled, making the skin color pattern glow. Elizabeth giggled. As he settled to the middle of the bed, she planted her feet beside her NESS man, pushing his hips into the bed. He grunted as he went all the way into her and she ground her pelvis into him. Her hands supported her weight by her hands on his chest.

Elizabeth smiled and AI'd Micha'el, *This is going to be fun. I wanted you from the very first moment I saw you.* She raised her hips above him and slowly slid him back into her. *Did you want me when you saw me the first time?*

He moaned while lifting her off the bed and AI'd, *YES.*

Elizabeth smiled. *Good.* She kissed him and AI'd, *I am very curious. What is this blending thing?*

Micha'el smiled as he lifted her off the bed and AI'd, *This is blending.*

OH MY, she thought, as she fell on his chest. Sometime later, looking at him from under her wet, tangled hair, she AI'd, *Do you want more?*

Micha'el smiled and he AI'd, *Yes.*

I do, too. My turn to blend. He groaned and she laughed. *Yes, NESS man, you are mine.*

Elizabeth smiled as she sat up the next morning. *Are you hungry?*

Smiling, he answered, *Yes.*

Well, let's go and get some breakfast.

Micha'el walked to the kitchen with Elizabeth. She had put the shirt back on, swinging her hips back and forth as women do.

He AI'd, *You are beautiful.*

You like my butt?

Yes, I do. She swayed even more.

Well, let's see. Juice, fruit, milk and cereal. Sound good to you?

He laughed and AI'd, *Sure*, as he grabbed the cups, utensils and bowls and sat beside her.

As they finished breakfast, Elizabeth AI'd, *I am going to sit in your lap* and she plopped in his lap, facing him. She laughed, wiggling and AI'd him, *Well?*

NESS man threw her shirt off. *We are going to make love all through this house, Elizabeth.*

Yep, you are right and she slid him into her.

GIFT is inside you. What else does it do?

He AI'd back, *Well, let me show you, my love.*

He rolled her on top of him; she smiled *this is fun* as he slid into her.

Now, I am going to extend my nerve ending into you. I will not hurt you. Alright.

Do you feel something.

Uhh! What are you doing?

Slowly lift off me and look down between your legs and mine.

Elizabeth looked down and the golden threads were attached to her clitoris and every major nerve bundle. She looked up and had an immediate orgasm as she again slid him into her.

Uhh! That feels fantastic!

You can do this, too. Just extend and grab me here.

Elizabeth did and he groaned while laughing. Elizabeth rolled him on top of her and AI'd him, *Come here, Micha'el.* He was wringing wet as he collapsed onto her chest, spent once more. She smiled. She rolled him under her and grabbed him again with her golden threads; he groaned and rose to the occasion.

The next several days were blissful for them. Elizabeth found herself watching Stardrifter sleep, with her hands crossed on his chest and her chin resting on them. When his eyes opened, he saw that Elizabeth was looking at him, grinning.

Well, Micha'el, my love, what are we going to do today?

How about this for starters, as he AI'd her a plan.

Oh yes, she said, as he slid into her. *That will do nicely for starters.* Elizabeth smiled to herself. Her Micha'el was in her, very nice and slow, from behind her. She opened her legs a little wider and moved to her side. He grabbed her hips and slid into her all the way. She could feel his build up. She AI'd, *Nice* and he smiled back as he let go into her. Two of Elizabeth's eggs were waiting in her fallopian tubes. Bathed by Micha'el's sperm, the spark of life began in her womb.

Three weeks passed. Elizabeth lay draped across him with one leg playing in his chest hairs in their bed. She AI'd, *Micha'el?*

Yes?

How do feel about children?

Stardrifter looked at her and considered this. *I am scared, but not frightened by children. Why do you ask?*

She smiled and AI'd, *My mother drops two eggs a month for babies in her uterus, my sisters do the same and I do, too; it runs in my family.* She smiled at him, shyly. *I missed my period. I am pregnant and have two babies in me.* She put his hand on her belly. *Can you feel the twins, my NESS man?*

He sampled her down to the atomic level.

Oh, my God.

Stardrifter beamed at her. He grabbed her and gently put her on his chest and AI'd, *Life from you and me.*

Elizabeth watched her mate light up. She smiled and AI'd him, *Well, you're going to be a dad in nine months, you better study up.*

Are you alright? Can I do anything for you?

Why, yes you can. She smiled and moved her hips to position over him; it rose to the occasion. She gently slid onto him.

You are doing it now, Micha'el.

He only nodded yes at her. She smiled.

You are doomed, she AI'd. He nodded yes and she pressed him harder into her then grabbed his small mind with her golden threads. *And now, we are going to have a very nice afternoon.* She had a GAT smile plastered over her face.

A week later, Elizabeth laughed as she watched Stardrifter put his armor on in the pond at the back of their house. She AI'd him, *Will your armor flow over you like that?*

He looked down and laughed. *It might, but I will not chance it.* He sat down in the water. *It might take a while.*

She laughed and AI'd, *Right, the water is very cold.*

It folded up and hid as the armor flowed around him. He laughed. *My armor is fully fed and charged.* As he stood up, the armor expanded and solidified. He still had a slight bulge in his waist. He AI'd Elizabeth, *Well, I'll be damned. It does flow around it.*

She laughed. *Well, if we survive, can we try it with the armor?*

Smiling, he replied, *Yes, that is going to be fun.* With his helmet in his hand, he got serious. *I am to report for the hearing. Are you ready?*

She nodded. *Where you go, I go.* He smiled, picked her up and kissed her deeply.

His head disappeared into the armored helmet. She watched as it sealed. He held out his hand and she grabbed it. She then went to the front door and opened the house door. Jeremiah was there, waiting for him. He AI'd Stardrifter, *Submit.* Ness surrounded the house. These

NESS knew he could kill all of them without breaking a sweat before they could blow his armor off, so they had their weapons out for their own comfort. Stardrifter nodded, went down on both knees and held his armored arms apart. Jeremiah went behind him. He locked all systems except life support and left him with very limited armor mobility.

Jeremiah looked at Elizabeth, *Did this NESS guard you correctly?*

She said, *Yes.*

He nodded. *This NESS Moriah will guard you and she will take you to the gathering.*

Jeremiah AI'd Stardrifter, *Stand up. Slow March.*

Stardrifter complied and slow marched to the transport. The NESS boxed him in with their weapons still out as protocol demanded. Their armor energy could be released at once. This would blow a ¼-mile wide chunk of earth out into space; the NESS knew from bitter experience.

Elizabeth watched as they loaded Micha'el into the transport. Moriah asked her. *Can you hear inner speech?*

Elizabeth AI'd, *I am getting used to it; still weird though, but very nice.*

I will slow down my thought patterns. We are to go for gathering. If at any time you do not hear the charges or debate, you can ask for outer speech, if you so desire. I can relay this to the FOLK.

I would prefer that. It can get very confusing with everyone around talking.

Moriah AI'd, *Yes, it takes practice to sort out the noise. Here is our transportation.*

Elizabeth sat in silence. The steam car was built for normal NESS armor and it had blacked out windows. The drive was short. She heard noise from the outside, but it was muted. When the motion stopped, NESS Moriah exited.

Please wait here; I will be right back.

Elizabeth waited. When the door re-opened, Moriah was out of her armor and was dressed in NESS combat fatigues; she motioned

Elizabeth to follow her. She stepped out and looked around. She was in a glass, half-dome. The sun was bright and she saw mountains with snow on the peaks in the distance.

NESS Moriah AI'd, *We are in the NESS FOLK city; this is Gathering. The FOLK are judging Stardrifter's attempted murder charges. Please follow me.* Elizabeth looked everywhere. *This city is laid out with precision and a lot of thought.* She felt like a tourist gawking at wonders.

NESS Moriah smiled. *Elizabeth's mind is leaking, but that is alright; we all have to learn.* She AI'd Elizabeth, *Can you hear me?*

Elizabeth AI'd, *Yes, but it is very noisy.*

Moriah AI'd the FOLK and asked them to tone down the chatter. It stopped abruptly and Elizabeth's face eased a little. Moriah AI'd the FOLK, *Thank you.*

They entered a large, round room that was packed with FOLK and NESS. In the center was Stardrifter standing on a platform. NESS Moriah AI'd, *The FOLK judges will enter on the left; do you see the chair in the middle splitting the circle?*

Yes.

When they are seated, they will ask you to come forward.

Then what?

You will need to answer, with truth, the questions presented to you. I will wait with you until you are called. Do you need some water or drink?

Elizabeth AI'd, *No, thank you.*

Well, let's sit down; it could be awhile.

Two hours later, the doors opened and everyone in the gallery stood up. Twelve FOLK judges walked to the chairs and sat down. "This is Gathering," the oldest said "We are here to judge Micha'el Stardrifter House Searle(e) on charges of dereliction of duty and attempted murder on one Elizabeth Pameddin. Since our witness has very limited ability with inner speech, we will use outer speech." He then proceeded to read the charges. When he was done, he said that the floor was open for debate.

Elizabeth listened. *They are just like us; some vindictive, some nasty, some nice, and some just like the show.* She looked at Moriah and AI'd, *Moriah, you are like us in many ways.*

Moriah AI'd back, *Yes, we are human. Stardrifter is our best general, not to mention a good leader.* She laughed out loud. *Though, he has his faults.*

Before she could finish, Elizabeth heard her name being called.

"Elizabeth Pameddin, please approach the platform."

When she was standing before the FOLK judges, the eldest stated, "In our society, 'Your 'Word is your Life'. Do you fully understand its meaning?"

She said, "YES."

"Please be seated then and we will ask the questions."

The questioning ended up lasting another hour. Elizabeth answered them all. At the end, they stated, "Stardrifter has admitted to giving you full blown GIFT. He is not permitted to do this without FOLK approval." The judges nodded at that statement. "However, he did it anyway because you asked him. You are an Outlander. Laws differ from people we have not judged because we were not the victim of GIFT. You were, so his life is yours to decide. Death or forgiveness? Do you have anything to say before you relay your judgment to the FOLK and NESS?"

Elizabeth stood up from the chair and looked around the chamber. She reached into her pocket and held up a crystal stone. She cleared her throat before speaking.

"One of our ancestors from the old world, MAY IT BE BLESSED, held up a similar stone and told them 'HE WHO IS WITHOUT SIN CAST THE FIRST STONE'. This happened to me on your warship, recently. She went over to each judge, holding the stone under their noses; not one reached for the stone. She said in her outer voice, "That's what I thought."

Elizabeth spun around, put the stone in her pocket and raised her voice to the gallery. "Stardrifter is not perfect; as a matter of fact, he needs a lot of work." That brought smiles to the faces of many FOLK and NESS. "But, when he offered me GIFT in his house, he told me I could be killed. Well, I have been blown up, shot at and damn near drowned by Stardrifter, but he never lied to me. I am a free person on this planet, so I chose GIFT. I wanted first-hand knowledge and validation of your claim that everyone has it on our planet, so I put it to the test with my life.

"Test and validation of a theory is the cornerstone for science," she said, smiling at the gallery. "It nearly killed me, I was told six days later, but I would never trade the experience. GIFT is unique; it is a being that has unlimited mental power. Since Stardrifter opened the gates to me, I have been talking to GIFT. It has vast knowledge that spans the universe. Just in my field alone, I have been what you call a 'mind dump' or FOLK schooling from GIFT. I have just scratched the surface in my field. I am one of the best on this planet in my chosen field, but I feel like a seven-year-old child looking forward to exploration of the world."

Her smile began to brighten up the gallery.

"I like this feeling; it has renewed me and stripped away the excess garbage that has been piled up on me as an adult. I will spend the rest of my life as a student. I have marveled at GIFT's intelligence and humor. I consider GIFT a friend, teacher and a student."

Elizabeth pointed her hand and slowly swung around the gallery, stating, "Maybe you are not aware, but let me set you straight about GIFT; you cannot control it, period. The armor, the inner speech, everything you think makes you masters is a **JOKE**. This is a first step to see if we, as a species, are mature enough to handle the next step that GIFT has in store for us."

NESS and FOLK looked shocked at that statement. Elizabeth thought, *Let's see if they can listen.*

"I am a scientist, one of the best in my field, and I am telling you that you had better work with GIFT or it will kill all of us and start again with our survivors or another species." She nodded to the crowd as they roared disapproval. "I am speaking; be QUIET." The gallery fell silent.

Elizabeth continued "GIFT is driven by a core belief to kill Devastation and to achieve that, it will pursue this quest until the universe dies. So, are we humans on board or not? Well, I am, but all of you are not on board, yet."

Elizabeth AI'd, *GIFT.*

Yes? GIFT answered.

Do you love me?

Yes.

What is your purpose?

To protect all life.

How?

Get life prepared to defeat and vanquish Devastation for eternity.

What are humans to you, GIFT?

You are First Premier Soldiers. You were built for this purpose two point five billion axis turns in the past.

GIFT.

Yes?

Who is first?

In your language, 'God'.

GIFT smiled in all the NESS and FOLK minds in the gallery.

What Elizabeth has asked should have been asked by all of you, FOLK and NESS, GIFT AI'd. *Your evolution is very old. I am your guardian and teacher. My duties are for blooming of life, so I have turned on limited abilities with your built-in switches from God. Your species was in hibernation until 175 axis turns ago; it is not now. Evaluation is done for the ongoing defeat of devastation. I need friends and allies; I cannot do this crusade alone. You will choose to join or not, but before you choose, I want to show all of you a vision from Jeremiah.*

Gift AI'd Jeremiah, *Please give me the pine forest memories.* Jeremiah opened his mind to GIFT for the vision.

All of us will witness GOD.

The NESS and FOLK screamed and fell over in the gallery, along with the FOLK and NESS wherever they were on the planet. GIFT fully expanded the vision, with no NESS filter, to show what Devastation was and what it did the last time and will do in the future.

One of my creators showed me recently what had happened. They released all memories locked up inside of me from 2.5 billion axis turns in the past. Now, I am fully functional; new systems have come online. It laughed. *I am one of your old legends, embedded deep into your minds from GOD, so I am turning on all switches within the FOLK and NESS minds now.*

While the NESS and FOLK worked on picking themselves up off the floor, Elizabeth remained standing and had not been affected by GIFT.

GOD is very real and my people are archangels to GOD in your language.

A vision of wings spread across a body and swept through the NESS and FOLK minds.

You are chosen by us for Illumination or Devastation CHOOSE NOW!

Elizabeth spun around. Most NESS and FOLK were kneeling, some were standing and others were on the floor, holding their heads. She noticed two of the judges on the floor not moving and AI'd, GIFT, *are they alright?*

GIFT said, *No, they are dead. I killed them. They chose Devastation. Not a wise move on their part.*

The NESS and FOLK were moaning in the gallery. Elizabeth AI'd, GIFT, *did you kill them?*

No, I have just turned on the switches. They will be alright in a few minutes, their minds just need to adapt to the new knowledge.

Why not me?

You are stealth to me. I can talk to you and be your friend, but I have no direct control. Free will is what I need from people. I have made many mistakes with people so far, but with this new knowledge, it has given me more options as to how I apply the GIFT. So, in that light, Elizabeth, my friend, I need Stardrifter whole and healed. Do you love him?

Elizabeth smiled and said, *Yes, but he needs a lot of work.*

GIFT laughed. *Yes, we all do. I like this passage. It explains what happened and will happen for him in the future.* GIFT looked at Elizabeth in her mind and said, *You both will make mistakes. That is life, but it will be fun and filled with love, too.*

Gift looked at her in its mind and stated,

O Lord Most High, help me to dwell in your secret place and abide under Your shadow.

Help me to believe and say out loud for everyone to hear that You are my refuge and my fortress, that You are my God and that in You I put my trust.

O Lord God Almighty, please deliver me from hidden traps and diseases.

Father God, cover me with your camouflage, hide me under Your wings and let Your truth be my shield and buckler against the fiery darts—the lies—of the enemy.

Lord Jesus, help me not to be afraid of terrorists' attacks in the night; or weapons that fly by day; or sicknesses that walk in darkness; or destruction that wastes at noonday.

O Holy God, though a thousand fall at my side, and ten thousand fall at my right hand, please let it not come close to me and my companions.

O Lord Most High, let me live to see the reward of the wicked because You are my refuge and my home. Let no evil conquer me and let no plague come into my house or near my family.

O Lord, my Strength and my Redeemer, please set angels over me to keep me in all Your ways, to bear me up in their hands and to keep my feet from stumbling.

Father God, help me to tread upon the lion and adder and trample the young lion and the dragon under my feet.

Lord Jesus, I love you with all my heart and I know your name. Deliver me and lift me on high to soar with the eagles. I call upon you to be with me in times of trouble to deliver and honor me because I know your name. Please show me your salvation and satisfy me with a long life.

I ask this prayer in the name of Jesus Christ.

GIFT smiled. *His path is set; here is the vision from my friend, Jeremiah.* Elizabeth gasped after the mind dump and said, *My God, is this true?*

Yes, he willingly stepped into this path. He would never submit any life to this Devastation; it is in his nature to be gentle and the berserker. All NESS, soldiers, police, firefighters, humans, any life who will not submit to evil are blessed by God. GIFT smiled sadly. *We will die together way in the future; he will kill it once and forever and his faith will carry life forward.*

GIFT sighed. *I hope I have a soul; it would be very nice to go to illumination with him and you and all the rest of my friends.* GIFT smiled at Elizabeth. *Have you chosen what you want with your life?*

Elizabeth smiled back and AI'd, *Yes. GIFT, you are in my crosshairs; you will not get off as easily as Stardrifter.*

GIFT laughed. *I am in good company then!*

The FOLK and NESS had picked themselves up off the floor in the gallery. They could see in their minds that Elizabeth was talking to GIFT, but it was private and there was no mind leakage; she had mastered the privacy.

Elizabeth AI'd all the FOLK and NESS, *GIFT is deadly and will not be swayed.* She pointed and said, *These FOLK judges paid with their lives; there is no compromise with GIFT. On this point, I agree. If we lose this war, all of life will be exterminated, period.*

Elizabeth raised her voice and spoke in her outer voice. "We have been entrusted by GIFT to use this inner speech for starters. This would unite our planet, it would strip away all the mistrust and it would kill all the psychopaths who hunger for the endless **WARS** on our planet and in the universe, or lust for power." She pointed to the dead judges as she said this. "NESS would not be needed to kill humans, and they would be pointed at the real enemy, Devastation. It is a PRISON for them, these men and women in the armor protect you so you can live in the fantasy world of your own making and feel safe while they sacrifice everything for you."

She pointed to the NESS in the gallery. "Yet you condemn them to death for being human. She pointed at Stardrifter and said, "This NESS is very human and frail. From what I gather, he is your best warrior and yet, you treat him like SHIT! Since he carries death in his hand, you fear him, yet I have seen his mind. He hates the armor, yet assumes the burden and responsibility of the armor. You are his people and he loves all of you."

Elizabeth's passion hit the FOLK and NESS like a hammer from God. "You demand a lot and give nothing back to him and his kind of people; the NESS ARE HUMAN." Elizabeth's mind was like a thunder storm. She AI'd, *You FOLK should be kissing all of the NESS's feet; they are the best of you.*

Elizabeth stomped over to the platform where Stardrifter was immobile in the armor. The judges told Stardrifter, "Get in the position of forgiveness, NESS. You are being judged."

She spun around suddenly. "Shut the FUCK UP and sit down or I will go over there and kick your sorry asses." They all sat down.

She nodded at Jeremiah. He came forward and released Stardrifter's knees and limbs. Stardrifter's right knee was on the ground and his left arm was on his knee with his palm up. Jeremiah then released the armored helmet, which folded back. Her NESS man looked at her, his expression calm. Jeremiah went and released the armored glove on his left hand, which peeled away from his hand.

Elizabeth looked down at Stardrifter and said to him, "Do you love me?"

"Yes."

"Will you marry me?"

"Yes."

"You're mine forever?"

"Yes."

"I forgive you." She looked at the gallery and grabbed his hand. "Can someone release my idiot husband now?"

The FOLK judges looked at her, dumbfounded, and she smiled. "Well, do it now, you idiots."

FOLK judges nodded and stated, "All charges are dropped," and released the NESS to full status.

Jeremiah went behind Stardrifter, released the safes for his armor and handed the key back. He was fully restored. "Thank God you are back; I really hate being C&C."

Stardrifter laughed. "I am taking a honeymoon and a very long vacation with my wife. You are stuck with it for now." Jeremiah swore up a storm. His daughter, Jessica, came up to him and Stardrifter told her in his outer voice, "I am sorry for my behavior towards you in my house."

She smiled. "That is alright, Micha'el. Seems we all learn from mistakes, so you will be in FOLK therapy when you return."

"Yes," he said, beaming a smile at her. "So, a wedding for Elizabeth and I?"

Jessica nodded. "Yes, just stay the hell out of the way and nod a lot." Jessica winked at Elizabeth and AI'd, *You sure about this?*

Elizabeth AI'd, *Yes, we will need to plan something, and these two men could not plan a picnic.*

Jessica laughed out loud. "Dad, go find my husband. Elizabeth and I have a wedding to plan."

Stardrifter smiled at his wife and Elizabeth leaped into his outstretched armored arms. Stardrifter lifted and kissed her. *Damn, my underwear is wet again.*

She AI'd him, *What are we going to do about that, my husband?* He AI'd a plan to her and she replied, *Yes, that sounds very fun. Will your armor fit in the car?*

Let's try, he answered, as they headed for the steam car.

Jeremiah smiled at the antics. *Thanks, Zoë.*

He felt lips on his lips, echoes of laughter and he thought, *Come here, my extremely cute NESS.* He had a very big grin on his face.

Elizabeth walked naked on OLD NESS decks. Stardrifter watched her move. He looked from her feet to her head; three months had passed and she was starting to show. He patted the very large towel and she came over and looked down at him. She AI'd, *You like me all pregnant.*

He AI'd, *Yes, you just glow.*

She smiled. *Right answer, my NESS man.* She sat down and threw her legs over him, covering her eyes with her left arm from the sun. *Your northern part of your country is nice. Too bad I could not get across to the northern continent. My studies are needed, but you are right, it is too dangerous for now.*

Stardrifter nodded. He looked at his left hand. The ring on his finger felt very good. Elizabeth grabbed that hand with her left hand and she admired how their rings matched. She placed his hand on her belly and he felt the kids moving in her. She AI'd, *The babies are hungry. Please go get some juice and fruit.* He got up to retrieve it. When he returned, she sat up on her elbows and her breasts swayed in the air. She noticed his eyes looking at her breasts and smiling, she thought, *Men are all the same.*

He smiled as he fed her some fruit and juice. He AI'd, *The crew will be coming back in a few days. Where do you want to go, Elizabeth?*

Well, Jeremiah showed me an area from one of the deserted cities around here. I would like to see how the planet is filling in the ecosystems.

No problem. Let's get the comp working on it; you do a plan, then we have fun.

"You will be in armor?"

He nodded. "My duty is to protect FOLK, and you." She smiled at him. *We had company last night; it was taken care of this morning while you slept.*

Are we alright?

Yes.

I know that look. Elizabeth AI'd her husband with a plan.

Smiling at her, he said, "That is a very fun plan." He picked his wife up and went below to implement the plan.

The lone surviving scavenger was running for his life. *Damn NESS killed everyone.* As he turned, he saw the glitter of the blade swinging at his head before it was severed from his body.

NESS Haldor nodded. "That was the last one." As he searched the body, he spotted a leather book in a pack. *Hmm, scavengers are feral, not educated. This is different… plasta-glass pages.*

When his armored hand touched the glass, the pages started to flow. *What the hell,* he thought. *Armor cinching power leads cinched down, load complete, index manual tesla jump drive.* He looked at the title, 'Engineering Tesla Jump Drive'. His hands shook as he flipped through the book. *Equation diagrams, specifications, where is it… oh my God.*

Jeremiah AI'd, *What is it?*

Haldor AI'd, *I have found a book on Tesla Jump Drives.*

We find that trash all the time.

NO, this is a real engineering book. The date is 2150, OLD Earth date. It is from the United States. It has a label on it, 'ultra-secret book 1 of 3 from TJD, New York' and it is plasta-glass storage unit. Looks very old and is damn near indestructible and wrapped in a leather binder.

Can it be? Jeremiah asked. *New Earth had several space ports that had been repeatedly nuked with city busters by someone. The radiation was no issue for the NESS, but it was blasted to ruins, nothing lived there.*

Jeremiah, hold tight, the NESS are moving to you now. He waited. A NESS APC ground to a halt and the NESS piled out and he handed it to Jeremiah

Oh shit, he thought as he scanned the pages. *I am not an engineer, but we have many in the city. Mount up, we are heading back now.*

As he mounted, he pointed to two NESS and AI'd, *John and Luke, fan out. Do a pheromone trace on this one. Track his movement. Do not engage anyone; you are on deep scout, as of now. Find the rest of these books, if possible.*

They nodded. Sampling the scavenger, the armor chameleon blended into the surrounding area. Both smiled and said, *Yes,* while running through the countryside and hid. They started the hunt for the spacecraft books.

FIVE

Oceana

Oceana Diplomat Seton was looking out on the Deep Ocean from the armored flying wing section in the ballroom on the Republic cruise liner, Traveler.

He was contemplating what he had just heard from Ambassador Michael Destroses while talking privately before the conference started regarding what the FOLK had presented to him from inside their city. His wife was also thinking hard with her hand in his.

I am glad the NESS FOLK are driven by peace. They would kill us all if they get really put into a corner. Fight or die is not a very good option and they have the tools to kill this planet. They both ran the story in their minds.

Ambassador Destroses was astounded by the FOLK city; it was very different. When they entered the armored door, another one was set further into the tunnel. Haldor AI'd Stardrifter, *We are in the outer tunnel.*

Stardrifter smiled and AI'd back, *Your helmet. We will hide nothing from the ambassador.*

Haldor said in his outer voice, "Ambassador Destroses, Sharon Destroses, I am going to roll my helmet back. Please do not be startled. I mean you no harm; can I do this in front of you?" They both nodded and Haldor AI'd the helmet back and smiled at them. They both gasped and looked at him in wonder. His colors glowed in the semi gloom of the tunnel.

Sharon Destroses told him, "We know you are NESS, but your skin is a wonder."

Haldor laughed and said, "Yes, I am colorful, but not like some of the NESS."

Haldor AI'd NESS Genève. She laughed from the driver's seat and AI'd back. In her helmet, her hair was pulled back to a titanium blond ponytail. She told them, "I can change my pattern at will, watch." Ambassador and Sharon Destroses laughed as she showed a colorful children's illustration book that was known to them on her head as they waited for the second armored door to open into the city.

Sharon laughed. "I know that book. I read it to my grandchildren."

Genève nodded. "I read it to mine, too, but I make the illustrations animate. Makes reading really fun. I have a captivated audience in my house and school."

The second armored door opened and NESS Genève said, "Here we go." She put the steam car in drive and Ambassador and Sharon Destroses gasped. The road went down into a floor. They stopped in front of a small barrier and the car was turned off.

Both NESS came around and opened the doors on the vehicle. "Please come with us. The NESS and FOLK welcome you to our city." They stepped forward, "Please look around from here." When they looked around, they saw massive buildings that soared into the air, blending into the granite walls of rocks.

Haldor said, "What you are seeing is a design from a very ancient architect, Paolo Soleri. We took his design and our architects were inspired to create this world for the FOLK and NESS."

Ambassador and Sharon Destroses looked around. Everything blended and had purpose, and nothing was wasted. They saw huge buildings with nothing but green coming from them. Ambassador Destroses asked, "What are those buildings?"

Haldor replied, "Oh, those are some of the many hydroponics' buildings. We grow almost all our vegetable food stuffs in them and besides, that is the structure for processing the vegetables for storage. Next to that is the recycling plant. We use that building for fish aquaculture. What you see is an enclosed ecosystem that can feed the NESS and FOLK for thousands of axis turns."

Ambassador and Sharon Destroses marveled. "Is this where you live?" Sharon asked.

The NESS both laughed. "No, this is one of the smaller processing plants. We have several hundred of these modules just for food. Now, we are going to show you where we live. Here is our ride now." A huge clear tube ascended to the platform. "Please just step into the tube and relax." As they stepped into the tube, it built seats to accommodate the guests. Ambassador and Sharon Destroses looked startled as the chairs formed seemingly out of nowhere. The NESS said, "Please sit down, these are for you."

THE NESS smiled as their armor blended to the tube. "Here we go."

Ambassador Destroses and Sharon Destroses sat down and the acceleration of the tube was not detectable. They both felt like a bird flying across the landscape. Everywhere they looked, buildings extended into the sky. The NESS smiled and said, "What you are seeing now is an industrial section; we build material from minerals.

Ambassador Destroses said, "I do not see any steel furnaces."

Both NESS nodded. "We do not use that manufacturing technique. It destroys our planet with pollution and it is very wasteful of material. We use NANO manufacturing; everything is used to the last atom." Ambassador and Sharon Destroses could see steel being moved into storage buildings.

The NESS said, "Look up." They could see what looked like a large dome. "This is a sun focuser; it tracks the sun and focuses the light into clear, enclosed light guides. The natural sunlight is piped to the building for our people who work in this section of the city."

Ambassador Destroses asked, "What about at night?"

Both NESS smiled. "We use a very old technique. Nikola Tesla invented a steam turbine that, coupled with a drilled pipe deep into the mantle, could extract heat from boiling water pumped to the bottom of the pipe. Then, the supersaturated steam would rise to power the turbines. Our scientists and engineers used his pioneering work and perfected his design. All electrical power is derived for this system to power our city."

Ambassador Destroses asked, "How are we doing this flight?"

"There are electromagnets in the tube that are built in real time for us. As we pass, a tube forms like an ocean wave with the tube. We are in the tube now; if you look behind us, the tube just goes back to its normal state of water. We find it useful; no roads to maintain, the water is very abundant and we have multiple uses for it when not used in this manner."

Sharon Destroses asked, "But, how do you do this?"

Both NESS smiled. "We are not scientists or engineers, but we use NANO technology in virtually everything we build. We find it most useful in every endeavor of the human experience."

The ride started to slow down. "Ambassador Destroses, Sharon Destroses, we are arriving."

They both noticed the buildings seemed to blend into the granite rock. Both NESS stepped out of the tube and helped Ambassador Destroses and Sharon Destroses onto the platform. They watched as the tube sank down to the floor and became water.

Both NESS stepped towards a rock wall and put an armored glove to it. It folded back to reveal a clear tube. "Please, Ambassador Destroses, Sharon Destroses, step in with us," the NESS smiled, "Please face forward. We think you will like the view."

Ambassador and Sharon Destroses stood in wonder. The lift went up as they passed through the bedrock till it hit the surface. The glass then opened up and they could see forest meadows, wildlife, birds, native, and non-native life as far as their eyes could see. Ambassador and Sharon Destroses both asked, "What?"

The NESS laughed and said, "We have rebuilt half a million square miles of habitat since the troubles. We like to think we are God's gardeners; this is life to us. Our city is underground, so we can rebuild this for all of us in the future."

The lift went up the side of the granite cliff and stopped.

"We have arrived at the villa. Please step into this place."

The door opened and the FOLK council was waiting for them.

"Welcome Ambassador Michael Destroses and Sharon Destroses to our city. We welcome our friends to our house." They both looked at the council. They all looked very normal; they had no color at all. One of the FOLK council members stated, "We are the ruling body for the FOLK and NESS; we will speak in the outer speech to you."

Ambassador Destroses said, "I do not understand. I always speak like this."

The FOLK council laughed. "We are sorry. We have not talked in outer speech for many axis turns. We use the inner speech among our people, so NESS Diplomat Ulysses will speak for us. His outer speech is very eloquent." NESS Diplomat Ulysses stepped forward and beamed at his friend.

Ambassador and Sharon Destroses were very startled to see him. "Have you buried your parents?"

He shook his head. "No, I am still grieving, but my people need my experience with Outsiders, so I have been asked by the FOLK council to speak for them. Is this acceptable with you and Sharon?" Both nodded. "Okay then, please follow me. We will sit beside the big window to look out at the rebuilt areas. We are several hundred feet off the floor of the valley, but you are very safe. Is this acceptable to you?"

Ambassador and Sharon Destroses smiled as they sat down. A bird hopped onto the railing, looking for treats. Ulysses smiled and said, "She is looking for Stardrifter; he always has treats around. Ahhh, here it is." He set the birdfeeder on the railing. The bird hopped onto the perch to eat and throw birdseed all over the place.

NESS Diplomat Ulysses cleared his throat. "Before we begin, do you need some refreshments?"

Ambassador Destroses said, "Yes, do you have some coffee and water?" Sharon asked, "Could I have some tea?"

"Absolutely. Would you like spice apple tea with sugar and lemon? And coffee, we have Mesopotamia dark roast with whole milk and sugar, is this acceptable?"

Both Ambassador and Sharon Destroses laughed out loud. "You have done your homework," Sharon said.

"Yes, I strive very hard; it is endless homework for me." They sat enjoying the refreshments.

Michael said to Ulysses, "The FOLK council wants something from me; it must be very important. I know you have not shown your city to Outsiders ever, so my question is why me and my wife now?"

The FOLK council AI'd Ulysses, *Ambassador Destroses is very sharp and honest. We will answer with all the truth as we see it fit to any of his or his wife's questions.*

Ulysses smiled. "You have heard from the FOLK 'Your 'Word is your Life'?" They both nodded. "I am under strict orders to tell the truth to you; if I lie to you, I will be killed." Ambassador and Sharon Destroses looked very startled by this statement. "You may ask any question, and I mean anything, and I will answer it. Do you understand my words?"

Sharon looked at her husband, who nodded and said, "Ulysses, we do understand the words."

Ulysses smiled at his friends. "You're right. My people have never opened the city to any outsider until now. We are very concerned with the state of affairs on our shared planet, so the FOLK council, on my recommendation, would like to be honest with you. Personally, we, as a people, wanted to meet you in our world to show you that we are not NESS." He pointed to the surrounding area. "What you see is FOLK works in progress. Our people have taken a vow to advance knowledge without using violence."

Sharon stated, "But the FOLK are guarded by the NESS and they are extremely violent in the world."

Ulysses nodded. "Yes, they are, I will explain. NESS are designed by GIFT to combat an enemy that destroyed the universe billions of axis turns in the past. We still do not have all the information, but NESS sense this devastation. If they find it anywhere, they will kill it. Some humans have been found with this disease, even in the FOLK. This devastation is extremely active; it is real and running wild in the universe."

Ulysses looked at both Michael and Sharon. "NESS are FOLK who have been asked to be NESS. It is an extreme honor to be one, but it is a horror, too. Let me show you." He set a crystal on the table and said, "This is NESS GENOME REBUILD. You are looking at Stardrifter. He is First of the NESS." He AI'd for the crystal recording to commence. "This recording is from GIFT."

Michael and Sharon hid their eyes behind their hands and whispered to Ulysses, "We have seen enough, please turn this recording off." The screaming ended from the recording.

Ulysses looked at both of them. "NESS are designed to be warriors; the coloring denotes their status as warriors. Once GENOME REBUILD is started, it is irreversible. The aging slows down tremendously in the NESS. Stardrifter is 728 years old in the old record keeping systems and the average age of the NESS is 400 years of age. We have never seen a NESS die of old age, period. The NESS die in battle not diseases."

Sharon nodded and said, "But we have documented records showing NESS killing everything that moved during the troubles."

Ulysses nodded. "I will tell you, NESS are now under very strict guidelines. We call them 'Life Protocols'. For our people, this came, as you stated, by NESS running wild over the planet."

Ambassador and Sharon Destroses nodded. Ulysses continued, "The killing stopped about 160 axis turns ago when your nation formed."

"Ahhh," Sharon said. "I see law and order were instituted by your FOLK Council."

"Yes, we gave the NESS purpose, along with hope, that they were not freaks to the rest of the humans. We, the FOLK, have welcomed them into our family. FOLK have many families that have NESS in them. We are seeing vast improvements in the minds and hearts of NESS since most have married and settled down to be family men and family women. It is most gratifying for the FOLK.

"FOLK never mention the horrors that happened during the troubles; we had a civil war between NESS during two axis turns. We lost nearly one million NESS, along with three million FOLK who were killed in that butchery. It was so painful to the existing FOLK that we resorted to wholesale slaughter of each other. The NESS FOLK that perished would not submit to law and order. We, as a people, had to constrain the wild NESS FOLK; they were going to kill the whole planet."

Ambassador Destroses asked, "What are Wild NESS FOLK?"

"Well, Wild NESS FOLK were arrogant, self-serving elitists. They would have exterminated anyone – and I mean anyone that did not fit the GENOME profile of their people. The NESS FOLK that had this line in them are extinct in the NESS FOLK now; we made sure that nothing survived from that NESS FOLK line."

Ambassador Destroses asked Ulysses, "Did any Wild NESS FOLK survive this civil war?"

"As far as we know, none survived, but in war, many miracles happen that we cannot explain. We have been looking for 160 axis turns for one NESS who started the whole civil war. His name is Temple. So far, we think he is dead, but we have no body. We have been sampling DNA profiles in the Outsiders, sorry, other humans on the planet and as far as we know, that NESS line is extinct."

Sharon nodded. "If he is alive, what does that mean to you and us, Ulysses?"

Ulysses shuddered. "He will kill this planet in war. He utterly hates the FOLK NESS, along with just about everyone else. His whole family perished in the troubles with GIFT's release. Let's just say vengeance rules his heart.

"In that light, I have been told by the council that I could tell you anything, so here goes. We have two groups of new NESS: offensive NESS and defensive NESS. Right now, we have 500,000 defensive NESS active and 1,000 offensive NESS."

"What's the difference?" Sharon asked.

"Defensive NESS are FOLK, so genetically, they follow our thought patterns. Protection of FOLK costs our family men and family women NESS. That is why we sank the ten ships from New World, but did not go on the offensive. However, offensive NESS are very different. They are survivors of the troubles. They are combat veterans who survived the wars from all over the planet, along with winning the civil war. We have them in suspended animation for now. The FOLK have one million in the suspension process; they are FOLK citizens.

Ulysses suddenly looked very serious. "Offensive NESS are extremely dangerous; they make GATS look like a pet for your children. We have found that once released, they are extremely violent. Killing makes up almost every facet of their lives. They were the ones that ran wild on the planet. FOLK have great misgivings of releasing them on this planet, but we have activated the 1,000. So far, they have our most advanced weapons on them."

"Why, if they are as violent as you say they are in the world, give them the means to burn the world to the ground?" Ambassador Destroses asked.

"We FOLK do not advocate violence. The civil war showed us very stark results, but we are being pushed to invoke life protocols by other groups on this planet. The FOLK council has been debating for months, but just a few days ago, we voted to go on a passive war footing. This means we are gearing up the offensive NESS with new weapons to release them to kill all nuclear, biological and chemical weapons systems on our planet. That means they can burn whole cities to the ground to kill these systems."

Ambassador and Sharon's faces couldn't hide their shock, while Ulysses' face revealed pain. "They are also under orders to kill the humans who order these weapons of mass destruction unleashed. They will kill all participants from politicos to the lowest trooper."

Sharon Destroses exclaimed, "Oh my God."

Ulysses nodded grimly. "To make sure you understand, here is the recording of the sea battle using one of these new weapons."

They listened with their hands covering their mouths in shock. When the recording ended, Sharon murmured, "Those poor seamen, your FOLK NESS."

Ulysses sighed. "Violence is a dead end for us as a species. FOLK NESS are very serious; we will not be nuked, gassed or biologically poisoned again by any nation or entity, ever. The FOLK NESS are united in these statements of fact for our people; WE WILL NOT BE EXTERMINATED."

Ambassador and Sharon Destroses both nodded. "We see the FOLK council fear."

The FOLK council AI'd Ulysses, *Tell him about inner speech then bring up the world hologram with FOLK projections of the coming war.*

Ulysses cleared his throat. "Michael and Sharon, I will divulge a FOLK secret during the troubles. GIFT was released on the planet during the ensuing wars. Everyone thought GIFT had been killed. This is not the truth. Our NESS are the prime carriers of GIFT. It is sentient."

Ambassador and Sharon Destroses nodded. Ambassador Destroses said, "We have had scattered reports that GIFT is active, but it was never confirmed as our people are deathly afraid of GIFT reoccurrence with the ensuing destruction of our populace. We are just now getting over the near extinction level event from that time."

Ulysses nodded and said, "My people were affected, too. We have inner speech now from GIFT's release.

"What is inner speech?" Sharon asked.

"My people communicate to each other across the whole planet directly, mind to mind, using GIFT. We have no need to use standard radio or what is called 'electromagnet spectrum' for communications."

"Can you read minds?"

"No, that is science fiction. We talk to each other like in outer speech, but our minds are private. We have developed mental barriers that keep our thoughts private unless we want to share them with NESS FOLK. My wife can literally read me, so we share everything because I like a happy wife, plus I need guidance from her."

Sharon Destroses laughed. "We have been married a long time. This inner speech would be nice, but he does this already so, Ulysses, what is the issue?"

"I am going to bring up a projection of our world. In it is the analysis from the FOLK economic diplomatic, along with NESS military projections for a coming war. We think this will happen in the next axis turn of our world." He set a crystal on the table and continued. "This crystal will project our world in three dimensions. Here we go." On the table, the hologram revolved, showing a very detailed map of the existing countries on the three continents.

Ambassador Destroses asked, "Is this real?"

"No, this is a comp-driven projection of our world, but everything is as exact as we can make it at this time. I am going to bring up the data in a format that you can read. Here is the first section, please read it. I will answer any question that you bring to me or the FOLK council." Ulysses sat quietly while they read.

The FOLK council smiled and AI'd Ulysses, *NESS data stream is coming in for Ambassador Destroses and Sharon Destroses; their neuron firing pattern shows extremely high understanding. Nearing unity, it is now achieved by them.*

Ambassador and Sharon Destroses nodded. "Please bring up the next section." This analysis lasted until supper time. Ulysses suggested a break for dinner. Ambassador and Sharon Destroses both laughed. "Well, Ulysses, what have you planned from your homework?" Ambassador Destroses asked.

Ulysses laughed. "Well, for an appetizer, Caesar salad, soup is clam with potato, the main course is sole steamed in water with a touch of butter and herbs, along with steamed asparagus. Dessert is a simple cherry tart, drinks are a fine white wine and after supper coffee and tea will also be served. Is this acceptable?"

Ambassador and Sharon laughed. "Ulysses, you really have done your homework."

Ambassador Destroses cleared his throat. "We see the issue. The underlying fear is loss of sovereignty over one's affairs. We agree with the FOLK council's assessment and I have a few recommendations to add. It would give me more lateral movement for a base understanding," he asked, "How do I do this to add to the document?"

Ulysses said, "Just speak and it will update."

Ambassador and Sharon Destroses took turns adding in the sections with their knowledge.

The FOLK council was very impressed; they nodded and said, *Very logical recommendations to the assessment.*

The FOLK council AI'd Ulysses, *We are very pleased with you, Ulysses. You are hereby promoted to 1st premier diplomat. More schooling is allocated starting after your grieving leave. You will not report before then; we want you whole and healthy.*

Ulysses AI'd his wife, *Did you hear?*

Maggie AI'd back, *Yes, but I need you home. I am having contractions.*

NESS Diplomat Ulysses said out loud, "Crap." Michael and Sharon looked at him and Ulysses said, "I am sorry, my wife is having contractions. Maggie just AI'd me."

"AI'd what?"

He laughed. "She used the inner speech on me."

Ambassador and Sharon Destroses shooed him away. "Well, Ulysses, go. We are done here, we think." They looked at the FOLK council.

All nodded. "We agree, we are done. We are most pleased with this agreement assessment. Would you like anything else?"

Ambassador and Sharon Destroses nodded. "Yes, since Ulysses lost his parents, can we fill in as god parents?"

Ulysses' jaw hit the table. His wife AI'd, *It is most acceptable to me. My parents are dead, too. The twins will need good grandparents.*

Ulysses said, "Hell yes! Come with me to the FOLK hospital." They all left together.

The FOLK council laughed. *Well, humans are humans. Time to go home.*

They all AI'd their spouses who all responded with things like, *Well, you are running late* or *Please pick up the kids* or *We need some paper.* The council was just as wrapped up in the daily affairs as any human being.

James was in a NESS bar in the FOLK NESS city, waiting on his cousin. He was enjoying himself – the NESS were human, after all. He was steered by several NESS to this very nice bar. He looked down at NESS Octavia who he had been drinking with. She had on a very skimpy outfit that showed off her nice legs, full breasts and blonde hair cut short. On the floor, her coloring was just a spectacular rainbow.

James thought, *All in all, a very nice looking woman. Can't hold her liquor, though. She's passed out on the floor.* Octavia had toppled from the bar stool when she threw a drink down her throat. James asked her running mate, "Is she like this every night?"

The female NESS said, "No, we just got back from patrol."

James nodded and thought, *Well, maybe I can lift her off the floor.*

He grabbed her and set her on the stool, arranging her clothes so they covered most of her body. When he let go, Octavia wobbled.

Damn, she is really out. Hmm. James laid her head on the bar top. He laughed and propped her arms on the bar so she would not roll off the stool. *There, much better,* he said to himself.

Her running mate was impressed. James had picked her friend off the floor, was gentle and did not do anything inappropriate. She smiled at him and asked, "So, are you a warrior?"

He nodded. "Yes, retired. I guard the ambassador. I am his cousin, James Destroses."

The sober NESS nodded, "Well, pleased to meet you, I am Lora."

James smiled and sized her up. Lora was the biggest female he had ever encountered in his life. Lora's uniform left him wondering what was under it. She was very beautiful, with her dark, chestnut hair and big brown eyes. He was even drawn to her wild skin pattern. James liked any woman and the NESS women in this bar were very beautiful. Drooling mentally and drinking from his glass, he thought, *Yes, very nice looking woman.*

"Well, Lora can I buy you another drink?"

Lora smiled. "Yes, you can."

James waved his hand at the bartender. "Two more rounds, whatever Lora is drinking."

The FOLK bartender smiled and he AI'd, *Lora, he will eat you alive.* She laughed and AI'd, *I hope so, he is cute.*

They were on their second round when a NESS fight broke out. The FOLK bartender said, "Here we go again," as he ran around the end of the bar. James smiled.

Lora was watching the bar fight erupt. Smiling, James hopped over the bar and stooped behind the counter. *Hmm, this looks good,* he thought.

James shouted at Lora above the noise, "Hey, Lora!" James waved the prize, "Look what I found, you like?" Lora laughed and started to hop over the bar when a chair smashed into her back, which sent her toppling over the bar top and crashing James to the floor. James fell hard onto the bar floor with Lora on top of him. *Oh, this feels mighty fine*. Lora was a foot taller than him. Her breasts had smashed his head into the floor, too. Lora started to get up off of him, but James smiled, saying above the noise, "Lora, I want to kiss you."

Lora smiled and settled on him. "So, James, you do. Well, have you ever kissed a female NESS?"

Laughing, he said, "Just you, I hope." She smiled and kissed him.

James looked at her after they broke apart. "Can we do that again?" he asked, as he grabbed her harder. Lora nodded. There was glass breaking, hooting and hollering going on all around them, but they both were oblivious to the distractions.

Lora looked at him and thought, *Damn that was very nice*. She could feel him stir against her. "Well, James," she said in her outer voice, "I like you. I have a place really close, so do you want to go home with me?"

James said, "Yes."

They got up and ducked as a body smashed into the wall with a shelf above them that held liquor. James grabbed Lora's hand and grabbed another bottle of something. Giggling, they both ran to the end of the bar. Peeking around the end of the bar, James and Lora scouted the terrain then made a dash for the window, which had been convenient- ly smashed by a NESS who had been tossed through it onto the walk- way. They stepped out the window, took a couple of hits of whatever they had grabbed and laughed. Lora pointed down the alley and said, "That way." They staggered off into the night toward Lora's place.

When they arrived, Lora opened the door and pulled James in. He looked around and said, "Nice place."

Lora closed the door, spun him around and kissed him. James dropped the bottle and kissed her back. They broke apart, giggled and then, stripped off each other's clothes.

James looked at Lora and thought, *My God*. The uniform had hid- den her curves. Lora laughed and turned around, showing all of her- self. He marveled. She was big, but very proportional. Lora had deep, flaring hips, a nice waist and very nice breasts that were not heavy, but very firm. Lora asked him in a low voice, "You like?" James, smiling, stepped over to her, gently pulled her to him and kissed her long and deep.

Lora smiled as they both crashed to the floor. Lora settled on top of him on the floor. Her arms were above his shoulders and her breasts dangled in front of him. Lora smiled and said in her outer voice, "James, you are my first man in over 3 axis turns." *But, that is going to change*, she said to herself. She put her full weight onto him and grinned. "James, do you like this with me?"

James had a very big grin on his face and he said, "YES!"

"We are going to have a lot of fun tonight."

James woke up in Lora's bedroom, which was in shambles. Lora's right leg lay draped across him. *Hmm, that looks nice*, he thought, as he started to kiss her.

She stirred and opened her eyes before smiling and saying, "Want more, James?" He kissed her right breast. Lora moaned and thought, *Yes, that is a very nice.* She rolled James on top of her.

Octavia staggered in the late afternoon to her shared apartment looking around. Lora's clothes and someone else's were all over the place. *What the hell*, she wondered. Her commander was such a straight lace that her having sex was not possible. Smiling, she smelled the sex on the floor, on the clothes in the air and thought, *Ahhh, evidence.* She found the bottle of liquor and picked it up, examining the label.

As she took a swig, Octavia heard noises coming from Lora's bedroom. She staggered over to the bedroom door.

Hmm, I could run a tank through here and my commander would not hear with all the noise they are making. She saw that the door was slightly ajar and she couldn't resist taking a peek. There was her commander with the cute Outsider, James Destroses. Lora had thrown the bed sheets on both of them and there was a lot of giggling coming from beneath them. She watched them both crash onto the floor with the bed sheets wrapped around them.

Oh, *they are doomed,* she giggled to herself. Lora and James were still oblivious to her presence. Laughing, she took another swig.

Lora whispered in her outer voice, "Well, you are not going anywhere for a while," as her golden threads grabbed James.

Well, Lora, about time, Octavia thought.

She took the bottle, staggered to her room, closed the door and plopped down in the chair. Octavia had duty in another two cycles and she wanted to party with some men. *I wonder if there are any more cute Outsiders running loose in the city.*

James looked at Lora and said, "God, I love this woman." Lora laughed and pulsed again around James. Lora then moved around and sat face to face with him and said, "Lift me up back to bed." James lifted her to the bed.

Octavia smiled when she heard more laughter erupt from the bedroom; Lora was definitely making up for lost time. Laughing, she took another swig.

Ambassador and Sharon Destroses waited all night for Ulysses. He came out and said, "We have two healthy babies, one boy and one girl. Maggie said it would be alright to visit now. Do you want to be god parents?"

Both smiled and answered, "Yes!"

Maggie looked tired, but she smiled. "Welcome. This is Prima, our girl, and this is Seneca, our boy." Both babies were wrapped in her arms. Maggie smiled and asked, "Would you like to hold them?" Michael and Sharon Destroses each took one and sat down with their newest grandchildren. Ulysses and Maggie AI'd each other, *They look good together.* Ulysses smiled and said, *That is why we all strive, for our children for a better future.*

Ambassador and Sharon Destroses read the letter again in their bed in the cruise liner while laughing. James Destroses had fallen hard for a NESS, Lora, whom he had met in a bar fight, of all places. Reading through the letter, they laughed harder. Both had met Lora before departure; she was a very beautiful and very large women.

James and Lora eventually married. Whenever Lora looked at her husband, James would just melt. The hardcore, woman chasing, permanent bachelor relative had settled down with a NESS. The letter from Lora stated that they were due to have a child next year. James had put a PS note, "I am very happy, my brother is very good at security. Please hire him. He needs to meet a NESS female. When you return next axis year, we can introduce him to Lora's friend, Octavia. She saw the picture of him and said she wanted him. Love, James."

Ambassador Destroses smiled at the memories as he looked at the gathering. "In closing, we have provided all of you NESS FOLK initiatives for trade. I know this is a very solid deal and there are no hidden agendas. The FOLK do not want war, period. They believe it would lead to our extermination on this planet."

Oceana Diplomat Seton thought, *The New World has stirred up all the animosities around the planet that have been festering for at least 24 axis turns.* His people were stretched across half the globe called the Belt, which was the island chains that stretched between two of the three continents. *Damn the New World. They are going to suck us into the planet conflagration and we will not be able to remain neutral this time.*

His people had chosen a strong defensive posture in their island fortifications; since founding, it had been fairly safe. *We have built the massive defensives along with our heavy industries to support world trade, but, as always, food is the problem for our people. With the industries, food production has diminished due to environmental damage, so we have to import more food from Minoans. If they go under, we will, too. We cannot eat steel.* He sighed to himself.

Oceana Diplomat Seton's wife, Ula, approached and he asked her, "What do you think of the information from Ambassador Destroses?"

"Sean, I think we should read the report in detail, but from first impressions, the FOLK are sending a message to the aligned nations that if they see it coming, it will happen unless we all steer it away from a global conflict."

Sean said, "That is my impression, too. We can gear up armaments, but we trade with other non-aligned nations that would send a negative message, too. Preparing for war is not in our best interest. It takes too much money without enough return.

"We also will be seen as a fat target, due to our industrial strengths. Along with our lack of an ocean navy, this would open us up for multiple attacks from many nations."

"True, our military is not geared for ocean warfare; we are a land-based military. We do not have naval force projection mobility, so we might have to start limited construction of small warships for convoy duty. We cannot have our trade routes blocked."

Ula replied, "Raiding and pirates have been with us since founding. The small-timers are easily handled now, but if they are given letters of marque and reprisal with semi-modern ocean warships, even second-hand ones, that would be very hard to control. They will prowl for victims in our waters. It would disrupt our food supplies with a plausible denial from our enemies. This would leave us starving to death in under one axis turn."

Sean agreed. "You are right. Being under a boot heel would not be in our best interest. So, in that light, in the presentation, the FOLK showed Ambassador Destroses a machine they called Iron Rations."

"Yes, it is fascinating. It uses something called Spirulina," she said as she pointed to the document. "Arthrospira is a planktonic, blue-green algae (Cyanobacteria) found in warm water, alkaline volcanic lakes, and is rich in raw protein and seven major vitamins: A1, B1, B2, B6,

B12, C and E. This plankton naturally contains beta-carotene, color-enhancing pigments and a whole range of minerals. I am a trained engineer, but even with my limited knowledge on nutrition, I know this could help us in the long run."

Sean looked at her and stated, "Yes, added to the granaries and fish tanks, we could possibly feed our people for extended periods of disruptions .The FOLK are asking for pure refined ores at 99.9% in vast quantities in under three months for the knowledge and the algae starter."

"I think we can make a deal with the FOLK. We have the capacity and the industrialists will go with this since it is in their best interest for money and freedom." Both of them laughed. "Yes, it is like herding GATS with our business people, but it can be done this time."

Oceana Diplomat Seton thought, *This cannot wait. I will encrypt my recommendations and send it wireless to the parliament. I also think we should include the royal families on the islands, too.* He looked at his wife and whispered, "We have to get a message off now."

She nodded. "Yes, should I gather the twins?"

He looked at his kids, Narissa and Nerida, and said, as he smiled, "They seem to be enjoying the party and the detail is guarding them.

Oceana Diplomat Seton motioned over his head to his detail, Miles. "We are going back to the suite. Can the detail handle watching the kids?"

"Sure," Miles said.

"Excellent. I will call second watch on now to cover. Please wait until we have them here."

Oceana Diplomat Seton looked around the gathering and thought, *The GATS smell blood and mayhem in the water; I wonder how many will be alive come next axis turn.*

Miles said, "Second watch has arrived. We can move now, Sir." With that, Sean and Ula departed the gathering.

SIX
Phoenician

Phoenician Ambassador Europa watched as Oceana Diplomat Seton left the diplomatic gathering.

Hmm, scuttling off to confer with your masters to the news from the FOLK.

Europa was thinking hard. *The FOLK presentation was very interesting. They are playing a very dangerous game in the arena of politics. On one hand, they are offering technology that will keep the Oceana people from buying our grains at a very nice profit for us and limiting our ability to wield the food club at them. On the other hand, they are gearing up a for world conflict. They offer upgraded capabilities for night actions for our farms and forests on the border with New World and the Romans. They must see a conflict coming. They need trade to survive in the lifestyle they like, so why the three headed hydra coming from them now? Hmm, the FOLK might be peaceful, but their pet NESS are not. My sources told me of the action just before we left New Hope; the NESS showed their capabilities.*

The Republic assault team was one of the best and the NESS had them for lunch, so they are extremely dangerous and my people have no clue as to their true abilities. She made a mental note to get more research on the NESS. *We also share the northern continent with New World and Romans and those two are at each other's throats. That keeps them ours for money, so even if the rumors are true for a peace initiative, we are going to gain more trade since, war or peace, it is still expensive, which is very good for my business. How can I keep the conflicts going? What idiots can I manipulate?*

Undersecretary Swellings noticed that Phoenician Ambassador Europa was currently alone.

She is beautiful, he thought. *Her dossier picture does not do her justice, but let's see what she thinks of the FOLK initiatives.*

Phoenician Ambassador Europa noticed Undersecretary Swellings approaching and thought, *Ahhh, my newest idiot; may the gods be on my side tonight.*

"Undersecretary Swellings, it is nice to see you. How are you doing?"

He bowed. "Very well, I have a new assignment starting next year."

"I have heard a rumor that you will be the next ambassador to New Hope for the FOLK enclave."

Undersecretary Swellings thought, *She is very well-informed. The former Ambassador Sir Felling was being held incognito for this voyage, the PM was not happy with the FOLK diplomatic protest, along with a body and parts of several bodies being tossed around in broad daylight for the diplomatic street to watch in our enclave, most embarrassing for Ambassador Sir Felling.*

"It is not official, yet, but I have been told my resume is being looked at for the replacement. It's too early, but thank you for your insights."

Europa smiled to herself. *He is young and nice looking. I wonder what he would look like with no clothes on. I might be able to peel that orange in due time.* "So," Europa asked, "what do you think of the FOLK initiatives?"

Undersecretary Swellings thought, *I have to watch her. She is has been in the game for almost 10 axis turns since her husband was killed by the Outcasts.* "Well, I think it is great for their favored 'yes people', but for the rest of us, not much. The FOLK will steam roll you down to a smooth surface so you're the road for their commerce," he answered her.

Europa thought, *I like this young man, honest, forthright; it will be fun on this voyage.*

Undersecretary Swellings thought, *I am going to have some fun tonight* as Europa lead him out to one of the armored wings to discuss his point of view.

Europa draped across Zacarias Swellings' chest, playing with his chest hair while they were in her suite. Smiling in the dark, she thought, *A very nice orange to peel* as she rolled on top of him. Phoenician Ambassador Europa started putting on her work outfit, which was a nice silk blouse and pants set with matching sandals and an embroidered jacket with her family's crescent on it. When Zacarias nibbled on her neck, she sighed, *Well, I can be late for breakfast.* Zacarias lifted her onto her bed.

Ambassador Destroses' detail was waiting for her in the hallway. She noticed they had not even raised an eyebrow when Zacharias left the suite. Nicolas, her head of security just plodded down the hall to the breakfast wing reserved for her diplomatic people.

Sipping her coffee, her cousin came over and plopped down into the chair with her notes on the FOLK initiatives. Europa looked at Grace and thought, *Hmm, I wish she was grace in motion, but my cousin has as much grace as a bog hunter. Oh well, she is a good accountant; numbers are her game.*

Europa asked, "Well, Grace, what do the numbers tell you?"

Grace looked at her notes and cleared her throat. "If the FOLK initiatives go through, we will be broke in under 5 axis turns; all the families from imperial to common merchants."

"How?"

"Well, as you know, we trade worldwide, but our main revenue is in gold and silver, the imperial houses. We have the largest mine deposits in the world. We manipulate the reserves, so demand is high for a scarce commodity."

Europa nodded. "We are one of the imperial houses. I have the figures, but what is different this time?"

"With the FOLK trading directly with technology, it bypasses the money houses that we control. It basically cuts the middle men out, namely, our interlocking Phoenician banking system."

"Well, that is just lovely," Europa exclaimed as she looked at Grace, but Grace was oblivious to her cousin's rage.

She snickered in her mind, *Serves you right, you old hag. Sleeping with pretty boys has dulled your mind. May the gods sweep you into the ocean for the GATS to feed on your bones.* Grace continued. "As I said, we will no longer be solvent. Whoever the FOLK have in their business modeling group is very sharp; we should hire them." She smiled at her cousin and thought, *Take that, you hag.*

Phoenician Ambassador Europa's hand swept the coffee cups onto the floor as her rage burst out for a few seconds. When she sat down, she had control and looked at her cousin and said, "No, Grace, we will not hire the FOLK for anything. Is that clear?"

Grace's smile dropped. "Sorry, Europa, I was just getting all the information out."

"I know, Grace, so go work the numbers with our best banking brains. We have to get over, around or through this trap."

She looked for the waiter. As she approached, she said, "I am sorry for the mess. Could I get another setting for more coffee?" The waiter rushed into the kitchen for another setting.

Europa pointed to her cousin, Michele, and approached her. Michele asked herself, *Now, what does the GAT want this time?*

Europa told her, "Please, ask Undersecretary Swellings if he could come and have coffee with me, and see if Ambassador Sir Felling could avail himself, too."

FOLK Mia came back with the coffee and a new setting for the ambassador. She smiled as she set up the arrangement. She planted the Omni-directional recording flower vase on the table then swept the fragments from the first vase, coffee cups and saucers into her pan. She was back in the kitchen when she pocketed the sliver plastic recording device into her work pants. She smiled to herself. It was nice, not to be noticed, just a faceless worker. When she was called to clear the ambassador's table, she pulled the whole setting off, brought it in for cleaning and then pocketed the other recorder.

FOLK Mia went off shift, got some lunch and went to her quarters. She pulled the bunk curtains for privacy and placed the two plastic devices on her neck. She AI'd her friend, *Ready for transfer.* She nodded in her mind and the information flowed to her FOLK people. Once the information was sent, the slivers broke down and became dust. She smiled. She liked the duty. Once docked, she could sunbathe and get some swimming in on the fabulous beaches. The men would chase her on the beach, but she would be busy hunting men in the casinos; she liked taking their money at the gaming tables. That was always fun, but she had no interest in men.

Her girlfriend AI'd while laughing, *Yes, you will never change.*

Nope. Do you want something while I am here?

No, you just be safe, my love. She smiled as she fell asleep.

Undersecretary Swellings, after talking to Phoenician Michele, went back to the suite. He asked security to bring out Ambassador Sir Felling. The ambassador approached, his chains rattling and the mouth gagged, as was proper for someone who had almost gotten them into a shooting war with the NESS FOLK.

Undersecretary Swellings said, "Roger, we are removing the gag. You will not speak, just listen. If you do not, we will throw you off this ship. Do you understand, Roger?" He nodded yes. When the security detail removed the gag, Undersecretary Swellings told them to retire to the next room and close the door. When they were gone, he spoke.

"I am with the Intelligence Service. The samples Elizabeth gave you are based on common blood, so the expense, time and effort has not brought us closer to the NESS technology and has alerted them to a higher state of readiness. The NESS and FOLK smashed our intelligence network; we lost all of our cells, due to your lack of vision.

"Your cousin, Elizabeth, played you. So, Roger, your life will be over once we reach home. You are going to be thrown into a very deep prison cell. If you are lucky, you might get out when you're a very old man, but you are going to do one last service for us. I will not go into details, but you have been requested for a coffee with Phoenician Ambassador Europa. You are attending, but you are sick, so the doctor is going to anesthetize your throat and wrap your mouth in a cough cloth. You will listen and take mental notes. We have documented proof that you have a photographic mind, so when the chat is over, you will come back here and write your notes down, along with your impressions. Roger, are you going to do this?"

He nodded yes.

"You have five minutes to get showered, dressed and ready. Can you do that, Roger?"

He nodded yes again.

Undersecretary Swellings called the detail in. "Get Roger ready; he has one last performance to do for our country."

After the ambassador was all cleaned up, he was escorted to Phoenician Ambassador Europa's chambers. She greeted Undersecretary Swellings and Ambassador Sir Felling at her table. "Please sit. Would you like something to drink, Undersecretary Swellings?"

He answered, "Please, some coffee."

"And you, Ambassador Sir Felling?

He just shook his head and pointed to his throat.

Phoenician Ambassador Europa got to the point. "The folk have proposed several items that might interest you since you had a misunderstanding at your compound and missed the presentation."

Undersecretary Swellings said, "Yes, it was very unfortunate that the incident happened. A rogue element was not happy with our government and tried to lay the blame on our government's doorstep. We are pursuing that line of inquiry and at the next opportunity, we will give our answer to the FOLK accusations."

Phoenician Ambassador Europa smiled and thought, *Yes, that is a line of GAT poop, but very well done. Hmm, seems Zacarias is a lot more than undersecretary.*

"I am sure a solid answer to the FOLK accusation will be finalized and your country returned to New Hope next year," she said. "So, in that light, here is a copy of what was presented to the select few. I would be most interested in your analysis."

Undersecretary Swellings sipped his coffee and thought, *Phoenician Ambassador Europa is very sharp. Why would she help us now that the Phoenicians are interlocked with each other? So, what has them running around like they are being chased by GATS* . He looked through the document. *Hmm, I am not a financial wizard, but it is always financed with Phoenician.*

Undersecretary Swellings said, "I think we should take this to our suite and look this over, don't you agree, Ambassador Sir Felling?" He nodded in agreement. "Phoenician Ambassador Europa, would you like to dine at 20:00 hours tonight? I am sure we can bring some insight along with us, if that is acceptable."

"Yes, most acceptable. Until then."

Undersecretary Swellings and Ambassador Sir Felling stood up and bowed to Phoenician Ambassador Europa and they left the dining room. Phoenician Ambassador Europa thought to herself, *Let the GATS of war loose; this is going to get interesting in a very short time.*

Undersecretary Swellings, looking at Ambassador Sir Felling, said, "What's your analysis? Do you think they will be broke in five axis turns?"

Roger nodded yes.

"Hmm, so what do you think they want, Roger?" He pointed at the last paragraph that contained the line, 'total annihilation of the NESS and FOLK, along with their allies.' "Will they finance it totally?"

Roger nodded again.

"That is a lot of money." Roger pointed to the line, 'estimated wealth column.' Undersecretary Swellings exclaimed, "Jesus, it would take 50% of their total wealth, a significant dent in their bottom line."

Roger nodded. He pointed to the very bottom to a place he had highlighted.

"They will make it all back by 20 axis turns after the war with agreements made with us and our allies."

Undersecretary Swellings and Ambassador Sir Felling met Phoenician Ambassador Europa for dinner on schedule. They were just finishing the third course of dinner when she asked, "I see your analysis is correct, so if we have an understanding of the same goals, would the Republic be interested in further negotiations with Phoenicians?"

Undersecretary Swellings looked at Ambassador Sir Felling who nodded. "It seems that we are interested, so once we dock, would you like a diplomatic reception set up in Oceana Neutral Section House for discussions?"

"That would be most agreeable. Let's say in one month then. Our staffs can do the detail work."

Undersecretary Swellings smiled and continued the small talk. It was a most pleasant dinner and he understood that his future would be set if he could get this accomplished without getting killed.

GIFT was mind cruising in the deep ocean when it blended with a six fin predator. *Hmm, she is very pregnant and she is very hungry.* As it looked through her mind, it noted, *Her offspring might have mind capabilities in several million axis turns. Let's see if she understands tools.*

Undersecretary Swellings and Ambassador Sir Felling were walking on the armored glass promenade deck, getting some fresh air after the dinner. Undersecretary Swellings told him, "This might get you a reduced sentence, so just keep it up and do not disappoint me… or I will kill you. I will need to call in favors from some friends when I talk to my council. Since I have lots of dirt on the rulers of my country, to clear the slate, they will sanction your death. You are a walking dead man now."

Undersecretary Swellings and Ambassador Sir Felling's smile faded when the warning alarm suddenly blared, indicating that there was an attack. Undersecretary Swellings swung around to look at the ocean and he saw a very large, six fin predator leap from the ocean and roll in midair before it smashed the armored glass with a very large rock gripped in one of it sucker tentacles. The rock shattered the armored glass and the tentacle propelled itself onto the promenade deck. It then dropped the rock and used the hook on the end of its sucker to dig into the wood deck; this allowed a second tentacle to whip onto the promenade deck.

Ahhh, crap, Undersecretary Swellings thought. *It holed the friggin armored glass.*

He ducked and leaped over the damn boulder as the second sucker pad swung above his head to slither along until it latched onto Ambassador Sir Felling. The six fin screamed its pleasure with its catch of prey by driving its spikes through the ambassador. As it yanked the sucker back, the curled ends hooked into the ambassador's back. He started screaming as he was pounded mercilessly into the deck.

Undersecretary Swellings ran and kept running until he was out of range of the tentacle, then he turned to watch what would happen. The second tentacle pulled Ambassador Sir Felling out through the hole in the armored glass, waved him around in the air and then stuffed him into its mouth. Bones audibly snapped above the noise of the ship and the predator's screaming coughed blood into the air from the six fin mouth. Undersecretary Swellings said, "Jesus" as he crossed himself.

The crew came onto the deck with guns, but before they could get set, it grabbed a crewman and pounded him into the deck. It pulled him out, waved him around and ate him, too. When the crew got over the shock of what was going on, they opened up at the holding tentacle. The bullets just bounced off the armor. The lead seaman screamed, "Shoot the wood deck!" The wood disintegrated and the six fin predator lost its grip and slid back into the ocean.

GIFT stayed blended with the six fin predator. It noticed that its hunger had been abated and she was pondering the rock solution to surface food. GIFT reflected. *Hmm, this will be fun. I will tag her and her offspring with this knowledge. Let's see if the human Darwin was correct about the fittest will survive.*

Undersecretary Swellings thought, *Well, that saved us the cost of prison for Ambassador Sir Felling.* He smiled, *Once we kill the NESS and FOLK and their allies, the Phoenician are next on that list. We will have the war machines and tooling in place for total domination.* With that, he returned to the suite to make a report for his country's preparation for war.

Phoenician Ambassador Europa thought, *Well, we are almost in Oceana. I think I will get some sun.* She sat down and took in the warmth from the sun. *Oh, yes, the tropics. Not a bit of cold water to be found unless it is in the drink, which is empty.*

She waved her glass in the air and an attendant came over.

"Would you like another?" he asked.

Phoenician Ambassador Europa smiled and answered, "Please, more ice this time."

Phoenician Ambassador Europa sipped her second drink and she gave barely a thought to the fate of Ambassador Sir Felling.

Oh, well. Undersecretary Swellings had been extremely fun that night. *Yes, danger is an aphrodisiac.*

Ambassador Destroses was walking the promenade deck when he passed the patched armored glass hole.

I wonder how in the world the six fin predator thought of a rock.

As he passed Phoenician Ambassador Europa, he smiled and nodded. *Too bad the six fin predator did not grab her. I bet she would have given the six fin a run for its own life.*

Eric was thinking about his first outing as he waited with Samantha for Ambassador Destroses. They were at the electric trolley stop for her housing area and he looked over at Samantha. He told her it had been a very beautiful day and that he really enjoyed spending it with her. Samantha studied his face as the setting sun played shadows with his features. She liked what Eric had in him. Plus, he made her laugh. It had been a very long time since she felt this way about anyone.

Samantha smiled to herself. *Well, scientist, let's see if his kiss fires me up.*

"Eric?" Samantha asked, "Can I give you some personal information about me?"

Eric smiled. "Whatever you tell me, I will never repeat it until you say I can. Is that fair?"

"Yes, my stop is here. I would like to invite you into my house for tea. Is that acceptable to you?"

Eric surprised by the offer answered, "Yes, it is, but I am a stranger to your customs. Is it all right to be alone with you?"

"Yes, it is. Shall we go?"

The two walked to Samantha's house. When Samantha opened the door into her house, Eric noted several pictures on her wall. *Ahhh, she has a daughter and husband,* he thought. God smacks the sinful in thoughts, but he was very interested about Samantha's information and her invitation. *I hope her husband will not take offense at me for my being here with his wife alone.*

Samantha sat down at her kitchen table and poured the tea into his cup. Samantha smiled and said, "Eric, in my society, it is all right to be alone with a woman." He nodded and she could see his relief.

"I am grateful," he said. "I saw the pictures on the wall; you have a very nice family."

"Yes, my husband was a NESS; Robert was his name. He was killed 4 axis turns ago in the line of duty."

Eric could see the pain in her face *and he kicked himself for dredging up the memories for her.* He closed his eyes and asked God for forgiveness. He nodded, "So, you are a widow now, Samantha?"

She nodded. "But I have my daughter, Joy. She is nine years of age now and she has a lot of her father in her; Joy's eyes are Robert's." Samantha smiled. "My daughter will be here shortly. She is very intelligent and sweet. She was curious about you and your countrymen. Would you like to meet her?"

Eric smiled. "It would be an honor."

"Alright, more tea?"

Eric watched Samantha in the sunlight. *I wonder if she even knows how exotically beautiful she is. In my country, she would be sought after for businesses to endorse their products. I am very lucky she is talking to me.* He asked about her work, her life with Robert and her daughter, Joy. She answered all his questions and shared her life with him in her kitchen.

Joy heard her mom talking to someone when she got home. Her inner voice was shaky, so she had to talk in the outer speech. She had another bad day at the FOLK school. The teaching was based on inner voice knowledge. It was literally dumped into their minds and absorbed like a sponge. Her teachers told her that she was falling way behind the other students. The teachers were also very concerned about her handicap. Full GIFT would be on her after she reached puberty and it might kill her if her inner speech was not working.

Joy came in the kitchen and Eric was amazed. She looked like her mom, but she had some NESS color patterns to her skin. All in all, she looked like a normal nine-year-old kid except that her head was bigger and her eyes were large and colored with a deep, emerald green that radiated intelligence.

Joy smiled at him and asked, "Are you Eric?"

He smiled. "Yes. I am Eric Stein from New World."

She looked at her mom and said, "This is the one I saw in my dream."

"Your dream?" Eric asked.

"Yes, I was doing my Quantum physics." She pulled out her notebook and showed it to him. It was very neat and orderly, but the equations made no sense to him. He had made it to geometry in school and that had been a struggle for him. "Then, Dad appeared to me and said you would be good for Mom and me. Are you?"

"I am confused. I have just met you, yet you have seen me?"

Joy nodded. "Yes. In my equations, we exist in discrete time or Many Worlds. In this theory, whenever a measurement takes place, the entire universe divides as many times as there are possible outcomes of the measurement. All universes are identical except for the outcome of that measurement. I think GIFT exists in this realm, so I see my dad or any one of him in an infinite number of universes, but the cool thing my equations say is that we can jump to any number of universes. Since they have discrete time for each of them, we just have to tune the frequencies since each universe resonates in and out of phase state to each other."

Joy looked at him, climbed into his lap and started her homework. Eric was speechless. As he looked over her shoulder, the equations just flowed from her with no hesitation or erasing. It looked complete to him. Eric understood that he was watching a genius working. He looked at Samantha and asked, "Can I have more tea? I think I will be here for a while."

Samantha put her daughter to bed after dinner. Joy insisted on sitting in Eric's lap throughout the evening.

"I'm sorry, my Joy is different. She normally does not sit in strangers' laps."

"Joy seemed normal to me. Her mathematics made no sense to me, even as she explained it, but math has never been really strong with me. I had to pull my shoes off to count past ten in school."

Samantha laughed and said, "Well, I am a trained scientist and my math is solid, but this is very high order mathematics. So, I asked her if I could get a copy and take it the physics professors to see if they could use it for their courses."

"And?"

"Well, they fell on the floor, laughing. 'This is gibberish,' they told me. She has no proof. The numbers look good, but we cannot even test the theory to see if it would work, so it is gibberish to us and to the physics departments."

Samantha huffed. "I was very pissed. My daughter's IQ is off the charts. We cannot even measure it in mathematics for her. I came home and told Joy they did not believe her and she told me that it wasn't a problem. She came back later with a shopping list, asking me

to buy the materials on the list. It was quite extensive, but very common. So I did. My Joy just finished building it last month. Can I show you what she built for me?"

"Sure."

"Follow me."

She went to the back door and down into the basement. She pointed at four small platforms lined up.

"Eric, see that switch? Throw it." Eric did and he felt a pressure hit him suddenly then disappear. "I am going to step on each platform. Watch." She stepped on the platform. "Now watch this."

She turned and leaped at the next one. Eric's mouth dropped open. As Samantha moved, she slowed down, only to reappear on the second platform, but he could see her on the first in mid leap. On the second platform, her clothes had changed. She was in a city, but not on this planet. She smiled at him and stepped again on the third platform. She was dressed in heavy clothing with winter all around her. On the fourth platform, she was in a jungle and she waved. Then, he saw her step out of thin air dressed as a FOLK in her basement.

Samantha smiled at Eric and stated, "What you are seeing is me in several universes." Eric was speechless. She threw the power switch off and said, "My Joy just built a proof of concept machine for me."

Samantha led Eric back up to the kitchen where he sat down and murmured, "Jesus."

Samantha nodded. "Yes, that sums it up. Would you like something stronger than tea?"

"Yes."

Samantha smiled. "My Robert liked this rum drink." She poured some in two glasses and held hers up to his glass. "Cheers."

Eric sat contemplating what he had just been shown. He looked at Samantha who said, "Joy explained to you about being in phase. Well, I was in each universe, but not really in this one or the surrounding universes either, so I exist somewhere in between. Plank time."

"What the hell is Plank time?"

"One Plank time is the time it would take for a photon travelling at the speed of light to cross a distance equal to one Plank length. Theoretically, this is the smallest time measurement that will ever be possible, roughly 10^{-43} seconds."

Eric held up his hand and said, "My math ability is with my shoes off my feet. Can you explain it so I can understand it?"

Samantha laughed. "When you see rain hitting water in a pond, the one drop makes a circle. This circle expands at a certain time rate. This is you. Now, my raindrop lands, let's say 8 inches away, but at a different time. When my circle intersects your circle, it forms an interference pattern. They blend and form a new pattern. Joy's machine grabs this new interference pattern and creates a stable universe at that frequency. When you saw me, I was on this plane, but at different frequencies, so there are different outcomes from an infinite number of possibilities."

"JESUS! She built a portal to other universes for our planet?"

"Yes, she solved the issue and is going further with her mathematics for us. It opens up vast potentials for us in this universe." Samantha suddenly looked frightened. "I am scared for my daughter. She is a child prodigy. I have seen her notebook and she has other machines designed and, to my core, I know they would work, too. I have not shared this with anyone except you."

Eric looked at Samantha. "Please look at me," he said, as he set the glass down on the table. "I am a stranger, but what you have shown me scares me, too, Samantha. I will not say a word to any person as long as I live, but... I am honest with people, so here goes. I find you very attractive. As a matter of fact, I find you stunningly beautiful, and so I want to know what is it you want from me? I am not handsome, nor rich, and I am a low-level diplomat who barely makes it in my country."

"When I saw you the first time, my heart beat faster. You are handsome to me," she said, smiling. "As a matter of fact, my mind was asking me about how you would look naked under me. So, I took a chance on you, Eric. My daughter had a vision in which she saw you. She said you would make us happy. And I trust my daughter's judgment. I am black in my country, but it makes no difference. We are FOLK, but your country does not allow this to happen; you are blond, white and part of the ruling regime."

Samantha could see Erik's shock on his face and she smiled a little. "I find you very attractive, but I am hiding from life since Robert died. So, I showed you my daughter to see if her abilities, her looks or mine would matter to you. From my observation of you, it does not matter. I would like to kiss you to see if there is anything between us. I am not loose with my feelings and body, but before you go home, I would like a kiss from you."

Eric smiled. "I would like that very much." His heart was trip hammering in his chest as she approached him. He stood up, gently put his hand around Samantha's waist and pulled her to him. As she made contact with him, Samantha tasted Eric's lips on hers and she thought, *Oh yes.*

Eric thought the same thing as they broke apart. He was sweating and he was also getting aroused.

Damn it, go back down. Samantha took notice of his response. She grabbed his hand and led him to her bedroom. Eric's hands were shaking as he stood before her. She smiled as she started to undress him.

"Are you afraid?" she asked. He admitted that he was and she smiled. "Well, it might help if you got my shirt buttons started."

He laughed. "Sorry." He started with the top button and worked his way down. He gently pulled the shirt off her and dropped it to the floor. He let his hands snake down her body and he worked her pants down around her ankles. She stepped out of them and stood before him in her underwear. Samantha smiled as she dropped her bra and underwear on the floor. He was amazed. Her figure was stunning and he let his eyes travel along the flat planes of her muscles down the curves of her body.

"Do you like me this way?" He nodded and smiled. She looked down at the bulge in his pants. She smiled and looked into his eyes as she stripped his shirt off of him, then pulled his pants and underwear off him. "Let's go to bed, Eric."

They took two steps and got into the bed. "I like it nice and slow. It has been a long time for me, Eric. Can you do that for me?"

"Yes," he answered.

Joy got up the next morning and slowly opened her mom's door. She saw Mom and Eric asleep. Eric had his arms around her mom. Joy smiled and went to go get breakfast. She had more equations to solve before she would go play dolls with two of her best friends.

Eric smiled at Samantha who smiled back at him. As the door closed, she rolled him on top of her. She nibbled his ear and he whispered, "Can we try that golden thread thing, again. I promise not to scream this time." She extended the golden threads and Eric's toes immediately curled.

"Like that?" Samantha whispered in his ear, He smiled and said, "Yes." Samantha thought, *This is very nice.*

Eric smiled and thought, *Samantha is my life and Joy just gives wonders. My country can go take a swim with a GAT, for all I care, with the NEO laws about who I can marry in our world. The FOLK have accepted my citizenship and I have a diplomatic ID, now, for them. I will be very careful. The thumper does not care if it's a lunatic, it just wants to eat you and NEW World is a thumper.*

Eric Stein was waiting for Ambassador Destroses as he finished his morning walk on the aft deck. Ambassador Destroses asked, "Morning, Eric, how are you today?"

Eric replied, "I am fine so far, but I have concerns with the proposal that you handed me."

"The NESS FOLK understand from the sea battle that it was a mistake and they don't want to make future mistakes for your nation or theirs."

"It is not a NESS and FOLK issue. As I said to you, we would like to trade the equipment for more food from your country for at least 12 axis turns until we get the country back to normal production levels."

Ambassador Destroses offered, "Yes we can help you out, but we are asking for at least three axis turns from your country to refrain from aggression on the northern continent."

Eric Stein sighed. "That is the problem. The Romans will not settle for protracted peace in my lifetime."

"I am working on the Roman's issue. It is early for optimism, but it might come about, so please, take my recommendations to your council. The Republic cruise liner, Traveler, will dock at Oceana capital Poseidon tomorrow. We would hope to hear from your council in the coming month since we have to go to the fishing grounds in my country and will be out of touch from then until winter sets in. So, till then, peace."

As Ambassador Destroses walked away from Eric Stein, Phoenician Ambassador Europa thought, *what is that idiot proposing to the New World?*

SEVEN

Roman

Equestrian Lucius Rutilius Sura watched the Republic cruise liner, Traveler, docking at Oceana capital Poseidon on the major quay, Dolphin. *My people have arrived from New Hope enclave. I wonder what word they have brought about the NESS and FOLK answer to our request for assistance from the damage of the war.*

Equestrian Lucius Rutilius Sura wore the tunic with narrow stripes, along with his Toga, which made him stand out in the crowd, showing in the posture and status as a Roman. His guard was dressed in modern garb: desert shorts, shirt, light boots, along with built-in body armor and assault rifles. Many people gave them a wide berth on the quay since Romans were considered very touchy or crazy; it depended on which nation group you talked to.

Equestrian Appius Marcius Milo disembarked. He was overjoyed with the weather, that was warm and pleasant, and he had finally thawed out enough to put on his traveling tunic with narrow stripes, along with his Toga.

Ah, proper clothing, finally, he thought as he saw his friend and comrade in arms waiting for him. Both smiled and gripped each other's arms. "Welcome Appius! I see you have finally thawed out enough to wear proper clothing,"

Appius laughed. "Yes, being warm takes precedent over form."

Equestrian Lucius Rutilius Sura replied, "I have brought the steam car to take us to the villa and your guards will be properly outfitted when we reach the villa."

"Good, the NESS and FOLK are extreme in their no weapons; it is a strange concept to wrap my mind around, but it works for them. Lucius, on the voyage..."

Lucius whispered, "Not here, my friend," as he nodded toward the shadows. "They have ears and eyes."

Oceana was a tropical climate with easy swimming beaches, along with world renowned tropical fruits, so it was a vacation destination for the moneyed people of New Earth.

Equestrian Lucius Rutilius Sura handed a cup of Roman wine, chilled to perfection, to his friend. They both sat back in the steam car, enjoying the people and scenery. Equestrian Appius Marcius Milo commented, "These are very soft people, but the bikinis make it bearable." They both laughed and waved at the women.

Arriving at the villa, the security team swept the villa for security risks to the Equestrians, and then proceeded to open the arms room to outfit the secondary security team for second watch.

Equestrian Lucius Rutilius Sura called out to his houseman, "Set up a late night meal at 18:00 hours. Tell my wife and children that I will expect them, too."

Milo looked at his friend and asked, "Shall we take a bath and relax in the steam room?" Lucius nodded to his headman to get it done, too.

Appius looked at his friend Lucius in the steam room. The heat was forcing the poisons from their bodies while also relaxing the Romans. Appius put some more water on the heated rocks and continued with his report.

"The NESS and FOLK will trade with us for converting saltwater to fresh water technology on an industrial scale. This would meet all our needs for our people. With this system, we will not have to depend on the New World letting a trickle of water out of the mountains from their accursed hydro dams for our agriculture."

Lucius thoughtfully nodded. "Yes, that would give us a very good break from continuous war with New World."

They both knew that this last war for control of the mountainous regions water resources was devastating to their country. "Whole regions were laid to waste; many indentured servants had left the farms, been freed by the New World, or had run away to be only food for the native predators."

Lucius asked, "What do the NESS and FOLK want in return?"

Appius said, "They want us to deliver in several areas, but the two that matter are no warring with New World for 12 Axis turns, and that they want this phosphorus, arsenic, selenium or tellurium anions and iron delivered to our docks in vast quantities within three months for FOLK ship transport."

"Well, I have full senate authority to make treaties and we still have the mines and railroads intact, so we can deliver, but I do not see how the NESS and FOLK can get the water systems online."

Appius smiled. "I went to see a ship that the NESS and FOLK had on hand for water. It can produce 20 million liters of water a day, so based on the agriculture and people, we would need four ships until the FOLK have the land based units online in six months."

"I take it they have these ships already?"

"Yes and they can be at the docks two weeks from signing the treaty with New World. What about the land units?"

Milo answered, "They have the modules on hand."

Lucius asked, "Modules?"

"Yes. They are buildings, prefabricated and ready to turn up. They called it a production line system; it was amazing to watch. So, we would need a pipeline built to the aqueduct system from the dock. That's about 10 kilometers, which is very easy for us to do. The legions can get that going and, by my calculations, have it ready in two weeks."

Lucius smiled and said, "Yes, we will finally get a break to get our own houses in order."

They both smiled. They could rebuild their estates and acquire more estates from the death sales from the war. Seems they would be in the mining and water businesses in short order, along with their patrons in the senate.

Equestrian Lucius Rutilius Sura's dinner was a Roman feast to welcome his friend back from the wilds. His wife, Lucia Rutilius Sura, looked at her husband and contemplated what he had told her in their cubiculum. *Hmm, Lucius is looking at just the now, but what do the FOLK and NESS really want from us?* She closed her eyes and started the mental training regime. She had been taught by her Celtic people and had taught all their children, as well.

GIFT heard her call and blended with Lucia. *These Celtics have a very ordered mind; their mental training is outstanding, on par with the NESS and FOLK.* GIFT was watching her mental processes break down the issues with her country. GIFT was very pleased with her; she was doing projections out to five hundred axis turns. *Yes, the program is going nicely with these wild humans.*

GIFT looked deeper at her and at the eggs she carried in her womb. They had been marked and it was now time to tweak them again. GIFT added new and improved strands of DNA that the FOLK and NESS had in them. It then said *hello* to her.

She smiled and asked, *My old friend, what brings you back?*

Life, you have life in you, but it needs your husband, too.

Yes, he will be very fun tonight, she said, as she looked at her love.

Lucius looked at his wife. *I love my wife, but she scares the crap out of me when she goes in the damn Celtic trance.* As she opened her eyes, he could see the color change in her pupils, gold flecks appeared. She smiled at him and he felt like a mouse with a cat. *My god, she is going to be a handful tonight after the feast.* He sighed. *I sometimes would rather be in combat; it is safer. But, it is very fun, too.*

Lucia had taken Lucius to their cubiculum after the feast. She had built him up during their lovemaking. As she leaned down, she whispered into his ear, "I will have your seed deep in me." He looked at his wife and nodded. Her eyes, the pupils were wide open and the gold flecks had fully expanded. She continued, "We are going to have twins and they will change the course of our world." She smiled at him and whispered, "You and I are not finished."

He smiled and said, "I was hoping you would say that," as he rolled Lucia under him.

GIFT spotted the sperm he wanted to change, so it added the DNA strands that would improve the nerve synapsis, along with the other NESS and FOLK improvements it had in mind for these people.

GIFT smiled at Lucia. *I am leaving now.*

She nodded. *It is alright, my friend; till the next time.* Lucia's orgasm hit a peak, she saw the sperm enter her uterus; the eggs in her womb were in place, waiting. Her husband saw it, too. As his orgasm peaked, she noticed that the gold flecks faded from his pupils. As he collapsed on Lucia's chest, spent and looking at his wife, he smiled.

Definitely worth it.

Equestrian Lucius Rutilius Sura's house in the morning was a riot of noise. Of their five children, three were busy with their studies. His oldest son was being trained in unarmed combat by his free man, Micon, his wife, was taking care of their one-year-old and his friend was lounging at the breakfast table with his newest friend from last night, a stunning Celt from his wife's clan who was in the city for studies at the university.

Lucius nodded at Appius. He had seen his friend in many ways, but not like this. He was totally distracted by Moya. He looked at his Lucia, who smiled and mouthed to him that he was doomed. He laughed.

"Yes, I know that one." As he turned back, Moya kissed Appius. *Yes, he is no longer a bachelor. I see his heart is captured by Moya. Well, I will talk to Lucia about a wedding in the future for my friend.*

Moya turned to leave and her eyes were totally golden with green flecks in the pupils. She smiled and grabbed Appius' hand to walk her to the university. As they left the house, his security team took up positions to cover both of them.

Lucia was breastfeeding their one-year-old. She raised her voice and said, "Lucius." He looked up from his reading of the treaty from the NESS and FOLK. "I think the treaty would greatly benefit all our people and here are the reasons…"

When she finished twenty minutes later, he nodded and said, "Yes, I did the projections out for only 10 axis turns, but my wife has always been on the mark with longer projections."

Lucius thanked the gods every day that his family had had the foresight to set him up in a marriage with Lucia and her clan. The last twenty years had been very happy for him and his house. Lucia nodded.

"Yes, you are very lucky, my husband. My people see into the future. You were picked by us along with your clan; it has been studied, too. You are honest and well-respected in war and business and you love me and I love you, too." Her daughter burped from her breast and she smiled, "Yes, I think the treaty will be very beneficial to our world."

EIGHT

Old World

Oceana diplomatic row hosted every nation or group in this section of the Poseidon capital. They boasted first class accommodation to diplomats as long as they behaved in their capital.

Old World Diplomat, Her Royal Princess Patricia Leonis Minoris, was talking to her general in residence about the upcoming conference for which Oceana Diplomat Seton had sent an invitation scheduled for Friday at the costliest resort in the capital.

General David Centauri informed her, "Our intelligence indicates that all of the major powers are building up armaments, armies, and fleets and stock piling vast quantities of food. Due to our lack of fore-sight since the peace party has been in parliament for the last 31 axis turns, they have cut the budget to less than 1% of GDP for military expenditures. We are going to go under if the world erupts in war; we are not ready, Princess."

Princess Patricia Leonis Minoris thought of her father, Crown Prince Victor Leonis, who had been disgraced 35 axis turns ago by Outcasts. He had not made King and had been asked to step down for the good of the crown. He had accepted on one condition: that he remain the leader of the Royal Marines. His condition had been accepted.

Her marines were the only fighting force in her country that was in-tact. She had continued her grandfather's secret program and she read the books and his journals. She smiled. He was in his 45 axis turn, now and his body was barely functioning, but he was still sharp in his mind. She paid attention to his wisdom.

Princess Patricia Leonis Minoris asked her general, "Can we defend our home waters with what is in the naval fleet and land based home guard?"

General David Centauri answered, "No, princess, since our last ocean battle 32 axis turns ago with Republic, our fleet has been gutted. We have no modern naval vessels, period, so along with the home coast guard, they would be used for target practice before our numerous enemies blew up our coastal cities."

"So, rape, murder, pillaging and slavery would be in store for our 15 million people."

"Yes, Highness, Outcast are hired for this type of butchery. They have experience. They carry very modern warships along with amphibious assaults, they are vicious, have no mercy and are very good. The home guard has maybe 10,000 regular, army personnel and, on paper, we have one million men and women ready for active duty, but who have no combat experience. This, along with antique equipment, means we would suffer massive casualties." He sighed. "Even the Celts could wipe the floor with us in our state of preparedness."

Princess Patricia Leonis Minoris thought, *I knew it. Has my family even listened to the generals? No, they are so wrapped up in self-delusions of greatness that we are going to have our heads chopped off, literally. Damn, parliament just flaps their lips and sucks the money from the treasury to line their own pockets.* General David Centauri watched her beat her chair with her hand.

Princess Patricia Leonis Minoris looked at her general and said, "I know you have plans, General, but what would you suggest? That the treasury is controlled by parliament?"

General David Centauri said, "Your family has wealth, but it is not enough to get even one warship built, so I think we need to get the land forces equipped immediately."

She nodded. "I do control that committee for funding, so what is needed right now?"

"We need to move the old government armaments, tooling factories, and munitions away from the coast; put them into the mountains, literally."

She nodded. "We have old mining tunnels that can be used for this purpose. We can stockpile the raw materials for at least a five axis war production cycle. That includes food storage, too. This is all well and good, but how can we keep this out of the media and keep parliament from knowing?"

"That's easy," he said. "We just tell the parliament we are moving this old equipment to the caves to get rid of it in the proper way. We could use the slogan, 'beating weapons into pruning hooks' and, what is nice is that we can use the home guard to move it during the next month-long exercise."

"Go on."

"We can have the engineering battalions build the complexes to the old tooling machines once they are set up. Your company, Engineering Dynamics, comes in and fully CNC's the facilities with minimum staffing. We can make up to 155mm cannons, but I think if we tool up with heavy infantry weapons, anti-tank weapons, machine guns, mortars, etc., as well as billions of rounds of ammunitions stockpiled in underground bunkers throughout our mountain range, it would be a good start for our country."

Princess Patricia Leonis Minoris said, "Let me see the figures." As she read them she answered, "Yes, this will be very nice, but I have concerns, General. Our people have no combat experience, so how are they going to get this experience?"

General David Centauri answered, "Well, I have read in the history books something called a 'foreign legion'. They are mercenaries, but are controlled by one country, so we put our best officers and enlisted in this legion and loan them out, say to the Balkans. These countries or tribes are ripe for this type of venture; small unit tactics, rough terrain, vicious combatants, and a very deep hatred for any form of government. We will then rotate them back into home guard with a new training regime based on actual combat lessons from the survivors."

Princess Patricia Leonis Minoris said, "I see. We need warriors, not ticket pushers."

Her general nodded. "That is why the Republic kicked our asses. Our armchair admirals sunk our fleet before it sailed out by gross incompetence. They have never been shot at in their entire careers and faced with 16-inch naval shells hitting your ship, they panicked and ran for home."

Princess Patricia Leonis Minoris ordered, "Approach me." When he was eye to eye with her, she told him, "Alright, you will get what you need from me, but do not fail me, General. If my head goes to the block, I will see your family get the head man axe on the oak before I do. You are now in the arena of Kings and Queens; victory or death is the only outcome. Are you in or out General?"

General David Centauri answered, "In, Your Highness."

Princess Patricia Leonis Minoris smiled. "Good, General, you will attend the conference, along with me. Tell your wife that she will be there. No excuses this time."

Princess Patricia Leonis Minoris went to her chambers. She took off the heavy clothing of state and put on her judo outfit. She smiled as she warmed up and thought, *Yes, it is going smoothly for now for the crown.* She spotted her three opponents and launched her attack without warning. The melee lasted one minute.

She had bested two of her three opponents, but when she came to on the floor, her childhood friend, Johnny, smiled at her.

"Not bad, Trish. I got lucky that time," he said, as he helped her up off the floor. Your footwork is good, but not excellent. So, let's begin with that, shall we, Your Highness?"

She nodded as she rubbed her shoulder. *Damn, that is going to bruise.*

Princess Patricia Leonis Minoris' steam car approached the resort. She looked at Johnny. "Well, let's get the show on the road."

He smiled and said, "You are beautiful."

She smiled. "You look handsome to me, but it is all business tonight. I need you very sharp and focused. Our nation depends on what we gather tonight."

Johnny stepped out and held his hand out for Princess Patricia Leonis Minoris to take. The red carpet reporter's newspaper people were snapping pictures and asking a myriad of questions about this diplomatic ball. She nodded and waved as Johnny escorted her into the reception area. General David Centauri waited for her with his wife, Natasha. Both bowed to her. She smiled and said, "Please walk with me." They both fell in behind her.

Princess Patricia Leonis Minoris walked into the ballroom. She noted all the cast of characters were in place. The caller announced their entrance. She smiled and greeted the ambassadors in the line until the last one, Outcast Ambassador Yorktown, bowed to her and smiled.

I have read the history books about Yorktown, she thought. *I am not as stupid as the royal English King George III. His pride got in the way of sound judgment, plus he had bad ministers who played both ends against the middle. These are self-serving bastards like we have now. Once I am in power, I am going to kill our bastards.*

She smiled and said, "Pleasure to meet you, Ambassador Yorktown."

"Pleasures all mine, Princess Patricia Leonis Minoris. I have heard that this is going to be the greatest event of the season."

Trenton Yorktown thought, *This is a very dangerous person to have as an enemy.*

One of her sparring partners was turned by the Outcast when one of his daughters was attacked by the crown regular constables. She was nearly beaten to a pulp. He smiled.

Yes, we paid the cop off for his services then blackmailed him, too, he thought.

Outcasts paid for the hospital recovery, but they wanted favors from him. He gladly gave them the information. He knew he was in their web, but the Outcasts had delivered on his daughter. She had recovered and was walking now.

Princess Patricia Leonis Minoris smiled pleasantly. "Yes, I have heard there will be some announcements that will give us hope in the world for peace." She thought, *Take that, you sack of shit. I will gladly slit your throat in the near future. The Outcast are out for blood and it will not be mine, nor my people's.*

Johnny De Lorne smiled and nodded to the Outcast ambassador. *How did our patrols miss this asshole? I will need to talk to the coast guard; they are asleep at the helm. He should have been sunk or at least hanged. Hmm, hanged would be better. Much slower and I could be the one to pull the lever.*

Trenton Yorktown thought, *Yes, you are a pair, but you will be last. We are going after your country, not you. We will kill the elites using those who do not have a voice in your country, which is about 99% of your beloved people. Oh yes, arming them will be very fun. Mayhem and blood for your average man and women with rage in their hearts. No hope and an empty belly with very modern weapons. 'Tis fun to be released at you. Oh yes, you will be very busy in the near future with a civil war. It will make the old French revolution look like a picnic.*

Equestrian Appius Marcius and Milo Equestrian Lucius Rutilius Sura laughed as they danced with their women. Appius was dancing with Moya; she was stunning. Her long, dark, brown hair was braided down her back and she was wearing a simple evening dress that was open in the back. She had only the Celtic clan emblem threaded through her hair. It showed her totem in a circle; the craftsmanship was stunning, but it dimmed in comparison to her.

She smiled and said, "Well, Appius, what are your intentions with me?"

He smiled and stuttered, "Well... I... oh..."

Moya, laughing, said, "That is what I thought. Just dance; do not think, I will do that for you."

Lucius laughed with Lucia.

"Well, that is that," Lucia stated.

Her husband nodded. "Yes." He might as well surrender now under favorable terms.

"You were very easy in your surrender."

He laughed. "Yes, my parents beat some sense into me. I am slow, but not dimwitted."

Eric Stein had met with Eric Von Liddell, Ambassador Destroses, Diplomat Seton, Equestrian Appius Marcius Milo and Equestrian Lucius Rutilius Sura. The ambassador had read Elizabeth Pameddin's dispatches and recommendations regarding the FOLK treaty with all the parties. It was an open discussion and all parties agreed to the FOLK treaty; it was very fair.

"Yes, all the players are here at the banquet. The people," Oceana Diplomat Seton noted, "everyone, are just finishing the dinner." He stood up, went to the podium and addressed the assembly.

"Ambassadors and dignitaries, ladies and gentleman, I am glad you could all attend and enjoy the final ball for the season. Oceana always strives to meet the best in all areas of human endeavor, so in that light, I would like to make an announcement for our countries and the world."

The crowd went silent.

"I would like to introduce Ambassador Eric Von Liddell from New World. He has some very startling news."

Eric stood up. His left leg was in a leg cast and his left arm was gone. Smiling, he slowly went over to the podium.

He looked at the crowd and said, "I will be brief. As of today, all hostilities have ceased between New World and the Roman Republic." Stunned silence filled in the ballroom. "A peace treaty has been signed for 12 axis turns and extensions, if we so desire.

"Secondly, since both our countries were extensively damaged, our countries have just finished a new business alliance. We would like to gratefully extend a very warm welcome to our new trading partner, the Minions. They have stepped up to help us with our food production for the short and long term. We are very grateful for their concern and generosity.

"Lastly, I also would personally like to thank Secondary Ambassador Eric Stein of the FOLK for his diligence, fortitude and honesty in getting all parties to agree to this binding treaty. He has saved many lives with this very fair treaty. God bless all of you." The whole ballroom exploded with applause.

Ambassador Eric Von Liddell sat down with his wife, Adal. She smiled, grabbed his right hand and said, "Eric, you did the right thing for our people."

He nodded. "Yes, you have read the dispatches from Elizabeth?"

She nodded and said, "Yes, that changed the PM's mind along with the parliament. It finally sunk into our thick heads what she and others had been saying to us all along."

He smiled. "We have dropped the NEO from the party. The die-hards are being rounded up for new services to our country. Railroad work was very dangerous. Now, we have started open elections once again in our country." He looked at his wife and whispered, "It feels like spring to me, the earth smell when I plow the fields for wheat." He sighed. "I miss our farm and children that are still alive."

She studied her husband. He was wounded physically, but mentally, he had changed deeply. He was more introspective, more open to her. She could see his mind and heart now. She liked the change in him.

Adal's prayers had been granted. She had her husband back. Leaning forward, she whispered to Eric, "I want you in my bed tonight."

He smiled. "I am an ugly sight. My wounds, my missing arm…"

His wife smiled. "Tonight, husband." She smiled inwardly when she spotted her husband looking down her dress when she leaned forward. *Yes, I still have it*, she thought while settling in her chair.

That night, Eric smiled to himself. *Well, damn, I did not need that arm anyway.* His wife smiled while lying on his chest. *Yes, I have my wife back.*

"I would like to retire from the service," Eric said. "What are your thoughts on this matter?"

She smiled as she slid closer into his arms and said, "Yes, Eric, I would like that very much. Our life needs rebuilding."

"Yes, I think we will do that, but this is a lot of fun."

She laughed as she threw her shift on the floor. *Oh yes, Eric, you and I are going to practice a lot to perfect this, too, on our farm, my love.*

Eric Stein smiled and went over to the Romans and held out his arm. Equestrian Appius Marcius Milo and Equestrian Lucius Rutilius Sura grabbed him. Eric smiled and stated, "The ships sailed yesterday and the modules have gone into production.

The Romans smiled. "Yes, your minerals have been mined and were shipped. The quantities you have asked for will be waiting. We are very pleased and the Roman senate is very pleased. If you want a posting or a vacation, let us know; we will make it happen."

Eric smiled. "I have just married, so a honeymoon would be nice. What is a horse ride like in the Roman vineyard countryside?"

They all laughed. "That can be arranged, no problem. As a matter of fact, there are land sales coming up. Would you like to bid on one in the vineyard areas?"

"Yes, but I will have to get permission from my wife. He AI'd Samantha, *Well, beautiful?*

I have never, but here is our budget.

Well, maybe we will go for a honeymoon.

Good call, cutie.

He looked around and said, "I will write my wife, then let you know."

The men smiled and thought, *Good call on that one.*

Phoenician Ambassador Europa thought, *I am livid that that son of a bitch, Eric Stein, pulled it off and he is a damn FOLK diplomat. Now, where is my head of Intelligence? I will personally kill her.*

Princess Patricia Leonis Minoris laughed as she saw the look on Europa's face. Johnny De Lorne smiled. *Yes, we have breathing room now.* That faded, however, as he watched the Republic diplomat look at Europa's secondary ambassador. He nodded and she nodded twice. *Those assholes are meeting in two days or two weeks.* He made a note to have the secondary followed. *They are plotting and a lot of people are going to die. Money and weapons walk hand in hand during war.*

Natasha whispered to David, "This was fun, husband. I have not danced with you in a long time."

He smiled and replied, "Yes, it was fun."

As they sat in the closed chauffeured steam car, Natasha smiled, hiked her dress up and slid onto David's lap. "Well, husband, I am going to have you right now."

He laughed and said, "Well, alright," as they threw their clothes out of the window.

The chauffer laughed and thought, *They are at it again.* He took the long route back to the villa.

Natasha smiled in their bed; she was pregnant by David and she liked life. She was almost 13 axis turns of age and this put her at risk for normal humans. However, she was a NESS and internally, she was 7. *Yes, I can still have more children.* She rolled onto David. "Wakey, wakey. I want you."

He smiled and groaned, "Woman, I am tired."

She laughed as she slid down his chest and said, "Not for long."

NINE

Outcast

Natasha was furious at the start of the ball, but it had cooled with the announcement from New World. *Yes, that takes out two of the players, for now,* she thought, but she still hated all the pomp and ceremony, especially royalty pomp and ceremony. Looking at her husband, she thought that he was still good looking and cut a fine figure in his State Tux; he was perfect. *Yes, I should enjoy my visit.*

She grabbed David's hand, smiled and asked him, "Dance?" He smiled and they went out on the ballroom floor.

My husband is wasted on these assholes, she thought, as they waltzed. She knew from experience that these types of people would slaughter him and her without thought, just like they did to her father. He had tried to organize and unionize the dock workers for better wages and benefits in the major coastal cities and had thought that with royalty, it would supposedly help.

Natasha's father's head had arrived in a pickling jar from the royal jail. The label had been to the point: he had been found guilty of Sedition to the Crown. He was used to get the ringleaders, the people who wanted a better future without creating revolution in their country, for all the people. So, her mother was thrown out in the street, their property confiscated and sold and her two brothers and one sister were sent to the orphanage. Natasha had run away, but the Crown had found her trying to escape. She was sentenced to five years of hard labor in one of the small colony islands as a farm hand. She was fourteen years old at that time.

She was chained up on an Old World trader ship, Thumper, a rust bucket of a ship, but the owners were paid to transport crown prisoners alive. How alive was debatable. Natasha's living quarters was a very loud statement as to her place in the world. She was chained to the bulkhead along with 35 other prisoners; all of them ate, pooped and peed in the same spot for three weeks.

When they arrived somewhere, Natasha stumbled out of the hold of the ship into the bright tropical sunshine. They were beat and lead to the dock. The tropical heat hit them and many passed out. The guards used shock sticks to motivate them to get off the ground. She noticed that three prisoners did not move. The guards went for a medico when she arrived and confirmed that they were dead. The guards picked up the bodies and threw them into the harbor. Large eels had a field day with the protein from their bodies; they always hid under the wharf looking for snacks. The prisoners were herded into the jail that was setup for them. Natasha's clothes were cut off. She was washed, her hair completely shaved off, washed again, deloused and given striped work clothes with two round circles containing a cross in each, one circle was located over her heart and the other over her spine; targets for rifle aiming points.

Just great, another lovely day as a slave, she thought. *Well, at least I am eating better food.* It was good and hot for the first three days.

On the fourth day, she was herded into a holding pen. Each prisoner was lead around a corner to the auction block; she could hear bidding going on for each prisoner.

When her turn came, she kicked the jailer between his legs. They released the heavy ankle chains and she made a dash for freedom. She didn't see the shock stick hit her. When she came to, she was being dragged up the stairs then tossed into the middle of the platform where she was chained solidly to the holding rail.

Bidding started at one crown for her. An old planter liked what he saw. He had heard she had kicked the crap out of a jailer by booting his crown jewels to the first moon before being subdued. He laughed to himself and started the bid at two crowns. The bidding went to 10 crowns before he was able to buy her.

Natasha was in the holding cell when Planter Trolling came up to her. He pointed to her and said, "I will make this simple; I just bought you for two axis turns for my plantation. You have an option: you can work in the fields 14 hours a day or work in my house."

Planter Trolling was surprised by her answer. "I will choose the fields!"

He said, "So be it." His head man hit her with a shock stick. When she awoke, her feet had light weight ankle chains, her hands were cuffed and she was tied into the bed of the steam truck slave rail holding bar.

Natasha's life was field work from sunup to sundown and the work sculptured her. She was all angles, no fat and extremely strong. One of the field hands tried to rape her once. She had picked him up, broke his back across her knee and smashed his windpipe so he would not scream in the slave quarters. Looking at the other slaves, Natasha asked, "Does anyone have a problem?"

They all shook their heads no.

She smiled then tossed the body for the scavengers to finish. She remembered her father's unarmed combat lessons. So, when Planter Trolling had found what was left of his expensive missing slave the next day, he was furious. No one knew what had happened, but he could guess. She was hit by three of the devices, but all the field hands had suffered from the shock stick that day.

She was seventeen when her world changed, again. She was sleeping in the slave quarters when she heard thunder. When they all looked through the bars, they could see orange, rolling clouds moving in from the harbor area.

The next morning, they heard heavy clanking sounds coming up the road. They all looked out the window and saw something from a nightmare. They saw bodies draped on the front end of a tank. It was covered in blood and guts and there were trucks of prisoners behind the tanks. They were screaming as the Outcasts cut heads off and threw the bodies into the ditches.

"Outcasts," one of the slaves screamed. She saw the turret swing toward the planter's house and let a shell fly. She laughed as it blew the house apart. Planter Trolling opened up with a machine gun from his bunker. Bullets hit the tank and several trucks; she could see an Outcast get blown off the truck. She laughed. As they got pissed, the tank fired another shell that hit the bunker, but he still kept the machine gun death dance on the Outcasts.

Planter Trolling's head man opened up from the other bunker. The Outcasts were chewed up pretty quick in the trucks, but the tanks began blasting any structure that was standing indiscriminately. She hit the floor as the tank gun swung toward their building. All she remembered was a flash of light then darkness.

Natasha awoke to just a crackling sound. It was dark and she crawled out of the debris and bodies from the slave quarters. She checked herself and found no damage, but she was covered in blood and guts. None of the slaves had survived attack except for her. She looked around and saw Planter Trolling and his head man stretched between two tanks, the Outcasts looking at them, smiling. Both were suspended near a fire pit. She slowly slithered back into the shattered building, draped a body across her, and watched the Outcasts.

The Outcasts were just finishing a pig for supper and had started on the wine they had liberated from Planter Trolling's cellar.

The leader of the Outcasts was talking, saying, "You killed one of my people today. For that, you are going to be roasted, slowly, but before that happens, we have a show for you."

He pointed to the show. His whole family had been lined up between the Outcasts and Planter Trolling. The leader smiled and had him moved to be dangling over the fire pit. The Outcast leader said, "Start the first act." His wife's clothing was cut off her until she was standing naked in front of him. The Outcasts tied her hands and feet and threw her into the fire pit. She screamed in terror as she hit the bottom of the pit; it was still very warm from the embers.

For the second act, his son was thrown on the ground and the Outcast women had fun with him before he was tossed into the pit, as well.

For the third act, his 13-year-old daughter was stripped and the Outcasts laughed while they tied her hands and feet.

"We have mercy in us," they said before tossing her into the tank. Her screaming was cut short.

The Outcast leader hopped on the fighting deck and yelled into the tank, "Is she alive?"

"Yes," a voice came up from the turret.

"We will sell her on the market," the Outcast said. "No touch. She will fetch a very handsome price." He turned and nodded. For the last act, all the rest of the children were tossed into the fire pit.

Then, the Outcasts gathered the furniture and any scrap of wood from the house and tossed it into the fire pit. They pulled Planter Trolling's head back to look at the pit, tied it into place and set the furniture on fire; Planter Trolling's family's screaming did not last long. The Outcast sipped wine from the crystal glasses and watched the show with Planter Trolling. They piled more wood into the fire pit tossed the chairs they had been sitting on, finished the wine and then, for the final curtain, they set the whole plantation on fire.

Starting up the tanks, the Outcast leader looked at the planter, smiled and cut Planter Trolling loose. He fell into the pit, screaming, and the Outcasts' smiles disappeared. He nodded to the other Outcasts, cut the planter's head man down and threw him to the side, while he was still breathing and alive.

"We are leaving you alive," he said. "Say hello to your beloved royalty, from the Outcasts."

Natasha was praying as the Outcasts mounted up. She looked at the area; it looked like hell on New Earth with the flames highlighting them.

He pointed down the road toward the harbor. As the tank came abreast of her hiding spot, it stopped. The Outcast leader jumped off the tank and approached Natasha's hiding spot.

"Natasha Temple, I am your Uncle Zacharias Temple. I have come for you. It took us three years to find you. I have your mom, your sister and brothers on my ships. I mean you no harm. My brother gave you a phrase I will say the first portion to show you that I am your uncle."

"God forbid we should ever be twenty years without such a rebellion.

The people cannot be all, and always, well informed. The part which is

Wrong will be discontented, in proportion to the importance of the facts

They misconceive. If they remain quiet under such misconceptions,

It is lethargy, the forerunner of death to the public liberty.

And what country can preserve its liberties, if its rulers are not

Warned from time to time, that this people preserve the spirit of Resistance?

Let them take arms. The remedy is to set them right as to the facts, pardon and pacify them.

What signify a few lives lost in a century or two? The tree of liberty must be refreshed from

Time to time, with the blood of patriots and tyrants.

It is its natural manure."

Who and where was this said??

Natasha Temple finished it, "Thomas Jefferson (1743-1826) Old Earth date, US Founding Father, drafted the Declaration of Independence, 3rd US President."

Zacharias Temple had tears in his eyes. "I am sorry it took us so long to find you," he said as helped her up and out of the hiding spot.

She nodded. "I am alright, Uncle. My father mentioned you, but never talked about you much. I can see why he did not."

"Yes. I hate doing this, but fear does work on a lot of occasions. Our people are hunted for sport, so being feared has certain advantages to our people."

"I thought I was dead when you shot the slave building."

He laughed. "No, we hit it with a flash bang round then we pulled you out and fired a real round. We then put you back; we had to test you to see if your dad's training had worked. I say it was successful. The slaves you thought were on top of you were locals who condone slavery. He pointed to the tanks. "We have every slave in these tanks. They are free to choose and they have accepted our proposal."

One head popped up and Shelia, the house slave and sex doll, waved at her.

"I am free now," she called out.

She was told to get back inside. Natasha saw the burn marks on her back from the shock sticks and god knows what else as she dropped into a fighting hatch. She knew the bastard and the whole family were perverted.

He pulled her up onto the tank. "We are leaving now. Let's see if we can burn this whole island to the ground."

She went into the tank and saw the planter's daughter. She remembered the taunting and shock stick from this bitch. She smiled at her and whispered, "Welcome slave. You will wish they had killed you." The girl, Terry Trolling, was weeping; she had peed all over herself when Natasha dropped into the compartment and approached her. She knew Natasha would kill her with no effort.

I am dead, she thought as she closed her eyes.

One of the Outcasts shouted, "Hand me a shell, now." Smiling, Natasha turned away from Terry and handed rounds to the crew for the cannons. This act released her from her fury at what had happened to her and Terry Trolling's life was saved, for the time being.

The Outcast tanks rolled up to the quay two days later. The amphibious landing had gone well. They had secured mountains of fuel, food, ammo, weapons, clothing and a large mountain of supplies. These came from the Crown Armory and there was enough to go around. They had secured a half ton of gold and two tons of silver. They had given other slaves a choice.

"Come with us where you are free or stay here to be slaughtered by the Crown." There was no issue; all of them went with the Outcasts.

The locals who were left alive had another show to perform for their king. When the Old World warships arrived, the carnage was unbelievable. Targeting optics from all the task force weapons were ready to deal with whatever had done this. All they saw was utter devastation. Buildings were smoldering and the whole island was in flames. The task force radars showed no ships, nothing. As they approached the harbor, Crown Prince Victor Leonis used his telescope to view the harbor. There were too many flames and too much smoke, so he demanded to go first on the quay with his ship. His captain had asked for caution; the prince almost shot him for his timidity. He pointed to the carnage.

"Timidity?!" he screamed. "You are relieved of command. CO, you are in command. When I return, you will have this crew on war footing. Do I make myself clear?"

The CO snapped to attention, "Yes, Prince."

"Good." He pointed to his guard. "I will go first. I want armor and a full war load kit, now." He stripped and put on his combat fatigues. He then loaded his automatic weapon, jacked a round in the chamber, and ordered, "Kill any thing that is not our citizens. Is that understood?" His royal marines nodded as the battleship locked into the quay. The boarding ramp slammed down into the quay and the prince ran off the ship with his marines.

The prince pointed to the captain and shouted, "Take point, I will follow in the middle."

The captain said, "Company, move and cover."

They moved down the quay; the smoke was very thick in the harbor. The captain, a few minutes later, said, "Shit," over the TACNET. The prince moved up to him. "Sir, you should not see this."

His marines were hardened veterans; they thought they had seen everything in war. They were very mistaken. The marines loved their prince. He risked his life with them on many occasions, so they knew he was the real deal. They tried to shield the prince from the view. The prince said, "Please move." They moved aside.

"My God," he exclaimed as he moved up the quay to the first body. Every Old World citizen was crucified or shot to pieces on the quay. Everywhere he looked, there were bodies of men, women and children.

He said, "Move up. Let's find these bastards."

They approached the end of the quay and found a sign that had been placed on the gate leading to the city. It read, "Dulce et decorum est pro patria mori." The prince was well-versed in Latin; he read the inscription out loud to his marines.

"It is sweet and proper to die for one's country." He turned to his people and said, "Find these monsters and kill them all. They are not far, Captain. You stay, pull the whole battalion with you and secure this island."

"Sir," the Captain answered and he went about his business. For the rest of the day, the prince could hear the APC trucks tanks rumbling from the ship transport from the beach as the marines spread out in the city. He heard the reports, not one citizen had been found alive, yet.

The next day, Crown Prince Victor Leonis sat in the field tent. One of the scout patrols had found a survivor. He went over to the medical tent. Jarvis Meadow was burned badly and the prince asked one of the doctors if he would live. They said, "No, we have made him comfortable with morphine. He would like to talk to you, sir, at your convenience."

Crown Prince Victor Leonis sat down beside Jarvis. Jarvis said, "Sir, I am sorry I cannot rise."

The prince told him, "No problem, Jarvis. Who did this to you?"

Jarvis whispered, "Outcasts, sir. They came in the evening out of the setting sun. They had huge battleships, amphibious ships with assault tanks, APC, artillery and heavy infantry trucks. They overran the Crown Garrison in hours. Five hundred home guard were slaughtered about an hour after the Garrison fell.

"Sir, I was there. Our cannon shots just bounced off the tank armor, sir!" He looked at his prince with wide eyes. "I have seen pictures of these 120 ton tank monsters. I have never seen one in the flesh until now. Just one blew us apart in the reinforced armor bunkers systems in the harbor. Home guard just died in place. The few survivors fell back. I grabbed a steam truck and loaded it with 12.5mm ammo. I wound up back at the plantation." He smiled. "I am not going out without a fight. I opened up with my heavy 12.5mm machine gun. I hit some of the trucks from my bunker, but the damn tanks just blew holes through the bunker, sir, I mean in and out. The concussion knocked me out. When I awoke, I was tied between two tanks along with Planter Trolling, my employer, on his plantation."

Jarvis looked at the prince and said, "Sir, the Outcasts ate a pig, drank wine and put a show on for him." His tears began running down his face. "They threw his family into the fire pit and set it on fire. They had hung him upside down, pulled his head back and tied it in place so that he had to watch his family burn alive under him."

Crown Prince Victor Leonis gasped, "Jesus Christ."

"I am an old man, sir. I have served in the royal marine's honorably giving quarter and mercy when an enemy is defeated, but I have never witnessed this type of savagery in my life."

"I..."

Jarvis interrupted him. "Sir! As one soldier to another, please listen." The prince nodded. "When I was discharged from service, the Crown paid for my education. I was a full professor in history at New Cambridge when I retired. I came out here to write more on my research and work at a slow pace."

He smiled at the prince who thought, *He is hideous, his lips are gone.*

Jarvis continued. "But these Outcasts are the Genghis Khan horde of our world." He looked at the prince, "Have you heard of this group?"

The prince said, "No, Jarvis."

"Sir! On Old World in the old time keeping, they overran and slaughtered most of the known world in less than 20 axis turns in the 12 century AD. This horde utterly destroyed civilizations that had stood for 250 axis turns. They were utterly ruthless. They give no quarter once engaged in battle; it is to the death. An old warning is, 'I will make your cities into my horse pastures'. A country, China, was utterly destroyed by this group; whole cities disappeared to become their horse pastures. Sir –"

Crown Prince Victor Leonis said to him, "Call me Victor."

Jarvis laughed. "Victor, in my shirt, pull out the two books." The crown prince pulled out the 'History of the United States of America' and the other, the 'Life history of Genghis Khan'.

The prince asked, "I have read about the United States. What has that to do with this horde?"

Jarvis coughed before speaking again. "Whoever the leader is has combined the divergent theories. Genghis Khan never lost a battle, war or empire, but he lacked structure for a stable government after his death." The prince nodded. "Royalty always faces this problem with power. The American model is based on individual initiative with very little overhead government. It is a framework that is very easy to address. People need structure and the Outcasts have done this to their culture."

The prince had an "Aha" moment and Jarvis smiled. This was his best lecture and his student was paying attention.

"When the patrol found me, I asked them to get these books. They are yours now." He coughed up blood. "I do not have much time, so listen." He sounded like a sergeant telling a private to pay attention, that what he would say would keep them alive. He said, "At New Cambridge is my thesis and follow up research on the Outcasts, please read it. Look at it critically with these two books. We, as a people, are going to feel the full brunt of the Outcasts first on our world. We control the ocean passages for now, so the Outcasts are contained, but God help us, if we do not prepare for them, they are arming themselves to the teeth and we will be first on their list."

Victor nodded. He looked down at Jarvis's dried blood on the covers.

"Victor, the Outcasts came for only one person. She was an indentured field hand girl named Temple; blond, tall at 6 foot 1, extremely strong, smart and mean as a GAT. She broke the back of another field hand that tried to have fun with her and the shock stick barely worked on her. When we found out who killed the field hand, it took three people to subdue her. She must be important to the Outcasts; they risked ships and lives for her."

Victor nodded. "I will make a mental note on that name. She must be in the records. The Crown was very meticulous regarding prisoners of the Crown."

Jarvis was slipping into the night and he murmured in a weak voice, "Victor, one more point before I go. Do not board your battleship; you will be killed if you do. Our country needs your leadership for the coming wars." And a second later, he was gone.

Crown Prince Victor Leonis stood up, stood at attention and saluted. He turned to his aide and said, "Bury Royal Marine Jarvis Meadow with full honors."

Crown Prince Victor Leonis put the books in his war pack and went back to the quay. The reports had come in: no survivors, over 3,500 Old World people; men, women, and children had been butchered and almost 10,000 indentured people had disappeared with the Outcasts.

On the third day, he sat beside the blown-up warehouse near the quay, eating lunch and drinking some water with his marine, Captain Charles Dunkley. He was looking at his warship, Blue Whale it was called. He laughed and thought, *Yes, but it is my deadly blue whale.* He pondered what Jarvis had said to him.

He noticed the pompous captain with all his gleaming medals on the ramp. He pulled his binoculars out and focused on him.

"Shit," he murmured.

His Captain said, "Sir!!" He stood up. "I had relieved that idiotic captain who let him out of the brig. I will court martial the jailer and then, hang him and then I..." Crown Prince Victor Leonis' Blue Whale warship suddenly exploded in his face. Both he and his captain were slammed into the warehouse.

Outcast Neil Kidd smiled. Being severely wounded, his life was over, but his family's was not. After spotting the prince prance around on the stern near the ramp, Neil set the heavy ship mines off at the quay and in the harbor. Neil smiled as the prince was blown to pieces, along with his battleship. Several cruisers were on fire and the Outcast gave the one hand salute to the late prince of the Old World.

Regimental Sergeant Major Dunning was looking down at Crown Prince Victor Leonis when the prince opened his eyes and moaned. "That hurt. Regimental Sergeant Major Dunning, you are still ugly, even in heaven."

Lee smiled at him and said, "I bet it did. This is not heaven and my wife thinks I am beautiful, sir!"

Victor moved around. He was intact, but bruised. Lee pulled him out of the debris. "Do you have some special water Regimental Sergeant Major Dunning?"

"Sir! Just a wee sip to calm the nerves." He handed the flask to his prince, who took a swig and handed it back his captain.

He climbed out of the debris and sat back down on the rubble. Victor smiled, "Charles, do you need some special water from Regimental Sergeant Major Dunning?"

"Yes sir, I think I do." Lee smiled at his charges as the captain handed the flask back.

"Regimental Sergeant Major Dunning, report!"

"Sir!" We have lost your battleship, three cruisers and two transports." The prince looked at the harbor. His ships were exploding all over the place.

"What about the marines?"

"Ten dead, thirty wounded, but we are intact, sir. All our armor field pieces are intact, active.' He looked out and saw that he still had eight cruisers, along with four transports waiting in the ocean.

Victor said, "Get the mine sweepers going. Find the bloody mines. It was a remote, detonated attack. We have Outcasts watching us; find them and kill them."

The Outcast hunter-killer group watched the prince giving directions, "We missed Crown Prince Victor Leonis. From their briefing, that SOB is very dangerous," the Outcast leader pointed, "but, the warships are toast in the harbor. Millions of crowns went to the bottom of the harbor." They all smiled, "Yep, just beautiful."

The Outcasts asked the leader, "Can you hit the SOB with the slayer?"

He nodded and said, "Yes, but it will give our position away." They all agreed. "We are dead anyway." All could see the royal marine patrols fanning out looking for them.

Orders from the Outcast leader stated, "Set the machine guns up overlapping the fields, the clays set for the approaches. I will shoot then drop mortar rounds on his majesty's marines. One more thing," smiling, he pushed the second mine field to active, "these were homing torpedoes in the ocean; they were set for very large game."

The Outcast leader went behind the big fifty caliber rifle, and thought, *The armorers dug this design up from a very ancient old book.* He settled in. Through the powerful optical scope, he could see all three. He pulled out the photo, confirmed the prince and started the ritual. His spotter said, "1,500 meters, crosswind 10 left, the right temp 90." Through the scope, he dialed the settings, moved the rifle to compensate and slowly pulled the trigger. He could see the laser reflecting off the prince's chest.

Crown Prince Victor Leonis' laser indicators went crazy. He dropped just as the Outcast pulled the trigger. The bullet punched a 6-inch hole through the wall where he was just standing. The rifle report came from the hill 1,500 meters away. He scrambled into the building, followed by his Regimental Sergeant Major who said to him, "Someone does not like you, Sir!"

"Tell me something I don't know, Regimental Sergeant Major Dunning." Another hole punched above Lee's head.

"Oh shit," they both said, as they heard the 80mm mortar round whistling toward them. "Time to go, Sir!"

They both dived out the back of the building, landing on their backs as the mortar round landed on their last position. The warehouse exploded, debris was falling around them. Both men got off the ground and sprinted as fast as they could away from the warehouse. Victor heard another round and thought, *That bastard is leading us.* They hit the ground and debris mushroomed 50 meters away.

Captain Charles Dunkley just laid there as the debris rained around him. He got on TACNET and commanded, "Get some damn artillery on that hill." He gave their coordinates and listened for their acknowledgement. The TACNET abruptly ended. He looked in the direction of the APC command vehicle and it suddenly exploded from a direct hit.

Bloody hell, he thought as he switched to artillery battery control. "Did you get my orders?"

"No, sir."

He repeated the coordinates and called back to him, "'Tubes one through four are engaging, sir."

"Damn it! Move the cannons."

"Sir, we are swinging them now. One minute to realign." The crawlers were moving the carriages and they had to swing them around 180 degrees.

He got his tanks and asked, "Can you hit the coordinates?"

"Yes, sir."

"Then kill that fucking sniper and mortar team."

The Outcast leader smiled. His spotter had moved to the other position. All AI'd, *Set.*

He nodded and said, *Hold fire. Do the plan. Acknowledge.*

They AI'd back, *Set. Ready. Holding fire plan.*

Hitting the foot pedal, the Outcast leader dropped eight more rounds into the tube while laughing. He saw his pattern explode among the royal marines. They were being lifted up in the air.

Just beautiful, he thought. A bonus hit the APC command center. He set another 10 stonk; number one was a fast nerve gas agent. *This should be fun*, he thought as he targeted the hospital. The laser came back with the range. *Hmm, just in range.* He set the angle. *Gas away*, he AI'd his team and the shell left the tube.

The Crown Prince Victor Leonis saw the shell explode above the hospital and he screamed, "Gas!" into his command net. His marines had been trained for chemical warfare. They had their BCN suits on in 20 seconds. The hospital staff that had not received such training screamed as they died.

Crown Prince Victor Leonis and Regimental Sergeant Major Dunning ordered, "Kill that bloody mortar now!"

Royal marine tanks fired at the hilltop with 120mm rounds. The Outcast leader hunkered down as the hillside erupted; he was behind solid granite. Wily Pete hit the designated target with 20 barrels of napalm. Crown Prince Victor Leonis screamed, "Jesus Christ," as he saw the napalm set the whole waterfront district on fire again.

Regimental Sergeant Major Dunning asked, "How come that mortar is still firing at us?"

"Working it, Sergeant Major," was the response from the artillery.

The Outcast leader fired the last round. He laughed as the nerve gas hit the quay between the high explosive Wily Pete and nerve gas; his majesty had his hands full. The scanner picked up the orders for the marine cannon naval barrage. Leaping off the back side of the hill, he dropped 30 feet, rolled as he landed and leaped for the deep hidey hole.

Holding his mouth open, he screamed as the 8-inch naval shells blew up his last position. Rocks and trees exploded up in the air. *Well, at least their navy can shoot right.*

Crown Prince Victor Leonis watched the enemy mortar being lifted into the air; there were no bodies *they're still alive.* "Captain Charles Dunkley."

"Sir!"

"Wily Pete that hill and set a one-mile perimeter on fire, now."

On the way, the royal marine batteries fired Wily Pete and napalmed the hill. The cruiser added its own special blend, an aerosol that lit up the whole area. The Outcast smiled as he rolled the fire proof cloth around him and stuck the air tanks' mask on his head. *Yes, by the book. Oh well, time to have some more fun.*

Two hours later, the Royal Marines went up the hill. They found the mortar and a very big rifle. The two Outcasts smiled as the Royal Marines came into the killing zone. They opened up with the belt feed 50 on them.

"Yes, old technology sure does work," one said, as they punched the marines off the hill at 700 meters in a cross fire.

Crown Prince Victor Leonis thought, *Those are big machine guns.*

He directed the artillery onto the positions. The Outcasts smiled, the shells just hit the granite but they were upset by missing the marines. As the ground moved, it made shooting harder, but they liked a challenge. The prince saw the weapons open up through the barrage and he said, "Alright, spread out. Small teams, hunt these bastards, I want the sniper scouts to swing around and box these bastards in. You have ten minutes."

The Outcast leader laughed. Now, both started to fire 90mm preset auto loading mortars; they had 40 shells apiece. The remote worked wonderfully. Both watched as the shells hit among the buildings; it also kept the royal marines busy. They laughed as one of the rounds hit an ammo truck.

Royal Marine Sniper Mark Little's team heard the gunfire. They moved and scouted, looking for the Outcasts. He smiled and thought, *A little different than catching poachers.* He found the minefield. He was a former game keeper in his home county. His father had taught him how to stalk as a child and the marines had taught him how to kill. His fellow marines kidded him on his small stature, but when it came to stalking and shooting, they shut up.

Hmm, if I was crazy, what would I do? I would ride out the pounding and do a sneak on the prince; he is the target, the other two are the distraction. Siren call. He calmed his thoughts down and went into 'NO mind' as his father had taught him. *Become one with the forest, the trees, the water. Relax, observe, then strike.* He signaled his team to wait. They nodded and spread out. He then moved like a shadow, stepping over the tripwires. He moved around the beams and settled in the exact middle of the Outcast's mine field and waited; his Ghelli suit blended into the forest floor.

The Outcast smiled, his second slayer was in position. He had inched forward until he felt the butt. *Ah yes, his majesty is going to be dead in a few then I will set the mine field to kill some more royal marines.*

Royal Marine Sniper Mark Little noticed the movement. His eyesight focused on the slight movement then he let his mind go back to 'NO mind'. *Yes, it is moving.* He slowly swung the rifle from his position; it was a downhill shot at 300 meters.

He dialed the range in and settled in for the shot. The Outcast thought, *His majesty is going to get a surprise with his party gift.* He settled in at 400 meters. The bullet would cut him in half. He slowed his breathing and slowly pulled the trigger.

Royal Marine Sniper Mark Little was surprised by the report of his rifle. He saw the bullet strike the Outcast and flip him over a couple of times. He jacked another round into the rifle, laid the scope on the Outcast's head and fired another round to make sure. Once the echo died, he waited for several minutes to make sure it was just one Outcast. He then crawled up to the body and pulled his pistol, just in case, but the Outcast was not faking death; he was very dead.

Mark searched the body, carefully. He found the remote, disarmed the device by pulling the battery and shoved it into his crawl sack. He waited until he returned to 'NO mind', then slipped back out the same way he had come. His team waited. He pointed out the next target. They moved and blended with each other through the forest, moving to the sounds of the artillery fire.

The Outcasts knew their leader was dead; he was not laughing in their minds. They had failed in killing the prince. One nodded and sent the coded message to the Outcast fleet. They knew their time was up, so after leaving the machine guns on full auto, they blended on the run between artillery loading to go meet their new friends. The two groups felt each other and opened up with all their weapons. Bullets were flying around between the two groups. The Outcasts were very fast, they had lost two people to their weapons. Royal Marine Sniper Mark Little had left his long rifle on the tree and his assault weapon on the run, so he drew his father's Gurka and leaped as his friends engaged the other two Outcasts.

The first Outcast was wounded. He kept the two surviving marines pinned down as his buddy moved in for the kill. *Where is that other small bastard?* He saw movement. *There that shit is,* he thought, as he swept the barrel toward the movement. The two marines rolled from behind the boulder, one high and one low. Their bullets punched into the first Outcast. The impacts drove him into the tree behind him; he slid down the trunk, very surprised and very dead. Both marines switched and pinned the second Outcast with full auto from their assault rifles. Mark's blade whistled through the air at the last Outcast. He heard the whistle, jumped, and flipped over him drawing his own blade to deflect the strike from Mark.

The Outcast bounced his blade off the Gurka blade to strike Mark as he landed on the forest floor. Mark rolled, slowed the blade down, parried and slashed the leg of his opponent. The Outcast reversed his strike to kill Mark. He slowed the Outcast, moved to him, went under the slash, moved inside the arc, spun and took the head off the shoulders. He let the blade swing up and over head then slammed the blade through the chest pinning the Outcast to the tree trunk.

His two marine buddies topped the boulder, eyes following the head as the Outcast head hit the ground. Mark smiled and said, "You owe me a pint."

"How many?"

"Just one each," he said as he pulled his father's blade from the enemy. He wiped the blood off the blade on the shirt, slashed it through the air to remove any more blood and settled it in the scabbard.

"Let's go."

They got his weapons and reloaded. They all smiled, started the lope, and blended to continue the scout to make sure these were the last Outcasts on the island.

Five days passed and Crown Prince Victor Leonis was not happy.

"Sir, we lost 38 marines and we have 125 wounded out of 1,200 men," Regimental Sergeant Major Dunning reported. "All by four Outcasts. The medical section is wiped out, the navy lost six cruisers, your battleship lost four transports and we lost a mine sweeper. We have two cruisers damaged, but still afloat and the dead are still being reported; just the battleship was over 500 casualties, sir."

Crown Prince Victor Leonis nodded at the report. *Not good. I have my ass handed to me by being careless. These Outcasts are very well-trained. Whoever leads them is very devious and dangerous.* He pondered the books that Jarvis had gifted him *I will read them most carefully on the voyage home.*

He nodded to Regimental Sergeant Major Dunning. "Do you have the sniper scout team outside?"

"Sir! Yes."

"Please bring them in and retire to the outside. I will call you when I am done with them."

Regimental Sergeant Major Dunning said, "Report to the prince now," to Royal Marine Sniper Mark Little, Royal Marine Sniper Jim Bentley and Royal Marine Garcia Mendoza.

All reported to their prince.

"At ease," he told them. "I have read your report so tell me what this blending is." They all looked at each other.

"Sir," Jim explained, "When we are in combat, we hear each other's thoughts; we blend, move as a team. When we engaged the Outcast, we could feel them approach. Our response to them was fast and deadly; our combat lasted twenty seconds at most, sir!"

So, five of you engaged these Outcasts and two members of your team were killed outright, but all of you shot apart one Outcast, kept the other busy, and then Royal Marine Sniper Mark Little killed him in one-on-one combat with his personal Gurka knife in less than 5 seconds."

All nodded at their prince. He looked at Mark.

"Mark, when you engaged the Outcast, what were your thoughts?"

"I entered 'NO mind' sir. My father was a combat veteran and a hand-to-hand instructor. He taught me to empty my mind. No distractions, flow with the problem, I just exist in the now, sir."

The prince asked, "Did your families have a history with GIFT during the troubles?"

They all nodded. "We have talked among ourselves. Our families immigrated to Old World from the NESS/FOLK area of control when the wars were waging on that continent! All of our families suffered from GIFT but not many died to the plague, sir."

Crown Prince Victor Leonis said, "I see. Are any of you married?"

They all said, "No."

Hmmm, I will rectify that issue.

"Attention!" They all snapped to attention. "Kneel." They went to the ground. "I, Crown Prince Victor Leonis, am giving you a battle field promotion to third lieutenant, effective immediately." He drew his sword and said, "You are all now, 'Sir'!" as he knighted them.

"Rise, gentlemen," he said, smiling. They looked like deer that had been shot in a poacher's lantern. "I have your DNA profile; all of you are Wild NESS. As a matter of fact, about half my royal marines are Wild NESS. You have no clue what that means, but you will. So, I have three distant nieces that need husbands; you three are chosen." He pulled out three slips of paper and placed them in his right hand, "Each of you will pull a paper." When they did, he said, "You will board a transport with my seal and you will present your selves to these addresses in full uniform. You will propose to my nieces and they will accept. Then, all of you will report to Marine OC training school for full training; is this understood by you?"

"Yes, sir!" came the reply.

"Good." He shook all their hands. "Welcome to the Zoo, gentlemen. You have you orders. Move." They all spun about and left the tent.

The prince bellowed for Regimental Sergeant Major Dunning when he came to attention. "Did you get my speech to my newest relatives?"

"Every word, sir!

"Well, make sure they get going. How many NESS were killed in this engagement?"

"The four Outcast and we lost three total in the dustup, sir!"

"Hmm, not good odds. We need to get better with our NESS. These three are full blown NESS. I want a detailed genealogy report on them. They will donate sperm to my Royal Marine breeding program once they are done with OC School. We have many widows. This time, I want more NESS in my ranks."

Regimental Sergeant Major Dunning nodded. He was a Wild NESS. He understood the problem the Outcasts and many other nations had with the NESS genome in their societies. The Outcasts had no color pattern and could hide in plain sight within the population. They could marry, have children, and have careers, but if provoked, they could also explode and kill many people. It had happened in their country too many times. *This is a very serious problem*, he thought. *You were either a very good NESS or a very bad NESS; the NESS genome did not have a middle ground.*

Crown Prince Victor Leonis pulled the two books. *I will need to get a copy of the Jarvis Meadow thesis and research. I have much work to do. My nation is not ready for this kind of slaughter.* As his marine details were burying their people in mass trench graves, he could hear the bulldozers doing their work as he went to the quay.

Natasha watched the island fade into the ocean. She could see the orange flashes highlight the smoke rising from the harbor as her people killed their enemies. She turned to her uncle. He nodded and said, "Neil Kidd and the other three missed the crown prince, but blew up his battleship along with six cruisers. The Royal Marines got pasted, from the report; all four families will get the bronze star, food and housing, along with education."

Natasha asked, "Where is my family?" Her uncle took her to his cabin, opened the cabin door and her heart leaped out of her chest when she saw them. Her uncle closed the door, smiled and went back to the bridge.

Three weeks later, the Outcasts went into a fjord. Natasha was not used to snow and she shivered. Her mom came up to her and said, "You will get a cold if you stay out here."

Natasha hugged her mom. "I will be alright. Where are we?"

Her mom laughed. "Home."

They turned up a smaller fjord and she almost missed the opening. The 20-ship flotilla went under a massive ledge and turned 90 degrees. The cave opened up into a very large fjord. She saw thousands of warships at anchor, hundreds of transports, fishing ships, floating docks and a city rising from the water's edge. Her mom smiled and said, "Welcome to Freedom City."

One year later, Natasha was summoned to the Outcast council. She was very nervous; she had no clue as to what they wanted from her.

Zacharias Temple smiled at her in the council chambers. "Natasha, please be seated. We have watched your progress this last year. Your training instructors have given you extremely high marks in every aspect of schooling and espionage craft that they can devise for you. So, are you wondering why we have given you this training?"

She said, "Yes."

"Our people are hunted worldwide. "Our greatest threat is Old World. They control the ocean passages from here to the rest of the world." She nodded. "So we want you to go into the lion's den, so to speak. We have a very long-term mission for you. It will mean years away from your family."

"Go on."

"We know what happened to you, so you do not have to do this for us. You have other abilities that are needed, so it would be your choice."

She looked at her uncle and nodded. "What is the long-term assignment?"

"We want you to marry this person, David Centauri. He is in the ruling family, but a lower status. We think he will rise to the upper crust of the Old World military in about twenty years."

As she looked, she saw from his picture that he was handsome. She smiled and thought, *At least he is my age.*

"Go on."

"Since it would be an arranged marriage, we will slip you into this woman's place." They showed her another photograph. It was like looking in a mirror. "Her family is dead, so no one can positively ID her. We plan to kidnap her and put her in the slave auction."

Natasha interrupted. "No," She remembered her own terror. "Just kill her; it would be more merciful."

The council nodded at that statement. "So be it. Since you were born in Old World, you have all the mannerism, plus the knowledge. She was and will attend Old World University for classic studies this coming season."

Natasha asked, "So once in place, then what?"

"We want their military intelligence so we can plan accordingly. There is great interest in destroying Old World from other major powers and they pay very well. We might be able to get out of this cold weather, too."

"Can I give you my answer after talking with my family?"

"Yes. How about tomorrow, same time?"

"Alright."

Lazarus Temple smiled when Natasha left. He addressed the council and said, "She will do it."

They all nodded. "Good, the time table is a go then. We will kill GIFT from this planet in the next 50 axis turns, we will consolidate this planet, and then move to space to take the rest of the human planets, wherever they are in this universe and kill all the GIFTs!" All of the council nodded. "We will never be ruled by a non-human, ever." The council smiled and slammed their knives into the wooden table as an affirmative to the crusade; each had the pattern of their flag.

Lazarus Temple got up, limped to the door, and said, "Yes, I am coming for you, bastard GIFT. I will take the NESS and FOLK with us or they will be destroyed." He smiled and then, howled and the Outcast council howled at the night stars with him. From the council's outlook, many people around the globe had very bad dreams that night.

Natasha talked to her mom and siblings. They all agreed that it would help all of them if she accepted the assignment. The next day, she told the Outcast council she would do it. They smiled, "Well, your training just increased." They all laughed.

She nodded. "Yes, my work is just beginning for my country."

General David Centauri looked at his wife and thought, *I love her dearly, but she has issues with royalty. She will whine and plead not to be included in this affair, but I have my orders; she will trooper up and follow. After 5 axis turns of marriage, I know her.*

Natasha Centauri looked at her husband. She liked him and she loved her two kids by him. *Thank God they are out of the country studying at New Hope FOLK University before the shit hits the fan with the information that David had told her in their bed.* She smiled at him. *They have their minds in their small mind, so we might be able to destroy this country in one fell swoop before they move the factories.*

She had received the letter from Dagny. She smiled inwardly. Her daughter had fought bravely, been wounded severely, and her future mate had saved her life; it made her very proud of her.

In her daughter's letter, she told her mom what Stardrifter said to her. The NESS found her family Temple tree in her DNA. Natasha smiled at that, it was far too late. The Temple NESS were all over the planet in vast numbers within the human population; they would never be ruled by GIFT, ever!

The breeding program was going extremely well. The Temple NESS men, women and their human allies were having babies and exchanging eggs and sperm, along with arranging adoptions for children.

More wild stock humans are flocking to our flag due to injustice, economic slavery and real slavery from the ruling elites; they gladly had babies, too. NESS with wild human strains is a good thing for my people. Nature has weeded out the weak giving us new, stronger and improved NESS and very wild humans with NESS attributes: speed, strength and better minds.

She smiled. She had had several other children, but had told David they had been stillborn. The Outcast had paired her with other NESS and wild human sperm. Once they were delivered, they were moved and adopted. She also had donated eggs to the breeding program. David knew of the high mortality rate of children. GIFT is still active and the plague was still killing them regularly. He was very informed by the Crown and not surprised by her stillbirths. She hated the artificial means of conceptions; just put the tube in her, walk around for a day then throw it out. She frowned, no fun, but it made her lovemaking to David on those nights very fun and extremely horny to boot. She smiled. *Yes, David did like those nights.*

Wild Humans bring grim resolve with them; they are very tough fighters and they will never submit to authority. We have had great victories and great defeats with Wild Humans and they have never failed to step up to the line and let fly the cannons at our enemies. They bleed and die with us in war and peace 'We the people' the OUTCASTS are growing stronger every axis turn. Our exile is almost over.

She remembered the flag when she was picked up off the island many years ago – the yellow with a rattlesnake, and with the words on the bottom, 'Don't Tread on Me' flying high from the battle bridge.

She asked her uncle what it had meant. He replied, "From our history, we are the true Americans; we have not wandered from the roots as the NESS/FOLK have by GIFT." He recited from memory, *Benjamin Franklin Diverts an Idle Hour.*

"In December 1775, Old Earth date, 'An American Guesser' anonymously wrote to the Pennsylvania Journal. I observed on one of the drums belonging to the marines now raising, there was painted a Rattle-Snake, with this modest motto under it, 'Don't tread on me.' As I know it is the custom to have some device on the arms of every country, I supposed this may have been intended for the arms of America.

"This anonymous writer, having 'nothing to do with public affairs' and 'in order to divert an idle hour,' speculated on why a snake might be chosen as a symbol for America.

"First, it occurred to him that 'the Rattle-Snake is found in no other quarter of the world besides America.' The rattlesnake also has sharp eyes, and "may therefore be esteemed an emblem of vigilance.

"Furthermore, she never begins an attack, nor when once engaged, ever surrenders: She is, therefore, an emblem of magnanimity and true courage… She never wounds 'till she has generously given notice, even to her enemy, and cautioned him against the danger of treading on her.

"Finally, I confess I was wholly at a loss what to make of the rattles, 'till I went back and counted them and found them just thirteen, exactly the number of the Colonies united in America; and I recollected, too, that this was the only part of the Snake which increased in numbers…

"'Tis curious and amazing to observe how distinct and independent of each other the rattles of this animal are and yet, how firmly they are united together, so as never to be separated but by breaking them to pieces. One of those rattles singly, is incapable of producing sound, but the ringing of thirteen together, is sufficient to alarm the boldest man living."

With those words, her course had been set for her life. Natasha had studied hard and took all the great American works on government to task and applied them to her children. All Outcasts studied and applied the same lessons to their people. They had grim resolve never to submit to anything on this planet or the universe, live free or die was literally for their people.

TEN

Persian

Banu Goshasp smiled as the NESS Titan came up to the practice sand mat. He laughed, "Banu, seems you have come for a rematch."

She smiled, nodded and said to him, "Yes, Tiny, I am going to whip your butt today."

Titan stood 8 feet tall in his bare feet and he was all muscle and speed. She watched him stretch to get the kinks out and then, nod. They both pulled on the practice armor, gloves and helmets.

Banu flipped a coin and said, "Call it."

Tiny said, "Heads." It landed tails.

She smiled. "Shield and spear today, my whipping boy." Titan laughed. She had the speed on him, but not the reach. They both pulled the shields off the wall and got the spears with electrical muscle interrupter neuron taps. These could lock the muscles in a body if it touched you.

Banu hit the timer. "Comp-intoned countdown begins 5, 4, 3, 2, 1."

Both went in to 'NO mind'. She lunged at Titan; he barely managed to get the shield in place to direct the thrust away from him. He then shifted the spear to his shield hand, spun and used his great strength to kick the shield with her attached to it. As she spun away from the blow, he grabbed the butt end of the spear and whipped it at her head as he completed the spin.

Banu saw the blow with Tiny's huge foot coming, so instead of planting her foot to absorb the impact, she went with it. She heard the spear coming around at her head as she completed the spin, planted the shield at a 45-degree angle, and used the impact to help roll backwards. She noticed his left leg planted from his turn. She whipped the end of her spear at his knee, it contacted the flesh. As she rolled away from Tiny, the shock stick made the muscle cramp the knee for a minute.

Tiny said, "Well, that is not good," as he set the shield with the spear over the top and shuffled back to get more reach. Banu did not let up, she leaped at him. She thrust again; Tiny used the shield to deflect the thrust. She saw him move, she used her momentum to deflect the thrust of the spear with hers past her helmet. She then hit his shield and slid down it. She smiled using the edge of the shield to smash his left foot, she got his big toe.

Tiny grunted, *Now that hurt.* Banu leaped back, but Tiny was pissed. He lunged at her without letup. He smiled as he smashed his shield into hers. As Banu set for the blow, it lifted her. Shield up, Tiny saw the opening. He dropped and spun, catching her left foot with his right leg and upended her. She landed heavily and he continued his spin, using the end of his spear and thrust at her stomach. When it contacted, the shock stick locked her stomach muscles as it made contact.

Tiny laughed as he stood up to finish her. Banu overrode the pain and thrust at his right knee. It locked that one up, too. Tiny crashed down, pinning her under her shield when the buzzer sounded.

Banu said, "Get off me, Tiny, you big idiot."

He said, "I wish I could but my knees are locked." He laughed and then groaned as he slid off the shield. He sat up and started to massage his knees. He could see the muscles spasm. *Jesus*, he moaned as his big toe started to throb.

Banu's stomach muscles had seized up. *I hope I don't throw up*, she thought as she tried to endure the pain. Banu smiled from the sand mat at Tiny. *I won, I think.*

Tiny pointed at the contact score.

"3 to 1 in your favor," he said, grimacing at the pain in his knees. *Next time, I am wearing my combat boots*, he thought.

Both of them helped each other up and limped over to put the weapons back on her combat wall. He bowed to her, "Next week, same time?"

Banu smiled, "Yes, and bring a friend, I need the exercise. You're getting slow, old man."

Tiny laughed as he limped for the shower and a long soak in the mineral springs. He was stationed at the FOLK diplomatic house for the last two axis turns in her country. His age was about 50 years and his skin pattern was a spectacular rainbow of colors.

Her country had many treaties and marriages with the NESS and FOLK over the past 175 axis turns; they had hid the NESS in the opening shots of the troubles from the old existing governments. She smiled. Her great-great grandfather was very wise; he saw into the future for his people.

Tiny AI'd his buddy NESS Lester. *Well, she beat the crap out of me today.*

Lester AI'd, *Serves you right. She is NESS, you idiot. Her speed alone is way above average and dexterity is off the charts, so you're lucky she only got one hit.*

Titan groaned as he got into the mineral springs. The heat loosened his aching muscles. He worked on his toe, the NANO bots had repaired it but it was still sore. He laughed and said, *Serves you right. Combat is unforgiving.* He closed his eyes and groaned some more. *Yes, I am getting old.*

His friend laughed at him. *Dinner tonight and some fun at the café's in the city?*

He smiled. *Yes, I think so, but dancing is out for tonight.*

Lester pouted and said, *The girls want to show us some moves on the dance floors.*

He laughed. *Right, but if I crash into things, you are paying damages.*

Tiny sighed. After about an hour in the bath, he called his armor. It slithered over and rolled onto him. It was very happy; the minerals and heat had completely recharged the systems.

NESS Titan AI'd, *I am back on duty* as his sensors came online. He stepped out of the springs and strode into the night from the NESS mineral baths.

Banu Goshasp watched him go. *Yes, I am very glad for the NESS being here, but NESS Jeremiah at the FOLK diplomatic enclave is asking for an audience with my family tomorrow, most interesting. I have not seen Jeremiah since my aunt died. I wonder if he is still in mourning.*

She headed for home chambering the .50 NESS caliber rifle with an armor-piercing round and started the walk back to her guard. The critters in the desert would be out in a few minutes for a drink at the spring; the NESS always left the spring open to any life for water.

She smiled *NESS and FOLK are tuned to the natural world. They accept and embrace life's challenges much like my people, Magi.* She smiled to the setting sun. She sensed the desert; she was safe for now. The burrows were still hibernating from the sun, but they would be out looking for snacks and water in the night.

The city was about five miles away from the spring. Normally she would have hiked the rock ridges to hone her night skills, but her father had insisted she take her guard this time.

The sand halftrack drew a lot of unwanted attention from the very large Scorps and Sandcats. *It might get very interesting going home,* she smiled as she dropped from the cleft into the fighting compartment. Her guard, Captain Aga, smiled from her helmet. *How was Tiny, Banu?*

She smiled and said, *Old and slow.*

Aga laughed. *In some ways. Some others, not so slow.*

All the women in the Sand halftrack laughed. They had flipped coins to see who would ambush the NESS at the Cafés with dancing and other fun activities. The poor NESS would be very tired the next morning. Banu smiled and pointed to the city.

Aga, over the Sand Track LANCOMM fighting network radio, said, "All weapons active and all three double 40mm cannons went active as the driver engaged the drive systems."

The 500-pound female Sandcat, Whisper, watched the humans from its daylight hide. She focused on the lone human that had just dropped into the Killer of Sandcats. Her clan would like to hunt and eat that one *she is very dangerous to my clan. We have lost two, Stalker and Sunbright to her claws.*

Whisper thought, *The human females are dangerous. I wonder if their males are just as lazy as my own males.* Before she could finish the thought of killing the laziest, she saw movement toward the water.

Sand Grazers were two tons, all armor and teeth, and ate sand plankton. They ran in large herds so they were very hard to kill. Whisper AI'd her clan, *Time to hunt.*

All fifteen females smiled back at her, *Yes, human or normal?*

Whisper smiled, *Just normal for tonight.* As she stretched and padded into the rocks, her clan moved with her to see about food for the week.

GIFT smiled. His work was coming along nicely with the Sandcats. In another million axis turns, they will be building machines.

Whisper smiled as her clan took a Sand Grazer. Its screaming was silenced as she clamped her jaws on the windpipe. When it stopped thrashing, they all dragged the body up into the high rocks to keep the others away from the kill. All the Sandcats ate their fill then hauled the rest to the cave for the offspring to eat.

Whisper took a large front leg to her offspring, one male and one female, to eat. When the male showed up demanding food, she growled at him and extended her claws. Whisper AI'd him, *You will wait or we will kick you out to hunt by yourself.*

He AI'd back whining, *But I am the clan leader. It is my right for the food.*

Whisper AI'd, *That is going to change. The females want strong offspring, not lazy ones. This is your last free meal. We females are going to train this generation to hunt, both females and males.*

But.

Your 'but' is done.

She AI'd her females and they all approached him. *Your right is over,* as they ripped him apart.

Whisper threw the body down the cliff to the Scorps. It was gone in minutes. She turned to the last large male and AI'd, *Any questions on hunting and taking care of our clan?*

Death AI'd back, *No, I hunt but, not with females. No glory in it, just food.*

She AI'd back, *That is good, but humans will not feed us nor do we care about glory, so you will hunt with us, the females.*

Yes.

Good answer, you can eat now.

I have eaten, three days ago, as he showed the hunt for the lone human. It was dressed in rags and had tried to kill him with a spear. He showed the cut to his leg.

Whisper smiled, *It is a small cut, but one with honor. Yes, you will do. Next mating season, I will have offspring with you, but we are going to hunt the Killer of Sandcats one day. Your bravery will be tested on that day.*

Sand Grazer is much better. He padded over to the kill. Sitting down, he ate his fill and smiled, *Much tastier, too.* Death was plotting to kill the male offspring of his dead rival without himself getting killed by the females.

Banu Goshasp's father was named for an ancient hero, Rostam, from the long epic poem book Shahnameh brought from home world. He smiled. *The poem was very interesting. In fact, it showed humans never changed that much.* He delighted in the insights to human thinking as he looked at his daughter. *She is a very formable warrior. Her training was ongoing and the tutors were very pleased in her progress. Let's see if she understands politics.*

His son FARĀMARZ was a Full NESS. The skin coloring was spectacular, just like his wife's. He was training with the NESS with the armor. He had just about finished the process, so his obligation was almost done to the NESS and he hoped that the two axis turns would go by fast. He missed his son. He smiled at his wife, NESS Cwenhild, holding her hand as they waited for their brother-in-law Jeremiah. She AI'd him, *My love, you are nervous. What is the problem?*

He AI'd back, *Jeremiah is acting C&C for the NESS until Stardrifter returns from his honeymoon. I have not told Banu that he has married an outsider.*

Cwenhild AI'd back, *OH SHIT! She has had a crush on him since she was small girl. She will not be pleased at the news; God only knows what she will do with the news.* She started to pray for her daughter. She was a full NESS, her blood ran hot with her passions and there was no middle ground with her.

NESS Jeremiah waited in the grand hall with his fellow NESS, "Are we ready?" They all nodded except NESS Lester and NESS Tiny. They were very tired. Jeremiah laughed and said, "Late night, boys?" They both nodded.

Aga had whispered in his ear, "Hurry back, I still have more plans for you, Tiny." She then curled back under her bed covers, as his skin was feeding AGA essence into the armor sensors. He AI'd Lester, *My armor is hammering me with Aga.*

Lester AI'd laughing *and* said, *Yes, Nayyer and RavAn ran me ragged last night and my armor is just having a field day with me, too.*

NESS Jeremiah smiled at his NESS, *Show time.* All the NESS drank liters of water; they would need it. As he lined up with the great doors, he told his armor to reflect his color pattern and project the colors in the hologram. His 10 NESS lined up in a wing formation. They told their armor to project their own color patterns then all of them blended together.

Rostam nodded, the light faded, and his court went silent as the great doors opened. The NESS colors burst into the Kings Great Hall. The NESS moved slowly into the middle of the great hall. When they stopped, they formed a circle. Jeremiah smiled and the NESS blurred in a very complicated dance pattern that created a moving hologram of their world.

Rostam's court was mesmerized, the hologram kept changing. "Oh my," came from the crowd. Showing the deep ocean, NESS Tiny smiled and leaped from the circle, straight up, as he projected a whale breaching the ocean. The court's eyes followed the great whale. They could feel its height and majesty in the hologram. As Tiny landed, the hall boomed with the sounds of the ocean crashing back into the ocean from the whale.

NESS Lester leaped into the air projecting a falcon swooping in the air. As he completed the arc and fell back to the floor, the hologram showed the falcon in a dive on a rabbit in the Persian countryside. The royal court could feel the wind screaming around the falcon head; they could feel the thrill of the flight of the falcon as it picked up the rabbit off the ground.

Each NESS projected their favorite themes to the court. When Jeremiah's turn came, he projected his Zoe's greatest dance in the Grand Hall of New Hope at the top of her fame. It was breathtaking. *Beautiful*, Jeremiah laughed. Joy radiated from him to his fellow NESS, laughing, they blended with him. Joy emanated from all NESS. The royal court could feel and sense God's movement in the dance from Zoe. She was one of their own that had been trained from infancy for dance.

NESS moved faster than the eye could follow when Zoe landed. Held still under the one spotlight, the hologram collapsed to darkness. Many of the court were wiping the tears from their eyes, clapping and cheering from the dance and every presentation when all of a sudden, a light started to pulse from the center of the Kings Great Hall.

In the darkness, Jeremiah was being held by all the NESS and he whispered to the hall, "In the beginning, God created the heaven and the earth. And the earth was without form, and void; and darkness was upon the face of the deep. And the Spirit of God moved upon the face of the waters. And God said, Let there be light: and there was light." The New World sun burst from the center of the hall. NESS blended; Jeremiah, laughing, now said, "In the beginning, God created the heavens and the earth."

The NESS projected the solar system with all eleven planets, moons, asteroid belt and deep space. It filled the hall, all the court, wherever they looked; it was like flying in space with God. The royal court marveled at their planet beneath their feet.

Jeremiah boomed, "Behold our Home, Our Friends and Loved Relatives," to the Court. Jeremiah AI'd, *Now.* He brightened the sun, showing the NESS in the circle and all of Jeremiah's family smiling at Rostam from the circle. Rostam screamed with joy as his relatives swarmed him and all their relatives in the royal hall.

The court was rooted in place looking at the solar system. One child held the great one, the gas giant, in his hands. He laughed. He could hear the planet singing music, the notes rippled in the clouds, harmonies building to a crescendo. Jeremiah finished with this, "And God saw that it was good," then the hologram collapsed; the court blinked and screamed in joyous praise to the NESS.

The NESS AI'd their helmets back and kneeled while breathing very heavily and facing Rostam. He came over with Alexia on a hip and said, "Jeremiah this is the greatest gift I have ever received. The NESS are the most beautiful people I have ever had the pleasure to call friends and loved relatives. Please rise and join us now."

As Jeremiah and the NESS stood up, Rostam could see tears on Jeremiah's cheeks. He nodded. "Thank you for sharing Zoe with us, Jeremiah, and with all the NESS with the joy of what you find beautiful on our world." He looked at his friend. "I love my sister and talk to her every night in my dreams. Now come, it is time for catching up with all of us."

Rostam laughed as he saw his wife and daughter swarmed with relatives. They were laughing and whispering to each other of the latest gossip from both countries at the breakfast table. Rostam AI'd Jeremiah, *Are you all right?*

Jeremiah AI'd back, *Yes and no. I talked to my Zoe a few months ago after the dustup with Republic.*

Rostam nodded. *Yes, I read all the reports. It must have been joyous and very painful for you.*

God granted me a favor, one which I will gladly repay, and no, I almost lost Stardrifter to madness by my meddling. God always asks for balance from us; it's an ongoing lesson for me.

Rostam AI'd, *Well, Banu will not be happy with the news, Jeremiah, but I will tell her later when she can break things in private.*

Jeremiah laughed and said, *I am not going near that issue and I will be safe in the NESS diplomatic wing.*

Rostam AI'd, *I am not crazy, Cwenhild will break the news. I admit to cowardice with my daughter. Can I hide in the diplomatic wing, with you, too?*

Jeremiah laughed and said, *Yes, I think you should until the dust settles in your house.*

Cwenhild AI'd her husband, *I will talk to her later. You just go about being king and let me run this show.*

Holly came up to her grandfather. She AI'd, *Gramps, can I sit beside Uncle Rostam?*

Jeremiah looked at Rostam and AI'd, *She will have you the rest of the morning.*

Rostam laughed as he picked her up, *No problem.* He smiled at Cwenhild and AI'd her, *Children scampering around again. I miss it.*

Cwenhild nodded. *I miss it, too. We are lucky to have two from us. My numerous wounds took a toll on me, but I am happy. My husband...*

Yes.

I am very happy, she said, as Holly pulled her coloring book out and asked for help from her uncle.

NESS Tiny slipped out and went to Aga. As he slipped under the covers, she rolled on top of him and smiled, "Well, Tiny, have you decided to marry me?"

He laughed, "Never had a doubt about it, Aga, but kids scare the crap out of me."

Smiling, she replied, "That is alright, you can be trained. Just look at my sister's husbands."

He laughed. "God help me."

"Yes, you should always ask God for help, but adapt and overcome is a good motto for our marriage and the children that will follow." He laughed kissing her.

NESS Lester smiled. Nayyer and RavAn were in his bed asleep. As he slid in, they wrapped their arms around him, murmured, and went back to sleep. He smiled. *Yes, a very nice morning*, he thought as he wrapped his arms around both of them to fall asleep in his bed.

Jeremiah AI'd both Rostam and Cwenhild when the party broke up due to the heat, *I need to talk to both of you in private, along with several of the ministers.*

Rostam AI'd, *Please follow me.*

They went onto the balcony overlooking the desert. The wind was still moving enough to be pleasant, but they sealed the glass and chilled the room to a more comfortable temperature. Some sat and drank the cool glasses of fruit juice or water.

Well, Jeremiah, what is on your mind?

Jeremiah AI'd, *As you know, we intercepted the last of the scavengers' raiding parties in the interior. We will have no more issues with them.* The ministers smiled and said, *The enclosed aqueducts could go forward now to bloom the desert with fruit trees, cereals, grains, more food and better trading. Their departments would get better resource allocations along with hefty bonuses.*

Jeremiah said, "We found this on a scavenger's body. It is a copy from the original book, a real engineering book. This date 2150 Old Earth date is from the United States. The label on it is 'ultra-secret book 1 of 3 from TJD New York'." He looked around, "This spaceship existed and is real. We found old records in the comp systems from before the troubles. So, the Tesla Jump Drive in it opens up space for us, if we can find the wreck." They all nodded. "They could reverse engineer the drive, even a small one, for solar jumping. They could tap the vast resources in the solar system for industries, food, you name it and our home will not get destroyed in the process."

Rostam said, "I have heard of this TJD. We thought it was a just wishful thinking on our part. We have found old books, too, that have gibberish mathematics of a lunatic. My best minds just laugh at it."

Jeremiah said, "I thought the same until we found it on a scavenger then traced the path of them to an area here," as he pulled out a map. "We have narrowed it down to 100 square miles in the dead zone in your country, Rostam, so we NESS and FOLK would like permission to cross your borders along with your people to do the search. We can supply the vehicles to handle the lingering radiation and will gladly share any information that we both find on the hunt.

"Our scientists and engineers have found in the mathematics that it has three cipher key codes to unlock the actual mathematical equations in the books. We did scan the books and the comp did find the code written into the book, but without the other two keys, it will not decompress the files."

Rostam and Cwenhild sat back and AI'd each other.

Most interesting, Cwenhild AI'd. *If we get this TJD with the NESS and FOLK, we can lead the way off this planet and expand our families, reach into the stars.*

The NESS FOLK and Persian had scattered accounts or legends of spacecraft that had TJD star jumping capabilities, but during the last 175 axis turns, the knowledge had eluded them until this book on the table opened the option again for their people.

Rostam said, "Alright, let's mount the expedition. When can you have the vehicles here?"

Jeremiah replied, "Two weeks."

He nodded. "Ladies and gentlemen, let's begin."

All of them got to work and soon, the afternoon flowed into the evening. When dinner was done, Jeremiah went to the sleeping quarters in the palace.

Cwenhild AI'd her husband, *I suggest you make yourself scarce until I call you. I am going to talk to our daughter.*

Rostam nodded, *Good luck* and ran after Jeremiah to hide.

Banu was getting ready for bed. Her nieces had already spread across her bed and were asleep. She laughed and thought, *Well, they did leave me a sliver on the bed and a couple of dolls to keep me company.*

Her mom AI'd, *Can I come in?*

Banu AI'd, *Sure* as she brushed her hair. She looked at the mirror and thought, *Well, at least, it was an attempt.*

Her mom sat down behind her and said, "Let me try."

Banu handed her mom the brush; she got most of the tangles out. Banu closed her eyes; it felt good, her mom brushing her hair.

When Cwenhild finished, she AI'd her daughter, *I have some news from the NESS and FOLK. You have heard about Stardrifter?*

Banu turned to look at her mom and AI'd, *Is he dead?*

No, he is not, but you will not like this news.

What news?

You read the reports from the sea battle four months ago with New World?

Banu nodded.

When he pulled out 30 survivors from the battle, one of them was one Elizabeth Pameddin.

Banu nodded and AI'd her mom, *She is a world class scientist from the report.*

Cwenhild AI'd, *Yes, that is correct. So I will be blunt. He married her three months ago and from the reports, she is carrying twins from him. They are on a honeymoon in the northern part of our continent now.*

Banu's shock was apparent on her face. She looked at her mom then closed her face to her mom. She got up, went to the balcony and closed the soundproof doors. Her rage exploded out of her. She gripped the stone balcony cap, ripped it off the moorings screaming, and threw it into the night. The stone smashed into the roof below her, punching into the apartment below; it woke up the old couple.

They heard her screaming rage from the balcony above them. Across the street, both put on the night robes, stepped out into the moonlight and asked the night, "Are you alright, Banu?"

Through her tears, she said, "I am sorry, are you alright?"

They said, "We are fine. Do you want us to come over to bind your wound? We are healers."

She laughed a tired laugh. "No, it is not physical, but thank you for your concern. I will get the roof repaired tomorrow."

The old couple smiled to the night; they remembered being young. His wife smiled and said, "Well."

He laughed and said, "I cannot pick you up now, but let's just go back to bed and have some fun."

Banu smiled as she heard the exchange. *DAMN IT! He is mine. He is only nine years older than me, physically. I will kill this outsider.*

She sat down on the balcony. It would never happen; she was not a murderer, but she was still pissed. *I am beautiful. Why did he not see this? I made it very clear of my attraction to him at the last conference.* She covered her eyes. *Why! Why! Why!*

Banu opened the balcony doors sometime after first moon set. Her mom AI'd, *Daughter, I am here.* Banu threw herself into her mother's arms. *Let it out, Banu, it will be alright.* Sobs came from her daughter.

Cwenhild laid with her daughter through the night; the nieces had snuggled with Banu and she smiled as she drifted off to sleep. Cwenhild smiled and thought, *Yes, daughter the pain will ease, but the wound will be with you until you die.*

Cwenhild sighed. Being nineteen and losing a first love was rough. Stardrifter always considered Banu a sister, so she had zero chance with him, but young adults never listen to their parents. Cwenhild never did until she was a lot older and then, her parents were very intelligent. *Yes, my daughter, life lessons are hard, but you will be alright.*

Rostam AI'd Cwenhild, *Cupcake, how is Banu?*

Hide for few more days. Banu will be looking for you when she figures out you doctored the reports about Stardrifter.

Rostam AI'd, *Crap, thanks love.*

Banu woke up in the morning, looking at her mom; she looked tired and worried. Banu AI'd, *Mom, are you alright?*

Yes, just worried about you. I am sorry about Stardrifter.

Banu AI'd, *But he said he loved me. I am beautiful, smart and NESS. What is his problem with me?*

Cwenhild AI'd, *Listen to me very carefully.* Banu nodded. *When Stardrifter said he loves you, he does, but he is not in love with you. It is a subtle difference. I have loved many people and have had several lovers, but I am in love with your father. He is the one I want till I die.*

Banu knew the story between her parents. Her father had stood over her protecting her when she had been ambushed and shot apart by Outcasts that had supplied scavengers with very heavy infantry weapons and several tanks to see if these weapons worked against NESS armor.

His company had waded into the battle to rescue the NESS patrol in the northern part of the country. Her father's company was hunting the scavengers with the NESS. They had superior sensors, but the scavengers had laid out a well-planned ambush. The enemy had separated the NESS scout party from her father's heavy tanks support by using massed attacks of antitank missiles. He had lost most of the tanks and APC trying to get to the NESS to cover them. During the ensuing battle, her father's tank had been hit by an anti-tank missile which had blown the tank tread apart, so he ordered his crew to bail out into the wadi.

He was alone and took one last look in his optic systems. He noticed a NESS slowly moving and firing back at the enemy. He could see the armor had major rents and the NESS was bleeding all over the place. When the NESS went down hard by shrapnel from a near-miss explosion, it pissed him off. That was the NESS he wanted to ask out for a date. He loaded the last cannon shell while his tank caught fire from another anti-tank missile. Swinging the turret, he targeted the last Outcast supply tank that had fired at the NESS. He pulled the trigger and the hyper-velocity sabot round hit stopped the tank, but it did not kill the Outcast tank commander or the scavenger crew.

The Outcast and scavenger crew leaped out of the tank as it caught fire. They then popped back up and fired at the downed NESS with assault rifles from cover supplied by the burning tank. The NESS rolled over from her back and fired back. Her last round lifted the Outcast tank and flipped it on the Outcast and scavengers firing at her.

Her father smiled and thought, *She just might be alive* as the NESS rolled on her back. *I want that date with her.* As he lifted out of the hatch turret, he was slammed into the lip. When one of the NESS armor power systems failed, everyone hit the ground and 400 hundred yards of earth went straight up into the stratosphere. The earth quaked and moved as dirt and rocks pelted the area. Her father leaped off his tank, pulled his assault rifle and charged while the Outcast and scavengers had their heads down from the NESS blast. His whole company saw him charge. They followed their commander and king opening up with every weapon they had. Charging forward, both groups smashed into each other in the dust. His people waded into the enemy and went hand-to-hand combat with the Outcast and scavengers. Pulling their swords and screaming, "For GOD and Country," they fell upon the enemy. Of his 120 men and women, 50 survived that day; there were no Outcast or scavenger survivors.

Banu asked her mom why she had married her father; he was not NESS or FOLK. She smiled and said, "I was on a heap of scavengers and Outcast bodies, my armor shot to pieces. I was bleeding all over the place, so I said to myself, *Well, you are dead, so you might as well enjoy your last moments.* I rolled on my back after I had blown the tank apart and AI'd my helmet back. I wanted the sunshine on my face, along with the blue sky, before my armor blew me apart to meet God. Then, my partner's armor let go. Damn, the dust blotted out the sun and sky. When a shadow fell across my view, it was your father. He asked me, 'Why are you taking a break, Cupcake? There are Outcast scavengers to kill' and he winked at me.

"I thought, *This is pretty weird. I want some peace and quiet before I die and here I am getting pelted by hot brass flying from his assault weapon on my face.* Pulling his sword and screaming at the top of his lungs 'Not today, you S.O.B', he fought hand-to-hand with the Outcast and scavengers standing over me for hours it seemed, protecting me."

Cwenhild laughed and said, "That is when I knew I was in love with your father. He had seen me earlier in the week and wanted to ask me out, but being a NESS does put a damper on that type of social interaction. So, here was this handsome, crazy man standing over me, asking me off-the-wall questions in the middle of the battle while giving me a reason to stay alive so he could properly ask me for a date." Her mom laughed, "And I also wanted to know what the hell a cupcake was.

"Your father stayed at the hospital until I recovered, dated me and then, asked me to marry him."

Banu's mom's skin was horribly scarred. She was told she would never have children and would never be able to wear the armor, ever. She had told Rostam, her father, all this.

Cwenhild said, "Your father told me, 'I do not care. I want you in my life, by my side, so how about it, Cupcake?' I found out what a cupcake was and had the wedding cake made to look just like it."

Banu loved her mom and dad fiercely. They had never given up trying to have kids; she and her brother were proof that the medical people were full of shit. She smiled at that thought. Cwenhild looked at her daughter, brushed her hair out of her eyes and wondered where the smile came from.

"How about some breakfast?"

Banu's smile looked like a beautiful sunrise to her mom. "Sure will dad be there?"

Cwenhild said, "No, he is hiding from you."

Banu smiled. "He better hide for a while. I want to ask him why Stardrifter's, the C&C of the NESS, marriage was not in the report to me."

Before her mom could reply, the nieces woke up asking.

"What is for breakfast?" they squealed.

Banu laughed and replied, "Well, let's go find out." All the girls ran down the hall.

Cwenhild got up slowly; her back was giving her fits.

"I hate getting old, it is not for the weak," she said, laughing at herself. Her Nano bots needed replenishing. *Shit, I hate that needle. Hurts every time. Whereas with the armor, there is no pain and no needles.*

She looked down at her body. The burn pattern had swirled to new colors, but had never healed properly. *I miss the armor.* She sighed, put her old robe on and strolled down the hallway. She could hear the kids laughing in the kitchen. Bedlam was coming from that room as the cooks tried to cope with the maniacs.

Yes, it is nice to have screaming, happy children in the house. I miss it, she thought, as she entered the fray.

Several days later, Jeremiah laughed at Rostam as they sipped very strong coffee, "Banu will find you."

He nodded, "Yes, but it will take a while, so can I bribe you to keep the family here till we get back from the expedition? It will keep her busy."

Jeremiah laughed. "Yep, how about some honey wine? It is impossible to get it in New Hope."

"Done."

ELEVEN

Celtic

Vercingetorix smiled in his court and Moya was moving right along with the plans. He laughed and thought to himself, *How ironic.* He was named after the chieftain that led the resistance against Julius Caesar's attempts to conquer Gaul, but he was eventually defeated, brought to Rome and executed. He smiled and thought, *My daughter is going to wed into the Roman society here on New Earth.*

His wife, Geileis, moved with stately grace and sat beside him. "Well, husband, our daughter has informed me of her decision. We think it will lead us out of the mountain fortresses. Romans will need to keep sharp against other groups now, so we are pointing them to the Balkans; there is much gold and silver in the region. They need wealth to rebuild the country and they are the best at land war. They can break the hold from the Phoenicians banking infrastructure on us. Once married, Moya, a mining engineer, will suggest to her husband that she found a pre-troubles map of the region, which we have and will supply her, we think, 20 axis turns before this comes viable."

He nodded. "We will prepare for this. We can move some of our population and start a colony, for now, for support. Projections look very good. We will refine with more inquiries. I am working it now."

Vercingetorix looked at his wife. She was totally blind, but she had the inner mind. She touched many minds listening to the songs. She smiled at him, her eyes were totally golden. She AI'd GIFT, *Hello, my friend, where are we going today?*

GIFT laughed. *I was thinking of blending with a Tritop today and running with the herd, want to come?*

She laughed and AI'd, *You bet!*

GIFT laughed and both of them blended with the Tritop.

Vercingetorix watched his wife smile and thought, *I wonder where they are going today?*

GIFT laughed in his mind. *Tritop, want to come?*

You bet, and he blended, too.

His wife saw him through the Tritop's eyes. *Oh, you are mighty handsome, Tritop.* He laughed and said, *Let's mate.*

She laughed. *Later, big boy*, as they thundered on the plain.

He laughed. His people's minds moved around the planet with GIFT tinkering on their people. He smiled, *Yes, GIFT, you make life very interesting.*

GIFT laughed. *You bet. Just wait for more surprises.*

The CELTS laughed and said, *Yes, we will have fun*, as they all blended with Tritop herds.

TWELVE

Search

FOLK Full Professor Closter laughed from the FOLK armored train as it pulled into the city of Nippur. He looked at David Centauri the 5th and said, "Well, David, being a 5th year student in archaeology, tell me where Nippur came from."

"Hmmm." David laughed. "Old Earth Nippur: Sumerian City. Sumerian: Nibru; Akkadian: Nibbur, from the Sumerian for 'lord wind' (Enlil).

"Nippur was the first city built by Enlil, it is the most sacred of all the Sumerian cities. It was the special seat of the worship of the Sumerian god, Enlil, ruler of the cosmos with his symbol being the Horned Crown and the Tablets of Destiny. All Kings being first among many were anointed in this city. Without this, they had no blessing from Enlil to rule their lands."

FOLK Full Professor Closter nodded. "Yes, that is the book answer, but why and how does it apply here on our world?"

David Centauri smiled. "After the troubles, many people banded together to forge new identities. Persia, from the Old World, was a very stable monarchy. They realized freedom was needed along with trade, so it was geared for local control with extended family ties. So, on New Earth, it has worked very well. Persians have very deep ties with FOLK and NESS, Oceana, Minions, and even the Balkans

through families. I also think it gave hope to many when so many had died from GIFT's release in the troubles."

FOLK Full Professor Closter nodded and said, "Yes, you are right in your assessment. Just look at the architecture alone. Everything is geared for desert dwelling."

David looked. "Yes, the city was literally carved into the sandstone mesas. They were designed to remain at a stable temperature through the year. The Persians were master stone masons and architects."

FOLK Full Professor Closter nodded, "Well, we should unload the scientific gear and get it loaded into the heavy N.A.P.C. for the expedition."

David smiled. He hated the military period. His father was extremely embarrassed by him for not going into the Hill for a military education. He had chosen his passion for old dusty dead things, archaeology. His father was livid by his choice.

David looked at him one last time and said, "I am leaving forever and will not return. Mother, I love you. Come visit me in New Hope." She nodded as tears ran down her face. "FOLK Full Professor Closter has a student aid opening and I am taking it.

His father screamed at him, "You will not get any money from the family if you leave your home."

David nodded. "I have my inheritance money and Mom has released it to me since I am going to school. It is enough for the schooling I need and I will work for my room and board." He kissed his mother, picked up his little sister and gave her a hug.

Dagny was crying, "Don't go."

He sat her down. "Sis, I will miss you very much. Can you be brave and help Mom when I am away?"

She nodded and mumbled, "Yes," and grabbed her mom's hand.

"Mom, you and Dagny will always be welcome wherever I live and can stay with me forever, but Dad can fu–"

His Mom interrupted him, saying, "No matter what, he is your father, time will heal many wounds."

His father slammed the study door. "SOB, ungrateful snot, know-it-all," he screamed, as he went out into the garden. David nodded, turned and left his house and country forever.

FOLK Full Professor Closter laughed and said, "David, wake up."

David jumped. "Sorry, professor, just had a bad flashback about hating all military and all the war machines."

The professor nodded. "Yes, I do, too, but these will take the radiation for the expedition."

David laughed. "Well, let's go and get the instruments and go find these war machines."

NESS Jeremiah was arguing with Banu Goshasp. "You are not going, Banu, period."

Banu leaped up, landed on the crate and stuck her nose to Jeremiah's helmet. "WHY?!"

Jeremiah said, "ONE – we have limited space, TWO – water, THREE – you are not trained, FOUR – we need specialists, FIVE – YOU DO NOT HAVE PERMISSION FROM YOUR GOVERTMENT TO GO! Shall I keep going?"

Banu was livid and she spun around, leaped from the crate and smashed into David Centauri. She screamed at him, "Get the hell out of the way, Outlander."

David just looked at her screaming at him from the floor as she stormed by him. He looked up. A very large NESS loomed over him.

NESS Jeremiah reached down and said, "Sorry, David. Banu is upset." He picked him up off the floor and asked if he was alright. David grinned. "Yes, it's not every day you get run over by a beautiful woman."

NESS Jeremiah chuckled and looked at David. "I would steer clear of Banu Goshasp; she eats future professors for lunch. Speaking of which, I know a café that serves an outstanding dish. Ever heard of smoked lizard? No? Well, you are in for treat," he said, as he steered David to the café.

David was inventorying the scientific gear in the NESS Armored Personal Carrier (N.A.P.C.) later in the day. He halfway slid out a case and pushed it back with some force. *Damn thing will not latch.* Stooping over to grab the strap, the case dropped out of the holding slot, hitting his head. After bouncing off David's head, it hit the steel deck then bounced out onto the cavern sand floor. *SOB! Damn it, where is the case?* David walked down the rear ramp, looking for the piece-of-crap case.

Hopping down onto the sand floor, David dropped to all fours. *Damn it,* he thought, as he pulled his torch out and shined it under the N.A.P.C. body. *SOB, it is wedged in between the axles.* He threw the tools down and swore louder as he wiggled under the vehicle.

David saw an object attached to an axle and thought, *What the hell?* He pulled his torch light out and shined it on the object. It looked very weird. He looked farther down and saw that they all had these devices on all the axles. Something nagged his brain.

OH SHIT! He remembered something about shape charges when he was forced to go to that military prep school before being tossed out on his ear. Scooting back out, he ran over to the alarm button and hit it.

All hell broke loose. The NESS appeared in front of him. He pointed and explained, "I saw devices attached to the axles when I was retrieving the case. It had dropped and bounced under that DAMN vehicle; it looked like shape charges to me." The NESS Aage scanned him. He could see the bruise on his head. Aage looked around and saw the whole picture from the IR foot prints to his running to hit the alarm.

The NESS Aage blurred. David was literally moved from the area. When he was set down in the sand, he was 400 yards away. NESS Aage said, "Stay. Do not move. We will come back for you. Do you understand?"

David said, "Yes," as he plopped his butt onto the sand floor.

NESS swarmed the area, their sensors went online. They found all the vehicles had been booby trapped. It took several hours to clear the explosives, and then they scanned every piece of expedition equipment, personal gear and personnel, but no more issues were found by the NESS.

NESS Jeremiah looked at David. "How is your head, David?"

He laughed. "Well, it is sore, but I will live. What the hell did I find?"

NESS Jeremiah said, "It is a NESS matter; let's say someone does not want us to succeed in our endeavor."

David smiled. "Well, are we still going?"

NESS Jeremiah said, "Yes, we mount up in the morning. I suggest you get some sleep." David went to the hotel, got dinner then went to bed.

NESS Jeremiah AI'd, *Well, what did we find?*

The NESS AI'd, *We found the devices were set to only blow the drive trains, not kill the personnel. They were on a simple counter, so many revolutions and there goes the axle. They were so low tech, we would have never found them. Plus they were also in smell proof packaging, so someone knows we have that capability.*

NESS Jeremiah nodded. *This is only the first attempt. Hmm, we have two offensive NESS in the group. You will bring the heavy offensive assault packs with four reloads each.*

NESS Stan and NESS Bartholomew smiled. *Oh yeah, real weapons.*

NESS Jeremiah AI'd, *The rest of the NESS are to bring extended load out packs, eight each. I think we are going to be in heavy combat.* Jeremiah pondered for a moment. *We will need extra vehicles, drivers and gunners, and we do not have enough NESS if we get into combat.*

The next day, NESS Jeremiah went to Rostam and told him what they had found and needed. Rostam nodded and said, "I will release the heavy assault vehicles to you. They can take the radiation. We have the new weapons fitted now, per your request, but Banu is the commander of that group. She is well versed, along with having combat time in them."

Jeremiah nodded, but thought, *Can she take my orders? She will be under NESS military command systems as we have agreed with this endeavor.*

Rostam AI'd, *Banu did you hear?*

Banu said yes.

Rostam continued, *Since you agree to taking orders from NESS Jeremiah, you will be under NESS command decisions. His orders just might get you killed.*

Banu smiled, *Yes, I agree, Father.*

Rostam AI'd back, *Not me* and pointed to her new commander.

Jeremiah AI'd, *Attention.*

Banu snapped to attention in front of him. *I am asking for "Your Word is your Life."*

Jeremiah continued. *Captain Banu Goshasp, this is as real as it gets. You are subordinate to me. I might order your death, along with your crews to save people if we engage an enemy.*

Banu felt fear in her guts and she AI'd back, *Yes.*

NESS Jeremiah AI'd, *I am glad you felt fear. I do not want to bury you because you've been heroically stupid. This will get your crews and NESS killed. Combat is kill or be killed and there are no halfway measures, so you will instantly obey my orders or I will kill you on the spot for disobeying. Is this understood by you?*

Banu said, *Yes, sir!*

Good. Your assault vehicles will be fully loaded out. You are to report to me along with your crews. I will ask for their word, too, at 05:30 hours at the staging area. Now, move!

Rostam Cwenhild AI'd Jeremiah with their concern. He answered, *Both of you know combat is brutal. Your daughter is an adult, she has chosen this profession and it is not safe as you both know.*

Jeremiah continued, *NESS does not waste lives ever.* Jeremiah saluted to Rostam Cwenhild. *Sir!* He spun around and left the king's chamber. Banu's parents knew Jeremiah's words were true, but both were praying very loudly to God for their daughter's protection.

In the morning at 05:30 dark, NESS Jeremiah barked, "Attention!" Banu's crews snapped to attention beside their war vehicles.

Captain Banu Goshasp reported to Jeremiah and said, "Sir, crews fully manned, war stores in place and we are 100% effective."

NESS Jeremiah reported, "Persian soldiers, NESS are asking for 'Your Word is your Life'. This means if you disobey an order from the NESS command chain, we will kill you, but you, as a sovereign individual, always have free will. Since NESS are not your regular commanders in your army, we are asking you to volunteer. Step forward to state 'Yes' or 'No'." Each soldier stepped up as their name was called and said yes.

NESS Jeremiah AI'd his helmet back and smiled. "Comrades in arms, you bring great honor to the NESS and Persian duty. Honor Pride is noted in the NESS journals for each of you." Jeremiah barked, "Attention!" NESS and Persian crews all snapped to attention, "Mount your vehicles, commander's orders are in the comps, you are to open them, read and confirm orders to me. Move."

NESS Jeremiah looked at the civilian FOLK and Persian scientists and technicians. He smiled, "You are under NESS military operations. This means <u>One</u>: you will not pick up any weapons in any vehicle. NESS and Persian soldiers are the ONLY personnel to have weapons. <u>Two</u>: if you have personal weapons on you now, turn them over to the quartermaster. They will be sealed here to be returned to you when we return."

Several Persian technicians turned over their sidearms and swords. Many expressed concern, as their swords were family heirlooms. The FOLK quartermaster said, "We will seal them; NO ONE WILL TOUCH THEM."

"<u>Three</u>:," NESS Jeremiah continued. "NESS and Persian directives will be obeyed instantly. If we say it, we mean it. If you disobey, you will be charged with Dereliction of Duty. In NESS and FOLK, these are punishable up to the death sentence, but we are under Persian laws, so all civilian FOLK and Persian will fall under Persian law courts with full charges.

"And <u>Last</u>, NESS require 'Your Word is your Life' for this endeavor. By that, we mean that your life is forfeit if you disobey, on your word. This gives us leeway so that if you get many of us killed by disobeying an order… we can kill you on the spot.

"Per both countries' laws, I am recording this. As I call your name, step forward, state your full name then state 'Yes' or 'No' to 'Your Word is your Life'." Of the forty personnel, five said no. NESS Jeremiah told them, "Please leave the area." He went down the standby list and got the next five personnel.

NESS Jeremiah looked at his civilians and said, "We are here to protect you; we are not your enemy. NESS, along with the Persian soldiers, will die fighting to protect you, but we want your best from you. This is very important for both our peoples. Per that thought, you will report to FOLK Full Professor Closter. He is the head of scientific endeavors." They all nodded. Jeremiah smiled and said, "Please find your vehicle and belt up; we have a three-day journey to the area."

David looked at NESS Jeremiah from the crowd as he boarded the N.A.P.C. "I'll be damned, the NESS are very colorful." He looked at FOLK Full Professor Closter smiling. "NESS are very colorful."

His professor looked at him, but did not smile. "You will find out how colorful in many ways."

Banu Goshasp read the orders. *No wonder someone does not want us to find this object.* She reported, "Vehicle Persian Heavy Assault vehicle P.H.A.V. 12 read and complying with orders."

Jeremiah AI'd, *Battle orders, the NESS deploy crescent standard spacing. NESS BLEND IN 3…2…1*

NESS scout standard pattern sync to vehicles.

Banu Goshasp punched in the security code and twisted the crypto key. *NESS scout sync achieved.* Her comp systems released all weapons systems. Her crew put on the virtual reality helmets. Banu AI'd her crew, *SYNC in 3…2…1 BLEND Aga, Nayyer and RavAn.*

Banu smiled and AI'd, *Well, let's not get killed, shall we?* They nodded to that statement.

NESS Jeremiah AI'd the brigade, *Deploy. All 24 vehicles move out in good war order, form up, sensor passive, deploy the seekers.*

Banu's heavy tank fired the seeker. The rocket punched out from the tube, ignited, went vertical, and then leveled out after dropping the rocket booster. The turbine screamed to life and a boom echoed off the desert floor as it went mach 2 in two seconds. Someone had painted a GAT on the side saying, "Surprise," in Persian script.

NESS AI'd, *Seeker 0001 flying nape of the earth sensor in 3...2...1.* NESS sensors came online. All in all 8 seekers were launched to cover the area. *SYNC in 3...2...1 BLEND.* Data flooded into the vehicles.

NESS Jeremiah AI'd, *Combat blend in 3...2...1 position Alpha is first wayward point.* Acknowledgments flowed as they went toward the 100 square mile hot zone.

NESS Jeremiah AI'd all, *Commands chameleon effect in 3...2...1.* The whole armored column disappeared. *The seekers NANO bots reconfigure in 3...2...1.* They shimmered and went into passive mode.

David Centauri and FOLK Full Professor Closter were strapped into the combat seats. David looked at the professor and asked, "Are you alright?"

He looked up. "Yes, but these machines scare the crap out of me," he said as they both heard the seekers boom around them.

David released the seat belts, grabbed a hand hold and swung over next to the professor. After he belted in, he pulled his comp out. David said, "These ruins, what are we looking for? I'm confused."

Closter smiled and pulled out a chip. "Well, my orders were to open these when we started this grand hunt, so shall we?"

David nodded. The professor slid the chip into the slot and the screen read, ":>Voice print." The professor said his full name. The screen said, "Confirmed. :>Voice print match, thumb print." He did this and the screen read, "Confirmed :>Quote 'GOD HELP US' :>confirmed."

It was then David Centauri's turn. ":>Voice print confirmed thumb print confirmed :>Quote."

David sighed and said, "God save us from the military."

"Confirmed :>data release in 3...2...1."

Both read the orders, along with the reports and findings. Both said, "JESUS CHRIST." David's mind ran into high gear. *Oh yes, if we find this, I will publish.*

FOLK Full Professor Closter AI'd NESS Jeremiah. He asked, *You read the orders?*

Brian nodded and AI'd back, *We are going to get shot at by someone on this planet that knows what this object is and wants it left buried in the sands.*

David Centauri watched the three women gunners in the cupolas in the N.A.P.C. It had massive armor plate around their torsos. David noted that they were covered in heavy combat armor. *Nice butts*, he thought, but looking harder, he noticed golden threads under the VR helmet in their necks. *What the hell is that?* He looked at the professor.

Brian AI'd Jeremiah, *He is looking at GIFT in the warriors.*

Jeremiah nodded in his mind, *Do not say anything. Just tell him he is not FOLK NESS or Persian. By the way, David is a NESS in the Temple line.*

Brain AI'd back, *OH SHIT!*

But he has no clue that he is, so no answers. That is an order.

Brian AI'd back, *Acknowledged.*

Hmm, David thought. *What about us?* He looked around the APC and saw that all critical systems were heavily armored. He asked the professor, "What happens if we get shot at by someone?"

The professor smiled and replied, "Well, I plan to be flat on this floor, peeing in my pants, but there is a small armor belt that is like a bath tub around the N.A.P.C., mainly for mines." He pointed it out, "it will give us some protection."

David asked, "Professor, have you been shot at in the past?"

Laughing, he said, "Yes, many times, I am 23 axis turns old. If you live long, you will, too. It seems to be a normal state of affairs with humans."

David looked at him and said, "I thought NESS protected FOLK."

"They do, but sometimes, they are very late. I have been around when they are pissed off. It is not a pretty sight for the enemy."

FOLK Full Professor Closter smiled at David, "A bit of advice, NEVER piss off a NESS, they are crazy."

David laughed, "Well, they should meet my father; he is just as crazy as a NESS, I bet."

David opened the lunch box. "Apple, professor? I need good grade."

FOLK Full Professor Closter laughed. "Bribery always works with me, but show me your analysis of the data presented from the orders. Be very quick while I eat my lunch and yours, too."

FOLK Full Professor Closter looked at David and the N.A.P.C. sampled him. "Armor sample, subject David Centauri, neurons firing 10 to 8th power, 10 to the 9th power, armor losing data stream, engaging auxiliary processors, 10 to the 10th power."

JESUS CHRIST, he thought.

It was like a star going NOVA to the NESS.

Jeremiah nodded. *Thought so,* he AI'd the NESS. They all laughed and thought, *Here we go again.*

"Holographic system coming on line, SYNCING, data stream acquired, download started."

The NESS AI'd, *Someone has been GENOMEING WILD humans, analysis suggest Outcasts.*

Jeremiah AI'd the brigade, *Stay sharp people.*

David Centauri smiled. His fingers flew over the keyboard.

Yep, here is the hypothesis. Ten minutes later he showed his professor. FOLK Full Professor Closter AI'd Jeremiah, *Damn, he is at 97% accurate in the actual data. JESUS CHRIST, who is this kid?*

Jeremiah nodded and AI'd back, *Lazarus Temple is alive and moving very large chess pieces in our world, Brian. This kid is a product from him.*

David smiled at the professor and asked, "Can I have my apple back?"

Brian laughed and said, "Sure," as he handed it back. He had completely spaced it. He also handed David his lunch back. "Can you pass me mine? I will share with you."

"And I'll still be hungry."

"Yes, I know, David."

Banu Goshasp smiled as the column halted for the evening in a very large wadi system. She AI'd her command, *Standard over, watch chameleon affect, camouflage deploy.*

All the vehicles blended into the wadi. The overhead system made it look like a wadi was in place, but the crews could stretch and relax outside the vehicles. Banu smiled and AI'd, *Aga I see the ring on your finger.*

She nodded. *Tiny and I are married. His training is just starting.*

What do you mean? Banu asked.

I gave him a list. He looked at it and said he did not know the first thing about stone work, so I sent him to my sister's husband. He will get the material for our new house. Both have orders. They are to finish the base foundation before I get back. We are going to fill the house up with kids. He will be very busy and very tired from fun activities.

Banu bent over to pick up a crate. *Yeah, well, I wish you luck. NESS are sometimes very slow on the uptake.* Banu crew laughed.

NESS Jeremiah AI'd, *All commanders report.*

He listened to their reports and he thought, *Good, not many maintenance issues.* He digested the NESS scouting reports. *Nothing moving. Hmm, seekers loitering over several areas. They, too, had not found a trace of the object, yet .*

He sipped some water and AI'd FOLK Full Professor Brian Closter, *Bring yourself and David to me. I wish to discuss the orders.*

FOLK Full Professor Brian Closter asked, "David, please follow me to the NESS commanders P.H.A.V.2."

As they strolled over, David saw Banu Goshasp bent over, lifting a crate near the P.H.A.V. and addressing her troops. He smiled. He hated uniforms, but she filled hers in nicely. Then, he smashed into a rock outcrop, knocking himself out.

When he came to, he saw stars and a blurry face above him. Banu Goshasp looked down at him. She was barking at him, "You are a stupid, dumb ass Outlander. What is this idiot's name?" She looked harder at his name tag, "David Centauri you are a dumb ass –"

Her tirade was interrupted by NESS Jeremiah. "Captain Banu Goshasp, get your ass back to duties."

"Sir," she spun around and returned where she was.

Jeremiah looked at David. "Do not move, Persian. Medicos are checking you out." He AI'd Brian, *What was he doing?*

Brian AI'd back, while laughing, *Looking at Captain Banu Goshasp's ass, sir!*

Jeremiah groaned. *God give me strength. Well, when the medicos patch him up, bring him and get a combat helmet on his head. That is twice in the last two days.*

David sat in the P.H.A.V. with a bandage around his head and a combat helmet, too. He was paying very close attention to the conversation. Jeremiah had asked very detailed questions to his professor. Jeremiah AI'd his helmet back, looking at David, "Your analysis suggests this is a setup. Why?"

David looked at him, as well. "Easy, sir. Based on long term situations from the Old World, machinery disintegrates rapidly. The higher the technology, the more rapidly it disappears. Analysis suggests this area was nuked, not once, but repeatedly, so it brings up three possibilities.

"One: someone wanted us to stay on the planet, so they glassed the ships with multiple nuclear weapons. As you know, these systems exceed the surface of the sun temperature for a brief time, so this, along with the high radiation, leads to dirty nuclear weapons being used to permanently seal the area.

"Two: they were saturation bombing the area. Since someone had no firm fixed target, it suggests the latter; 100 square miles is a very large area to nuke.

"The third option is a honey pot, sir."

Jeremiah nodded and said, "Go on."

"Well, you put a legend in that says a device that exceeds your expectation is around. Leave clues, some solid and some vague and then, you see what it draws in to give a look. My analysis suggests this scenario, sir."

"Why?"

"Sir, before GIFT's release, we had several star ports legends that stated traffic was infrequent, but it was real. Then, GIFT was released, total records were destroyed en masse, all in high technology areas. My research suggests that we are back to the Old Earth Dark Ages when Rome collapsed their world. Civilization disappeared in that region, but the Far East region did not disappear. Math, sciences, medical studies and agriculture flourished, so someone wanted us to stay in the Roman Dark Ages."

David Centauri smiled.

"My best estimate, we were destroyed culturally and physically. My estimates put that we had 7 billion humans on our world with a very high technology, and then it was gone in 1 axis turn, around 175 axis turns in the past.

Jeremiah nodded, "Go on."

David stated, "Even looking at GIFT release, casualties only mounted to two percent of the population as a whole." He pointed and said, "The x/y display, based on our projections, now, with death rates from our databases, is still in my range of two percent of base. So, by my best estimate, we were suppressed, due to GIFT release extermination worldwide." David did not smile as he looked at the commander, "Sink the ship with all rats in the ocean. None survive, sir."

NESS Jeremiah nodded and said, "I agree, David. It is too easy. Hmm, we know it is a trap, so how do we trap the trapper?"

He AI'd the NESS, *We will hold here. I need a fast analysis of David Centauri's paper.*

NESS AI'd, *We are on it; time, 12 hours.*

NESS Jeremiah smiled. "Well, David, we are holding up for a day here. I want FOLK Full Professor Closter and you to work with the scientific groups using your honey trap. As to what we might face, no wild stuff, just solid science. You have 12 hours, move."

Banu Goshasp strolled by N.A.P.C.-4. David and several scientists were in a heated debate. "This is not your area of expertise."

David responded, "I do not care. My field uses many scientific disciplines. I have passed my exams being fully qualified. I have my views; your math is wrong." He got up, went over to the board, and wrote the equation. "Disprove it," and handed the chalk to his opponent.

The other scientist worked the math and said, "You second rate mind, your equation is wrong."

Banu Goshasp stuck her head in and asked, "What the hell is going on here?"

David turned to her and barked, "Shut the hell up; I am defending my paper in peer review." He went back to the board, looked at his equation. "You are full of GAT poop. Look at this, it clearly states…" Both of them began arguing and they totally ignored her.

She smiled and thought, *Well, maybe this Outlander has some balls* and she went about her business.

NESS Jeremiah AI'd the NESS, *We think the paper presented is correct, so what is your thought?*

Hmm, we will send in 2 N.A.P.C. and 2 P.H.A.V. to scout the region. NESS scouts will shadow along with the two assault NESS. We will provide an over watch. Let's see what we draw out of the dead zone.

NESS Jeremiah said, "David Centauri, I am asking you to volunteer to go into the zones. We need to find what is lurking there, or the object, I prefer the object. Here is the plan."

When he was done, David and Brian were worried.

"Sir," David said. "We are bait for a very large predator."

Jeremiah nodded. He AI'd, *Offensive NESS, report to me now.*

NESS Stan and NESS Bartholomew appeared at the P.H.A.V.-2

FOLK Full Professor Closter said, "David Centauri, these NESS are offensive NESS." Brian in the outer voice said, "OH SHIT."

David looked, stood up and held out his hand, "Pleased to meet you."

NESS Stan, smiling, AI'd his helmet back. Stan had many scars on his face from blast wounds, knives and shrapnel. He was very proud about his face and how it had never healed properly.

Stan picked up David in one armored hand, pulled him really close, and said in the outer voice, "Listen kid, I will eat you alive if you fuck up and some of us get killed."

David smiled. "Put me down you SOB or I will break your fucking arm."

Setting him down, Stan laughed. "Oh, yeah? Try it, I need the exercise."

David blurred. Stan saw his feet upended. He thought, *This is interesting. I weigh a ton and this kid has picked me up with no armor.* He AI'd his helmet back, which brought his weapons online.

Stan was slammed into the steel deck of the P.H.A.V.2. The impact shook the assault vehicle. Stan bounced up trying to get his feet under him. David blurred again, picked Stan up in mid bounce screaming, and threw him out the back of the tank onto his back.

Stan tucked, rolled and turned, facing him and screamed at his armor, *BOOST!* David had blurred, meeting Stan grabbing the weapon flowing out to kill him. David rolled down, taking Stan with him and, using his legs to push him off the sand, Stan thought, *What am I, a bird, now?* He smashed and rolled over the next parked tank turret, making it ring like a church bell.

Stan was pissed. Slamming his armored hand down on the tank, he grabbed a handhold. Bending it was enough to slow him. *Armor leg, boost.* Leaping back, his sensor had a lock and he thought, *I will kill this kid.*

David blurred, grabbed Stan in midair, and used his momentum to smash him into the ground. Stan's armor rang like a church bell. David swung and grabbing the left arm, landed on the NESS's back. He spun and planted his feet on the ground, screaming, and started to bend the left arm back. The armor groaned. Stan's armor informed him *failure in 5...4* Stan screamed *boost the left arm armor now.* The armor informed *NANO boost pressure holding, failure in 12...11...10.*

NESS Jeremiah quietly said, "Hold," from the ramp. Both Stan and David looked at Jeremiah. David's arms were bulging along with everything else and he said in a calm voice, "I will kill this SOB if he ever touches me again." David let go, blurred, and facing the NESS, backed up, shaking. His muscles creaked. As they relaxed he said, "Not again," and sat down on the sand, moaning to himself.

NESS Jeremiah AI'd the NESS, *WE HAVE A BIG PROBLEM!*

The NESS AI'd back, *NO SHIT.*

Jeremiah pointed and said, "Stay there, do not move, both of you." Both nodded. He AI'd the NESS, *NOW WHAT?*

NESS Stan's weapons flowed back into the peace position and Stan thought, *My commander is going to kill me this time.* He slumped into the sand. *I am screwed.*

Several minutes later, NESS AI'd, *Jeremiah, in looking over the data, David is a prototype. We think we have the armor; it is ours, so someone is designing humans to oppose the NESS using biological designs. The closest analogy is an ant. It has massive strength-to-weight ratio along with speed.*

The FOLK NESS AI'd, *We have the DNA profile, so GIFT is working with us, but it is running into problems. This NESS line is stealthed, so we are not happy, but we should have some results in two weeks. If it looks promising, we will integrate into the next NESS cycle. Your mission is still a go.*

NESS Jeremiah looked at both of them and pointed. "David, Stan, follow me, please. Everyone go back to your duties." Jeremiah told both of them to sit on the rock outcropping away from prying ears and eyes.

Jeremiah drummed his armored fingers on the rock; David started to speak. "Sir, I – " NESS Jeremiah held his armored glove up. David stopped in mid-sentence.

Jeremiah said in his outer voice, "NESS Stan, attention!" Stan stood rigid. "I should shoot you now to save myself grief, but that would bring paperwork and I hate paperwork, so did you learn anything tonight?"

Stan did not say a word; he knew he was in deep shit. First, there was the weapons release. Second, he had been handed his ass on a platter by a kid with no armor. Third, he had been taught a valuable lesson: never underestimate anyone, again.

"You are demoted to private when we get back, if you survive," NESS Jeremiah said. "You will go to FOLK therapy and they will evaluate you for active service. If they find you lacking, you will be stripped of the armor and returned to the FOLK. Is this understood by you, private?"

"Sir. Yes, sir!"

"Good, private. This kid that handed your ass to you is the one you will protect with your life on this mission. Do not come back without him alive and whole. Do I make myself clear to you, private?"

"Sir! Yes, sir!

"Now get out of my sight."

When he was gone, Jeremiah AI'd NESS Sergeant Tyron, *NESS Private Stan needs a refresher course in hand to hand combat. Make sure it is done.*

Tyron responded back, *Sir!*

NESS Tyron smiled an evil sergeant's smile as NESS Stan reported to him. Stan moaned and thought, *I am doomed!*

NESS Tyron AI'd his helmet back. *Private, strip your armor off per orders. We are going to use you as a practice dummy until you learn. Seems this David handed you your ass on a platter without armor. We want to see you do the same with us.* He called over his friends. *Meet the new dummy*, he told them.

NESS Jeremiah AI'd his helmet back, "David, you alright?"

David was still shaking, "No sir!" He looked at Jeremiah. "Sir! What am I? A normal person without armor cannot defeat a NESS in armor, at will, and toss them around like toys, like I just did to NESS Stan."

Jeremiah sighed and said, "David, listen to me. When your sister, Dagny Centauri, was wounded, we did DNA testing on her. We found that she is a direct descendent of the NESS GENOME Temple line when you donated bone marrow to save her leg, which did save her life." David smiled as Jeremiah continued. "You are a NESS of the same line."

David stated, "But I do not have the coloring of NESS; I look normal."

Jeremiah nodded. "Many people are NESS; they just do not know they are. A few minutes ago, you did not know, correct?"

David looked at Jeremiah and said, "No, I did know I was a NESS long before coming to New Hope."

"Then why conceal it?"

"Sir! I do research. I did DNA testing on myself, my sister and my mother. We are NESS. My father is NESS, too, but he is twisted; he likes pain in people, so to protect me, my mother insisted I train in unarmed combat." David smiled a little, "I like the exercise, but to me, it is a sport, not a road to becoming a trained killer."

Jeremiah was not surprised David wanted more from his life. He said, "So, you choose science."

"Yes, sir! I like it. I am good. It is combat, but at the mind level; much more satisfying to me. But, tonight my anger got away from me with this bully."

Jeremiah nodded. "I can see that, David. You had every right to protect yourself."

David was startled by that statement. "NESS Stan just reminded me of my childhood with my father. He is a bully. When he hit my mother before I left home, I lost it. I almost killed him in my rage." David's muscles creaked.

NESS Jeremiah responded, "Jesus Christ." His armor sampled David. *He has NANO technology built into his atomic structure.*

"Sir, I swore I would never hurt another being again like I did my father." David looked at Jeremiah, "I am sorry about this. I could have killed NESS Stan from my anger. I hate this ability. It is a curse on me and my sister." He paused for a moment before saying, "I hate all military services. I am sorry, but that is the way I think and feel about this predicament."

NESS Jeremiah said, "David, listen to me. I do not care about you being a NESS or the fact that you beat the crap out of NESS Stan. I want your mind. You were picked by the professor. He loves you and said that you were the best student he has ever had the pleasure to whip into shape for his replacement."

David looked surprised. "He is a grumpy SOB. I never knew."

Jeremiah laughed. "I will tell you, he was on my peer review for my PhD. He is a dictator." David laughed. "I am asking you to go, not ordering you to go. I want the scientist, not the warrior in you."

Jeremiah sat there waiting. David looked up after some minutes. "Sir! I will go. FOLK Full Professor Closter cannot do this alone; he is old and frail."

Jeremiah laughed a belly laugh. "I would not repeat it around him; I think he could whip your ass." David smiled and Jeremiah said, "Attention!" David stood up. "Your orders, science from you, get ready. You leave in the morning."

Banu Goshasp smiled and thought, *Well, David Centauri is quite different.*

She had missed the fight, but the NESS armor recorded it all for her. Her crew laughed when they viewed it in the VR system. NESS Stan had his clock cleaned by a 6 foot 2, 200-pound, young man without armor.

He is nice looking for an Outlander.

Aga laughed and AI'd, *You did run him over, then scream at him after arguing with Jeremiah.*

She nodded.

You are lucky that he did not kill you, her crew piped in.

NESS Jeremiah AI'd, *Banu Goshasp, you will take P.H.A.V.12 and P.H.A.V.3 with N.A.P.C.4 and N.A.P.C.2, work the western grid, run passive scout learn report. Assault NESS Stan and NESS Bartholomew will cover and kill anything that attacks us. Megaton release Code TZFC3BAT23 is authorized.*

Both NESS smiled and responded, *Armor engaging 99% speed of light, 100 12mm round loaded, 200 6mm rounds loaded, 400 3mm round loaded, 1000 1mm loaded, 2500 .25mm loaded. Cold Fusion plants coming online, countdown 3...2...1, power released, system Go. Enhanced sensors coming online, SYNC online, armor NANO diamond pattern engaged, build started 25, 50, 75, 100% online, SYNC to seekers online, spare water loaded online, spare ammo stored, food stored, enhanced oxygen flow online, medical online, engaged, NESS 100% efficient.*

David watched FOLK Full Professor Closter praying. "We have two lunatics with megaton weapons in their hands," he whispered to David.

David watched as the NESS in their armor had just grown by 25%. *We have two walking tanks and my professor is praying that that is a good idea.*

NESS Trevor and NESS Dolan AI'd, *Sir, NESS extended war load; protect the scientists and technicians.*

Jeremiah AI'd Banu Goshasp, *P.H.A.V. will be targeted probably, so megaton release code APTZZX4TC is authorized.*

Banu smiled. *Main engaging, 99% speed of light, prime gun 105mm 150 round, turret 2 and 3 88mm 500 rounds, turret 5/6 40mm 8000 rounds per barrel, 8 12.5mm point defense 15,000 rounds, vertical launch tubes 1 to 8 loaded 180mm hunters with two reloads. Cold Fusion plants coming online, countdown 3...2...1, power released, system Go. Enhanced sensors coming online, SYNC online, armor NANO diamond pattern engaged, build started 25, 50, 75, 100% online, SYNC to seekers online, spare water loaded online, spare ammo stored, food stored, enhanced oxygen flow online, medical online, engaged Persian 100% efficient, spare ammo train engaged, SYNC GO.*

David Centauri put the armor over his scientist's jump suit. *I hate this, but orders are orders.*

Smiling, he put the VR helmet on and slipped the gloves on in N.A.P.C.-4 science suit.

Commander all systems GO. FOLK Full Professor Closter put on the VR helmet, adjusted the strap, secured it, and slipped the gloves on in N.A.P.C.-2 science suit. He smiled once more into the breach. *I wonder if we will survive* he thought.

Commander all systems GO.

Banu Goshasp AI'd her crew, *SYNC in 3...2...1 BLEND Aga, Nayyer and RavAn.* Banu smiled once more into the breach and said, *Chameleon effect in 3...2...1.* The four war machines disappeared and moved forward into the hot zone.

NESS Jeremiah deployed the 20 war machines covering the scouts. He stressed the standing orders, "We shoot and kill anything that endangers our people, no hesitation. Acknowledge." All of them acknowledged. He AI'd the NESS, *We wait and pray.* The FOLK council prayed to all their gods.

David Centauri, after three days of searching, had not found anything in the massive ruins of the dead cities surrounding them. He asked Radiation Scientist Fair-Bell, "Well, how is our rad count?"

She answered, "We are fine. Not many levels, way below lethal levels, we thought, for the region." She continued to work on the issue.

David asked, "Any life signs?"

"They were all negative."

He thought, *Jesus, not even a single Scorps lives here and they are immune to this radiation.* He asked, "Any sonograms worth mentioning?"

"No, just massive junk under us."

He asked FOLK Full Professor Closter, "Well, sir, shall we move to the next sector?"

Brian AI'd NESS Jeremiah, *This whole area is full of ghosts.*

Jeremiah nodded and said, *Yes, but let's be thorough. Go to the next sector; you have three more weeks before we pull you out.*

The N.A.P.C. had basic accommodations. They slept in shifts and life was just work, eat and sleep. After two weeks, the N.A.P.C. had unique smells. David ignored all this; he was watching the sonogram display when it beeped. He queried the comp and typed, :> *what is the alarm?*

comp:> *underground echo looks shielded, active passive beams being intercepted, probability near unity for artificial construct.*

David typed, *Calibrate, run scans again.*

comp:> *working, need to return to this coordinate to run scans.*

He said to Banu Goshasp, "Commander, we would like to return to these coordinates and run the scans again. Comp has found an anomaly."

Banu said, "Granted." She AI'd, *We will cover on my mark 3...2...1.* She turned the four war machines in order to return to the coordinates from the comp system. This would take three hours to go back.

David was looking in the comp records and thought, *Hmm, let's see if I can rebuild this city.* He typed, *comp run simulation on city using these coordinates.*

comp:> *hold, working, 3d rebuild working.*

comp:> *hold loading program.*

A screen came up showing, *Earth Star Republic/ Exploration 2250/ New Earth password: Enquiry which password for ADMIN, GENERAL, ENGINEERING, MILITARY, POLITICAL, RESEARCH.*

He asked the professor, "Have you ever seen this program?"

Brian answered, "Yes, it is from very old records, before the troubles. We keep it for historical records. There is nothing in them, just clerk entries. Do you want the passwords?"

"Yes."

"Here they are, David."

He ran the program. comp:> *open word pad, write to word pad.*

He looked at the underlying software. David liked software. He played in the university's comp systems. The comp group had a formal protest in his records. He laughed. They said he was a hacker, an old term. He pulled up a program.

comp:> *search for this historical doc*, comp:> *found, load for viewing?*

David typed, *Yes*. Looking at the code two hours later, he smiled and thought, *Only a thousand line code change. Not bad, let's see if this works.*

comp :> *execute?*

David typed *yes*.

Well, let's see if I get some hits. He went back to the sparse kitchen. *Well, for dinner, we have fish, fish and more fish; NESS FOLK have gills, I swear to God; vegetables, canned bread, canned fruit. Hmm, well, canned fruit it is, and oh, coffee, canned, of course.* After he heated the coffee, he threw in lots of honey. He went back to the comp.

comp:> *password: Admin*

He laughed and thought, *No way, someone was real lazy.*

comp:> *Go?*

David typed *yes*.

comp :> *working files being unencrypted, run program?*

David typed *yes*.

Oh shit, oh shit. A very large database opened.

"Professor?"

FOLK Full Professor Closter answered, "Yes?" He sounded like he had been asleep.

"Those files you said were clerk entries?"

"Yes."

"They are not. It shows before this city was nuked, a very detailed database. I have just looked under military. According to this database, underground military bunker complexes were sealed before the troubles."

Brian looked over David's shoulder. "But not here. They are about a day from here near a thing called an 'air-car dealership' in the middle of a tenement building section."

Brian asked, "What the hell is a tenement section?"

David said, "Poor people were there; they could not afford housing, food, etc."

Brian said, "What the fuck? They did not take care of each other?"

"It was a thing called dog-eat-dog world."

Brian reflected, "Dog systems are built into the armor, a very good animal, sounds more like Scorps, winner take all, the rest are dead, and you eat them."

David laughed. "You are right, sir! But I think the echo that we saw earlier is EMP shielded power leads. Here is the 3-D rebuild."

"Good work, David."

NESS Jeremiah AI'd Captain Banu Goshasp, *Data dump coming in 3...2...1. Something is out here and it is not friendly.*

Jeremiah AI'd, *His command, David Centauri's sonic earth scans indicate massive power leads down nearly a mile below us. Attention to orders.*

Jeremiah then AI'd the battle group, *Slow turn, full stealth. NESS scouts go to this region, do not engage, find, report, return, move.* The NESS scouts Andy and Bella shimmered into the gloom.

NESS Andy and NESS Bella AI'd, *Armor stealth, passive sensor to MAX, no life sign, no power, AI'd Andy Bella 3...2...1 Blend ready, yes.* They moved after 36 hours in slow stealth. Armor AI'd, *Life signs human, sampling, no known genome on New Earth. Accessing NESS Archives DATA SYNC, Go.* They both had chameleon armor capabilities. *No known DNA sample in Archives, human species unknown, sampling wind, no pheromones in air samples.*

Andy's armor AI'd, *Engage optics 10 power record, scan all electromagnetic spectrum, armor scanning, lock FIR spectrum, running decryption protocols, working decryption, key lock broke, running stealth intercept, virus passive system engaged, SYNC 3...2...1. Armor information DATA DUMP 3...2...1, SYNC to NESS, holographic download started to NESS.*

Jeremiah AI'd, *Good data, NESS FOLK. We need fast scan.*

FOLK AI'd, *Working, one hour.*

Andy's armor AI'd, *Protocol changing, detection alarms indicated.*

Bella told the AI NESS, *Virus software adapt, hide, contact in seven days.*

Armor AI'd back, *Seeing power build up, search systems are engaging.* Andy's and Bella's armor rippled. Armor AI'd, *ECM match lock, we look like debris now.*

Andy and Bella AI'd Jeremiah, *Commander?*

Go!

We have stirred up a wild ass bee colony. We are in stealth, for now, but these humans are encased in space suits. Both their Armor AI'd, *Detecting unknown shield, working match, opening optical window, count-down 5 seconds.* Andy AI'd, *Visually record this, Bella. No weapons detected, scanning 250-meter ship, fusion power plant, warship that matches light destroyer or small cruiser from very old records. Losing window 2...1, last working flag on warship, working match.*

NESS Jeremiah AI'd, *What in the HELL?* He AI'd the NESS FOLK Persians; they looked at each other. *We have been fucked.* Earth Star Republic flag was in their minds.

NESS Jeremiah AI'd Banu Goshasp, *You are to withdraw immediately. Meet and regroup at waypoint C.* Jeremiah AI'd NESS Andy and Bella, *Observe and report, but do not engage. Long range stealth and map this SOB. Perimeter, stay loose and alive.*

Andy and Bella AI'd, *Acknowledge.*

They looked at each other and Andy AI'd, *The NESS are really pissed off, moving now.*

Two days later, NESS Jeremiah AI'd, *FOLK Full Professor Closter will present David's findings; he has no AI capability.*

Brian AI'd findings from David's research and the scientific group.

We think this is a scientific research post from the data. The destroyer matches general config of this model, Destroyer form ESN. It has three offensive ball turrets, two barrels, fusion-powered plasma weapon range, 10 light seconds, recharge rate 30 seconds and 10 megaton per barrel. Their point defense systems are from standard shell up to 88mm plasma weapons and the rest is a guess from the weapons scientists. This shield, we think, destroys GIFT. It uses interlocking fields to interfere with GIFT. The stealthiest AI we deployed cannot engage the system. We are getting no return and think we will need to use it for another one-shot penetration. The shield adapted and closed us out in the Nano time frame. Our findings from the area indicate an EMP weapon burst, followed by neutron weapons blasts across the area. Then, the area was nuked with dirty one megaton impact weapons 174 axis turns ago, but we have found new neutrino traces today, this kills all life.

The FOLK and Persian AI'd, *My God, that is why we did not find any life in the area!*

Brian AI'd, *Why they are here is a guess, but we have a theory. They are making sure GIFT never left the planet. Based on the past from the fragmented data and the new data base David found, our planet was systematically exterminated of human life.*

FOLK and Persian AI'd, *Go on.*

Brain cleared his mind mentally for a moment. *David's research suggests we are supposed to be dead or living in caves. This Earth Star Republic nearly killed all life on our planet based on the spotty existing data. The Earth Star Republic sent one lone starship to make sure we are dead. If they find GIFT, they will come back with a fleet to kill our world and this time they will succeed. We cannot match the military might of a star empire.*

There was much debate in the FOLK and Persian capitals, but they reached a consensus.

The NESS and Persian councils told NESS Jeremiah, *We would like to take the ship, along with the personnel in the research bunker, alive.*

FOLK council, what about the warriors? Jeremiah asked.

We are still debating the issue was the reply.

Four days later, NESS Jeremiah AI'd the FOLK Persian council, *What is your decision regarding any warriors that may be on the warship?*

FOLK Persian council AI'd, *We agree that life protocols are suspended for the warrior group. If they submit, they are to be given mercy. Is that understood?*

NESS roared with the Persian warriors, *We understand that NESS FOLK and Persian had lost 350 million citizens 174 axis turns ago along with almost 6 billion other people on their planet from the weapons carried on similar ships.*

Seven days later, NESS Jeremiah AI'd his command, *Your orders are in the comps. Life protocols are suspended for warriors. If they submit they are given mercy, is this understood?*

Sir.

NESS Jeremiah AI'd, *Chameleon effect in 3...2...1.* The whole armored column disappeared. *Seekers NANO bots reconfigure in 3...2...1.* They shimmered and went to active mode.

The next day, at 07:00 hours, NESS Jeremiah AI'd, *Deploy greeting Hologram projection.*

Starting. You are live 3...2...1 Go.

Earth Star Republic Command General Sir Thomas Stoddard was reading the reports.

We had a breach in the shield. No GIFT had gotten in, but it was close. His computer people were going over the ship, atom by atom. *It's been 700 years since we have been back here. The 13-star system quarantine was finally lifted 30 years ago.* He sighed. *Almost 100 billion people were killed during the outbreak; it took 56 deep space fleets to kill 13-star systems over a ten-year period. Four million deep space sailors, army and marine soldiers were killed during the operations.* He looked at the destroyed column. *15 fleets were destroyed outright, 10 had 50% loss.* The next column indicated that it had taken one century to rebuild the fleets back to operational status.

Even with the Tesla jump drive, it took 20 years to get here. His survey was almost complete. *The other 12 star systems are completely dead. No life, just very dead worlds. Thank God the Gift Electromagnetic Shield Machine (G.E.S.M.) killed the GIFT. It rips it apart, but also kills the host in the process. The engineers had made sure the planet-wide shields had been intact in the other 12 star systems.*

He nodded. This was the original outbreak planet. Coming into orbit, life scanners saw life here. He smiled because of the results of the scans. From orbit, they saw very small settlements dispersed around the planet, hell, even steam locomotives and very primitive radio was evident. He had leeway for GIFT protocols, this time he ignored the protocol. By all reports GIFT was dead on this planet.

Earth Star Republic had killed the original carriers; all six were dead, along with every infected human on this planet. With the breach in the shield, though, GIFT was still here.

Damn, the fleet will need to glass this planet, too, along with neutron bombardment. G.E.S.M. shielding took the power of the local sun to power. He smiled sadly and thought, *This is a very beautiful world. It would be cooked when the atmosphere was stripped off when the G.E.S.M. went active. It would use the solar winds to kill everything alive for centuries.*

We will need to report to the congress to see if...what the HELL, he thought, while looking from his command bridge on Destroyer ESN-12 12035 Lion as NESS Jeremiah's form appeared in front of the G.E.S.M. Shield.

The shield reported, *GIFT detected, all systems online, scanning, tracking, lock minds detected, 180 people infected within range. GIFT*

attack detected, killing GIFT atomic structure. Fusion plant online, boosting shield, GIFT approaching, shields at full power.

Earth Star Republic Command General Sir Thomas Stoddard screamed, "Bring on neutron weapon countdown to pulse in 120... 119." He hit the 'General Quarters' and 200 men and women scrambled to battle stations.

"Report."

"ECM systems online, scanning, sir. I am receiving a broadcast in these frequency ranges."

"Put it on the speakers."

"I am NESS FULL Commander Jeremiah Lee of the FOLK. We have a warrant for your arrest for murder from 174 planet axis turns in the past of 350 Million FOLK Persian citizens and 5.9 billion planet citizens. We ask you SUBMIT; you have 15 seconds. 14...13...12."

"Captain turn on offensive/defensive systems now. Track that signal; kill it."

Laser turrets swung into action. "Weapons, sir, have lock."

"Fire!" The display quickly disappeared into molten glass under a hail of gunfire.

Jeremiah smiled. He AI'd Commands, *Alpha Strike package NOW.*

NESS Andy and Bella AI'd, *Armor opening window for strike package, countdown 5...4...*

David Centauri's fingers flew over the keyboard. "Now."

Brian AI'd, *Sir, strike package delivered.*

Stealth AI'd, *Receiving. CONFIRMED.* It smiled as it shut down the G.E.S.M., along with ECM suite and active radar systems.

General Sir Thomas Stoddard asked, "What do you mean G.E.S.M. and ECM are down?

"Sir, the whole comp systems have crashed."

He screamed, "Go to manual system and isolate! We are under GIFT virus computer attack!"

The ship shimmered into view. Jeremiah nodded and thought, *Nice ship* and AI'd, *Assault strike package NOW.*

Banu smiled and AI'd her command, *Launch seekers.*

All P.H.A.V. fired.

Banu AI'd her command, *Reload, detach missile carrier, move to new positions, now.*

"General Sir Thomas Stoddard, sir! Optical tracking reporting. Multiple missile launch tracking 30 miles, configuration unknown, sir! Mach 2, Mach 3."

"DAMMIT! Kill those missiles!"

"Radar systems online, laser range radar online, ECM, G.E.S.M. rebooting, found virus, have killed it. Defensive anti air coming online, systems have rebooted, engaging missiles."

Jeremiah watched and smiled. *They are using standard explosive shells.* He AI'd, *Chameleon, engage.*

"General Sir Thomas Stoddard, sir, missile track is lost."

SOB

"Scanning, seeing air wakes, engaging. Laser systems coming online, firing, massive weapons fired from the destroyer."

92 seekers exploded. The whole area shook as the cold fusion weapons casing were released into the atmosphere. The last four missiles dived into the wadi. Massive chunks of the sandstone were blasted by the destroyer's weapons, but missed the seekers as they blew past the ship.

"Sir, a second missile has launched. Tracking, sir, we see dust being stirred up, we think they are vehicles. We have three hostiles sited in the turret targeting system. Now ECM is burning through their shielding, have them on target, lock."

General Sir Thomas Stoddard yelled, "Fire. Now!"

P.H.A.V. 11, P.H.A.V. 1, and P.H.A.V. 7 Persian Commanders AI'd Jeremiah, *We have lost chameleon. Destroyer targeting systems is painting us, evading.*

All moved behind destroyed scrappers. The destroyer's two-barrel, fusion-powered, plasma weapon, 10 megaton per barrel, fired one salvo at each target. Jeremiah watched as one square mile of the dead

city was fused instantly into glass. The plasma weapons fired at 5,505 centigrade, the impact exploded the cold fusion power plants in the P.H.A.V.s.; a mile of earth exploded into the stratosphere.

Jeremiah thought, *We have 30 seconds before they kill us again.* He moved his armor optical to 20 power. *Time to die for your country.*

General Sir Thomas Stoddard shouted, "Yes!" but he looked behind him just in time. "DAMMIT, they're going for the research center!"

He watched the four seekers' wakes dive into the underground complexes. The cold fusion weapons casing let go in the warheads. Massive amounts of earth went into the air as the concussion wave rocked the warship.

"Sir! Engage the second wave. More massive weapons have been fired from the destroyer. 94 seekers were destroyed."

The general screamed to be heard above the noise as the seekers exploded in the air, "Are these NUCLEAR WEAPONS?"

"No, sir. No radiation; conventional warheads. We think about half a megaton range."

General Sir Thomas Stoddard replied, "Non-nuclear? These people have COLD FUSION weapons?" He spun around, "Launch the distress torpedo, now."

"Sir! System is down and rebooting. GIFT attack detected. Killing it."

General Sir Thomas Stoddard pointed at the helmsmen and said, "Get the key, go to the distress torpedo and fire it manually."

"Sir, the complex is reporting many people severely wounded, machinery cooling systems are down, GIFT detected in the complexes, they are sealing the air intakes."

The people in the outpost were praying to God as the complex rolled, throwing them around into walls and floors as two more weapons hit them.

NESS Jeremiah AI'd all Commands, *Strike designated targets now.* The remaining nine P.H.A.V. stopped. They rotated the ball turrets toward the destroyer.

Banu AI'd Command, *Target all weapons systems, paint now.*

"General Sir Thomas Stoddard, sir," ECM station said. "We tracked the missile launches. Twelve are counted, we killed three. So far, we have the general area targeted for the other nine."

"GLASS THEM, NOW!"

"Main weapons recharging, 10...9...8, engaging turret targeting system, ECM is burning through their shielding, target lock."

General Sir Thomas Stoddard asked, "What the hell are those?" He pointed 250 meters from them. He watched as the things formed what looked like massive weapons from the body. He shouted, "Weapons, target those things, now. We are going to get shot at by them."

G.E.S.M. reported, "GIFT detected, 250 meters, two life signs, neutron weapon countdown to pulse, 90...89...."

Assault NESS Stan and NESS Bartholomew smiled then waved at the ship as their weapons flowed out of the armor. *Targeting main batteries, sir!*

"General Sir Thomas Stoddard, sir, unknown targeting signatures hitting our ship, vacuum forming, ECM jamming has no effect, radar has no return, and all of our weapons systems are being targeted."

Assault NESS blending, BANU command blending SYNC 3...2...1.

"Sir, we are seeing a vacuum forming on our three primary turret weapons systems."

"WHAT DO YOU MEAN?"

"Sir, like space! Sir! Very heavy tanks forming, ECM phased array, radar return, punching through the shielding, unknown origin, estimated mass 300 tons, four ball turrets, seeing unknown power source."

Jeremiah smiled and AI'd, *Fire!*

The whole starship rocked from the concussions before General Sir Thomas Stoddard was thrown to the deck. He saw number two turret's armor being blown out the back of the turret.

General Sir Thomas Stoddard stood up and thought, *JESUS CHRIST.* He looked out of the bridge windows. His primary weapons had massive holes in them. He could see the two 'things' fire

something; it hit number one and number two turrets, more armor punched out the back along with personnel. His weapon's officer confirmed, "All primary turrets are down."

General Sir Thomas Stoddard yelled, "Fire at the tanks and those two 'things' with everything we have left." Missiles leaped out of the destroyer seeking the tanks.

All Persian P.H.A.V. tank commanders blend for anti-missile defense.

The smaller turrets swiveled seeking the missiles. Massive fire erupted, the sky lighted up as the NESS slivers vacuum disintegrated half a mile around them. The concussion set a wall in front of the destroyer's missiles homing onto the tanks. When they hit, the missiles exploded harmlessly.

General Sir Thomas Stoddard looked at the Weapons Officer and said, "Reload missile tubes, attack using pebbles strike package from space. Let's see if they can hit MIRV warheads going 16,000 feet a second , weapons confirmed, start configuring 5...4...3...."

Banu's tank rocked as it took hits. *Keep moving,* she AI'd her crew. *Remain steady.*

Jeremiah AI'd the brigade, *Kill all smaller weapons now on the destroyer.*

Banu smiled. *Engaging time to die.* Massive gunfire erupted from the tanks.

NESS Persian slivers passed the medium fusion-powered, beam weapons from the destroyer. The city's old steel structure melted a little more with each hit from the beam weapons. Banu screamed as she put another 120mm round into her primary gun and fired back at the turret that had fired at her; it hit the barrel, blowing it off the turret. Banu's AI informed her that her missile battery had a 90% probability of hitting. Pulling the trigger on her main weapon, a 120mm round hit the destroyer's missile battery; the whole ship rocked as the war heads exploded on the ship.

General Sir Thomas Stoddard responded, "DAMMIT, kill those tanks," as chunks of his ship were landing on the planet's surface. The missile battery blast shielding had channeled the explosion away from the ship keeping it from breaking the spine of the destroyer.

Aga, Banu commanded, *Kill all secondary turrets on our side.* Aga smiled. Her 6mm rounds punched through the turrets. Banu AI'd Nayyer, *Cut a hole for the assault, NESS Stan, now.* 3mm holes punched into the bow of the destroyer. *RavAn kill the Radar and ECM.* 1mm hit the side of the destroyer taking out the systems.

RavAn said, *Yes* as she watched her weapon blow the systems apart. Her tank rocked as it was hit by a small fusion-powered beam weapon. RavAn screamed as it blew into her turret.

Banu AI'd RavAn, *Report.* There was nothing but silence.

Banu AI'd HedAyat, *Sir! Get out of the driving position pull RavAn out of the turret then get in that turret to reengage targets on the ship.*

HedAyat moved. The tank was rocking hard from the destroyer weapon hits. He opened the turret door; RavAn was hanging in the harness. He released her from it and dragged her out onto the deck. He looked at her left leg and saw that it had been completely blown off. He reached and felt a pulse on her neck. Smiling, he opened the armored medical locker, pulled out the cuff and slid it over the stump. He AI'd it to start medical.

Engaging, the cuff AI'd him. *Left leg gone, hole in right leg, no major blood vessel damage, punctured left lung. Need packs two and three.* He pulled them out and slapped them into the cuff. *Medical engaging, patient stable, inducing coma, need pack one for plasma.* He pulled it out and slapped it on the cuff. It AI'd back, *No further treatment.*

HedAyat climbed into the turret and put the combat harness on, along with the VR helmet. *Blending, engaging targets,* he reported to Banu.

She AI'd back, *Target these.*

On it.

After pulling the trigger, he watched as he shot apart the laser range finders. RavAn's blood soaked into the armor from the harness as more shrapnel pinged around him. He prayed; the hole was two feet across on the turret.

General Sir Thomas Stoddard prayed, as well. Every turret and every weapons system was taking massive hits and the tanks just kept firing into his ship. Armor exploded off the tanks as his weapons hit them. *Jesus*, he thought, *he sank enemy destroyers with his weapons with one salvo. These tanks just took the pounding.* Looking down along the length of his ship, he saw that chunks of armor were exploding off his ship.

P.H.A.V.1 and P.H.A.V. 2 exploded. Jeremiah was seething as he picked himself up from the blast wave from P.H.A.V. 2. He AI'd, *Let's end this now. Assault NESS kill the bridge, too.*

David Centauri and FOLK Full Professor Closter in N.A.P.C. 4 were thrown to the floor as the N.A.P.C. was hit with the blast wave from the exploding P.H.A.V. 2; they had tried to cloak the P.H.A.V.

The destroyer had punched in with a medium fusion-powered beam weapon to hit the cold fusion reactor. The N.A.P.C. had spun around, stopped, then the cloak failed and they became a target.

David hit the floor in the N.A.P.C. 4 as the war machine rang, then groaned from a hit from a small fusion-powered beam weapon. The armor melted as the beam punched in, and then out of the side leaving a two-foot hole.

The N.A.P.C. had let loose with the 40mm cannon slivers hitting around the small fusion-powered beam weapon before it could fire again. David screamed in the helmet, "Get us in the ditch before we get hit again." The driver floored it; the second shot glassed the rock behind them.

Brian laughed and looking at the holes, thought, *Damn big hole.* They went airborne, and then smashed into the ditch; the third shot went over the top of the turrets.

The commander screamed, "Get the assault troopers out now for deployment!" David hit the back ramp button and it clanged into the rocks. The NCO screamed, "MOVE!" as twenty heavily armed Persians went out into the hell of combat.

The 40mm cannons shot at the destroyer. Debris thumped on the top of the N.A.P.C. 4; the nearest gunner suddenly jerked, then slumped in the harness. The driver screamed, "Get her out of the harness, I will come back to man the gun" David reached up and released the harness as the gunner slid out; he was sprayed with blood.

David said, "Shit," and pulled her farther away from the gun. Brian showed up with a medico's bag. David grabbed the scissors and noted blood from under her arm. Hitting the release on the armor, it fell away. "Damn it, she is bleeding all over the place."

David ran the power scissors, cut her uniform off and looked at her arm. He stuck his finger into the hole and said, "Professor, I do not have the ability to use the cuff."

Brian grabbed the cuff and slapped it on her arm. He AI'd it, *Start medical.*

Started. Hole right arm, hole chest, lung open, broken right arm, shrapnel in right torso, need two each, pack 1, pack 3, pack 4, pack 5. Brian slapped all of them on the cuff. Medical AI'd back, *No further treatment.*

The driver came back, climbed into the harness and put on the VR helmet *Blended.* He blew apart the turret that had wounded his girlfriend who was in serious trouble. He had heard the cuff AI *give probability of surviving 20 percent.*

David looked at his professor. He went back to the seat and patted it for David to follow. When David sat down, Brian told him, "You saved that woman's life. She will make it. Another load explosion rocked the N.A.P.C.; shrapnel pinged the outside.

David did not grin. "Well, professor, this is not fun."

Brian looked at him and said, "No, and it is about to get much worse," as another tank exploded smashing them into the roof. As David was knocked out, his last thought before oblivion was, *At least I have a helmet on this time.*

David woke up and the N.A.P.C. was choking with dust and dirt. The interior lighting was on emergency battery systems. He rolled over and looked at his professor; Brian was breathing, but out cold.

Moaning, he got up and noticed there was no noise. He shook his head, his ears were ringing. Going over to the driver, he shook his leg. The driver bent down and smiled.

"Are we alright?" David screamed.

The driver nodded, pointed to the driving position, and made the universal sign "you drive".

David nodded and plopped into the driver's chair and put the VR helmet on his head.

HUD:>*reboot?*

David yelled, "Yes!"

HUD:> *Reboot started system online 3...2...1* then the HUD :> *AI?*

David screamed, "No!"

HUD:> *Manual boot 3...2...1* then David witnessed Virtual Reality through his eyes in the helmet. HUD:> *System started Yoke engaged.* HUD:> *Orders?*

David asked, "Commander, where do we want to go?"

HUD:> *Answer report to Captain Banu Goshasp.* HUD:> *Map overlay waypoint D.*

David muttered, "Alright, let's back up; get this piece of crap going." He backed out of the ditch then spun the N.A.P.C. "Flooring it. I hate the military!" screaming out loud. The gunners were still firing at the destroyer.

David saw a large blue beam glass a destroyed building 100 meters away. Spinning the yoke, he skidded the N.A.P.C. to the right between two large buildings. 100 meters in front, another large blue beam blew another destroyed building apart. Slamming on the brakes, he swung N.A.P.C. to the left and floored it as another blue beam blew the building to his left apart. He was screaming and driving like a maniac to get away from the weapons fire.

"Sir! We have destroyed three more tanks. They have other vehicles. We have killed four of those, too."

General Sir Thomas Stoddard watched as half the skyline went up with thousands of tons of dirt and rocks. His ship was shoved several feet back from the concussions; the air waves slapped all of the bridge personnel off their feet.

General Sir Thomas Stoddard looked up from the deck at a monitor hanging above him. The medical people were screaming into the monitor's voice pickups, "Half the ship's compliment is dead from one hit; we have never seen this type of wound. It just pulped the sailors."

General Sir Thomas Stoddard watched as his chief medical officer was blown apart in the monitor from behind 6 inches of armor.

"Sir!" General Sir Thomas Stoddard picked himself up off the deck. "Weapons reported. We have no more effective weapons." He looked around, punched in destruct code on the fusion engines and set the countdown. The timer began: 60... 59...

He went on the speakers and said, "Release the weapons' locker; we are going to get a ground assault attack."

Jeremiah AI'd Assault NESS, *Kill all the lesser warriors. Bring command warriors to us. Leave the ship intact. We are seeing destruct command.* He AI'd, *Comp is trying to override destruct authorization. Now slap on more AI comp system packages when you get on board the ship. Acknowledge.*

They AI'd back, *Acknowledge, sir!*

NESS Stan and NESS Bartholomew went under the ship as the weapons opened on them. Stan smiled in his helmet and thought, *Just like the old days; everyone trying to kill you.* He rolled out in the open firing a burst at the bridge with 1mm NESS slivers.

General Sir Thomas Stoddard saw holes appearing in the armored glass. He thought, *That is impossible, that is diamond glass* ducking as it shattered then blew the shards onto the bridge. The helmsman was pulped along with the key for the distress torpedo manual launch. His

blood splattered onto the general's space suit and the other personnel located on the bridge.

NESS Stan and NESS Bartholomew blurred; one went to the stern, one went to the bow. *Armor engaged, targets blending, 'NO mind'.* Earth Star Republic command General Sir Thomas Stoddard watched as the things cut through eight inches of armor in six seconds. In his monitor, Banu smiled and AI'd Nayyer, *Nice hole. Stan is a very big NESS.*

NESS Stan and NESS Bartholomew watched as the destroyer's armor was blown apart. Stan AI'd his assault team, *On me now.* 20 troopers blurred to him. Stan AI'd, *Set weapons for infantry, no armor piercing.*

The assault team responded, *Sir!*

Sir! Armor breaches in bow along with one forward of engine room; the Marine's navy personnel responding to penetration. Last sensors reporting 40 GIFT enemies under our hull with very heavy weapons.

General Sir Thomas Stoddard peeked over the shattered bridge window *SOB here they come!*

Captain Robert Stork fired from his assault rifle and dropped an enemy trooper, but firing on the thing had no effect as it stepped over his fallen comrade

NESS Stan smiled. *Armor 20mm grenade 2,000 feet a second, no penetration.* Smiling, he raised his rifle and AI'd *.25mm no damage to ship. Alright, the old fashioned way.* Picking up the warrior, he slammed him into the bulkhead then used his knife and drove it into the warrior then flung him down the corridor.

Stan smiled as he yanked the knife back from the enemy soldier it trailed intestines down the corridor Stan stepped over the late Captain Stork going toward the bridge as his strike team killed everything in their path.

Captain Robert Stork exclaimed, "Sir, we are getting slaughtered!" He screamed then there was silence.

General Sir Thomas Stoddard heard more screaming and massive gunfire being reported from the engine room. He turned as the armored door blew off, something entered his bridge and crewmen died before he could blink. This 'thing' yanked his radio woman off the seat and threw her out the bridge's shattered armored glass window. Her screaming ended as she hit the ground 100 feet below them.

NESS Stan's armor reported, *Three warrior officers, eight lesser warriors, targets are painted*; he smiled, killing all eight lesser warriors. General Sir Thomas Stoddard, as well as two others, was alive when the 'thing' looked at him; it was covered in blood along with massive impacts. As he watched, the armor drew in the blood and the impacts filled in. It pointed a rifle between his eyes and said, "Submit." General Sir Thomas Stoddard heard gibberish as he raised his hands in the air.

NESS Stan thought, as he put the handcuffs on their wrists, *Bunch of 'name only' warriors.* He felt nothing but contempt. *David would have beaten me to death with my own weapons if he had been in command of this warship.* Stan had great respect for David's abilities He finished by also cuffing their feet together, "Stay, do not move, if you do I will kill you." General Sir Thomas Stoddard did not understand a word, but he saw the weapon pointed between his eyes; message was received loud and clear.

NESS Stan slapped another NANO comp and AI'd, *Take over this ship; seal the comps now working.*

Comp AI'd, *Simple protocol, have control destruct command stopped at +4.*

NESS Stan AI'd Jeremiah, *Self-destruct aborted, all systems under NESS Persian control.*

NESS Jeremiah returned, *Bring up hologram recording systems, dump all comp information, SYNC data stream, engaged 2...1* and several minutes later, AI'd, *Reported, done.*

General Sir Thomas Stoddard looked at the 'thing'. It disappeared. Hearing more screaming and gunfire, he looked at his captain and said, "We are dead, Charles."

He nodded. "I think so, sir. Whatever they are, we are going to find out real quick." When the 'thing' came back, his knife flowed out of the armor.

General Sir Thomas Stoddard and two other captives were suddenly grabbed. It cut the bindings on their legs and pointed to the door. NESS Stan smiled in his helmet and said, "My commander wants a long talk with you," still gibberish from the 'thing' waving massive weapons at him. He went out the blown-off armored hatch; the interior passage was covered with blown-apart crewmen, blood pooled on the deck. Nothing was alive on the ship.

He neared the surface hatch when he saw the last of his crew members being herded out in front of him. The 'thing' was pointing at the normal-looking enemy humans. As he stepped out onto the planet's surface, gunfire erupted. He spun and watched his entire surviving enlisted crewmembers being shot down. Screaming, he rushed the 'thing'.

Stan smiled and thought, *At least he has bravery in him.* He backhanded General Sir Thomas Stoddard into unconsciousness. He AI'd his Persian comrades, *Still stupid.* They picked him up to go to their commander.

They all answered, *Yep, lucky for us, we could have been slaughtered if this human had any warrior in him.*

NESS Stan and NESS Bartholomew dumped 22 officers in front of NESS Jeremiah Lee. He AI'd NESS Stan, *Good work. You are reinstated to your former rank, but FOLK evaluation is still on.*

Sir!

NESS Bartholomew, good work. You are promoted to chief master sergeant, further schooling is authorized.

Sir!

Go get the scientists in the underground complex. Do not kill them, bring them to me, they are like FOLK. Life protocols apply to them.

Sir!

Banu AI'd HedAyat, *We are to report at the starship, get back to the driving position, be ready to move our tank, Sand Stalker.*

She AI'd Persian medicos, *I have one wounded N.A.P.C.-4*

Commander AI'd back, *Sir, we are one click behind you; we will be there in two minutes.*

Banu AI'd the main turret hatch open. Popping her head up, she looked at her tank. It was chewed up with gaping holes in the armor. The Jell Shot dribbled out the holes *hmmm*. She AI'd support, *Need temporary bulwarks, bring the Jell tanker, too.* She smiled. *But still 100% effective. Defensive perimeter, nothing gets in or out.*

Her command AI'd *Sir!*

David Centauri walked over to Banu, "Sir! I can help."

She nodded. "The Persian medicos are working on my crewman; they need an orderly to help move her."

"Sir!" He went into the tank; it smelled like a slaughterhouse. RavAn looked very pale and the medicos were working on her in a pool of blood.

One of them motioned him over and said, "Hold the plasma up for us."

As he watched, they worked hard. Medico Aref pointed and said, "David, hand me the plasma, then go get a stretcher with a three on it." He ran into the N.A.P.C. 4, pulled it down, and ran back. Aref said, "When I say we are going to lift her, slide it under her. Ready? 3...2...1 lift." David saw that the blown off leg was showing bone, as he slid the stretcher under RavAn.

Aref said, "Step back."

They engaged the thermo stretcher. RavAn stopped thrashing. Medico Aref pointed to David and said, "Pick up the front; we are moving her now." David bent and lifted her. Persian medico P.A.P.C. was waiting. They slid her in and left him in the dust.

Banu came up behind David; he had just finished throwing up behind the N.A.P.C. Banu stated to his bent over back, "David, you are to report to the underground complexes."

He turned, put his head against the N.A.P.C. and turned his head to Banu, asking her, "Is that your friend?"

Banu nodded and said "Yes."

David had contempt on his face. "How do you cope with the slaughter of people?"

Banu looked into his eyes and said, calmly, "YOU DON'T. You just do your duty, then, when you have time to think, you throw up and get very drunk."

Banu knew David could see her pain. She had lost many people today, but she is a commander and responsibility was hers alone. She would have further duties with the surviving people today. "You have your orders, now move."

"Sir!" David went into the N.A.P.C. *I really hate the military*, he thought, as he hit the switch to the armored door; it shut out the scene from hell.

David sat in the combat chair covered with grime. He threw the combat helmet on the floor and noted half the destroyed city was on fire, again. He looked out of the armored window; it looked like a nuclear winter. From his reading, he figured the dust was still falling. Closing his eyes, tears ran down his cheeks. FOLK Full Professor Brian Closter grabbed his hand and said, "David, we have a duty to save the Earth Star Republic civilians. The FOLK need you to be brave. These people are under Life Protocols, can you do that for us?"

David looked at the professor that he loved and answered, "Yes, Father, I will be brave." As he wiped his tears away, he said, "I will not forget this stupidity." He looked out the window and thought, *There has to be a better way than killing each other because we are different in looks, beliefs, speech or have GIFT.*

David smiled. "Professor?

FOLK Full Professor Brian Closter said, "Yes, David?"

He replied, "I see you did not hit the deck when the shooting started." He pointed to a massive hole beside them in the N.A.P.C. 4 war machine.

"David, you can call me Brian, and to answer your question, I am not a coward. I was a NESS before I came to my senses after the troubles." David was very startled. "I gave up the armor forever. I will never kill another human being for the rest of my life." Smiling at David, he said, "Look," as he rolled up his sleeve, he showed him his skin color. David was shocked. It was not normal NESS coloring; he had rather lewd tattoos running up his arm.

Brian laughed. "Well, GIFT has a sense of humor. It matched the tattoos to my skin and added others after it went through the data bases for human sex. I was a deep space sailor in astronavigation, as a matter of fact, before I got stuck on this planet with GIFT release." Brian's eyes twinkled at David. When he saw David just stare at him with disbelief, Brian laughed and said, "I am from the Constellation Carina, Star name HR 3138, or 'damn it is hot here'."

David just stared. Brian pulled a cooler to him and asked, "Ever had a beer?" As he pulled a glass jug out with the golden liquid, Brian's eyes twinkled. Talking to the beer, Brian said, "My baby, not a scratch after being tossed around by crazy people with guns."

"No, what the hell is beer?"

Brian laughed. "Well, I have a friend who is a lab rat in New Hope. We make it using Old World instructions."

"Old World?"

"Yes, Earth, the original planet of humans." David's jaw hit the N.A.P.C. 4 deck. Brian continued while laughing, "David, hold the two frosted mugs for me, that's it," as he poured the beer into the glasses. Brian set the beer like it was a precious jewel in the cooler. "Hand me one. Now, hold up the glass, that's it," he smiled. "A toast, David, may you find a beautiful woman to share your lives together," he clinked his mug to David's. Smiling as he sipped the beer, he sighed and said, "Ah, nectar of the gods." David eyed the beer, took a sip and smiled as it went down.

He said, "Brian, this is very good."

Brian laughed. "I am your professor. I would not steer you wrong. Just don't tell Jeremiah; he will drink my stock out in days. The man loves fine liquor, one woman and plants."

David laughed as he leaned back sipping his beer and said, "I have much to learn, Professor."

Brian nodded. *Yes, the universe is wide and mysterious. I miss staring out into vastness from a starship bridge.*

Earth Star Republic civilians were in shock. Some were injured and several were dead. In the emergency light, they looked at each; fear was very real on their faces. Jody Sanatoria was holding her friend, Sasha. Her arm had been broken in two places and there was a big tear on that arm; the atmosphere had penetrated her breathing systems.

Sasha was looking at her with very big eyes. "I am going to die; the atmosphere has penetrated the G.E.S.M. shielding." Jody tried to patch the suit, but it was leaking.

Jody said, "Be quiet. I have stopped the bleeding, the splint is working, and we will be alright." *But,* Jody smiled, *be brave.* Before she could finish her thought, holes appeared on the armored door, through the door, and then blew through the back wall.

The door was wrenched off the blast hinges. Metal screeched as it disappeared back toward the tunnel then a 'thing' entered. It moved with no sound, was 10 foot tall and encased in green armor. It screamed, talked gibberish and waved the rifle at the people. All of them screamed while running to the back of the bunker.

Jody picked Sasha up and said, "Run," she screamed as she looked over her shoulder. It screamed more gibberish while advancing toward them. There was no place to run. The 'thing' looked over its shoulder, more gibberish. A normal looking human being appeared before them, looking at them.

NESS Stan was having fun. His scream, along with saying, "BOO," worked. He loved the old cartoon films. He smiled while waving the rifle around, it had the same effect on non-warriors panic which was very good; made it easier for them to listen to reason while David interpreted.

"I am David Centauri. I am in service to the NESS FOLK and Persians. You will not be harmed by this NESS unless you have any weapons on you. I mean, anything that is considered a weapon and that kills, if you have anything like that then drop them on the floor now!" He talked to the 'thing'. He nodded. David pointed to a woman and said, "You have a pistol under your right arm and one behind your back. This is NESS Stan, he is an assault NESS. He will kill you if you do not submit to being disarmed, now. If not, Stan will consider you a warrior, so spread your arms apart, now." She reached for the weapon from under the right arm of her space suit.

"Die!" she screamed.

NESS STAN smiled. *Warrior armor targeting.* His rifle blew her torso in half. The people screamed and hit the floor as the woman splattered over them.

David did not smile. *God, almighty; I hate the military,* he thought. "I will not tell you again, any weapons, NESS Stan will kill you!"

NESS Stan said, while scanning, "David, no more weapons; knives, but that is it."

"Thank you, Stan, please refrain from killing these people. But, since I do not have any armor, if I get wounded or killed by a knife, you will die."

NESS Stan said, "Oh shit." He pointed one out.

David pointed and said, "You in the back, the one with the broken arm, we see a knife. Drop it on the floor, now." Sasha pulled it from its scabbard and dropped it on the floor. David nodded. "Very wise move. Stan, any more weapons?"

Stan said, "No."

David nodded. "Please refrain from killing anyone else. We need these people, is that understood?"

"Yes, David. I am sorry for being a shit head toward you; I ask for forgiveness."

"You are forgiven, Stan. I am sorry for beating your sorry ass to a pulp. I ask for your forgiveness."

Stan laughed. "You are forgiven, my friend."

David smiled and looked at the group. "You have wounded?"

"Yes."

"How many?"

"Around twenty."

David nodded. "We have medicos that will assist the injured now."

Jody marveled. More normal people arrived with stretchers. Her friend was put on one.

David said, "Follow these people. They will not harm you." Another NESS stepped in who was smaller than the first. "This NESS will take you to the assembly area. YOU WILL NOT BE HARMED BY HER."

David looked at Stan. "Let's round them up." When the complex was emptied, some 200 were still alive. David noted, *They all had space suits on them, even the 22 officers.*

NESS Jeremiah Lee smiled in his helmet; David Centauri and FOLK Full Professor Closter were beside him. Jeremiah turned and said, "You will speak in their language for me."

David said, "Sir!"

"Yes"

David replied, "We speak their language."

He smiled. "I want fear in their hearts. Plus, we have spies among us from these people, remember the axles?"

Jeremiah's armor AI'd, exploding with data. Jeremiah laughed, for the new NESS FOLK label for these types of people was Nova's.

NESS Jeremiah stated in his language while David interpreted, "I am the NESS Full Commander who took your ship along with your complexes; you are now guests of the NESS FOLK and Persian countries. We will treat you fairly and humanly if you behave. This will be explained to you in detail in the next few days. If you don't behave, we will kill you on the spot."

He replayed the recording of the woman who would not submit. Jeremiah finished by pointing at the Earth Star Republic.

"Is this understood? For now, say 'Yes' or 'No'. If 'No', we will explain it to you again."

They all said, "Yes."

He nodded and said, "Good. We understand you are not from this planet, but work here." He laughed, "What a concept. So, we are going to take your space suits off of you, all your clothes. You will be scanned and given Persian clothing."

David looked at them. They were crying and screaming. "Jeremiah, they are saying they will die from plague!"

NESS Jeremiah stated, "I understand your concern, but it is too late. You will submit or we will kill you now." His armor flowed with massive weapons. The Earth Star Republic civilians in front laid flat on the sand. Jeremiah continued, "Do I make myself clear on this subject? Strip, now, sit in the sand and wait. You will be asked your name, you will be scanned, and you will have a DNA scan."

Sasha was on the stretcher; she looked at the normal human medico, Yelena, and smiled. Pointing to her badge, Sasha looked at her and spoke Russian. Yelena jumped back, a startled look on her face. Sasha smiled and looked at Jody. "Told you Russians rule the galaxy."

Yelena smiled and told her in Russian, "I am going to remove your clothing; we need to scan you, and we will not hurt you." Yelena looked at Jody, "You help?" Jody nodded and helped her friend.

Yelena AI'd her team, *I will need a cuff with bone repair.* Her team arrived, put the cuff on her and the diagnostics flowed, *Compound fractures. We will wait to see if she survives GIFT.* Yelena told her in Russian, "We are going to wait, for now, then repair your arm in a more sterile area. Your fractures are alright, for now, with the temporary splint."

Jody Sanatoria took her space suit off beside her friend and thought, *JESUS CHRIST, we are truly screwed. I knew it, I should have stayed in my lab, but no, five million credits was a lot of money. Easy duty, adventure and more science equipment in my hot hands. It was fun until now.* She pulled her jumper off, pulled her underwear off, and kicked it all away. She sat away from the group, naked in the sun and sand.

Several hours later, Jody was looking at the sand when a shadow covered her. She put her hand over her eyes in order to see. She was surprised; this was the man who addressed them. David Centauri lowered his hand.

"Miss, I am David Centauri. I will not hurt you. Would you please stand up? I would like to ask for some information." She grabbed the offered hand and he lifted her with no effort. He smiled and asked, "Miss, your name?"

"Jody Sanatoria."

"Your occupation?"

"Ecological biologist," she said.

"What planet?"

"Orion Arm, New Edennnaradie. Do you need galactic coordinates?"

He smiled and said, "That will come later. Your age?"

"25."

"Married?"

"No."

He smiled. She wondered, *Why is he smiling? I am going to die anyway.* "David Centauri, why are you smiling? I am naked, standing in the sun and scared to death. Does that sound like fun to you?"

David smiled and really looked at her. *About 5 foot 8, dirty blond hair. Jody Sanatoria is very beautiful.*

"No, I think you are the most beautiful woman I have ever encountered, naked or clothed, in my life." He smiled broader. "We are not going to harm you; the scans work better without clothes. If you wish, I will take my clothing off, too, I have nothing to hide."

She thought, *He is cute.*

"I will go through the scan first if it will ease your worry," he offered.

She laughed and said, "Well, thank you, David Centauri, for your offer. My friends call me Jody." She held out her hand.

"My friends call me David," he said, gripping her hand. *Oh, God,* he thought.

Jody thought, *Oh my God, David is very handsome.* Still holding his hand, she asked, "David, you are not a soldier?"

He replied, "No, I will never be a soldier. I will not kill life, period. I am a student working on my Master's degree in Archaeology."

Jody felt her mind/body responding to David. *What the hell? I am going to kiss David.*

"I wish to kiss you for not letting that 'thing' kill us in the bunker."

David said, "Alright."

She pulled him to her, while thinking, *Damn, this feels real good.* She pulled him into her harder. When they broke apart, both were red and panting.

David looked down and thought, *Damn it, go down, you little mind.*

Jody stated while smiling, "David, I am not sorry. I wanted to kiss you before I die. It was very nice."

David's mind was racing. He had never, ever responded to anyone like this. His DNA screamed at him for this woman. "Jody, I would like to ask you for a date, with your clothes on. I know a café in the city of Nippur that serves a very good local dish."

She laughed and said, "I think I am going to die, but if God grants wishes, I accept your date proposal."

Sasha rolled onto her side, "Where is Jody?" She had watched her friend kiss this David character and she smiled. Jody was an Orion. They were considered very wild, rough explorers, miners and a no-holds-barred group. Her crowd would sooner start a bar fight just for the hell of it, to see what would happen to the more sophisticated worlds. All the other Galactic arms considered them crazy, deep space crazy. She laughed as she saw David's character rise to the occasion.

David pointed from the bent over position, "This is NESS Brenda. She is going to scan you. She will not hurt you. Just stand, legs apart, arms apart."

Jody complied while looking down and laughing. "I think, David, you should stay bent over for a while until you can get it under control."

David smiled. "I will take your advice, Jody."

NESS Brenda laughed and said in her outer voice, "David, I am scanning." Several minutes later, the scan was finished with results, *Jody Sanatoria, armor sampling, no issue.* NESS Brenda leaned over and whispered, "David, Jody Sanatoria might not make it, but I will pray for her. You two are very cute."

David slowly straightened. Jody was watching him with a big smile on her face while not hiding anything from him. NESS Brenda laughed in her outer voice and said, "David, I will give Jody Sanatoria the clothing or she is going to throw you on this sand and have you for lunch."

David stated, "I am brave."

NESS Brenda suppressed a laugh and thought, *You men are easily fooled. Jody Sanatoria is going to eat you alive and you are walking right at her oblivious.* Shrugging, she held up the clothes. David smiled and took the clothes over to her.

Jody grabbed David and threw him over the small sand dune rise. They rolled to the bottom; Jody landed on top of him, smiling. She held her fingers over his lips and whispered in his ear, "Do not move." She ripped his clothing off, smiling at him on the sand.

Sasha laughed as she saw Jody grab David and toss him over the small sand dune. She watched as David's pants were tossed up in the air, along with his other clothing. Sasha laughed harder when she saw her friend's head just above the dune popping up and down over the sand dune crest.

"Well, at least Jody will be happy when we die." She looked at the NESS 'thing'. She swore it was laughing at her friend's antics. Rolling flat on her back, she started to pray.

NESS Jeremiah AI'd NESS Brenda, *What is the hold up? Where is David Centauri?*

She AI'd back, *Ahh, sir! He is kind of busy now, sir!*

Jeremiah AI'd, *Explain.*

Brenda AI'd, *I will just show you, feeding data.*

Jeremiah saw Jody taking David at the bottom of the sand dune. Jeremiah laughed and thought, *I like this Jody Sanatoria, no hesitation in her. I will pray she lives with GIFT. Well, continue.*

Brenda thought, *Jody is not going to run.* She bent down and picked up her comp pad. *Yes, you men have your brain between your legs,* as she went over to Sasha.

Jody Sanatoria smiled as they both got up, "Well, David." He had a very dazed look on his face, "What is next?"

He looked at her and said, "We will go back over to the group."

As he handed her the clothing, she laughed and turned around. *Hmm, this looks like a bra?*

"David, is this a bra?" she asked, while waving a strip of cloth.

"Bra?"

"Yes, for women," Jody said, pointing at her breast.

David laughed and said, "Yes, here." He reached around to her front. "It will adapt to your breast shape."

Jody turned and said, "Oh, I see. Yes, put it on me." He smiled, slid it on her and wrapped it to her back. It sealed. She examined it and said, "Yes, that is very nice." Grabbing the rest of the clothes, she put them on. He was still dazed; she grabbed his hand. "David, you are naked."

He looked down. "Well yes, that seems to be no problem because I like being naked."

Jody laughed. "Well, so do I, but the NESS is coming back, so clothes would be alright." David laughed and pranced around, picking his clothes off the desert floor.

He got dressed and continued. "We will sit in the group; the NESS will touch you. Do not be frightened because you are going to meet GIFT."

Jody looked at her feet. "It is going to kill me."

David lifted her chin up. "No, Jody, have faith. I will sit beside you."

Jody put her hand in his. "Alright, let's go and meet this GIFT."

Sasha smiled as Jody and David sat beside her. She put her good arm over her eyes; her friend smelled like sex. She laughed to herself and thought, *I hope heaven has sex.*

All of the Earth Star Republic personnel took off their clothing. They were scanned, given clothing, and told to sit.

Jeremiah brought the officers in front of the crowd. Brian stated for Jeremiah, "You will witness GIFT. First, I am NESS. I am the primary carrier of GIFT. It is my friend. These men and women around you are also with GIFT. We on this planet have thrived with GIFT but it needs new friends, too."

Brian pointed to Jeremiah, he AI'd his helmet back and all the Earth Star Republic looked at him. Jeremiah AI'd the NESS, *AI your helmets back, too.* He pointed, "These are NESS, too, we are going to sample you with GIFT."

NESS touched all. Jody Sanatoria watched as the people passed out around her. Jody looked at her friend as the NESS broke contact asking, "David, is my friend alive?"

The NESS nodded to David.

David said, "Jody, your friend is alive and well; she will be asleep for two days."

Jody was last gripping David Centauri's hand, hard. Her knuckles were white. NESS Brenda knelt in front of her and looked at David. "I am her friend I will not hurt her." David repeated what she had said to him.

NESS Brenda smiled. Her sensors showed extreme fear. *I will ease that fear.* She liked this woman. Stepping back, she AI'd her armor to disengage from her.

Jody Sanatoria watched as the armor fell away. The NESS pulled the helmet off and set it on top of the armor. Brenda stepped forward and her breasts swayed on her very pregnant belly. Jody looked from her feet to her head. Brenda was as naked as the day she was born with very colorful skin, a rainbow of colors, along with being a natural brunette, too.

Brenda smiled and said, "Tell her I am eight months pregnant from my husband." David did. Brenda got down on her knees, slowly held her belly up to get better settled and took Jody's hand to put it on her belly. She said, "Life starting."

Jody could feel the baby moving under her hand. The skin felt smooth and supple. Jody smiled as she saw a hand stretch on the NESS's side. Brenda pulled a picture from the armor and handed it to Jody. It showed her husband; he looked normal to Jody.

"You are human?"

Brenda laughed and nodded. "I am human, just different. Are you ready?" David told her.

Jody Sanatoria nodded and said, "Yes."

NESS Brenda AI'd GIFT, *I am praying for Jody Sanatoria.*

GIFT smiled and thought, *Here we go.* Brenda held her palms up and golden threads appeared. Jody looked into Brenda's eyes; there was no malice and no hatred, just patience. Jody bit her lip and put her hands into Brenda's looking down at her hands. Golden threads ran up her arms; she was not frightened. The scientist watched and observed.

GIFT went into her mind; it said, *Hi, I am GIFT, my friend.*

Jody said, "You are GIFT?"

GIFT AI'd, *Yes.*

She laughed. "I was told you kill everything you touch."

GIFT laughed and said, *No, I treasure life. Jody Sanatoria, I am going to look at you, relax you have passed the test.*

Jody felt less fear. "So you're saying I am not going to die?"

GIFT said, *Nope* then giggled. A few minutes later, GIFT said, *Jody Sanatoria, bye, for now. Our minds will adapt to each other, you have plenty of reserves, build is complete.*

NESS Brenda sat back. Jody Sanatoria's eyes opened. She looked at David who had a very startled look on his face. He seemed very surprised, so she said, "Well, are you going to kiss me?"

David Centauri, smiling, said, "You bet." When they broke apart, David smiled and said, "Jody, as a matter of fact, I would like to ask you to go the N.A.P.C. 4 with me to take a nap in my bunk. You look very tired."

Jody laughed, "Well, if you insist, but I am going to take your clothes off again while we sleep. Do you mind?" He picked Jody up in his arms and blurred. Jody laughed and said, "Not bad."

When they arrived, he set her on the bed. She took his clothes off and threw hers off the bunk. "In here now, David." Closing the curtains, she had fun with David.

NESS Trudy saw her leg sticking out from the closed curtain. She scanned the area; her armor reported, *Jody Sanatoria, asleep; David Centauri asleep.* She laughed. *Not for long, armor,* as Jody pulled her leg back.

"David," Jody moaned. "Do you like that, David?" She laughed and said, "I see that you do, David."

NESS Brenda reengaged her armor laughing and AI'd Jeremiah, *Jody Sanatoria is awake and fully functional.*

Jeremiah AI'd back, *What do you mean? She should be out cold for another two days."*

Brenda AI'd back, *Well, Jody woke up. She said she wanted David to kiss her, he did, and then he blurred. I think he is in the N.A.P.C. 4 with Jody now.*

Jody Sanatoria, NESS Jeremiah AI'd, *I like her, very Zoe like.* He laughed to himself. *God grants many things to good people. Well, let's get the rest into the N.A.P.C.s. They will be out for two days.* Everyone was surprised that only three Earth Star Republic people died.

All the rest were out cold, GIFT AI'd, *Rebuild going normal.* When asked, GIFT AI'd them *I have been given more options,* so when it ran into artificial suppression of human reproductions, it destroyed the means, not the human. The three that did not make it had cancer, it was far too late to rebuild them so it mercifully killed them.

FOLK Persian medicos were very busy. GIFT AI'd Jeremiah, *Well, these new human genomes will make very fine additions to our home.*

Jeremiah smiled, *Well, good luck, GIFT.*

It rubbed its golden threads together, *Yep, starting analysis.*

NESS Jeremiah watched the Earth Star Republic civilian personnel move out of the area. When that was done he turned to the officers, "You, on the other hand, are warriors and do not fall under life protocols since you take life." He AI'd his armored hand back and showed them, "This is GIFT in my palm." Golden threads waved, "I will ask you to submit, if you do, you might wake up with a massive headache with no damage to your minds. GIFT will kill you outright by finding a flaw in you or if you make me fight my way into your mind, and then you might wake up with the mind of a three-year old; choose the easy or the hard way."

He pointed to General Sir Thomas Stoddard and said, "Who and what rank are you?"

He looked, smiled and said, "Go FUCK YOURSELF." FOLK Full Professor Closter smiled and interpreted this with all the emotion for Jeremiah.

Jeremiah laughed. "Nope, I was married, am a widower now, and I really like women."

FOLK Full Professor Closter relayed this back with the same enjoyment. Jeremiah put his armored foot on the general, pushed him into the sand, and AI'd GIFT, *Ready.*

"You have no concept of what is going to happen to you. You will not like it." The golden threads penetrated General Sir Thomas Stoddard's mind. He screamed as GIFT ripped his mind apart.

The sun set. The entire complement of officers would not submit. Jeremiah nodded. *Warriors never did throughout history.* He pointed to the ruins on the map. *Put these warriors and the civilian dead there, no need to bury; it is a wasted effort.*

NESS threw them in the ruins of a once great city. They did not want scavengers around the complexes or spaceship. The NESS washed the N.A.P.C. 1 and 2 out with soap and water to clean the blood, and then left the area.

A lot of bodies were tossed during the night, the blood drifted on the air enticing many that were hungry. The whole area seethed with animals fighting over the bodies. Two Scorps grabbed the late General Sir Thomas Stoddard to feed on; a huge fight broke out between them. The third Scorp ate the three carcasses for several days.

Officer Engineer Conner O'Kelly screamed as the thing attacked him. He fought it, and then passed out. When he awoke, it was night and he was cold and had a screaming headache.

Rolling over, he looked for his brother, thinking, *Where is that shit?* Science Officer Ian O'Kelly was a few feet away. Conner crawled, put his finger on his neck and felt a pulse on his brother. *Mother will kill me if he got killed*, then he remembered the NESS, the battle, another NESS with golden threads in his palms, and then waking up here.

His brother moaned, "My head."

Conner asked Ian, "How are you?"

"Well, Conner, getting shot at and attacked by NESS 'things', then smaller NESS 'things' trying to kill me, I have had just a lovely day, you?"

A voice from the darkness said, "Maybe I can help."

They both turned around. "Who are you?"

It smiled from the rock perch and said, "I am not one of the NESS that attacked you. This is the third day and I have dragged you both under this rock outcrop to keep you from being dinner."

Conner and Ian held their heads in their hands. "My head," they both moaned.

The stranger tossed two bottles of a blue liquid drink to them. "Now drink the liquid; it will relieve the headache." Both brothers finished it. Their headaches eased.

"Whatever this is, thanks."

The stranger nodded and said, "You are welcome."

Conner asked, "How come you can speak our language?"

The stranger laughed. "I have been here a long time. Your language is known to me."

Ian asked, "Why did you save us? The 'things' thought us dead."

The stranger nodded, "Let's say I am one of your country men and I need your help." They both looked at him.

"The NESS 'things' will find us and kill us this time, for sure," Ian said.

"No, both of you, and I, are immune to GIFT."

Ian said, "Jesus Christ, the plague kills everything."

"No, some humans have a built in immunity to GIFT. It is very rare and tends to run in families. I take it you are related." They both nodded and it stood up. "Be still, I am going to run a scan; I will draw some blood."

They felt the needles. After several minutes, the stranger thought, *No GIFT.*

"Your names?"

They answered, "Engineer Officer Conner O'Kelly and Science Officer Ian O'Kelly."

The stranger stated, "Well, brothers, you are on a very hostile battle front. The people that took your ship are the most dangerous human beings in this galaxy." The stranger nodded at the looks on the brothers' faces, "You still do not believe me? Well, they captured a fully armed destroyer that can glass a planet in days; and did it with only 96 soldiers and 24 vehicles. This is unprecedented, even from your histories." Smiling, he said, "I'd say that they are very lethal."

The stranger asked, "How many people were in the lab complex?"

Ian said, "About 300."

The stranger said to them, "They are waking up now and I counted 200, so all the information that was in their minds are now in the NESS FOLK and Persians collective archives."

Ian and Conner asked, "Who are you?"

"I am deep scout Andrew Lee, Earth Star Republic, and you will follow my orders, exactly or I will kill you. Is that understood?"

"Yes, sir!"

He smiled, "Welcome to N.E.S.S. or New Earth Star Systems."

Both stood up asking where the rest of the officers were. Andrew said, "I will ask the questions to you." Looking at them, he ordered, "Attention!" They both snapped to attention. Andrew stated, "You are to observe, listen, evaluate and then act; what did you observe?"

"Well, they treated the civilians totally differently; gentle, kind, no aggressive moves for the most part. The naval and marines lower ranks personnel were killed outright by two 'things', what you call NESS."

Andrew continued, "Good, now what did you hear?"

They both thought about it and said, "The civilian speaker told us what would happen to the civilians and the last navel people, the officers, what would happen to us."

"Good, evaluate?"

Both said, "They have different standards for different people; something called 'life protocols'."

"Good, now act on that information.

They both looked at him. "We are going with you, sir!"

Andrew smiled, "You might make it here, too early to tell."

Ian asked, "Sir! Before we move, what happened to the officers?"

Andrew replied, "They are dead. I moved you here to get you away from the flying Wasps and other predators."

"WASPS!"

He nodded, "GIFT changed all life on the planet. Everything is very large, tough, and aggressive. The minds have increased, as well. Your former comrades, along with the civilians who were killed, are being eaten. There will be nothing left; they are bee shit, along with many other forms of shit, now."

He nodded. "Now, be still and listen. Do you hear sounds on the wind?"

"Yes."

"Predators are out looking for food. You will follow my orders exactly. If you do not, you will die."

Two days later, they were in a natural cave. He led them further down into the cave, the floor was just sand. He smiled, a door popped open after he pushed a rock to get in, he closed it and said, "Follow me," the door sealed shut and the sandy floor moved until the footprints disappeared.

They entered an underground bunker. Andrew twisted a light tube; natural sun light flooded into the cave. Chairs, a couch, and several bunk beds were bolted to the rock. They looked to the left, a massive library went down the tunnel, and thousands of books lined the shelves going into the gloom. He smiled, pulled a book, and said, "Sit, want some water?" They both nodded. Andrew went around another rock face and brought some water in cups. "Drink, it is natural spring water." Andrew sat down. "You are wondering about this?" They nodded. "Alright, 700 years ago, a non-human entity was released on this planet. You know what happened from the history disk?"

They both nodded, "Earth Star Republic killed 13 star systems to stop the plague from spreading."

He laughed, "Yes, that is correct, but what was not told is that the original planet was not totally destroyed. We needed to know what this nonhuman entity is, what its plans were for humans."

"What the hell are you talking about?" Ian asked.

Andrew laughed and said, "GIFT is sentient and extremely old. This one is a least 4 billion years old."

Ian asked, "What do you mean this one?"

Andrew smiled. "We have killed four, so far, in this galaxy."

"We learned from this one that GIFT is extremely hard to kill. The Gift Electromagnetic Shield Machine 'G.E.S.M.' is one defense; there are others, but humans like you are prime weapons. GIFT does not see us, period. When it attacked you, it thought you were dead after blend and told the NESS to throw you on the pile with your dead friends, and then it went about its merry way." Andrew smiled at both of them; he was busy putting a lizard into the stove. "Genetically, we are very different, we kill GIFT. Naturally, you both survived by being hibernated, making you appear dead. Why this happens, we have no clue, but it works, so your education begins now.

Andrew went over to the solar stove, pulled out the steaming lizard cooked in a sauce, smiled, set it on the table, put in more spices and then put it back in the stove.

"I will teach you how to survive here. I will be blunt: these people are extremely intelligent, fast, very deadly and they have been genetically altered by GIFT. Let's say Darwin on steroids. The fittest survive, the rest are food." Smiling, he said, "You are not on the top of the food chain on your new home."

Andrew continued, as he put other food on the table. "The humans that attacked your starship are NESS, New Earth Star Soldiers, with the Persians. NESS come in two groups; remember the two 'things' that boarded the ship?" Both brothers nodded. "Well, that is an Assault NESS; they are bigger, more aggressive, meaner, and have more armor along with massive weapons; a walking, thinking tank. Your captain should have hit those two with the primary weapons, first." Shrugging, he continued, "Oh well, your commander is dead. You may wish God had granted you that favor."

Andrew went over and got dried dates and pomegranates and set them on the table. "The others were Defensive NESS; they protect the civilians and are smaller, but extremely fast. They blur."

Ian asked, "What the hell is 'blur', sir!"

Andrew smiled, "When the NESS moves, you visually lose sight of them. That means they can cut you in half before you finish an eye blink." He finished setting more food on the table and continued, "Persians, during the outbreak, hid the NESS founders group; this joined them at the hip, literally." He laughed at himself, "They have many family ties."

"NESS Jeremiah Lee married a Persian." He sighed, "Zoe was very beautiful and gentle and she was the best dancer this planet has ever produced." He smiled as he set more water on the table, "Zoe loved him, utterly," he smiled sadly at them, "and they had many children together. Taming Jeremiah made him care about life which is a good thing for our planet."

Andrew pulled a photograph showing Jeremiah with Zoe. Ian and Conner looked. Zoe was extremely beautiful, she had her arm wrapped around Jeremiah, and along with their five kids, they looked happy. Andrew smiled, "I wish I could marry, but it is too dangerous, so you two are living with a hermit but I digress." He said, "Persians have been breeding with NESS and FOLK for a very long time. He looked at the brothers, "Some look normal while others have very colorful skin; they are very wild NESS. The gentleman that had GIFT in his hand is Jeremiah Lee. He is extremely dangerous, one of the three surviving original NESS."

"But," the brothers said, "The records indicated the entire original NESS were destroyed."

Andrew smiled, "I was born here, I am certain of his identity since I am his twin brother."

Conner and Ian both said, "Shit," at the same time.

He nodded, "Now, my very dangerous brother, by the gracious gift from Earth Star Republic just handed to the NESS FOLK and Persians, has a working, fully armed starship with Tesla jump drive. Now, report." Both Ian and Conner snapped to attention. "What were your orders?"

Ian and Conner told him. Andrew swore a blue streak, "I told them to never come back until I sent for them, those bloody idiots." He threw a cup against the rock wall, turned around, and waved his finger under their noses, "If these people break out of this star system, the whole milky way will burn, then beyond. We are in a universal war that started 10 billion years ago. Humans like my brother are frontline soldiers. You witnessed a small atom, when they took your starship, of their capabilities."

He asked Conner, "Was the TJD disabled per orders?"

Conner replied, "We thought this planet was sterilized, the general overrode that protocol. When we arrived during the winter season, he was very interested in the life that survived here."

Andrew screamed, "SOB! Was he killed by my brother?" They both nodded. "He deserves it, but it still works out the same, they have all his memories, along with all the officers."

He looked at them and stated, "The NESS are extremely fast and they will have fleets of starships built within 20 years or five axis turns here."

Conner asked, "Sir?"

"Yes?"

"How come you are not dead? Seven hundred years is a long time to live for a human."

Andrew smiled and pulled his sleeve up, he had NESS coloring, "My body changed, but not my mind. GIFT lived in your mind during the troubles, I was infected, too. When I woke up, my brother tried to blend with me, but he could not see me, nor could any others with GIFT. To them, I am a walking ghost." Andrew explained, "GIFT slows NESS metabolism down, so that I age very slowly. I am about 70 years of age, now, so I volunteered to stay to see if I could help my people." He laughed then looked at them. "Before we eat, I want to show you something." Pulling his clothes off, he said, "My color pattern is unique. It identifies me as a warrior. Attention privates." Both snapped to. "I want you to strip your clothes off now." When done he said, "Relax, look at yourselves. Do you see anything?

Both saw the beginning of color in their skin and they looked at each other with wide eyes.

Andrew nodded. "You will be alright; GIFT left its mark. Your color will be NESS since you are warriors. But it will take about four weeks, so we are going to eat and you will be getting P.T. to improve the muscle tone, and then you can start unarmed combat training. Your strength will increase to about three times normal for a standard human. Now sit, eat."

Both brothers were very frightened as they started to eat. He got the lizard from the solar oven and asked, "Would you like some? It is very good."

Both brothers said, "No, thank you."

Andrew continued, "Any junk DNA is being rebuilt. Key proteins are being turned on; I wonder what your color pattern will be?" He laughed out loud. "But the key is that GIFT is not in you and does not see you, so it leaves one avenue open. We are joining the Outcasts."

Conner asked him, "The what, sir?"

"The Outcasts hate GIFT; they are on a crusade to kill it." He smiled. "My kind of people. Outcasts take no prisoners. Once engaged in combat, you win or die; that is where we are going once you finish transforming."

Andrew pointed to the table. He had set out massive amounts of food while talking, "Now eat everything, you will need it." He watched and ate sparingly. The lizard was excellent; they had cleaned their plates of all the food and water on the table. Smiling, he said, "Good, how is your stomach?" Both could barely move; their stomachs bulged.

Ian asked, "Sir! Why are we eating like this? My stomach aches."

"See the blue coloring?" They both nodded. "You are in for a ride." Both screamed and fell to the sand floor as they looked at their hands and arms. He informed them, "Everything has GIFT in it, your bodies, the air, water, food, your piss, EVERYTHING. It will convert every morsel for the process of NESS from the food you eat to the water you take in for the next coming weeks, but do not worry. You are human, but different, now."

Both brothers were screaming as their muscles rippled, then cramped. They screamed until the pain made them pass out on the sand floor.

Andrew went over to the rock ledge and stretched out, enjoying the afternoon sun through the glass. He fluffed a pillow and opened a book to read. *Yes, you will learn or you will die. Where was I... here we go, W.B. Yeats the Land of Heart's Desire.*

Two weeks later, FOLK Full Professor Closter told David of the cost for taking the Starship along with the complexes. They had lost six P.H.A.V. as well as four N.A.P.C.; they had lost 125 soldiers from both brigades in the engagement. David Centauri looked at FOLK Full Professor Closter, "Professor, I really hate a military uniform."

Brian nodded and smiled. "David, I know you do, but this is not about the military, this is remembering all the dead. We give them honor so their families will have closure for their deaths."

David was very surprised by FOLK Full Professor Closter. When he showed up, his patch showed 'fons et origo' meaning 'source and origin', NESS First Army; he had Full Commander stars on his collar. David looked at his chest and it showed the Medal for 'The Pass'; only four had been given out on that day of slaughter. Brain smiled. "Yes, I am a NESS FOLK Founder; there are not many left of the Old Guard." Brian looked into David's eyes and said, "We meet every axis turn on the same day in the pass to honor the dead from both sides of the civil war."

David said, "Sir!"

Brian looked at David who came to attention and snapped a salute to him. Brain went to attention and returned the salute. Smiling, he grabbed David's hand and said, "Shall we go be in a parade?"

David smiled and said, "Yes, Professor."

Jody had said the same thing to him when she had adjusted his uniform. Jody smiled and told him her father had been killed in the Orion Deep Space Navy. His body was never recovered from space. Her family felt very grateful for the Navy ceremony; it had closed the wound for them.

Jody smiled at David, kissed him and said, "You look very handsome in this uniform."

He stood back. "I will be at the ceremony to honor all the dead."

NESS Full Commander Jeremiah Lee smiled. All the civilians that survived the battle were in the brigade formation, even David Centauri. Jeremiah's armor reflected Gold with NESS FULL Army

Commander, five stars, the only medal for 'The Pass', was on his armor. He strode out to face the brigades. When he was 10 feet way, he stopped and went to attention.

NESS Full Commander Jeremiah Lee said, "Attention." NESS FOLK and Persian snapped to attention on Nippur's largest army base. He then said, "NESS Full Commander Brian Closter, front and center."

Brian marched to the front and center and snapped a salute. "Sir! NESS Full Commander Brian Closter reporting, Sir!"

NESS Full Commander Jeremiah Lee stated, "You will do the Honor of Colors. Are these orders clear?"

NESS Full Commander Brian Closter replied, "Sir! Clear." Brian spun around, marched to front ranks and took the Colors; spun around and stated, "NESS Full Commander Jeremiah Lee, sir! Colors are ready, sir!"

NESS Full Commander Jeremiah Lee spun around and said, "Slow March," and the command was repeated by all officers, and then noncoms. Jeremiah said, "MARCH," and as one, the whole brigade stepped in parade stride. He then ordered, "Wheel right," and the order was repeated. The whole brigade wheeled right; the crowd could hear the marching cadence of the boots hitting the ground. Next he ordered, "Unfurl the colors," and the order was repeated. The NESS First Brigade Persian First Brigade colors were unfurled waving above them. A roar came from the crowds. He continued. "Unfurl the Earth Star Republic Destroyer Lions captured standard," and the order was repeated. The flag unfurled showing it shot full of holes. The crowd screamed roaring approval of the enemies captured flag. The next order, "Wheel right," was given; and the whole brigade marched toward the reviewing stand. NESS Full Commander Jeremiah Lee ordered, "HALT." The order was repeated; the whole brigade stopped. Finally, NESS Full Commander Jeremiah Lee ordered, "Battle standard for the captured Earth Star Republic Destroyer Lions front and center," and the order was repeated.

Captain Banu Goshasp marched with the Earth Star Republic Destroyer Lions battle standard. When Banu was in place, NESS Full Commander Jeremiah Lee ordered, "Present the captured standard to the Persian government." The order was repeated. Captain Banu Goshasp marched to the reviewing stand, stopped in front of the stand, and then came to attention.

NESS Full Commander Jeremiah Lee said, "Brigade, kneel," and the order was repeated. The entire brigade went to their right knee left hand on the left knee. He then said, "The brigade presents the captured Earth Star Republic Destroyer Lions standard; it was won with blood and bravery."

Rostam came to attention and stated, "The Persian government accepts this standard won with blood and bravery from the brigade." He then stated, "We understand the sacrifices made by the brigade in that we are putting this standard in honorable viewing for the warrior's hall for all our people to remember and cherish." He continued with, "We have a new battle standard for our starship. Captain Banu Goshasp, bring the Earth Star Republic Destroyer Lions standard forward." Banu marched forward and halted in front of her father. Lastly, Rostam stated, "I take this battle standard from the brigade and present the brigade with this new battle standard." They exchanged the battle standards, Captain Banu Goshasp did an about face, and marched to her place in the brigade with the flag not unfurled.

NESS Full Commander Jeremiah Lee ordered, "Rise brigade," and then, "Attention." When they were at attention, he stated, "Swing right, swing left." The commands were repeated. The crowd was very silent; they could hear the cadence when the line formed facing the reviewing stand, the boots slammed in step. It sounded like one crack as they stopped. He then ordered, "Salute." The brigade snapped a salute. Rostam snapped to attention, returned the salute, and then all went back to attention.

Jody Sanatoria smiled and thought, *David Centauri, no matter how much he hates the military, is a good citizen.* She could see pride in him for saving people's lives, no matter where they came from, as an enemy or friend.

NESS Full Commander Jeremiah Lee ordered, "Brigade wheel left, form brigade," and the orders were repeated. The brigade formed. The people could hear the boots marching in cadence. He continued with, "Wheel left," and the orders were repeated. Again he ordered, "Wheel left," and his orders were repeated. He then ordered, "brigade unfurl the new battle standard," the orders were repeated, and a roar come from the crowds as their brigade went down the middle of the parade ground. The flag showed their national flag a Sandcat on a star field with the NESS Persian brigade patches in the top corners. The name N.E.S.S. Stalker in gold script was displayed between the brigade patches.

A month later, Jody Sanatoria found herself sitting with David Centauri, eating smoked lizard.

"Well, David, this lizard tastes like chicken."

David asked, "What is a chicken?" She laughed and drew a picture. He looked at her, "This is not a chicken, this is a runner and it weighs 180 pounds. It eats anything that moves and they are extremely hard to kill." David pulled up a picture; it looked like a fossil record of a dinosaur with feathers.

Hot damn, I need samples. She asked, "Where do they live?"

He laughed and said, "Well in the northern continent."

Smiling, she asked, "Well, David, what are the plans for you and me?"

David smiled. "I would like you to come to New Hope with me. I need to finish my studies, pass exams, face peer review, and then look for work."

She smiled. "Well, I like that, and one more issue."

"Yes?"

"Do they have a hospital there?"

He laughed and said, "One of the best on the planet, why?"

"Well, David, I am carrying a child from you."

David fell out of the chair. Jody got up and went over to him, "Are you all right?"

David was stuttering, "Yes, ah no, ah yes,"

Jody laughed, "Well make up your mind," as David got up from the floor. Jody Sanatoria smiled at him, "Yes, you are going to be father; no need to be frightened."

David smiled, "When?"

Jody laughed, "We have been having sex since day one, silly, so four weeks ago in the sand dunes." Jody smiled and told David, "I asked GIFT about that when we arrived at New Earth, part of the stipulation was 'no children' for the expedition. It is a standard clause in the contract for this type of work. The shot last for the years we would have been on the planet and awake, so when I meet GIFT, it removed the barrier for life. Jody smiled at David's confusion, "David do you want children from me?"

David gently held her hand, "Yes, I do. I fell hard for you that first day. I am still falling hard; I hope to fall hard for the rest of my life. I am in love with you, Jody Sanatoria. You are the only woman I want in my life." David smiled, "I am going to ask you something." Jody nodded. "My people have arranged marriages by their parents. It works in most cases, but I declined this way of life for me. I left my home country to carve my own life in the world." David watched Jody's face. "I would not submit to my father's wishes for marriage. He was also very angry by my decision to follow a non-military way of life." David looked at Jody, "I would never marry anyone that did not love me for who I am."

Jody smiled and thought, *Here it comes. David will ask me to marry him or tell me to get lost.*

"I have a stubborn streak as wide as the Deep Ocean. Until I met you, my life was my studies for knowledge, but this time I want you in my life any way I can have you, so I am asking, would you marry me? I work hard, and can provide for us now and in the future.

Once my schooling is finished, I can secure a small post as an associate professor."

Jody beamed at David, "Yes, I will marry you, David Centauri."

David lifted her up from the floor, dancing around in the café stating, "I was so afraid you would say no to me."

Jody smiled from the air and stated, "David, I want my life with you, so can we finish lunch then I will show you how much I want you in my life. I am very horny."

David was still dancing around with her in the air. "What is horny?" he asked as he set Jody back on the floor. Jody smiled, grabbed his head, and whispered in his ear the explanation. David laughed, "I like this horny idea."

Jody laughed with him, "Well, I am feeding two so I need to eat." Both sat back down smiling. They finished, went back to the hotel, and David found out how horny.

Brian watched David spin Jody in the air. He AI'd Jeremiah, *David Centauri is marrying Jody Sanatoria.*

Jeremiah AI'd back smiling *Jody Sanatoria's scans indicate an IQ at the top of the scale and that is without GIFT meddling.* Jeremiah continued, *David needs to be tamed by a woman. I think Jody is up for the task.* (pausing) *Before I go, one more question, what is beer?*

Brian snorted out his mug of beer in the Café, swearing. He had forgotten the N.A.P.C. recorded everything inside. Jeremiah AI'd smiling, *I will trade you some honey wine for beer.*

Later in bed Jody told David, "The FOLK have asked me to work a contract for one axis turn today, when you were out in the city; it is in my science field. So, I am asking you, my future husband is this alright for us? I am still a stranger in a very strange land."

David smiled, "Yes, the FOLK are totally different from the NESS. So, what did they offer?"

She said, "A salary of one gold ounce a month; is this a good salary?"

David laughed, "Yes, it is. We can buy farm land, build a house and raise the baby with that salary alone."

Jody asked, "You are not mad at this offer from your government to me?

David laughed, "No, we are mated partners; married decisions are based on our best interests." He looked at her, "Let's discuss this again by being horny."

Jody laughed, "Yes, that is what I was thinking, too," as Jody rolled David on top of her.

Sasha was in the Nippur hospital. Her arm had healed but she was in for a checkup. The FOLK medico Yelena asked, "What is your degree?"

Sasha laughed and said, "Astrobiology. GIFT's release is my life's work. Now, I have a captive audience with the character."

"Well, we have an enclave at New Hope. You are most welcome to come with us. Did the FOLK offer you a job?"

Sasha nodded. "Yes, a princely sum of one ounce of gold per month. Is that a lot of money?"

Yelena said, "That is a very large sum of money on our world."

Hmm, I wonder if I could get a science lab going in New Hope, Selena thought.

Yelena laughed, "Just ask the FOLK or do you want me to?"

"Where is the communication's desk so I can talk to someone in the government?"

Yelena looked at her, puzzled. "No outer speech. I will ask using inner speech. Is it alright for me to do this for you?"

Sasha said, "Yes."

Yelena AI'd FOLK, *Well?*

The FOLK AI'd, *No problem. From her scans, she is no threat to us. Her science training will be very useful so, yes.*

Yelena looked at her new friend. "No problem for the lab. We are going back tomorrow, so get packed, and see you at the train."

Sasha thought, *What the hell is inner speech? Well, time to find out in the coming years.*

NESS Brenda was at duty when her water broke. The Armor said, *Birth has started.* Brenda groaned and responded, *Ya think? Armor release.* It folded down. She stepped away, threw her helmet on the floor, and AI'd her husband, *Daniel, I am in labor.*

Daniel was a FOLK electronics' technician. Smashing into the office on the run, he looked around and saw water, blood and fluid all over the place. *Shit,* he thought. He AI'd. *Hun, I do not think we can make it to the clinic.*

Brenda said, "Ya think?"

Daniel looked around and saw a cot with sheets on it. "Brenda can you move?"

She screamed at him, "NO."

"Shit." Grabbing the sheets, he threw them on the floor next to her, helping her down. "Lean back," he said as he stuffed pillows under her back. "Spread your legs, I want to see how much you are dilated. Shit."

He could see the contractions rippling her. She grunted and screamed again at him. He said, "Damn, near seven."

Brenda looked very scared and she gripped his hand. "The baby is coming! Do something!"

Daniel AI'd his medico friend, *Beth, I need help.*

She smiled. *Baby?*

Yes, damn it, the head is crowning.

Beth AI'd, *Put pillows under her ass and get her hips up off the floor. Then, put your hands under the baby's head and tell her to push.*

Daniel, in his outer voice, said, "Brenda, push." She lifted her hips higher, screaming, and the head of the baby slid out.

Beth AI'd, *Blend now, Daniel.* Beth looking through his eyes and said, *You are doing fine, no cord wrapped around the neck, one more push from Brenda.*

Daniel said, "Push," to Brenda pushing. She grunted, and the baby slid out.

Beth AI'd Daniel, *Do not cut the cord. I am on the way. Is the baby breathing?*

Yes.

Just put the girl on her chest, face down, watch the baby's breathing and then, cover both your wife and new baby; we will be there in one minute.

Brenda was soaking wet; she fell back on the floor exhausted. David put their baby girl on her chest and smiled.

"Welcome to the world, little one." Daniel covered both of them to keep them warm.

The medicos arrived. Beth smiled and AI'd Daniel, *I need to work on Brenda.*

Beth asked Daniel, "Do you want to cut the cord?"

"Yes". Daniel's hands were shaking and Beth helped him.

Checking Brenda, Beth AI'd Daniel, *Did the afterbirth come out?*

David bent down and checked. *Yes, it slid out onto the sheets.*

Beth AI'd, *Good, move over to the other side of me, let me look. Good, no bleeding. Also, we will not have to stitch her up* and then she AI'd the rest of the medicos.

Beth said in her outer voice, "Brenda, we are going to move you now. 3...2...1 lift." Behind them the medicos lifted both onto the gurney. "We will get you cleaned up in a jiffy."

Brenda smiled very tiredly. "David, stuff the armor in the helmet and bring it along to throw in the pool for me, and then get your cute butt to the recovery room." She had the girl tucked on her chest as they left the guard room.

Daniel reached down for the armor; it was finishing up eating the afterbirth. Daniel just rolled his eyes. *The armor will eat anything.*

Picking up the armor, he stuffed it into the helmet, walked to the pool and threw it in with the rest of the armor. Armor slithered around, sniffing the others, then settled to feed in the nutrients. Armor sighed, "Oh well, back to rations."

Brenda was being cleaned up and the baby was asleep, healthy in her arms, beaming a smile at her husband. Brenda AI'd Daniel, *The name we chose?*

Ya think?

Yes.

David laughed and AI'd, *Yes, our first after so many tries and disappointments, 'Hope' is a wonderful name for our daughter."*

Three weeks later, FOLK Persian councils AI'd the NESS, *Stalker is not ready to lift. It will need extensive rebuild for space operation. The question is where are we going to move it for the rebuild? FOLK council suggests in our city. We have a spare factory that can repair the destroyer. Is that acceptable to the councils?*

Persian council would like to transfer scientists, engineers, technicians and shipbuilding trades to the new facility for hands on training. We then suggest production runs in both capitals. FOLK Persian councils agree on this point.

FOLK Persian councils AI'd, *We will split the Earth Star Republic personal offer of very big incentives, then rotate the groups in one axis turn. We have lost ten from suicide, but the rest are adjusting, FOLK therapy is helping along with GIFT. It is showing them that it is not a monster. The data from the science complex is vast. We have started a complete record analysis, too. On this end, we are rebuilding the complex. We hope the Earth Star Republic personnel will continue since they are very familiar with the equipment. This will be completed in small axis turns.* They all smiled. *We have a treasure trove of new technology.*

Persian and NESS FOLK are going to rebuild the star port in the destroyed city construction. We will start after winter season. They all smiled then AI'd Jeremiah, *Asking on the progress for the Starship.*

NESS Jeremiah AI'd the FOLK NESS, *Persians, we have the starship patched. Where do we want to hide it?* They all smiled and told him. *Oh, that is really wild.*

NESS blended with the ship *SYSTEMS ONLINE.* The Captain AI'd, *Persian, NESS FOLK crew, prepare for lift 3...2...1 fire main engines.* Massive fusion engines screamed as they lifted the ship using water converted into hydrogen and oxygen, the thunder could be heard for miles in the desert. After 700 years New Earth had a working starship.

NESS Persian warriors had drawn for who would be the first N.E.S.S space captain; a name had been drawn. Everyone had a very good laugh. NESS Space Commander Bill House Ocean smiled and said, *Sure beats bilge cleaning duty!*

NESS Space Commander Bill House Ocean AI'd his Officer of the Deck, *Set course for FOLK CITY the HUMP fortress.* Officer of the Deck AI'd, *Helmsman.*

Sir!

Set course speed for FOLK CITY the HUMP fortress.

Helmsman AI'd his response, *Aye, aye, sir. Setting course speed for FOLK CITY the HUMP fortress.*

FOLK NESS Persians council's well orders have gone into the factories. We will rebuild the destroyer then build more for a fleet. Then next a moon base for the fleet. This will secure our planetary system based on this design. The Councils inner speech faded back in his mind. NESS Jeremiah smiled and said, *I will buy the first round of drinks back home. I think I need to party, no more C&C.* He danced across the train station in Nippur.

Andrew Lee watched the starship lift through his telescope and thought, *Yes they are going, but it is not space worthy.* Smiling at his charges, he said, "Pack up the gear."

He pondered his next move as the spaceship disappeared over the mountains. The brothers groaned in unison. They were very sore from running all morning. Both groaned more as they packed their gear into ruck sacks. Andrew smiled an evil sergeant smile. "You look like proper NESS, so we are going to run back to the hide, MOVE!" They had a four hour run at fifteen kilometers an hour pace and the packs on their backs weighed 80 pounds apiece.

Andrew suspected there was only one place in New Hope to hold the starship for repair. He had to kill it before the NESS FOLK and Persians got it functional or the galaxy would burn from his failure.

Looking at his charges, he noticed that they were now 7 foot 6 and 450 pounds of muscle and sinew and they were still filling out. *Yes, you are in for some fun with me,* he thought. "Tomorrow, we will do a three-day run to meet the Outcast warship on the coast." All three ran hard in the desert.